Dover Thrift Study Edition

A Portrait of the Artist as a Young Man

JAMES JOYCE

DOVER PUBLICATIONS, INC.
Mineola, New York

Copyright

Bibliographical Note

This Dover edition, first published in 2011, contains the unabridged text of a standard edition of *A Portrait of the Artist as a Young Man,* as published by B.W. Huebsch, New York, 1916, plus literary analysis and perspectives from *MAXnotes®* *for A Portrait of the Artist as a Young Man,* published in 1996 by Research & Education Association, Inc., Piscataway, New Jersey. The footnotes were prepared especially for the present edition.

Library of Congress Cataloging-in-Publication Data

Joyce, James, 1882–1941.
    A portrait of the artist as a young man / James Joyce.
        p. cm. — (Dover thrift study edition)
    This Dover edition contains the unabridged text of A portrait of the artist as a young man, as published by B. W. Huebsch, New York, 1916, plus literary analysis and perspectives from MAXnotes, published in 1996 by Research and Education Association, Piscataway, New Jersey.
    ISBN-13: 978-0-486-48249-1
    ISBN-10: 0-486-48249-9
    1. Dublin (Ireland)—Fiction. 2. Young men—Ireland—Fiction. 3. Artists—Fiction. 4. Joyce, James, 1882–1941. Portrait of the artist as a young man—Examinations—Study guides. I. Title.

PR6019.O9P63 2011
823'.912—dc22

2010053661

Manufactured in the United States by Courier Corporation
48249902
www.doverpublications.com

Publisher's Note

Combining the complete text of a classic novel or drama with a comprehensive study guide, Dover Thrift Study Editions are the most effective way to gain a thorough understanding of the major works of world literature.

The study guide features up-to-date and expert analysis of every chapter or section from the source work. Questions and fully explained answers follow, allowing readers to analyze the material critically. Character lists, author bios, and discussions of the work's historical context are also provided.

Each Dover Thrift Study Edition includes everything a student needs to prepare for homework, discussions, reports, and exams.

Contents

A Portrait of the Artist as a Young Man

JAMES JOYCE

"Et ignotas animum dimittit in artes."[1]
Ovid, Metamorphoses, VIII., 18.

Chapter I

Once upon a time and a very good time it was there was a moocow coming down along the road and this moocow that was down along the road met a nicens little boy named baby tuckoo. . . .

His father told him that story: his father looked at him through a glass: he had a hairy face.

He was baby tuckoo. The moocow came down the road where Betty Byrne lived: she sold lemon platt.

> *O, the wild rose blossoms*
> *On the little green place.*

He sang that song. That was his song.

> *O, the green wothe botheth.*

When you wet the bed, first it is warm then it gets cold. His mother put on the oilsheet. That had the queer smell.

His mother had a nicer smell than his father. She played on the piano the sailor's hornpipe for him to dance. He danced:

> *Tralala lala,*
> *Tralala tralaladdy,*
> *Tralala lala,*
> *Tralala lala.*

Uncle Charles and Dante clapped. They were older than his father and mother but Uncle Charles was older than Dante.

---

[1] [*"And he sets his mind to work upon unknown arts."*]

1

Dante had two brushes in her press. The brush with the maroon velvet back was for Michael Davitt and the brush with the green velvet back was for Parnell. Dante gave him a cachou every time he brought her a piece of tissue paper.

The Vances lived in number seven. They had a different father and mother. They were Eileen's father and mother. When they were grown up he was going to marry Eileen. He hid under the table. His mother said:

— O, Stephen will apologise.

Dante said:

— O, if not, the eagles will come and pull out his eyes. —

> Pull out his eyes,
> Apologise,
> Apologise,
> Pull out his eyes.
>
> Apologise,
> Pull out his eyes,
> Pull out his eyes,
> Apologise.

*   *   *

The wide playgrounds were swarming with boys. All were shouting and the prefects urged them on with strong cries. The evening air was pale and chilly and after every charge and thud of the foot-ballers the greasy leather orb flew like a heavy bird through the grey light. He kept on the fringe of his line, out of sight of his prefect, out of the reach of the rude feet, feigning to run now and then. He felt his body small and weak amid the throng of players and his eyes were weak and watery. Rody Kickham was not like that: he would be captain of the third line all the fellows said.

Rody Kickham was a decent fellow but Nasty Roche was a stink. Rody Kickham had greaves in his number and a hamper in the refectory. Nasty Roche had big hands. He called the Friday pudding dog-in-the-blanket. And one day he had asked:

— What is your name?

Stephen had answered: Stephen Dedalus.

Then Nasty Roche had said:

— What kind of a name is that?

And when Stephen had not been able to answer Nasty Roche had asked:

— What is your father?

Stephen had answered:

— A gentleman.

Then Nasty Roche had asked:

— Is he a magistrate?

He crept about from point to point on the fringe of his line, making little runs now and then. But his hands were bluish with cold. He kept his hands in the side pockets of his belted grey suit. That was a belt round his pocket. And belt was also to give a fellow a belt. One day a fellow had said to Cantwell:

— I'd give you such a belt in a second.

Cantwell had answered:

— Go and fight your match. Give Cecil Thunder a belt. I'd like to see you. He'd give you a toe in the rump for yourself.

That was not a nice expression. His mother had told him not to speak with the rough boys in the college. Nice mother! The first day in the hall of the castle when she had said goodbye she had put up her veil double to her nose to kiss him: and her nose and eyes were red. But he had pretended not to see that she was going to cry. She was a nice mother but she was not so nice when she cried. And his father had given him two fiveshilling pieces for pocket money. And his father had told him if he wanted anything to write home to him and, whatever he did, never to peach on a fellow. Then at the door of the castle the rector had shaken hands with his father and mother, his soutane fluttering in the breeze, and the car had driven off with his father and mother on it. They had cried to him from the car, waving their hands:

— Good-bye, Stephen, goodbye!

— Good-bye, Stephen, goodbye!

He was caught in the whirl of a scrimmage and, fearful of the flashing eyes and muddy boots, bent down to look through the legs. The fellows were struggling and groaning and their legs were rubbing and kicking and stamping. Then Jack Lawton's yellow boots dodged out the ball and all the other boots and legs ran after. He ran after them a little way and then stopped. It was useless to run on. Soon they would be going home for the holidays. After supper in the study hall he would change the number pasted up inside his desk from seventyseven to seventysix.

It would be better to be in the study hall than out there in the cold. The sky was pale and cold but there were lights in the castle. He wondered from which window Hamilton Rowan had thrown his hat on the haha and had there been flowerbeds at that time under the windows. One day when he had been called to the castle the butler had shown him the marks of the soldiers' slugs in the wood of the door and had given him a piece of shortbread that the community ate. It was nice and warm to see the lights in the castle. It was like something in a book. Perhaps Leicester Abbey was like that. And there were nice sentences in

Doctor Cornwell's Spelling Book. They were like poetry but they were only sentences to learn the spelling from.

> Wolsey died in Leicester Abbey
> Where the abbots buried him.
> Canker is a disease of plants,
> Cancer one of animals.

It would be nice to lie on the hearthrug before the fire, leaning his head upon his hands, and think on those sentences. He shivered as if he had cold slimy water next his skin. That was mean of Wells to shoulder him into the square ditch because he would not swop his little snuffbox for Wells's seasoned hacking chestnut, the conqueror of forty. How cold and slimy the water had been! A fellow had once seen a big rat jump into the scum. Mother was sitting at the fire with Dante waiting for Brigid to bring in the tea. She had her feet on the fender and her jewelly slippers were so hot and they had such a lovely warm smell! Dante knew a lot of things. She had taught him where the Mozambique Channel was and what was the longest river in America and what was the name of the highest mountain in the moon. Father Arnall knew more than Dante because he was a priest but both his father and Uncle Charles said that Dante was a clever woman and a wellread woman. And when Dante made that noise after dinner and then put up her hand to her mouth: that was heartburn.

A voice cried far out on the playground:

— All in!

Then other voices cried from the lower and third lines:

— All in! All in!

The players closed around, flushed and muddy, and he went among them, glad to go in. Rody Kickham held the ball by its greasy lace. A fellow asked him to give it one last: but he walked on without even answering the fellow. Simon Moonan told him not to because the prefect was looking. The fellow turned to Simon Moonan and said:

— We all know why you speak. You are McGlade's suck.

Suck was a queer word. The fellow called Simon Moonan that name because Simon Moonan used to tie the prefect's false sleeves behind his back and the prefect used to let on to be angry. But the sound was ugly. Once he had washed his hands in the lavatory of the Wicklow Hotel and his father pulled the stopper up by the chain after and the dirty water went down through the hole in the basin. And when it had all gone down slowly the hole in the basin had made a sound like that: suck. Only louder.

To remember that and the white look of the lavatory made him feel cold and then hot. There were two cocks that you turned and water came out: cold and hot. He felt cold and then a little hot: and he could see the names printed on the cocks. That was a very queer thing.

And the air in the corridor chilled him too. It was queer and wettish. But soon the gas would be lit and in burning it made a light noise like a little song. Always the same: and when the fellows stopped talking in the playroom you could hear it.

It was the hour for sums. Father Arnall wrote a hard sum on the board and then said:

— Now then, who will win? Go ahead, York! Go ahead, Lancaster!

Stephen tried his best but the sum was too hard and he felt confused. The little silk badge with the white rose on it that was pinned on the breast of his jacket began to flutter. He was no good at sums but he tried his best so that York might not lose. Father Arnall's face looked very black but he was not in a wax: he was laughing. Then Jack Lawton cracked his fingers and Father Arnall looked at his copybook and said:

— Right. Bravo Lancaster! The red rose wins. Come on now, York! Forge ahead!

Jack Lawton looked over from his side. The little silk badge with the red rose on it looked very rich because he had a blue sailor top on. Stephen felt his own face red too, thinking of all the bets about who would get first place in Elements, Jack Lawton or he. Some weeks Jack Lawton got the card for first and some weeks he got the card for first. His white silk badge fluttered and fluttered as he worked at the next sum and heard Father Arnall's voice. Then all his eagerness passed away and he felt his face quite cool. He thought his face must be white because it felt so cool. He could not get out the answer for the sum but it did not matter. White roses and red roses: those were beautiful colours to think of. And the cards for first place and third place were beautiful colours too: pink and cream and lavender. Lavender and cream and pink roses were beautiful to think of. Perhaps a wild rose might be like those colours and he remembered the song about the wild rose blossoms on the little green place. But you could not have a green rose. But perhaps somewhere in the world you could.

The bell rang and then the classes began to file out of the rooms and along the corridors towards the refectory. He sat looking at the two prints of butter on his plate but could not eat the damp bread. The tablecloth was damp and limp. But he drank off the hot weak tea which the clumsy scullion, girt with a white apron, poured into his cup. He wondered whether the scullion's apron was damp too or whether all white things were cold and damp. Nasty Roche and Saurin drank cocoa that their people sent them in tins. They said they could not drink the tea; that it was hogwash. Their fathers were magistrates, the fellows said.

All the boys seemed to him very strange. They had all fathers and mothers and different clothes and voices. He longed to be at home and lay his head on his mother's lap. But he could not: and so he longed for the play and study and prayers to be over and to be in bed.

He drank another cup of hot tea and Fleming said:

— What's up? Have you a pain or what's up with you?

— I don't know, Stephen said.

— Sick in your bread basket — Fleming said — because your face looks white. It will go away.

— O yes, Stephen said.

But he was not sick there. He thought that he was sick in his heart if you could be sick in that place. Fleming was very decent to ask him. He wanted to cry. He leaned his elbows on the table and shut and opened the flaps of his ears. Then he heard the noise of the refectory every time he opened the flaps of his ears. It made a roar like a train at night. And when he closed the flaps the roar was shut off like a train going into a tunnel. That night at Dalkey the train had roared like that and then, when it went into the tunnel, the roar stopped. He closed his eyes and the train went on, roaring and then stopping; roaring again, stopping. It was nice to hear it roar and stop and then roar out of the tunnel again and then stop.

Then the higher line fellows began to come down along the matting in the middle of the refectory, Paddy Rath and Jimmy Magee and the Spaniard who was allowed to smoke cigars and the little Portuguese who wore the woolly cap. And then the lower line tables and the tables of the third line. And every single fellow had a different way of walking.

He sat in a corner of the playroom pretending to watch a game of dominos and once or twice he was able to hear for an instant the little song of the gas. The prefect was at the door with some boys and Simon Moonan was knotting his false sleeves. He was telling them something about Tullabeg.

Then he went away from the door and Wells came over to Stephen and said:

— Tell us, Dedalus, do you kiss your mother before you go to bed?

Stephen answered:

— I do.

Wells turned to the other fellows and said:

— O, I say, here's a fellow says he kisses his mother every night before he goes to bed.

The other fellows stopped their game and turned round, laughing. Stephen blushed under their eyes and said:

— I do not.

Wells said:

— O, I say, here's a fellow says he doesn't kiss his mother before he goes to bed.

They all laughed again. Stephen tried to laugh with them. He felt his whole body hot and confused in a moment. What was the right answer to the question? He had given two and still Wells laughed. But Wells must know the right answer for he was in third of grammar. He tried to think of Wells's mother but he did not dare to raise his eyes to Wells's face. He did not like Wells's face. It was Wells who had shouldered him into the square ditch the day before because he would not swop his little snuffbox for Wells's seasoned hacking chestnut, the conqueror of forty. It was a mean thing to do; all the fellows said it was. And how cold and slimy the water had been! And a fellow had once seen a big rat jump plop into the scum.

The cold slime of the ditch covered his whole body; and, when the bell rang for study and the lines filed out of the playrooms, he felt the cold air of the corridor and staircase inside his clothes. He still tried to think what was the right answer. Was it right to kiss his mother or wrong to kiss his mother? What did that mean, to kiss? You put your face up like that to say goodnight and then his mother put her face down. That was to kiss. His mother put her lips on his cheek; her lips were soft and they wetted his cheek; and they made a tiny little noise: kiss. Why did people do that with their two faces?

Sitting in the study hall he opened the lid of his desk and changed the number pasted up inside from seventyseven to seventysix. But the Christmas vacation was very far away: but one time it would come because the earth moved round always.

There was a picture of the earth on the first page of his geography: a big ball in the middle of clouds. Fleming had a box of crayons and one night during free study he had coloured the earth green and the clouds maroon. That was like the two brushes in Dante's press, the brush with the green velvet back for Parnell and the brush with the maroon velvet back for Michael Davitt. But he had not told Fleming to colour them those colours. Fleming had done it himself.

He opened the geography to study the lesson; but he could not learn the names of places in America. Still they were all different places that had different names. They were all in different countries and the countries were in continents and the continents were in the world and the world was in the universe.

He turned to the flyleaf of the geography and read what he had written there: himself, his name and where he was.

Stephen Dedalus
Class of Elements

> Clongowes Wood College
> Sallins
> County Kildare
> Ireland
> Europe
> The World
> The Universe

That was in his writing: and Fleming one night for a cod had written on the opposite page:

> Stephen Dedalus is my name,
> Ireland is my nation.
> Clongowes is my dwellingplace
> And heaven my expectation.

He read the verses backwards but then they were not poetry. Then he read the flyleaf from the bottom to the top till he came to his own name. That was he: and he read down the page again. What was after the universe? Nothing. But was there anything round the universe to show where it stopped before the nothing place began? It could not be a wall but there could be a thin thin line there all round everything. It was very big to think about everything and everywhere. Only God could do that. He tried to think what a big thought that must be but he could think only of God. God was God's name just as his name was Stephen. *Dieu* was the French for God and that was God's name too; and when anyone prayed to God and said Dieu then God knew at once that it was a French person that was praying. But though there were different names for God in all the different languages in the world and God understood what all the people who prayed said in their different languages still God remained always the same God and God's real name was God.

It made him very tired to think that way. It made him feel his head very big. He turned over the flyleaf and looked wearily at the green round earth in the middle of the maroon clouds. He wondered which was right, to be for the green or for the maroon, because Dante had ripped the green velvet back off the brush that was for Parnell one day with her scissors and had told him that Parnell was a bad man. He wondered if they were arguing at home about that. That was called politics. There were two sides in it: Dante was on one side and his father and Mr. Casey were on the other side but his mother and Uncle Charles were on no side. Every day there was something in the paper about it.

It pained him that he did not know well what politics meant and that he did not know where the universe ended. He felt small and weak. When would he be like the fellows in Poetry and Rhetoric? They had big voices and big boots and they studied trigonometry. That was very far away. First came the vacation and then the next term and then vacation again and then again another term and then again the vacation. It was like a train going in and out of tunnels and that was like the noise of the boys eating in the refectory when you opened and closed the flaps of the ears. Term, vacation; tunnel, out; noise, stop. How far away it was! It was better to go to bed to sleep. Only prayers in the chapel and then bed. He shivered and yawned. It would be lovely in bed after the sheets got a bit hot. First they were so cold to get into. He shivered to think how cold they were first. But then they got hot and then he could sleep. It was lovely to be tired. He yawned again. Night prayers and then bed: he shivered and wanted to yawn. It would be lovely in a few minutes. He felt a warm glow creeping up from the cold shivering sheets, warmer and warmer till he felt warm all over, ever so warm and yet he shivered a little and still wanted to yawn.

The bell rang for night prayers and he filed out of the study hall after the others and down the staircase and along the corridors to the chapel. The corridors were darkly lit and the chapel was darkly lit. Soon all would be dark and sleeping. There was cold night air in the chapel and the marbles were the colour the sea was at night. The sea was cold day and night: but it was colder at night. It was cold and dark under the seawall beside his father's house. But the kettle would be on the hob to make punch.

The prefect of the chapel prayed above his head and his memory knew the responses:

> O Lord, open our lips
> And our mouths shall announce Thy praise.
> Incline unto our aid, O God!
> O Lord, make haste to help us!

There was a cold night smell in the chapel. But it was a holy smell. It was not like the smell of the old peasants who knelt at the back of the chapel at Sunday mass. That was a smell of air and rain and turf and corduroy. But they were very holy peasants. They breathed behind him on his neck and sighed as they prayed. They lived in Clane, a fellow said: there were little cottages there and he had seen a woman standing at the halfdoor of a cottage with a child in her arms, as the cars had come past from Sallins. It would be lovely to sleep for one night in that cottage before the fire of smoking turf, in the dark lit by the fire, in the warm dark, breathing the smell of the peasants, air and rain and turf and corduroy. But, O, the road there between the trees was dark! You would be lost in the dark. It made him afraid to think of how it was.

He heard the voice of the prefect of the chapel saying the last prayer. He prayed it too against the dark outside under the trees.

> *Visit, we beseech Thee, O Lord, this habitation and drive away from it all the snares of the enemy. May Thy holy angels dwell herein to preserve us in peace and may Thy blessing be always upon us through Christ our Lord. Amen.*

His fingers trembled as he undressed himself in the dormitory. He told his fingers to hurry up. He had to undress and then kneel and say his own prayers and be in bed before the gas was lowered so that he might not go to hell when he died. He rolled his stockings off and put on his nightshirt quickly and knelt trembling at his bedside and repeated his prayers quickly, fearing that the gas would go down. He felt his shoulders shaking as he murmured:

God bless my father and my mother and spare them to me!
God bless my little brothers and sisters and spare them to me!
God bless Dante and Uncle Charles and spare them to me!

He blessed himself and climbed quickly into bed and, tucking the end of the nightshirt under his feet, curled himself together under the cold white sheets, shaking and trembling. But he would not go to hell when he died; and the shaking would stop. A voice bade the boys in the dormitory goodnight. He peered out for an instant over the coverlet and saw the yellow curtains round and before his bed that shut him off on all sides. The light was lowered quietly.

The prefect's shoes went away. Where? Down the staircase and along the corridors or to his room at the end? He saw the dark. Was it true about the black dog that walked there at night with eyes as big as carriagelamps? They said it was the ghost of a murderer. A long shiver of fear flowed over his body. He saw the dark entrance hall of the castle. Old servants in old dress were in the ironingroom above the staircase. It was long ago. The old servants were quiet. There was a fire there but the hall was still dark. A figure came up the staircase from the hall. He wore the white cloak of a marshal; his face was pale and strange; he held his hand pressed to his side. He looked out of strange eyes at the old servants. They looked at him and saw their master's face and cloak and knew that he had received his death wound. But only the dark was where they looked: only dark silent air. Their master had received his death wound on the battlefield of Prague far away over the sea. He was standing on the field; his hand was pressed to his side; his face was pale and strange and he wore the white cloak of a marshal.

O how cold and strange it was to think of that! All the dark was cold and strange. There were pale strange faces there, great eyes like carriagelamps. They were the ghosts of murderers, the figures of marshals who had received their death wound on battlefields far away over the sea. What did they wish to say that their faces were so strange?

> *Visit, we beseech Thee, O Lord, this habitation and drive away from it all . . .*

Going home for the holidays! That would be lovely: the fellows had told him. Getting up on the cars in the early wintry morning outside the door of the castle. The cars were rolling on the gravel. Cheers for the rector!

Hurray! Hurray! Hurray!

The cars drove past the chapel and all caps were raised. They drove merrily along the country roads. The drivers pointed with their whips to Bodenstown. The fellows cheered. They passed the farmhouse of the Jolly Farmer. Cheer after cheer after cheer. Through Clane they drove, cheering and cheered. The peasant women stood at the halfdoors, the men stood here and there. The lovely smell there was in the wintry air: the smell of Clane: rain and wintry air and turf smouldering and corduroy.

The train was full of fellows: a long long chocolate train with cream facings. The guards went to and fro opening, closing, locking, unlocking the doors. They were men in dark blue and silver; they had silvery whistles and their keys made a quick music: click, click: click, click.

And the train raced on over the flat lands and past the Hill of Allen. The telegraph poles were passing, passing. The train went on and on. It knew. There were lanterns in the hall of his father's house and ropes of green branches. There were holly and ivy round the pierglass and holly and ivy, green and red, twined round the chandeliers. There were red holly and green ivy round the old portraits on the walls. Holly and ivy for him and for Christmas.

Lovely . . .

All the people. Welcome home, Stephen! Noises of welcome. His mother kissed him. Was that right? His father was a marshal now: higher than a magistrate. Welcome home, Stephen!

Noises . . .

There was a noise of curtainrings running back along the rods, of water being splashed in the basins. There was a noise of rising and dressing and washing in the dormitory: a noise of clapping of hands as the prefect went up and down telling the fellows to look sharp. A pale sunlight showed the yellow curtains drawn back, the tossed beds. His bed was very hot and his face and body were very hot.

He got up and sat on the side of his bed. He was weak. He tried to pull on his stocking. It had a horrid rough feel. The sunlight was queer and cold.

Fleming said:

— Are you not well?

He did not know; and Fleming said:

— Get back into bed. I'll tell McGlade you're not well.

— He's sick.

— Who is?

— Tell McGlade.

— Get back into bed.

— Is he sick?

A fellow held his arms while he loosened the stocking clinging to his foot and climbed back into the hot bed.

He crouched down between the sheets, glad of their tepid glow. He heard the fellows talk among themselves about him as they dressed for mass. It was a mean thing to do, to shoulder him into the square ditch, they were saying.

Then their voices ceased; they had gone. A voice at his bed said:

— Dedalus, don't spy on us, sure you won't?

Wells's face was there. He looked at it and saw that Wells was afraid.

— I didn't mean to. Sure you won't?

His father had told him, whatever he did, never to peach on a fellow. He shook his head and answered no and felt glad.

Wells said:

— I didn't mean to, honour bright. It was only for cod. I'm sorry.

The face and the voice went away. Sorry because he was afraid. Afraid that it was some disease. Canker was a disease of plants and cancer one of animals: or another different. That was a long time ago then out on the playgrounds in the evening light, creeping from point to point on the fringe of his line, a heavy bird flying low through the grey light. Leicester Abbey lit up. Wolsey died there. The abbots buried him themselves.

It was not Wells's face, it was the prefect's. He was not foxing. No, no: he was sick really. He was not foxing. And he felt the prefect's hand on his forehead; and he felt his forehead warm and damp against the prefect's cold damp hand. That was the way a rat felt, slimy and damp and cold. Every rat had two eyes to look out of. Sleek slimy coats, little little feet tucked up to jump, black slimy eyes to look out of. They could understand how to jump. But the minds of rats could not understand trigonometry. When they were dead they lay on their sides. Their coats dried then. They were only dead things.

The prefect was there again and it was his voice that was saying that he was to get up, that Father Minister had said he was to get up and dress and go to the infirmary. And while he was dressing himself as quickly as he could the prefect said:

— We must pack off to Brother Michael because we have the collywobbles!

He was very decent to say that. That was all to make him laugh. But he could not laugh because his cheeks and lips were all shivery: and then the prefect had to laugh by himself.

The prefect cried:

— Quick march! Hayfoot! Strawfoot!

They went together down the staircase and along the corridor and past the bath. As he passed the door he remembered with a vague fear the warm turf-coloured bogwater, the warm moist air, the noise of plunges, the smell of the towels, like medicine.

Brother Michael was standing at the door of the infirmary and from the door of the dark cabinet on his right came a smell like medicine. That came from the bottles on the shelves. The prefect spoke to Brother Michael and Brother Michael answered and called the prefect sir. He had reddish hair mixed with grey and a queer look. It was queer that he would always be a brother. It was queer too that you could not call him sir because he was a brother and had a different kind of look. Was he not holy enough or why could he not catch up on the others?

There were two beds in the room and in one bed there was a fellow: and when they went in he called out:

— Hello! It's young Dedalus! What's up?

— The sky is up, Brother Michael said.

He was a fellow out of the third of grammar and, while Stephen was undressing, he asked Brother Michael to bring him a round of buttered toast.

— Ah, do! he said.

— Butter you up! said Brother Michael. You'll get your walking papers in the morning when the doctor comes.

— Will I? the fellow said. I'm not well yet.

Brother Michael repeated:

— You'll get your walking papers. I tell you.

He bent down to rake the fire. He had a long back like the long back of a tramhorse. He shook the poker gravely and nodded his head at the fellow out of third of grammar.

Then Brother Michael went away and after a while the fellow out of third of grammar turned in towards the wall and fell asleep.

That was the infirmary. He was sick then. Had they written home to tell his mother and father? But it would be quicker for one of the priests to go himself to tell them. Or he would write a letter for the priest to bring.

Dear Mother,
    I am sick. I want to go home. Please come and take me home. I am in the infirmary.

                                                    Your fond son,
                                                                    Stephen.

How far away they were! There was cold sunlight outside the window. He wondered if he would die. You could die just the same on a sunny day. He might die before his mother came. Then he would have a dead mass in the chapel like the way the fellows had told him it was when Little had died. All the fellows would be at the mass, dressed in black, all with sad faces. Wells too would be there but no fellow would look at him. The rector would be there in a cope of black and gold and there would be tall yellow candles on the altar and round the catafalque. And they would carry the coffin out of the chapel slowly and he would be buried in the little graveyard of the community off the main avenue of limes. And Wells would be sorry then for what he had done. And the bell would toll slowly.

He could hear the tolling. He said over to himself the song that Brigid had taught him.

> *Dingdong! The castle bell!*
> *Farewell, my mother!*
> *Bury me in the old churchyard*
> *Beside my eldest brother.*
> *My coffin shall be black,*
> *Six angels at my back,*
> *Two to sing and two to pray*
> *And two to carry my soul away.*

How beautiful and sad that was! How beautiful the words were where they said *Bury me in the old churchyard!* A tremor passed over his body. How sad and how beautiful! He wanted to cry quietly but not for himself: for the words, so beautiful and sad, like music. The bell! The bell! Farewell! O farewell!

The cold sunlight was weaker and Brother Michael was standing at his bedside with a bowl of beeftea. He was glad for his mouth was hot and dry. He could hear them playing in the playgrounds. And the day was going on in the college just as if he were there.

Then Brother Michael was going away and the fellow out of third of grammar told him to be sure and come back and tell him all the news in the paper. He told Stephen that his name was Athy and that his father kept a lot of racehorses that were spiffing jumpers and that his father would give a good tip to Brother Michael any time he wanted it because

Brother Michael was very decent and always told him the news out of the paper they got every day up in the castle. There was every kind of news in the paper: accidents, shipwrecks, sports and politics.

— Now it is all about politics in the papers, he said. Do your people talk about that too?

— Yes, Stephen said.

— Mine too, he said.

Then he thought for a moment and said:

— You have a queer name, Dedalus, and I have a queer name too, Athy. My name is the name of a town. Your name is like Latin.

Then he asked:

— Are you good at riddles?

Stephen answered:

— Not very good.

Then he said:

— Can you answer me this one? Why is the county of Kildare like the leg of a fellow's breeches?

Stephen thought what could be the answer and then said:

— I give it up.

— Because there is a thigh in it, he said. Do you see the joke? Athy is the town in the county Kildare, and a thigh is the other thigh.

— O, I see, Stephen said.

— That's an old riddle, he said.

After a moment he said:

— I say!

— What? asked Stephen.

— You know, he said, you can ask that riddle another way.

— Can you? said Stephen.

— The same riddle, he said. Do you know the other way to ask it?

— No, said Stephen.

— Can you not think of the other way? he said.

He looked at Stephen over the bedclothes as he spoke. Then he lay back on the pillow and said:

— There is another way but I won't tell you what it is.

Why did he not tell it? His father, who kept the racehorses, must be a magistrate too like Saurin's father and Nasty Roche's father. He thought of his own father, of how he sang songs while his mother played and of how he always gave him a shilling when he asked for sixpence and he felt sorry for him that he was not a magistrate like the other boys' fathers. Then why was he sent to that place with them? But his father had told him that he would be no stranger there because his granduncle had presented an address to the Liberator there fifty years before. You could know the people of that time by their old dress. It seemed to him a solemn time: and he wondered if that was the time when the fellows in Clongowes wore blue coats with brass buttons and yellow waistcoats and caps of rabbit-skin and drank beer like grownup people and kept greyhounds of their own to course the hares with.

He looked at the window and saw that the daylight had grown weaker. There would be cloudy grey light over the playgrounds. There was no noise on the playgrounds. The class must be doing the themes or perhaps Father Arnall was reading out of the book.

It was queer that they had not given him any medicine. Perhaps Brother Michael would bring it back when he came. They said you got stinking stuff to drink when you were in the infirmary. But he felt better now than before. It would be nice getting better slowly. You could get a book then. There was a book in the library about Holland. There were lovely foreign names in it and pictures of strange-looking cities and ships. It made you feel so happy.

How pale the light was at the window! But that was nice. The fire rose and fell on the wall. It was like waves. Someone had put coal on and he heard voices. They were talking. It was the noise of the waves. Or the waves were talking among themselves as they rose and fell.

He saw the sea of waves, long dark waves rising and falling, dark under the moonless night. A tiny light twinkled at the pierhead where the ship was entering: and he saw a multitude of people gathered by the waters' edge to see the ship that was entering their harbour. A tall man stood on the deck, looking out towards the flat dark land: and by the light at the pierhead he saw his face, the sorrowful face of Brother Michael.

He saw him lift his hand towards the people and heard him say in a loud voice of sorrow over the waters:

— He is dead. We saw him lying upon the catafalque.

A wail of sorrow went up from the people.

— Parnell! Parnell! He is dead!

They fell upon their knees, moaning in sorrow.

And he saw Dante in a maroon velvet dress and with a green velvet mantle hanging from her shoulders walking proudly and silently past the people who knelt by the waters' edge.

A great fire, banked high and red, flamed in the grate and under the ivy twined branches of the chandelier the Christmas table was spread. They had come home a little late and still dinner was not ready: but it would be ready in a jiffy, his mother had said. They were waiting for the door to open and for the servants to come in, holding the big dishes covered with their heavy metal covers.

All were waiting: Uncle Charles, who sat far away in the shadow of the window, Dante and Mr Casey, who sat in the easy chairs at either side of the hearth, Stephen, seated on a chair between them, his feet resting on the toasted boss. Mr Dedalus looked at himself in the pierglass above the mantelpiece, waxed out his moustache ends and then, parting his coat tails, stood with his back to the glowing fire: and still from time to time he withdrew a hand from his coat tail to wax out one of his moustache ends. Mr Casey leaned his head to one side and, smiling, tapped the gland of his neck with his fingers. And Stephen smiled too for he knew now that it was not true that Mr Casey had a purse of silver in his throat. He smiled to think how the silvery noise which Mr Casey used to make had deceived him. And when he had tried to open Mr Casey's hand to see if the purse of silver was hidden there he had seen that the fingers could not be straightened out: and Mr Casey had told him that he had got those three cramped fingers making a birthday present for Queen Victoria.

Mr Casey tapped the gland of his neck and smiled at Stephen with sleepy eyes: and Mr. Dedalus said to him:

— Yes. Well now, that's all right. O, we had a good walk, hadn't we, John? Yes . . . I wonder if there's any likelihood of dinner this evening. Yes. . . . O, well now, we got a good breath of ozone round the Head today. Ay, bedad.

He turned to Dante and said:

— You didn't stir out at all, Mrs Riordan?

Dante frowned and said shortly:

— No.

Mr Dedalus dropped his coat tails and went over to the sideboard. He brought forth a great stone jar of whisky from the locker and filled the decanter slowly, bending now and then to see how much he had poured in. Then replacing the jar in the locker he poured a little of the whisky into two glasses, added a little water and came back with them to the fireplace.

— A thimbleful, John, he said, just to whet your appetite.

Mr Casey took the glass, drank, and placed it near him on the mantelpiece. Then he said:

— Well, I can't help thinking of our friend Christopher manufacturing . . .

He broke into a fit of laughter and coughing and added:

— . . . manufacturing that champagne for those fellows.

Mr Dedalus laughed loudly.

— Is it Christy? he said. There's more cunning in one of those warts on his bald head than in a pack of jack foxes.

He inclined his head, closed his eyes, and, licking his lips profusely, began to speak with the voice of the hotel keeper.

— And he has such a soft mouth when he's speaking to you, don't you know. He's very moist and watery about the dewlaps, God bless him.

Mr Casey was still struggling through his fit of coughing and laughter. Stephen, seeing and hearing the hotel keeper through his father's face and voice, laughed.

Mr Dedalus put up his eyeglass and, staring down at him, said quietly and kindly:

— What are you laughing at, you little puppy, you?

The servants entered and placed the dishes on the table. Mrs Dedalus followed and the places were arranged.

— Sit over, she said.

Mr Dedalus went to the end of the table and said:

— Now, Mrs Riordan, sit over. John, sit you down, my hearty.

He looked round to where Uncle Charles sat and said:

— Now then, sir, there's a bird here waiting for you.

When all had taken their seats he laid his hand on the cover and then said quickly, withdrawing it:

— Now, Stephen.

Stephen stood up in his place to say the grace before meals:

Bless us, O Lord, and these Thy gifts which through Thy bounty we are about to receive through Christ our Lord. Amen.

All blessed themselves and Mr Dedalus with a sigh of pleasure lifted from the dish the heavy cover pearled around the edge with glistening drops.

Stephen looked at the plump turkey which had lain, trussed and skewered, on the kitchen table. He knew that his father had paid a guinea for it in Dunn's of D'Olier Street and that the man had prodded it often at the breastbone to show how good it was: and he remembered the man's voice when he had said:

— Take that one, sir. That's the real Ally Daly.

Why did Mr Barrett in Clongowes call his pandybat a turkey? But Clongowes was far away: and the warm heavy smell of turkey and ham and celery rose from the plates and dishes and the great fire was banked high and red in the grate and the green ivy and red holly made you feel so happy and when dinner was ended the big plum pudding would be carried in, studded with peeled almonds and sprigs of holly, with bluish fire running around it and a little green flag flying from the top.

It was his first Christmas dinner and he thought of his little brothers and sisters who were waiting in the nursery, as he had often waited, till the pudding came. The deep low collar and the Eton jacket made him feel queer and oldish: and that morning when his mother had brought him down to the parlour, dressed for mass, his father had cried. That was because he was thinking of his own father. And Uncle Charles had said so too.

Mr Dedalus covered the dish and began to eat hungrily. Then he said:

— Poor old Christy, he's nearly lopsided now with roguery.

— Simon, said Mrs Dedalus, you haven't given Mrs Riordan any sauce.

Mr Dedalus seized the sauceboat.

— Haven't I? he cried. Mrs Riordan, pity the poor blind.

Dante covered her plate with her hands and said:

— No, thanks.

Mr Dedalus turned to Uncle Charles.

— How are you off, sir?

— Right as the mail, Simon.

— You, John?

— I'm all right. Go on yourself.

— Mary? Here, Stephen, here's something to make your hair curl.

He poured sauce freely over Stephen's plate and set the boat again on the table. Then he asked Uncle Charles was it tender. Uncle Charles could not speak because his mouth was full but he nodded that it was.

— That was a good answer our friend made to the canon. What? said Mr Dedalus.

— I didn't think he had that much in him, said Mr Casey.

— *I'll pay your dues, father, when you cease turning the house of God into a polling-booth.*

— A nice answer, said Dante, for any man calling himself a catholic to give to his priest.

— They have only themselves to blame, said Mr Dedalus suavely. If they took a fool's advice they would confine their attention to religion.

— It is religion, Dante said. They are doing their duty in warning the people.

— We go to the house of God, Mr Casey said, in all humility to pray to our Maker and not to hear election addresses.

— It is religion, Dante said again. They are right. They must direct their flocks.

— And preach politics from the altar, is it? asked Mr Dedalus.

— Certainly, said Dante. It is a question of public morality. A priest would not be a priest if he did not tell his flock what is right and what is wrong.

Mrs Dedalus laid down her knife and fork, saying:

— For pity sake and for pity sake let us have no political discussion on this day of all days in the year.

— Quite right, ma'am, said Uncle Charles. Now Simon, that's quite enough now. Not another word now.

— Yes, yes, said Mr Dedalus quickly.

He uncovered the dish boldly and said:

— Now then, who's for more turkey?

Nobody answered. Dante said:

— Nice language for any catholic to use!

— Mrs Riordan, I appeal to you, said Mrs Dedalus, to let the matter drop now.

Dante turned on her and said:

— And am I to sit here and listen to the pastors of my church being flouted?

— Nobody is saying a word against them, said Mr Dedalus, so long as they don't meddle in politics.

— The bishops and priests of Ireland have spoken, said Dante, and they must be obeyed.

— Let them leave politics alone, said Mr Casey; or the people may leave their church alone.

— You hear? said Dante turning to Mrs Dedalus.

— Mr Casey! Simon! said Mrs Dedalus, let it end now.

— Too bad! Too bad! said Uncle Charles.

— What? cried Mr Dedalus. Were we to desert him at the bidding of the English people?

— He was no longer worthy to lead, said Dante. He was a public sinner.

— We are all sinners and black sinners, said Mr Casey coldly.

— Woe be to the man by whom the scandal cometh! said Mrs Riordan. *It would be better for him that a millstone were tied about his neck and that he were cast into the depths of the sea rather than that he should scandalise one of these, my least little ones.* That is the language of the Holy Ghost.

— And very bad language if you ask me, said Mr Dedalus coolly.

— Simon! Simon! said Uncle Charles. The boy.

— Yes, yes, said Mr Dedalus. I meant about the . . . I was thinking about the bad language of that railway porter. Well now, that's all right. Here, Stephen, show me your plate, old chap. Eat away now. Here.

He heaped up the food on Stephen's plate and served Uncle Charles and Mr Casey to large pieces of turkey and splashes of sauce. Mrs Dedalus was eating little and Dante sat with her hands in her lap. She was red in the face. Mr Dedalus rooted with the carvers at the end of the dish and said:

— There's a tasty bit here we call the pope's nose. If any lady or gentleman . . .

He held a piece of fowl up on the prong of the carvingfork. Nobody spoke. He put it on his own plate, saying:

— Well, you can't say but you were asked. I think I had better eat it myself because I'm not well in my health lately.

He winked at Stephen and, replacing the dish-cover, began to eat again.

There was a silence while he ate. Then he said:

— Well now, the day kept up fine after all. There were plenty of strangers down too.

Nobody spoke. He said again:

— I think there were more strangers down than last Christmas.

He looked round at the others whose faces were bent towards their plates and, receiving no reply, waited for a moment and said bitterly:

— Well, my Christmas dinner has been spoiled anyhow.

— There could be neither luck nor grace, Dante said, in a house where there is no respect for the pastors of the church.

Mr Dedalus threw his knife and fork noisily on his plate.

— Respect! he said. Is it for Billy with the lip or for the tub of guts up in Armagh? Respect!

— Princes of the church, said Mr Casey with slow scorn.

— Lord Leitrim's coachman, yes, said Mr Dedalus.

— They are the Lord's anointed, Dante said. They are an honour to their country.

— Tub of guts, said Mr Dedalus coarsely. He has a handsome face, mind you, in repose. You should see that fellow lapping up his bacon and cabbage of a cold winter's day. O Johnny!

He twisted his features into a grimace of heavy bestiality and made a lapping noise with his lips.

— Really, Simon, you should not speak that way before Stephen. It's not right.

— O, he'll remember all this when he grows up, said Dante hotly — the language he heard against God and religion and priests in his own home.

— Let him remember too, cried Mr Casey to her from across the table, the language with which the priests and the priests' pawns broke Parnell's heart and hounded him into his grave. Let him remember that too when he grows up.

— Sons of bitches! cried Mr Dedalus. When he was down they turned on him to betray him and rend him like rats in a sewer. Lowlived dogs! And they look it! By Christ, they look it!

— They behaved rightly, cried Dante. They obeyed their bishops and their priests. Honour to them!

— Well, it is perfectly dreadful to say that not even for one day in the year, said Mrs Dedalus, can we be free from these dreadful disputes!

Uncle Charles raised his hands mildly and said:

— Come now, come now, come now! Can we not have our opinions whatever they are without this bad temper and this bad language? It is too bad surely.

Mrs Dedalus spoke to Dante in a low voice but Dante said loudly:

— I will not say nothing. I will defend my church and my religion when it is insulted and spit on by renegade catholics.

Mr Casey pushed his plate rudely into the middle of the table and, resting his elbows before him, said in a hoarse voice to his host:

— Tell me, did I tell you that story about a very famous spit?

— You did not, John, said Mr Dedalus.

— Why then, said Mr Casey, it is a most instructive story. It happened not long ago in the county Wicklow where we are now.

He broke off and, turning towards Dante, said with quiet indignation:

— And I may tell you, ma'am, that I, if you mean me, am no renegade catholic. I am a catholic as my father was and his father before him and his father before him again when we gave up our lives rather than sell our faith.

— The more shame to you now, Dante said, to speak as you do.

— The story, John, said Mr Dedalus smiling. Let us have the story anyhow.

— Catholic indeed! repeated Dante ironically. The blackest protestant in the land would not speak the language I have heard this evening.

Mr Dedalus began to sway his head to and fro, crooning like a country singer.

— I am no protestant, I tell you again, said Mr Casey flushing.

Mr Dedalus, still crooning and swaying his head, began to sing in a grunting nasal tone:

> O, come all you Roman catholics
> That never went to mass.

He took up his knife and fork again in good humour and set to eating, saying to Mr Casey:

— Let us have the story, John. It will help us to digest.

Stephen looked with affection at Mr Casey's face which stared across the table over his joined hands. He liked to sit near him at the fire, looking up at his dark fierce face. But his dark eyes were never fierce and his slow voice was good to listen to. But why was he then against the priests? Because Dante must be right then. But he had heard his father say that she was a spoiled nun and that she had come out of the convent in the Alleghanies when her brother had got the money from the savages for the trinkets and the chainies. Perhaps that made her severe against Parnell. And she did not like him to play with Eileen because Eileen was a protestant and when she was young she knew children that used to play with protestants and the protestants used to make fun of the litany of the Blessed Virgin. *Tower of Ivory*, they used to say, *House of Gold!* How could a woman be a tower of ivory or a house of gold? Who was right then? And he remembered the evening in the infirmary in Clongowes, the dark waters, the light at the pierhead and the moan of sorrow from the people when they had heard.

Eileen had long white hands. One evening when playing tag she had put her hands over his eyes: long and white and thin and cold and soft. That was ivory: a cold white thing. That was the meaning of *Tower of Ivory*.

— The story is very short and sweet, Mr Casey said. It was one day down in Arklow, a cold bitter day, not long before the chief died. May God have mercy on him!

He closed his eyes wearily and paused. Mr Dedalus took a bone from his plate and tore some meat from it with his teeth, saying:

— Before he was killed, you mean.

Mr Casey opened his eyes, sighed and went on:

— He was down in Arklow one day. We were down there at a meeting and after the meeting was over we had to make our way to the railway station through the crowd. Such booing and baaing, man, you never heard. They called us all the names in the world. Well there was one old lady, and a drunken old harridan she was surely, that paid all her attention to me. She kept dancing along beside me in the mud bawling and screaming into my face: *Priest hunter! The Paris Funds! Mr Fox! Kitty O'Shea!*

— And what did you do, John? asked Mr Dedalus.

— I let her bawl away, said Mr. Casey. It was a cold day and to keep up my heart I had (saving your presence, ma'am) a quid of Tullamore in my mouth and sure I couldn't say a word in any case because my mouth was. full of tobacco juice.

— Well, John?

— Well. I let her bawl away, to her heart's content, *Kitty O'Shea* and the rest of it till at last she called that lady a name that I won't sully this Christmas board nor your ears, ma'am, nor my own lips by repeating.

He paused. Mr Dedalus, lifting his head from the bone, asked:

— And what did you do, John?

— Do! said Mr Casey. She stuck her ugly old face up at me when she said it and I had my mouth full of tobacco juice. I bent down to her and *Phth!* says I to her like that.

He turned aside and made the act of spitting.

— Phth! says I to her like that, right into her eye.

He clapped a hand to his eye and gave a hoarse scream of pain.

— *O Jesus, Mary and Joseph!* says she. *I'm blinded! I'm blinded and drownded!*

He stopped in a fit of coughing and laughter, repeating:

— *I'm blinded entirely.*

Mr Dedalus laughed loudly and lay back in his chair while Uncle Charles swayed his head to and fro.

Dante looked terribly angry and repeated while they laughed:

— Very nice! Ha! Very nice!

It was not nice about the spit in the woman's eye.

But what was the name the woman had called Kitty O'Shea that Mr Casey would not repeat? He thought of Mr Casey walking through the crowds of people and making speeches from a wagonette. That was what he had been in prison for and he remembered that one night Sergeant O'Neill had come to the house and had stood in the hall, talking in a low voice with his father and chewing nervously at the chinstrap of his cap. And that night Mr Casey had not gone to Dublin by train but a car had come to the door and he had heard his father say something about the Cabinteely road.

He was for Ireland and Parnell and so was his father: and so was Dante too for one night at the band on the esplanade she had hit a gentleman on the head with her umbrella because he had taken off his hat when the band played *God save the Queen* at the end.

Mr Dedalus gave a snort of contempt.

— Ah, John, he said. It is true for them. We are an unfortunate priestridden race and always were and always will be till the end of the chapter.

Uncle Charles shook his head, saying:

— A bad business! A bad business!

Mr Dedalus repeated:

— A priestridden Godforsaken race!

He pointed to the portrait of his grandfather on the wall to his right.

— Do you see that old chap up there, John? he said. He was a good Irishman when there was no money in the job. He was condemned to death as a whiteboy. But he had a saying about our clerical friends, that he would never let one of them put his two feet under his mahogany.

Dante broke in angrily:

— If we are a priestridden race we ought to be proud of it! They are the apple of God's eye. *Touch them not*, says Christ, *for they are the apple of My eye.*

— And can we not love our country then? asked Mr Casey. Are we not to follow the man that was born to lead us?

— A traitor to his country! replied Dante. A traitor, an adulterer! The priests were right to abandon him. The priests were always the true friends of Ireland.

— Were they, faith? said Mr Casey.

He threw his fist on the table and, frowning angrily, protruded one finger after another.

— Didn't the bishops of Ireland betray us in the time of the union when Bishop Lanigan presented an address of loyalty to the Marquess Cornwallis? Didn't the bishops and priests sell the aspirations of their country in 1829 in return for catholic emancipation? Didn't they denounce the fenian movement from the pulpit and in the confession box? And didn't they dishonour the ashes of Terence Bellew Mac-Manus?

His face was glowing with anger and Stephen felt the glow rise to his own cheek as the spoken words thrilled him. Mr Dedalus uttered a guffaw of coarse scorn.

— O, by God — he cried — I forgot little old Paul Cullen! Another apple of God's eye!

Dante bent across the table and cried to Mr Casey:

— Right! Right! They were always right! God and morality and religion come first.

Mrs Dedalus, seeing her excitement, said to her:

— Mrs Riordan, don't excite yourself answering them.

— God and religion before everything! Dante cried. God and religion before the world!

Mr Casey raised his clenched fist and brought it down on the table with a crash.

— Very well, then, he shouted hoarsely, if it comes to that, no God for Ireland!

— John! John! cried Mr Dedalus, seizing his guest by the coat sleeve.

Dante stared across the table, her cheeks shaking. Mr Casey struggled up from his chair and bent across the table towards her, scraping the air from before his eyes with one hand as though he were tearing aside a cobweb.

— No God for Ireland! he cried. We have had too much God in Ireland. Away with God!

— Blasphemer! Devil! screamed Dante, starting to her feet and almost spitting in his face.

Uncle Charles and Mr Dedalus pulled Mr Casey back into his chair again, talking to him from both sides reasonably. He stared before him out of his dark flaming eyes, repeating:

— Away with God, I say!

Dante shoved her chair violently aside and left the table, upsetting her napkinring which rolled slowly along the carpet and came to rest against the foot of an easychair. Mrs Dedalus rose quickly and followed her towards the door. At the door Dante turned round violently and shouted down the room, her cheeks flushed and quivering with rage:

— Devil out of hell! We won! We crushed him to death! Fiend!

The door slammed behind her.

Mr Casey, freeing his arms from his holders, suddenly bowed his head on his hands with a sob of pain.

— Poor Parnell! he cried loudly. My dead king!

He sobbed loudly and bitterly.

Stephen, raising his terrorstricken face, saw that his father's eyes were full of tears.

*   *   *   *

The fellows talked together in little groups.

One fellow said:

— They were caught near the Hill of Lyons.

— Who caught them?

— Mr Gleeson and the minister. They were on a car.

The same fellow added:

— A fellow in the higher line told me.

Fleming asked:

— But why did they run away, tell us?

— I know why, Cecil Thunder said. Because they had fecked cash out of the rector's room.

— Who fecked it?

— Kickham's brother. And they all went shares in it.

But that was stealing. How could they have done that?

— A fat lot you know about it, Thunder! Wells said. I know why they scut.

— Tell us why.

— I was told not to, Wells said.

— O, go on, Wells, all said. You might tell us. We won't let it out.

Stephen bent forward his head to hear. Wells looked round to see if anyone was coming. Then he said secretly:

— You know the altar wine they keep in the press in the sacristy?

— Yes.

— Well, they drank that and it was found out who did it by the smell. And that's why they ran away, if you want to know.

And the fellow who had spoken first said:

— Yes, that's what I heard too from the fellow in the higher line.

The fellows were all silent. Stephen stood among them, afraid to speak, listening. A faint sickness of awe made him feel weak. How could they have done that? He thought of the dark silent sacristy. There were dark wooden presses there where the crimped surplices lay quietly folded. It was not the chapel but still you had to speak under your breath. It was a holy place. He remembered the summer evening he had been there to be dressed as boat-bearer, the evening of the procession to the little altar in the wood. A strange and holy place. The boy that held the censer had swung it gently to and fro near the door with the silvery cap lifted by the middle chain to keep the coals lighting. That was called charcoal: and it had burned quietly as the fellow had swung it gently and had given off a weak sour smell. And then when all were vested he had stood holding out the boat to the rector and the rector had put a spoonful of incense in and it had hissed on the red coals.

The fellows were talking together in little groups here and there on the playground. The fellows seemed to him to have grown smaller: that was because a sprinter had knocked him down the day before, a fellow out of second of grammar. He had been thrown by the fellow's machine lightly on the cinderpath and his spectacles had been broken in three pieces and some of the grit of the cinders had gone into his mouth.

That was why the fellows seemed to him smaller and farther away and the goalposts so thin and far and the soft grey sky so high up. But there was no play on the football grounds for cricket was coming: and some said that Barnes would be the prof and some said it would be Flowers. And all over the playgrounds they were playing rounders and bowling twisters and lobs. And from here and from there came the sounds of the cricket bats through the soft grey air. They said: pick, pack, pock, puck: little drops of water in a fountain slowly falling in the brimming bowl.

Athy, who had been silent, said quietly:

— You are all wrong.

All turned towards him eagerly.

— Why?

— Do you know?

— Who told you?

— Tell us, Athy.

Athy pointed across the playground to where Simon Moonan was walking by himself kicking a stone before him.

— Ask him, he said.

The fellows looked there and then said:

— Why him?

— Is he in it?

Athy lowered his voice and said:

— Do you know why those fellows scut? I will tell you but you must not let on you know.

— Tell us, Athy. Go on. You might if you know.

He paused for a moment and then said mysteriously:

— They were caught with Simon Moonan and Tusker Boyle in the square one night.

The fellows looked at him and asked:

— Caught?

— What doing?

Athy said:

— Smugging.

All the fellows were silent: and Athy said:

— And that's why.

Stephen looked at the faces of the fellows but they were all looking across the playground. He wanted to ask somebody about it. What did that mean about the smugging in the square? Why did the five fellows out of the higher line run away for that? It was a joke, he thought. Simon Moonan had nice clothes and one night he had shown him a ball of creamy sweets that the fellows of the football fifteen had rolled down to him along the carpet in the middle of the refectory when he was at the door. It was the night of the match against the Bective Rangers and the ball was made just like a red and green apple only it opened and it was full of the creamy sweets. And one day Boyle had said that an elephant had two tuskers instead of two tusks and that was why he was called Tusker Boyle but some fellows called him Lady Boyle because he was always at his nails, paring them.

Eileen had long thin cool white hands too because she was a girl. They were like ivory; only soft. That was the meaning of *Tower of Ivory* but protestants could not understand it and made fun of it. One day he had stood beside her looking into the hotel grounds. A waiter was running up a trail of bunting on the flagstaff and a fox terrier was scampering to and fro on the sunny lawn. She had put her hand into his pocket where his hand was and he had felt how cool and thin and soft her hand was. She had said that pockets were funny things to have: and then all of a sudden she had broken away and had run laughing down the sloping curve of the path. Her fair hair had streamed out behind her like gold in the sun. *Tower of Ivory. House of Gold.* By thinking of things you could understand them.

But why in the square? You went there when you wanted to do something. It was all thick slabs of slate and water trickled all day out of tiny pinholes and there was a queer smell of stale water there. And behind the door of one of the closets there was a drawing in red pencil of a bearded man in a Roman dress with a brick in each hand and underneath was the name of the drawing:

Balbus was building a wall.

Some fellows had drawn it there for a cod. It had a funny face but it was very like a man with a beard. And on the wall of another closet there was written in backhand in beautiful writing:

Julius Cæsar wrote The Calico Belly.

Perhaps that was why they were there because it was a place where some fellows wrote things for cod. But all the same it was queer what Athy said and the way he said it. It was not a cod because they had run away. He looked with the others across the playground and began to feel afraid.

At last Fleming said:

— And we are all to be punished for what other fellows did?

— I won't come back, see if I do, Cecil Thunder said. Three days' silence in the refectory and sending us up for six and eight every minute.

— Yes, said Wells. And old Barrett has a new way of twisting the note so that you can't open it and fold it again to see how many ferulæ you are to get. I won't come back too.

— Yes, said Cecil Thunder, and the prefect of studies was in second of grammar this morning.

— Let us get up a rebellion, Fleming said. Will we?

All the fellows were silent. The air was very silent and you could hear the cricket bats but more slowly than before: pick, pock.

Wells asked:

— What is going to be done to them?

— Simon Moonan and Tusker are going to be flogged, Athy said, and the fellows in the higher line got their choice of flogging or being expelled.

— And which are they taking? asked the fellow who had spoken first.

— All are taking expulsion except Corrigan, Athy answered. He's going to be flogged by Mr Gleeson.

— I know why, Cecil Thunder said. He is right and the other fellows are wrong because a flogging wears off after a bit but a fellow that has been expelled from college is known all his life on account of it. Besides Gleeson won't flog him hard.

— It's best of his play not to, Fleming said.

— I wouldn't like to be Simon Moonan and Tusker, Cecil Thunder said. But I don't believe they will be flogged. Perhaps they will be sent up for twice nine.

— No, no, said Athy. They'll both get it on the vital spot.

Wells rubbed himself and said in a crying voice:

— Please, sir, let me off!

Athy grinned and turned up the sleeves of his jacket, saying:

It can't be helped;
It must be done.
So down with your breeches
And out with your bum.

The fellows laughed; but he felt that they were a little afraid. In the silence of the soft grey air he heard the cricket bats from here and from there: pock. That was a sound to hear but if you were hit then you would feel a pain. The pandybat made a sound too but not like that. The fellows said it was made of whalebone and leather with lead inside: and he wondered what was the pain like. There were different kinds of sounds. A long thin cane would have a high whistling sound and he wondered what was that pain like. It made him shivery to think of it and cold: and what Athy said too. But what was there to laugh at in it? It made him shivery: but that was because you always felt like a shiver when you let down your trousers. It was the same in the bath when you undressed yourself. He wondered who had to let them down, the master or the boy himself. O how could they laugh about it that way?

He looked at Athy's rolled-up sleeves and knuckly inky hands. He had rolled up his sleeves to show how Mr Gleeson would roll up his sleeves. But Mr Gleeson had round shiny cuffs and clean white wrists and fattish white hands and the nails of them were long and pointed. Perhaps he pared them too like Lady Boyle. But they were terribly long and pointed nails. So long and cruel they were though the white fattish hands were not cruel but gentle. And though he trembled with cold and fright to think of the cruel long nails and of the high whistling sound of the cane and of the chill you felt at the end of your shirt when you undressed yourself yet he felt a feeling of queer quiet pleasure inside him to think of the white fattish hands, clean and strong and gentle. And he thought of what Cecil Thunder had said; that Mr Gleeson would not flog Corrigan hard. And Fleming had said he would not because it was best of his play not to. But that was not why.

A voice from far out on the playground cried:

— All in!

And other voices cried:

— All in! All in!

During the writing lesson he sat with his arms folded, listening to the slow scraping of the pens. Mr Harford went to and fro making little signs in red pencil and sometimes sitting beside the boy to show him how to hold his pen. He had tried to spell out the headline for himself though he knew already what it was for it was the last of the book. *Zeal without prudence is like a ship adrift.* But the lines of the letters were like fine invisible threads and it was only by closing his right eye tight tight and staring out of the left eye that he could make out the full curves of the capital.

But Mr Harford was very decent and never got into a wax. All the other masters got into dreadful waxes. But why were they to suffer for what fellows in the higher line did? Wells had said that they had drunk some of the altar wine out of the press in the sacristy and that it had been found out who had done it by the smell. Perhaps they had stolen a monstrance to run away with it and sell it somewhere. That must have been a terrible sin, to go in there quietly at night, to open the dark press and steal the flashing gold thing into which God was put on the altar in the middle of flowers and candles at benediction while the incense went up in clouds at both sides as the fellow swung the censer and Dominic Kelly sang the first part by himself in the choir. But God was not in it of course when they stole it. But still it was a strange and a great sin even to touch it. He thought of it with deep awe; a terrible and strange sin: it thrilled him to think of it in the silence when the pens scraped lightly. But to drink the altar wine out of the press and be found out by the smell was a sin too: but it was not terrible and strange. It only made you feel a little sickish on account of the smell of the wine. Because on the day when he had made his first holy communion in the chapel he had shut his eyes and opened his mouth and put out his tongue a little: and when the rector had stooped down to give him the holy communion he had smelt a faint winy smell off the rector's breath after the wine of the mass. The word was beautiful: wine. It made you think of dark purple because the grapes were dark purple that grew in Greece outside houses like white temples. But the faint smell off the rector's breath had made him feel a sick feeling on the morning of his first communion. The day of your first communion was the happiest day of your life. And once a lot of generals had asked Napoleon what was the happiest day of his life. They thought he would say the day he won some great battle or the day he was made an emperor. But he said:

— Gentlemen, the happiest day of my life was the day on which I made my first holy communion.

Father Arnall came in and the Latin lesson began and he remained still leaning on the desk with his arms folded. Father Arnall gave out the theme-books and he said that they were scandalous and that they were all to be written out again with the corrections at once. But the worst of all was Fleming's theme because the pages were stuck together by a blot: and Father Arnall held it up by a corner and said it was an insult to any master to send him up such a theme. Then he asked Jack Lawton to decline the noun *mare* and Jack Lawton stopped at the ablative singular and could not go on with the plural.

— You should be ashamed of yourself, said Father Arnall sternly. You, the leader of the class!

Then he asked the next boy and the next and the next. Nobody knew. Father Arnall became very quiet, more and more quiet as each boy tried to answer it and could not. But his face was black looking and his eyes were staring though his voice was so quiet. Then he asked Fleming and Fleming said that that word had no plural. Father Arnall suddenly shut the book and shouted at him:

— Kneel out there in the middle of the class. You are one of the idlest boys I ever met. Copy out your themes again the rest of you.

Fleming moved heavily out of his place and knelt between the two last benches. The other boys bent over their theme-books and began to write. A silence filled the classroom and Stephen, glancing timidly at Father Arnall's dark face, saw that it was a little red from the wax he was in.

Was that a sin for Father Arnall to be in a wax or was he allowed to get into a wax when the boys were idle because that made them study better or was he only letting on to be in a wax? It was because he was allowed because a priest would know what a sin was and would not do it. But if he did it one time by mistake what would he do to go to confession? Perhaps he would go to confession to the minister. And if the minister did it he would go to the rector: and the rector to the provincial: and the provincial to the general of the jesuits. That was called the order: and he had heard his father say that they were all clever men. They could all have become high-up people in the world if they had not become jesuits. And he wondered what Father Arnall and Paddy Barrett would have become and what Mr McGlade and Mr Gleeson would have become if they had not become jesuits. It was hard to think what because you would have to think of them in a different way with different coloured coats and trousers and with beards and moustaches and different kinds of hats.

The door opened quietly and closed. A quick whisper ran through the class: the prefect of studies. There was an instant of dead silence and then the loud crack of a pandybat on the last desk. Stephen's heart leapt up in fear.

— Any boys want flogging here, Father Arnall? cried the prefect of studies. Any lazy idle loafers that want flogging in this class?

He came to the middle of the class and saw Fleming on his knees.

— Hoho! he cried. Who is this boy? Why is he on his knees? What is your name, boy?

— Fleming, sir.

— Hoho, Fleming! An idler of course. I can see it in your eye. Why is he on his knees, Father Arnall?

— He wrote a bad Latin theme, Father Arnall said, and he missed all the questions in grammar.

— Of course he did! cried the prefect of studies, of course he did! A born idler! I can see it in the corner of his eye.

He banged his pandybat down on the desk and cried:

— Up, Fleming! Up, my boy!

Fleming stood up slowly.

— Hold out! cried the prefect of studies.

Fleming held out his hand. The pandybat came down on it with a loud smacking sound: one, two, three, four, five, six.

— Other hand!

The pandybat came down again in six loud quick smacks.

— Kneel down! cried the prefect of studies.

Fleming knelt down squeezing his hands under his armpits, his face contorted with pain, but Stephen knew how hard his hands were because Fleming was always rubbing rosin into them. But perhaps he was in great pain for the noise of the pandybat was terrible. Stephen's heart was beating and fluttering.

— At your work, all of you! shouted the prefect of studies. We want no lazy idle loafers here, lazy idle little schemers. At your work, I tell you. Father Dolan will be in to see you every day. Father Dolan will be in tomorrow.

He poked one of the boys in the side with the pandybat, saying:

— You, boy! When will Father Dolan be in again?

— Tomorrow, sir, said Tom Furlong's voice.

— Tomorrow and tomorrow and tomorrow, said the prefect of studies. Make up your minds for that. Every day Father Dolan. Write away. You, boy, who are you?

Stephen's heart jumped suddenly.

— Dedalus, sir.

— Why are you not writing like the others?

— I . . . my . . .

He could not speak with fright.

— Why is he not writing, Father Arnall?

— He broke his glasses, said Father Arnall, and I exempted him from work.

— Broke? What is this I hear? What is this? Your name is? said the prefect of studies.

— Dedalus, sir.

— Out here, Dedalus. Lazy little schemer. I see schemer in your face. Where did you break your glasses?

Stephen stumbled into the middle of the class, blinded by fear and haste.

— Where did you break your glasses? repeated the prefect of studies.

— The cinderpath, sir.

— Hoho! The cinderpath! cried the prefect of studies. I know that trick.

Stephen lifted his eyes in wonder and saw for a moment Father Dolan's whitegrey not young face, his baldy whitegrey head with fluff at the sides of it, the steel rims of his spectacles and his no-coloured eyes looking through the glasses. Why did he say he knew that trick?

— Lazy idle little loafer! cried the prefect of studies. Broke my glasses! An old schoolboy trick! Out with your hand this moment!

Stephen closed his eyes and held out in the air his trembling hand with the palm upwards. He felt the prefect of studies touch it for a moment at the fingers to straighten it and then the swish of the sleeve of the soutane as the pandybat was lifted to strike. A hot burning stinging tingling blow like the loud crack of a broken stick made his trembling hand crumple together like a leaf in the fire: and at the sound and the pain scalding tears were driven into his eyes. His whole body was shaking with fright, his arm was shaking and his crumpled burning livid hand shook like a loose leaf in the air. A cry sprang to his lips, a prayer to be let off. But though the tears scalded his eyes and his limbs quivered with pain and fright he held back the hot tears and the cry that scalded his throat.

— Other hand! shouted the prefect of studies.

Stephen drew back his maimed and quivering right arm and held out his left hand. The soutane sleeve swished again as the pandybat was lifted and a loud crashing sound and a fierce maddening tingling burning pain made his hand shrink together with the palms and fingers in a livid quivering mass. The scalding water burst forth from his eyes and, burning with shame and agony and fear, he drew back his shaking arm in terror and burst out into a whine of pain. His body shook with a palsy of fright and in shame and rage he felt the scalding cry come from his throat and the scalding tears falling out of his eyes and down his flaming cheeks.

— Kneel down! cried the prefect of studies.

Stephen knelt down quickly pressing his beaten hands to his sides. To think of them beaten and swollen with pain all in a moment made him feel so sorry for them as if they were not his own but someone else's that he felt sorry for. And as he knelt, calming the last sobs in his throat and feeling the burning tingling pain pressed in to his sides, he thought of the hands which he had held out in the air with the palms up and of the firm touch of the prefect of studies when he had steadied the shaking fingers and of the beaten swollen reddened mass of palm and fingers that shook helplessly in the air.

— Get at your work, all of you, cried the prefect of studies from the door. Father Dolan will be in every day to see if any boy, any lazy idle little loafer wants flogging. Every day. Every day.

The door closed behind him.

The hushed class continued to copy out the themes. Father Arnall rose from his seat and went among them, helping the boys with gentle words and telling them the mistakes they had made. His voice was very gentle and soft. Then he returned to his seat and said to Fleming and Stephen:

— You may return to your places, you two.

Fleming and Stephen rose and, walking to their seats, sat down. Stephen, scarlet with shame, opened a book quickly with one weak hand and bent down upon it, his face close to the page.

It was unfair and cruel because the doctor had told him not to read without glasses and he had written home to his father that morning to send him a new pair. And Father Arnall had said that he need not study till the new glasses came. Then to be called a schemer before the class and to be pandied when he always got the card for first or second and was the leader of the Yorkists! How could the prefect of studies know that it was a trick? He felt the touch of the prefect's fingers as they had steadied his hand and at first he had thought he was going to shake hands with him because the fingers were soft and firm: but then in an instant he had heard the swish of the soutane sleeve and the crash. It was cruel and unfair to make him kneel in the middle of the class then: and Father Arnall had told them both that they might return to their places without making any difference between them. He listened to Father Arnall's low and gentle voice as he corrected the themes. Perhaps he was sorry now and wanted to be decent. But it was unfair and cruel. The prefect of studies was a priest but that was cruel and unfair. And his whitegrey face and the no-coloured eyes behind the steel rimmed spectacles were cruel looking because he had steadied the hand first with his firm soft fingers and that was to hit it better and louder.

— It's a stinking mean thing, that's what it is, said Fleming in the corridor as the classes were passing out in file to the refectory, to pandy a fellow for what is not his fault.

— You really broke your glasses by accident, didn't you? Nasty Roche asked.

Stephen felt his heart filled by Fleming's words and did not answer.

— Of course he did! said Fleming. I wouldn't stand it. I'd go up and tell the rector on him.

— Yes, said Cecil Thunder eagerly, and I saw him lift the pandybat over his shoulder and he's not allowed to do that.

— Did they hurt much? Nasty Roche asked.

— Very much, Stephen said.

— I wouldn't stand it, Fleming repeated, from Baldyhead or any other Baldyhead. It's a stinking mean low trick, that's what it is. I'd go straight up to the rector and tell him about it after dinner.

— Yes, do. Yes, do, said Cecil Thunder.

— Yes, do. Yes, go up and tell the rector on him, Dedalus, said Nasty Roche, because he said that he'd come in tomorrow again and pandy you.

— Yes, yes. Tell the rector, all said.

And there were some fellows out of second of grammar listening and one of them said:

— The senate and the Roman people declared that Dedalus had been wrongly punished.

It was wrong; it was unfair and cruel: and, as he sat in the refectory, he suffered time after time in memory the same humiliation until he began to wonder whether it might not really be that there was something in his face which made him look like a schemer and he wished he had a little mirror to see. But there could not be; and it was unjust and cruel and unfair.

He could not eat the blackish fish fritters they got on Wednesdays in Lent and one of his potatoes had the mark of the spade in it. Yes, he would do what the fellows had told him. He would go up and tell the rector that he had been wrongly punished. A thing like that had been done before by somebody in history, by some great person whose head was in the books of history. And the rector would declare that he had been wrongly punished because the senate and the Roman people always declared that the men who did that had been wrongly punished. Those were the great men whose names were in Richmal Magnall's Questions. History was all about those men and what they did and that was what Peter Parley's Tales about Greece and Rome were all about. Peter Parley himself was on the first page in a picture. There was a road over a heath with grass at the side and little bushes: and Peter Parley had a broad hat like a protestant minister and a big stick and he was walking fast along the road to Greece and Rome.

It was easy what he had to do. All he had to do was when the dinner was over and he came out in his turn to go on walking but not out to the corridor but up the staircase on the right that led to the castle. He had nothing to do but that; to turn to the right and walk fast up the staircase and in half a minute he would be in the low dark narrow corridor that led through the castle to the rector's room. And every fellow had said that it was unfair, even the fellow out of second of grammar who had said that about the senate and the Roman people.

What would happen? He heard the fellows of the higher line stand up at the top of the refectory and heard their steps as they came down the matting: Paddy Rath and Jimmy Magee and the Spaniard and the Portuguese and the fifth was big Corrigan who was going to be flogged by Mr Gleeson. That was why the prefect of studies had called him a schemer and pandied him for nothing: and, straining his weak eyes, tired with the tears, he watched big Corrigan's broad shoulders and big hanging black head passing in the file. But he had done something and besides Mr Gleeson would not flog him hard: and he remembered how big Corrigan looked in the bath. He had skin the same colour as the turfcoloured bogwater in the shallow end of the bath and when he walked along the side his feet slapped loudly on the wet tiles and at every step his thighs shook a little because he was fat.

The refectory was half empty and the fellows were still passing out in file. He could go up the staircase because there was never a priest or a prefect outside the refectory door. But he could not go. The rector would side with the prefect of studies and think it was a schoolboy trick and then the prefect of studies would come in every day the same, only it would be worse because he would be dreadfully waxy at any fellow going up to the rector about him. The fellows had told him to go but they would not go themselves. They had forgotten all about it. No, it was best to forget all about it and perhaps the prefect of studies had only said he would come in. No, it was best to hide out of the way because when you were small and young you could often escape that way.

The fellows at his table stood up. He stood up and passed out among them in the file. He had to decide. He was coming near the door. If he went on with the fellows he could never go up to the rector because he could not leave the playground for that. And if he went and was pandied all the same all the fellows would make fun and talk about young Dedalus going up to the rector to tell on the prefect of studies.

He was walking down along the matting and he saw the door before him. It was impossible: he could not. He thought of the baldy head of the prefect of studies with the cruel no-coloured eyes looking at him and he heard the voice of the prefect of studies asking him twice what his name was. Why could he not remember the name when he was told the first time? Was he not listening the first time or was it to make fun out of the name? The great men in the history had names like that and nobody made fun of them. It was his own name that he should have made fun of if he wanted to make fun. Dolan: it was like the name of a woman who washed clothes.

He had reached the door and, turning quickly up to the right, walked up the stairs; and, before he could make up his mind to come back, he had entered the low dark narrow corridor that led to the castle. And as he crossed the threshold of the door of the corridor he saw, without turning his head to look, that all the fellows were looking after him as they went filing by.

He passed along the narrow dark corridor, passing little doors that were the doors of the rooms of the community. He peered in front of him and right and left through the gloom and thought that those must be portraits. It was dark and silent and his eyes were weak and tired with tears so that he could not see. But he thought they were the portraits of the saints and great men of the order who were looking down on him silently as he passed: Saint Ignatius Loyola holding an open book and pointing to the words *Ad Majorem Dei Gloriam*[1] in it, Saint Francis Xavier pointing to his chest, Lorenzo Ricci with his berretta on his head like one of the prefects of the lines, the three patrons of holy youth, Saint Stanislaus Kostka, Saint Aloysius Gonzaga and Blessed John Berchmans, all with young faces because they died when they were young, and Father Peter Kenny sitting in a chair wrapped in a big cloak.

He came out on the landing above the entrance hall and looked about him. That was where Hamilton Rowan had passed and the marks of the soldiers' slugs were there. And it was there that the old servants had seen the ghost in the white cloak of a marshal.

An old servant was sweeping at the end of the landing. He asked him where was the rector's room and the old servant pointed to the door at the far end and looked after him as he went on to it and knocked.

There was no answer. He knocked again more loudly and his heart jumped when he heard a muffled voice say:

— Come in!

He turned the handle and opened the door and fumbled for the handle of the green baize door inside. He found it and pushed it open and went in.

He saw the rector sitting at a desk writing. There was a skull on the desk and a strange solemn smell in the room like the old leather of chairs.

His heart was beating fast on account of the solemn place he was in and the silence of the room: and he looked at the skull and at the rector's kind-looking face.

— Well, my little man, said the rector, what is it?

Stephen swallowed down the thing in his throat and said:

— I broke my glasses, sir.

The rector opened his mouth and said:

— O!

Then he smiled and said:

---

[1] [*For the greater glory of God* (the motto of the Jesuit Order).]

— Well, if we broke our glasses we must write home for a new pair.

— I wrote home, sir, said Stephen, and Father Arnall said I am not to study till they come.

— Quite right! said the rector.

Stephen swallowed down the thing again and tried to keep his legs and his voice from shaking.

— But, sir . . .

— Yes?

— Father Dolan came in today and pandied me because I was not writing my theme.

The rector looked at him in silence and he could feel the blood rising to his face and the tears about to rise to his eyes.

The rector said:

— Your name is Dedalus, isn't it?

— Yes, sir.

— And where did you break your glasses?

— On the cinderpath, sir. A fellow was coming out of the bicycle house and I fell and they got broken. I don't know the fellow's name.

The rector looked at him again in silence. Then he smiled and said:

— O, well, it was a mistake, I am sure Father Dolan did not know.

— But I told him I broke them, sir, and he pandied me.

— Did you tell him that you had written home for a new pair? the rector asked.

— No, sir.

— O well then, said the rector, Father Dolan did not understand. You can say that I excuse you from your lessons for a few days.

Stephen said quickly for fear his trembling would prevent him:

— Yes, sir, but Father Dolan said he will come in tomorrow to pandy me again for it.

— Very well, the rector said, it is a mistake and I shall speak to Father Dolan myself. Will that do now?

Stephen felt the tears wetting his eyes and murmured:

— O yes sir, thanks.

The rector held his hand across the side of the desk where the skull was and Stephen, placing his hand in it for a moment, felt a cool moist palm.

— Good day now, said the rector, withdrawing his hand and bowing.

— Good day, sir, said Stephen.

He bowed and walked quietly out of the room, closing the doors carefully and slowly.

But when he had passed the old servant on the landing and was again in the low narrow dark corridor he began to walk faster and faster. Faster and faster he hurried on through the gloom excitedly. He bumped his elbow against the door at the end and, hurrying down the staircase, walked quickly through the two corridors and out into the air.

He could hear the cries of the fellows on the playgrounds. He broke into a run and, running quicker and quicker, ran across the cinderpath and reached the third line playground, panting.

The fellows had seen him running. They closed round him in a ring, pushing one against another to hear.

— Tell us! Tell us!
— What did he say?
— Did you go in?
— What did he say?
— Tell us! Tell us!

He told them what he had said and what the rector had said and, when he had told them, all the fellows flung their caps spinning up into the air and cried:

— Hurroo!

They caught their caps and sent them up again spinning skyhigh and cried again:

— Hurroo! Hurroo!

They made a cradle of their locked hands and hoisted him up among them and carried him along till he struggled to get free. And when he had escaped from them they broke away in all directions, flinging their caps again into the air and whistling as they went spinning up and crying:

— Hurroo!

And they gave three groans for Baldyhead Dolan and three cheers for Conmee and they said he was the decentest rector that was ever in Clongowes.

The cheers died away in the soft grey air. He was alone. He was happy and free: but he would not be anyway proud with Father Dolan. He would be very quiet and obedient: and he wished that he could do something kind for him to show him that he was not proud.

The air was soft and grey and mild and evening was coming. There was the smell of evening in the air, the smell of the fields in the country where they digged up turnips to peel them and eat them when they went out for a walk to Major Barton's, the smell there was in the little wood beyond the pavilion where the gallnuts were.

The fellows were practising long shies and bowling lobs and slow twisters. In the soft grey silence he could hear the bump of the balls: and from here and from there through the quiet air the sound of the cricket bats: pick, pack, pock, puck: like drops of water in a fountain falling softly in the brimming bowl.

Chapter II

UNCLE CHARLES smoked such black twist that at last his nephew suggested to him to enjoy his morning smoke in a little outhouse at the end of the garden.

— Very good, Simon. All serene, Simon, said the old man tranquilly. Anywhere you like. The outhouse will do me nicely: it will be more salubrious.

— Damn me, said Mr Dedalus frankly, if I know how you can smoke such villainous awful tobacco. It's like gunpowder, by God.

— It's very nice, Simon, replied the old man. Very cool and mollifying.

Every morning, therefore, Uncle Charles repaired to his outhouse but not before he had creased and brushed scrupulously his back hair and brushed and put on his tall hat. While he smoked the brim of his tall hat and the bowl of his pipe were just visible beyond the jambs of the outhouse door. His arbour, as he called the reeking outhouse which he shared with the cat and the garden tools, served him also as a soundingbox: and every morning he hummed contentedly one of his favourite songs: *O, twine me a bower* or *Blue eyes and golden hair* or *The Groves of Blarney* while the grey and blue coils of smoke rose slowly from his pipe and vanished in the pure air.

During the first part of the summer in Blackrock Uncle Charles was Stephen's constant companion. Uncle Charles was a hale old man with a well tanned skin, rugged features and white side whiskers. On week days he did messages between the house in Carysfort Avenue and those shops in the main street of the town with which the family dealt. Stephen was glad to go with him on these errands for Uncle Charles helped him very liberally to handfuls of whatever was exposed in open boxes and barrels outside the counter. He would seize a handful of grapes and sawdust or three or four American apples and thrust them generously into his grandnephew's hand while the shopman smiled uneasily; and, on Stephen's feigning reluctance to take them, he would frown and say:

— Take them, sir. Do you hear me, sir? They're good for your bowels.

When the order list had been booked the two would go on to the park where an old friend of Stephen's father, Mike Flynn, would be found seated on a bench, waiting for them. Then would begin Stephen's run round the park. Mike Flynn would stand at the gate near the railway station, watch in hand, while Stephen ran round the track in the style Mike Flynn favoured, his head high lifted, his knees well lifted and his hands held straight down by his sides. When the morning practice was over the trainer would make his comments and sometimes illustrate them by shuffling along for a yard or so comically in an old pair of blue canvas shoes. A small ring of wonderstruck children and nursemaids would gather to watch him and linger even when he and Uncle Charles had sat down again and were talking athletics and politics. Though he had heard his father say that Mike Flynn had put some of the best runners of modern times through his hands Stephen often glanced at his trainer's flabby stubble-covered face, as it bent over the long stained fingers through which he rolled his cigarette, and with pity at the mild lustreless blue eyes which would look up suddenly from the task and gaze vaguely into the blue distance while the long swollen fingers ceased their rolling and grains and fibres of tobacco fell back into the pouch.

On the way home Uncle Charles would often pay a visit to the chapel and, as the font was above Stephen's reach, the old man would dip his hand and then sprinkle the water briskly about Stephen's clothes and on the floor of the porch. While he prayed he knelt on his red handkerchief and read above his breath from a thumb blackened prayer-book wherein catchwords were printed at the foot of every page. Stephen knelt at his side respecting, though he did not share, his piety. He often wondered what his granduncle prayed for so seriously. Perhaps he prayed for the souls in purgatory or for the grace of a happy death or perhaps he prayed that God might send him back a part of the big fortune he had squandered in Cork.

On Sundays Stephen with his father and his granduncle took their constitutional. The old man was a nimble walker in spite of his corns and often ten or twelve miles of the road were covered. The little village of Stillorgan was the parting of the ways. Either they went to the left towards the Dublin mountains or along the Goatstown road and thence into Dundrum, coming home by Sandyford. Trudging along the road or standing in some grimy wayside public house his elders spoke constantly of the subjects nearer their hearts, of Irish politics, of Munster and of the legends of their own family, to all of which Stephen lent an avid ear. Words which he did not understand he said over and over to himself till he had learnt them by heart: and through them he had glimpses of the real world about him. The hour when he too would take part in the life of that world seemed drawing near and in secret he began to make ready for the great part which he felt awaited him the nature of which he only dimly apprehended.

His evenings were his own; and he pored over a ragged translation of *The Count of Monte Cristo*. The figure of that dark avenger stood forth in his mind for whatever he had heard or divined in childhood of the strange and terrible. At night he built up on the parlour table an image of the wonderful island cave out of transfers and paper flowers and coloured tissue paper and strips of the silver and golden paper in which chocolate is wrapped. When he had broken up this scenery, weary of its tinsel, there would come to his mind the bright picture of Marseilles, of sunny trellises and of Mercedes.

Outside Blackrock, on the road that led to the mountains, stood a small whitewashed house in the garden of which grew many rose-bushes: and in this house, he told himself, another Mercedes lived. Both on the outward and on the homeward journey he measured distance by this landmark: and in his imagination he lived through a long train of adventures, marvellous as those in the book itself, towards the close of which there appeared an image of himself, grown older and sadder, standing in a moonlit garden with Mercedes who had so many years before slighted his love, and with a sadly proud gesture of refusal, saying:

— Madam, I never eat muscatel grapes.

He became the ally of a boy named Aubrey Mills and founded with him a gang of adventurers in the avenue. Aubrey carried a whistle dangling from his buttonhole and a bicycle lamp attached to his belt while the others had short sticks thrust daggerwise through theirs. Stephen, who had read of Napoleon's plain style of dress, chose to remain unadorned and thereby heightened for himself the pleasure of taking counsel with his lieutenant before giving orders. The gang made forays into the gardens of old maids or went down to the castle and fought a battle on the shaggy weedgrown rocks, coming home after it weary stragglers with the stale odours of the foreshore in their nostrils and the rank oils of the seawrack upon their hands and in their hair.

Aubrey and Stephen had a common milkman and often they drove out in the milkcar to Carrickmines where the cows were at grass. While the men were milking the boys would take turns in riding the tractable mare round the field. But when autumn came the cows were driven home from the grass: and the first sight of the filthy cowyard at Stradbrook with its foul green puddles and clots of liquid dung and steaming bran troughs sickened Stephen's heart. The cattle which had seemed so beautiful in the country on sunny days revolted him and he could not even look at the milk they yielded.

The coming of September did not trouble him this year for he was not to be sent back to Clongowes. The practice in the park came to an end when Mike Flynn went into hospital. Aubrey was at school and had only an hour or two free in the evening. The gang fell asunder and there were no more nightly forays or battles on the rocks. Stephen sometimes went round with the car which delivered the evening milk: and these chilly drives blew away his memory of the filth of the cowyard and he felt no repugnance at seeing the cow hairs and hayseeds on the milkman's coat. Whenever the car drew up before a house he waited to catch a glimpse of a well scrubbed kitchen or of a softly lighted hall and to see how the servant would hold the jug and how she would close the door. He thought it should be a pleasant life enough, driving along the roads every evening to deliver milk, if he had warm gloves and a fat bag of gingernuts in his pocket to eat from. But the same foreknowledge which had sickened his heart and made his legs sag suddenly as he raced round the park, the same intuition which had made him glance with mistrust at his trainer's flabby stubblecovered face as it bent heavily over his long stained fingers, dissipated any vision of the future. In a vague way he understood that his father was in trouble and that this was the reason why he himself had not been sent back to Clongowes. For some time he had felt the slight change in his house; and those changes in what he had deemed unchangeable were so many slight shocks to his boyish conception of the world. The ambition which he felt astir at times in the darkness of his soul sought no outlet. A dusk like that of the outer world obscured his mind as he heard the mare's hoofs clattering along the tramtrack on the Rock Road and the great can swaying and rattling behind him.

He returned to Mercedes and, as he brooded upon her image, a strange unrest crept into his blood. Sometimes a fever gathered within him and led him to rove alone in the evening along the quiet avenue. The peace of the gardens and the kindly lights in the windows poured a tender influence into his restless heart. The noise of children at play annoyed him and their silly voices made him feel, even more keenly than he had felt at Clongowes, that he was different from others. He did not want to play. He wanted to meet in the real world the unsubstantial image which his soul so constantly beheld. He did not know where to seek it or how but a premonition which led him on told him that this image would, without any overt act of his, encounter him. They would meet quietly as if they had known each other and had made their tryst, perhaps at one of the gates or in some more secret place. They would be alone, surrounded by darkness and silence: and in that moment of supreme tenderness he would be transfigured. He would fade into something impalpable under her eyes and then in a moment, he would be transfigured. Weakness and timidity and inexperience would fall from him in that magic moment.

*   *   *

Two great yellow caravans had halted one morning before the door and men had come tramping into the house to dismantle it. The furniture had been hustled out through the front garden which was strewn with wisps of straw and rope ends and into the huge vans at the gate. When all had been safely stowed the vans had set off noisily down the avenue: and from the window of the railway carriage, in which he had sat with his red eyed mother, Stephen had seen them lumbering along the Merrion Road.

The parlour fire would not draw that evening and Mr Dedalus rested the poker against the bars of the grate to attract the flame. Uncle Charles dozed in a corner of the half furnished uncarpeted room and near him the family portraits leaned against the wall. The lamp on the table shed a weak light over the boarded floor, muddied by the feet of the vanmen. Stephen sat on a footstool beside his father listening to a long and incoherent monologue. He understood little or nothing of it at first but he became slowly aware that his father had enemies and that some fight was going to take place. He felt, too, that he was being enlisted for the fight, that some duty was being laid upon his shoulders. The sudden flight from the comfort and revery of Blackrock, the passage through the gloomy foggy city, the thought of the bare cheerless house in which they were now to live made his heart heavy: and again an intuition, a foreknowledge of the future came to him. He understood also why the servants had often whispered together in the hall and why his father had often stood on the hearthrug, with his back to the fire, talking loudly to Uncle Charles who urged him to sit down and eat his dinner.

— There's a crack of the whip left in me yet, Stephen, old chap, said Mr Dedalus, poking at the dull fire with fierce energy. We're not dead yet, sonny. No, by the Lord Jesus (God forgive me) nor half dead.

Dublin was a new and complex sensation. Uncle Charles had grown so witless that he could no longer be sent out on errands and the disorder in settling in the new house left Stephen freer than he had been in Blackrock. In the beginning he contented himself with circling timidly round the neighbouring square or, at most, going half way down one of the side streets: but when he had made a skeleton map of the city in his mind he followed boldly one of its central lines until he reached the Custom House. He passed unchallenged among the docks and along the quays wondering at the multitude of corks that lay bobbing on the surface of the water in a thick yellow scum, at the crowds of quay porters and the rumbling carts and the ill dressed bearded policeman. The vastness and strangeness of the life suggested to him by the bales of merchandise stocked along the walls or swung aloft out of the holds of steamers wakened again in him the unrest which had sent him wandering in the evening from garden to garden in search of Mercedes. And amid this new bustling life he might have fancied himself in another Marseilles but that he missed the bright sky and the sun-warmed trellisses of the wineshops. A vague dissatisfaction grew up within him as he looked on the quays and on the river and on the lowering skies and yet he continued to wander up and down day after day as if he really sought someone that eluded him.

He went once or twice with his mother to visit their relatives: and though they passed a jovial array of shops lit up and adorned for Christmas his mood of embittered silence did not leave him. The causes of his embitterment were many, remote and near. He was angry with himself for being young and the prey of restless foolish impulses, angry also with the change of fortune which was reshaping the world about him into a vision of squalor and insincerity. Yet his anger lent nothing to the vision. He chronicled with patience what he saw, detaching himself from it and testing its mortifying flavour in secret.

He was sitting on the backless chair in his aunt's kitchen. A lamp with a reflector hung on the japanned wall of the fireplace and by its light his aunt was reading the evening paper that lay on her knees. She looked a long time at a smiling picture that was set in it and said musingly:

— The beautiful Mabel Hunter!

A ringletted girl stood on tiptoe to peer at the picture and said softly:

— What is she in, mud?

— In a pantomime, love.

The child leaned her ringletted head against her mother's sleeve, gazing on the picture and murmured as if fascinated:

— The beautiful Mabel Hunter!

As if fascinated, her eyes rested long upon those demurely taunting eyes and she murmured devotedly:

— Isn't she an exquisite creature?

And the boy who came in from the street, stamping crookedly under his stone of coal, heard her words. He dropped his load promptly on the floor and hurried to her side to see. He mauled the edges of the paper with his reddened and blackened hands, shouldering her aside and complaining that he could not see.

He was sitting in the narrow breakfast room high up in the old dark windowed house. The firelight flickered on the wall and beyond the window a spectral dusk was gathering upon the river. Before the fire an old woman was busy making tea and, as she bustled at the task, she told in a low voice of what the priest and the doctor had said. She told too of certain changes they had seen in her of late and of her odd ways and sayings. He sat listening to the words and following the ways of adventure that lay open in the coals, arches and vaults and winding galleries and jagged caverns.

Suddenly he became aware of something in the doorway. A skull appeared suspended in the gloom of the doorway. A feeble creature like a monkey was there, drawn there by the sound of voices at the fire. A whining voice came from the door asking:

— Is that Josephine?

The old bustling woman answered cheerily from the fireplace:

— No, Ellen, it's Stephen.

— O . . . O, good evening, Stephen.

He answered the greeting and saw a silly smile break over the face in the doorway.

— Do you want anything, Ellen? asked the old woman at the fire.

But she did not answer the question and said,

— I thought it was Josephine. I thought you were Josephine, Stephen.

And, repeating this several times, she fell to laughing feebly.

He was sitting in the midst of a children's party at Harold's Cross. His silent watchful manner had grown upon him and he took little part in the games. The children, wearing the spoils of their crackers, danced and romped noisily and, though he tried to share their merriment, he felt himself a gloomy figure amid the gay cocked hats and sunbonnets.

But when he had sung his song and withdrawn into a snug corner of the room he began to taste the joy of his loneliness. The mirth, which in the beginning of the evening had seemed to him false and trivial, was like a soothing air to him, passing gaily by his senses, hiding from other eyes the feverish agitation of his blood while through the circling of the dancers and amid the music and laughter her glance travelled to his corner, flattering, taunting, searching, exciting his heart.

In the hall the children who had stayed latest were putting on their things: the party was over. She had thrown a shawl about her and, as they went together towards the tram, sprays of her fresh warm breath flew gaily above her cowled head and her shoes tapped blithely on the glassy road.

It was the last tram. The lank brown horses knew it and shook their bells to the clear night in admonition. The conductor talked with the driver, both nodding often in the green light of the lamp. On the empty seats of the tram were scattered a few coloured tickets. No sound of footsteps came up or down the road. No sound broke the peace of the night save when the lank brown horses rubbed their noses together and shook their bells.

They seemed to listen, he on the upper step and she on the lower. She came up to his step many times and went down to hers again between their phrases and once or twice stood close beside him for some moments on the upper step, forgetting to go down, and then went down. His heart danced upon her movements like a cork upon a tide. He heard what her eyes said to him from beneath their cowl and knew that in some dim past, whether in life or revery, he had heard their tale before. He saw her urge her vanities, her fine dress and sash and long black stockings, and knew that he had yielded to them a thousand times. Yet a voice within him spoke above the noise of his dancing heart, asking him would he take her gift to which he had only to stretch out his hand. And he remembered the day when he and Eileen had stood looking into the Hotel Grounds, watching the waiters running up a trail of bunting on the flagstaff and the fox terrier scampering to and fro on the sunny lawn, and how, all of a sudden, she had broken out into a peal of laughter and had run down the sloping curve of the path. Now, as then, he stood listlessly in his place, seemingly a tranquil watcher of the scene before him.

— She too wants me to catch hold of her, he thought. That's why she came with me to the tram. I could easily catch hold of her when she comes up to my step: nobody is looking. I could hold her and kiss her.

But he did neither: and, when he was sitting alone in the deserted tram he tore his ticket into shreds and stared gloomily at the corrugated footboard.

The next day he sat at his table in the bare upper room for many hours. Before him lay a new pen, a new bottle of ink and a new emerald exercise. From force of habit he had written at the top of the first page the initial letters of the jesuit motto: A.M.D.G. On the first line of the page appeared the title of the verses he was trying to write: To E —— C —— . He knew it was right to begin so for he had seen similar titles in the collected poems of Lord Byron. When he had written this title and drawn an ornamental line underneath he fell into a day dream and began to draw diagrams on the cover of the book. He saw himself sitting at his table in Bray the morning after the discussion at the Christmas dinner table, trying to write a poem about Parnell on the back of one of his father's second moiety notices. But his brain had then refused to grapple with the theme and, desisting, he had covered the page with the names and addresses of certain of his classmates:

> Roderick Kickham
> John Lawton
> Anthony MacSwiney
> Simon Moonan

Now it seemed as if he would fail again but, by dint of brooding on the incident, he thought himself into confidence. During this process all those elements which he deemed common and insignificant fell out of the scene. There remained no trace of the tram itself nor of the trammen nor of the horses: nor did he and she appear vividly. The verses told only of the night and the balmy breeze and the maiden lustre of the moon. Some undefined sorrow was hidden in the hearts of the protagonists as they stood in silence beneath the leafless trees and when the moment of farewell had come the kiss, which had been withheld by one, was given by both. After this the letters L. D. S. were written at the foot of the page and, having hidden the book, he went into his mother's bedroom and gazed at his face for a long time in the mirror of her dressing table.

But his long spell of leisure and liberty was drawing to its end. One evening his father came home full of news which kept his tongue busy all through dinner. Stephen had been awaiting his father's return for there had been mutton hash that day and he knew that his father would make him dip his bread in the gravy. But he did not relish the hash for the mention of Clongowes had coated his palate with a scum of disgust.

— I walked bang into him, said Mr Dedalus for the fourth time, just at the corner of the square.

— Then I suppose, said Mrs Dedalus, he will be able to arrange it. I mean about Belvedere.

— Of course, he will, said Mr Dedalus. Don't I tell you he's provincial of the order now?

— I never liked the idea of sending him to the christian brothers myself, said Mrs Dedalus.

— Christian brothers be damned! said Mr Dedalus. Is it with Paddy Stink and Mickey Mud? No, let him stick to the jesuits in God's name since he began with them. They'll be of service to him in after years. Those are the fellows that can get you a position.

— And they're a very rich order, aren't they, Simon?

— Rather. They live well, I tell you. You saw their table at Clongowes. Fed up, by God, like gamecocks.

Mr Dedalus pushed his plate over to Stephen and bade him finish what was on it.

— Now then, Stephen, he said, you must put your shoulder to the wheel, old chap. You've had a fine long holiday.

— O, I'm sure he'll work very hard now, said Mrs Dedalus, especially when he has Maurice with him.

— O, Holy Paul, I forgot about Maurice, said Mr Dedalus. Here, Maurice! Come here, you thick-headed ruffian! Do you know I'm going to send you to a college where they'll teach you to spell c.a.t. cat. And I'll buy you a nice little penny handkerchief to keep your nose dry. Won't that be grand fun?

Maurice grinned at his father and then at his brother. Mr Dedalus screwed his glass into his eye and stared hard at both of his sons. Stephen mumbled his bread without answering his father's gaze.

— By the bye, said Mr Dedalus at length, the rector or provincial rather, was telling me that story about you and Father Dolan. You're an impudent thief, he said.

— O, he didn't, Simon!

— Not he! said Mr Dedalus. But he gave me a great account of the whole affair. We were chatting, you know, and one word borrowed another. And, by the way, who do you think he told me will get that job in the corporation? But I'll tell you that after. Well, as I was saying, we were chatting away quite friendly and he asked me did our friend here wear glasses still and then he told me the whole story.

— And was he annoyed, Simon?

— Annoyed! Not he! *Manly little chap!* he said.

Mr Dedalus imitated the mincing nasal tone of the provincial.

— Father Dolan and I, when I told them all at dinner about it, Father Dolan and I had a great laugh over it. *You better mind yourself, Father Dolan,* said I, *or young Dedalus will send you up for twice nine.* We had a famous laugh together over it. Ha! Ha! Ha!

Mr Dedalus turned to his wife and interjected in his natural voice:

— Shows you the spirit in which they take the boys there. O, a jesuit for your life, for diplomacy!

He reassumed the provincial's voice and repeated:

— I told them all at dinner about it and Father Dolan and I and all of us we all had a hearty laugh together over it. Ha! Ha! Ha!

The night of the Whitsuntide play had come and Stephen from the window of the dressing room looked out on the small grassplot across which lines of Chinese lanterns were stretched. He watched the visitors come down the steps from the house and pass into the theatre. Stewards in evening dress, old Belvedereans, loitered in groups about the entrance to the theatre and ushered in the visitors with ceremony. Under the sudden glow of a lantern he could recognise the smiling face of a priest.

The Blessed Sacrament had been removed from the tabernacle and the first benches had been driven back so as to leave the daïs of the altar and the space before it free. Against the walls stood companies of barbells and Indian clubs; the dumb bells were piled in one corner: and in the midst of countless hillocks of gymnasium shoes and sweaters and singlets in untidy brown parcels there stood the stout leatherjacketed vaulting horse waiting its turn to be carried up on the stage and set in the middle of the winning team at the end of the gymnastic display.

Stephen, though in deference to his reputation for essay writing he had been elected secretary to the gymnasium, had had no part in the first section of the programme, but in the play which formed the second section he had the chief part, that of a farcical pedagogue. He had been cast for it on account of his stature and grave manners for he was now at the end of his second year at Belvedere and in number two.

A score of the younger boys in white knickers and singlets came pattering down from the stage, through the vestry and into the chapel. The vestry and chapel were peopled with eager masters and boys. The plump bald sergeant major was testing with his foot the springboard of the vaulting horse. The lean young man in a long overcoat, who was to give a special display of intricate club swinging, stood near watching with interest, his silver coated clubs peeping out of his deep sidepockets. The hollow rattle of the wooden dumb bells was heard as another team made ready to go up on the stage: and in another moment the excited prefect was hustling the boys through the vestry like a flock of geese, flapping the wings of his soutane nervously and crying to the laggards to make haste. A little troop of Neapolitan peasants were practising their steps at the end of the chapel, some circling their arms above their heads, some swaying their baskets of paper violets and curtseying. In a dark corner of the chapel at the gospel side of the altar a stout old lady knelt amid her copious black skirts. When she stood up a pink dressed figure, wearing a curly golden wig and an old fashioned straw sunbonnet, with black pencilled eyebrows and cheeks delicately rouged and powdered, was discovered. A low murmur of curiosity ran round the chapel at the discovery of this girlish figure. One of the prefects, smiling and nodding his head, approached the dark corner and, having bowed to the stout old lady, said pleasantly:

— Is this a beautiful young lady or a doll that you have here, Mrs Tallon?

Then, bending down to peer at the smiling painted face under the leaf of the bonnet, he exclaimed:

— No! Upon my word I believe it's little Bertie Tallon after all!

Stephen at his post by the window heard the old lady and the priest laugh together and heard the boys' murmurs of admiration behind him as they passed forward to see the little boy who had to dance the sunbonnet dance by himself. A movement of impatience escaped him. He let the edge of the blind fall and, stepping down from the bench on which he had been standing, walked out of the chapel.

He passed out of the schoolhouse and halted under the shed that flanked the garden. From the theatre opposite came the muffled noise of the audience and sudden brazen clashes of the soldiers' band. The light spread upwards from the glass roof making the theatre seem a festive ark, anchored among the hulks of houses, her frail cables of lanterns looping her to her moorings. A side door of the theatre opened suddenly and a shaft of light flew across the grassplots. A sudden burst of music issued from the ark, the prelude of a waltz: and when the side door closed again the listener could hear the faint rhythm of the music. The sentiment of the opening bars, their languor and supple movement, evoked the incommunicable emotion which had been the cause of all his day's unrest and of his impatient movement of a moment before. His unrest issued from him like a wave of sound: and on the tide of flowing music the ark was journeying, trailing her cables of lanterns in her wake. Then a noise like dwarf artillery broke the movement. It was the clapping that greeted the entry of the dumb bell team on the stage.

At the far end of the shed near the street a speck of pink light showed in the darkness and as he walked towards it he became aware of a faint aromatic odour. Two boys were standing in the shelter of a doorway, smoking, and before he reached them he had recognised Heron by his voice.

— Here comes the noble Dedalus! cried a high throaty voice. Welcome to our trusty friend!

This welcome ended in a soft peal of mirthless laughter as Heron salaamed and then began to poke the ground with his cane.

— Here I am, said Stephen, halting and glancing from Heron to his friend.

The latter was a stranger to him but in the darkness, by the aid of the glowing cigarette tips, he could make out a pale dandyish face, over which a smile was travelling slowly, a tall overcoated figure and a hard hat. Heron did not trouble himself about an introduction but said instead:

— I was just telling my friend Wallis what a lark it would be tonight if you took off the rector in the part of the schoolmaster. It would be a ripping good joke.

Heron made a poor attempt to imitate for his friend Wallis the rector's pedantic bass and then, laughing at his failure, asked Stephen to do it.

— Go on, Dedalus, he urged, you can take him off rippingly. *He that will not hear the churcha let him be to theea as the heathena and the publicana.*

The imitation was prevented by a mild expression of anger from Wallis in whose mouthpiece the cigarette had become too tightly wedged.

— Damn this blankety blank holder, he said, taking it from his mouth and smiling and frowning upon it tolerantly. It's always getting stuck like that. Do you use a holder?

— I don't smoke, answered Stephen.

— No, said Heron, Dedalus is a model youth. He doesn't smoke and he doesn't go to bazaars and he doesn't flirt and he doesn't damn anything or damn all.

Stephen shook his head and smiled in his rival's flushed and mobile face, beaked like a bird's. He had often thought it strange that Vincent Heron had a bird's face as well as a bird's name. A shock of pale hair lay on the forehead like a ruffled crest: the forehead was narrow and bony and a thin hooked nose stood out between the closeset prominent eyes which were light and inexpressive. The rivals were school friends. They sat together in class, knelt together in the chapel, talked together after beads over their lunches. As the fellows in number one were undistinguished dullards Stephen and Heron had been during the year the virtual heads of the school. It was they who went up to the rector together to ask for a free day or to get a fellow off.

— O by the way, said Heron suddenly, I saw your governor going in.

The smile waned on Stephen's face. Any allusion made to his father by a fellow or by a master put his calm to rout in a moment. He waited in timorous silence to hear what Heron might say next. Heron, however, nudged him expressively with his elbow and said:

— You're a sly dog.

— Why so? said Stephen.

— You'd think butter wouldn't melt in your mouth, said Heron. But I'm afraid you're a sly dog.

— Might I ask you what you are talking about? said Stephen urbanely.

— Indeed you might, answered Heron. We saw her, Wallis, didn't we? And deucedly pretty she is too. And inquisitive! *And what part does Stephen take, Mr Dedalus? And will Stephen not sing, Mr Dedalus?* Your governor was staring at her through that eyeglass of his for all he was worth so that I think the old man has found you out too. I wouldn't care a bit, by Jove. She's ripping, isn't she, Wallis?

— Not half bad, answered Wallis quietly as he placed his holder once more in a corner of his mouth.

A shaft of momentary anger flew through Stephen's mind at these indelicate allusions in the hearing of a stranger. For him there was nothing amusing in a girl's interest and regard. All day he had thought of nothing but their leavetaking on the steps of the tram at Harold's Cross, the stream of moody emotions it had made to course through him, and the poem he had written about it. All day he had imagined a new meeting with her for he knew that she was to come to the play. The old restless moodiness had again filled his breast as it had done on the night of the party but had not found an outlet in verse. The growth and knowledge of two years of boyhood stood between then and now, forbidding such an outlet: and all day the stream of gloomy tenderness within him had started forth and returned upon itself in dark courses and eddies, wearying him in the end until the pleasantry of the prefect and the painted little boy had drawn from him a movement of impatience.

— So you may as well admit, Heron went on, that we've fairly found you out this time. You can't play the saint on me any more, that's one sure five.

A soft peal of mirthless laughter escaped from his lips and, bending down as before, he struck Stephen lightly across the calf of the leg with his cane, as if in jesting reproof.

Stephen's movement of anger had already passed. He was neither flattered nor confused but simply wished the banter to end. He scarcely resented what had seemed to him a silly indelicateness for he knew that the adventure in his mind stood in no danger from these words: and his face mirrored his rival's false smile.

— Admit! repeated Heron, striking him again with his cane across the calf of the leg.

The stroke was playful but not so lightly given as the first one had been. Stephen felt the skin tingle and glow slightly and almost painlessly; and, bowing submissively, as if to meet his companion's jesting mood, began to recite the *Confiteor*. The episode ended well for both Heron and Wallis laughed indulgently at the irreverence.

The confession came only from Stephen's lips and, while they spoke the words, a sudden memory had carried him to another scene called up, as if by magic, at the moment when he had noted the faint cruel dimples at the corners of Heron's smiling lips and had felt the familiar stroke of the cane against his calf and had heard the familiar word of admonition:

— Admit.

It was towards the close of his first term in the college when he was in number six. His sensitive nature was still smarting under the lashes of an undivined and squalid way of life. His soul was still disquieted and cast down by the dull phenomenon of Dublin. He had emerged from a two years' spell of reverie to find himself in the midst of a new scene, every event and figure of which affected him intimately, disheartened him or allured and, whether alluring or disheartening, filled him always with unrest and bitter thoughts. All the leisure which his school life left him was passed in the company of subversive writers whose gibes and violence of speech set up a ferment in his brain before they passed out of it into his crude writings.

The essay was for him the chief labour of his week and every Tuesday, as he marched from home to the school, he read his fate in the incidents of the way, pitting himself against some figure ahead of him and quickening his pace to outstrip it before a certain goal was reached or planting his steps scrupulously in the spaces of the patchwork of the pathway and telling himself that he would be first and not first in the weekly·essay.

On a certain Tuesday the course of his triumphs was rudely broken. Mr Tate, the English master, pointed his finger at him and said bluntly:

— This fellow has heresy in his essay.

A hush fell on the class. Mr Tate did not break it but dug with his hand between his thighs while his heavily starched linen creaked about his neck and wrists. Stephen did not look up. It was a raw spring morning and his eyes were still smarting and weak. He was conscious of failure and of detection, of the squalor of his own mind and home, and felt against his neck the raw edge of his turned and jagged collar.

A short loud laugh from Mr Tate set the class more at ease.

— Perhaps you didn't know that, he said.

— Where? asked Stephen.

Mr Tate withdrew his delving hand and spread out the essay.

— Here. It's about the Creator and the soul. Rrm . . . rrm . . . rrm. . . . Ah! *without a possibility of ever approaching nearer*. That's heresy.

Stephen murmured:

— I meant *without a possibility of ever reaching*.

It was a submission and Mr Tate, appeased, folded up the essay and passed it across to him, saying:

— O . . . Ah! *ever reaching*. That's another story.

But the class was not so soon appeased. Though nobody spoke to him of the affair after class he could feel about him a vague general malignant joy.

A few nights after this public chiding he was walking with a letter along the Drumcondra Road when he heard a voice cry:

— Halt!

He turned and saw three boys of his own class coming towards him in the dusk. It was Heron who had called out and, as he marched forward between his two attendants, he cleft the air before him with a thin cane, in time to their steps. Boland, his friend, marched beside him, a large grin on his face, while Nash came on a few steps behind, blowing from the pace and wagging his great red head.

As soon as the boys had turned into Clonliffe Road together they began to speak about books and writers, saying what books they were reading and how many books there were in their fathers' bookcases at home. Stephen listened to them in some wonderment for Boland was the dunce and Nash the idler of the class. In fact after some talk about their favourite writers Nash declared for Captain Marryat who, he said, was the greatest writer.

— Fudge! said Heron. Ask Dedalus. Who is the greatest writer, Dedalus?

Stephen noted the mockery in the question and said:

— Of prose do you mean?

— Yes.

— Newman, I think.

— Is it Cardinal Newman? asked Boland.

— Yes, answered Stephen.

The grin broadened on Nash's freckled face as he turned to Stephen and said:

— And do you like Cardinal Newman, Dedalus?

— O, many say that Newman has the best prose style, Heron said to the other two in explanation; of course he's not a poet.

— And who is the best poet, Heron? asked Boland.

— Lord Tennyson, of course, answered Heron.

— O, yes, Lord Tennyson, said Nash. We have all his poetry at home in a book.

At this Stephen forgot the silent vows he had been making and burst out:

— Tennyson a poet! Why, he's only a rhymester!

— O, get out! said Heron. Everyone knows that Tennyson is the greatest poet.

— And who do you think is the greatest poet? asked Boland, nudging his neighbour.

— Byron, of course, answered Stephen.

Heron gave the lead and all three joined in a scornful laugh.

— What are you laughing at? asked Stephen.

— You, said Heron. Byron the greatest poet! He's only a poet for uneducated people.

— He must be a fine poet! said Boland.

— You may keep your mouth shut, said Stephen, turning on him boldly. All you know about poetry is what you wrote up on the slates in the yard and were going to be sent to the loft for.

Boland, in fact, was said to have written on the slates in the yard a couplet about a classmate of his who often rode home from the college on a pony:

> *As Tyson was riding into Jerusalem*
> *He fell and hurt his Alec Kafoozelum.*

This thrust put the two lieutenants to silence but Heron went on:

— In any case Byron was a heretic and immoral too.

— I don't care what he was, cried Stephen hotly.

— You don't care whether he was a heretic or not? said Nash.

— What do you know about it? shouted Stephen. You never read a line of anything in your life except a trans or Boland either.

— I know that Byron was a bad man, said Boland.

— Here, catch hold of this heretic, Heron called out.

In a moment Stephen was a prisoner.

— Tate made you buck up the other day, Heron went on, about the heresy in your essay.

— I'll tell him tomorrow, said Boland.

— Will you? said Stephen. You'd be afraid to open your lips.

— Afraid?

— Ay. Afraid of your life.

— Behave yourself! cried Heron, cutting at Stephen's legs with his cane.

It was the signal for their onset. Nash pinioned his arms behind while Boland seized a long cabbage stump which was lying in the gutter. Struggling and kicking under the cuts of the cane and the blows of the knotty stump Stephen was borne back against a barbed wire fence.

— Admit that Byron was no good.

— No.

— Admit.

— No.

— Admit.

— No. No.

At last after a fury of plunges he wrenched himself free. His tormentors set off towards Jones's Road, laughing and jeering at him, while he, half blinded with tears, stumbled on, clenching his fists madly and sobbing.

While he was still repeating the *Confiteor* amid the indulgent laughter of his hearers and while the scenes of that malignant episode were still passing sharply and swiftly before his mind he wondered why he bore no malice now to those who had tormented him. He had not forgotten a whit of their cowardice and cruelty but the memory of it called forth no anger from him. All the description of fierce love and hatred which he had met in books had seemed to him therefore unreal. Even that night as he stumbled homewards along Jones's Road he had felt that some power was divesting him of that sudden woven anger as easily as a fruit is divested of its soft ripe peel.

He remained standing with his two companions at the end of the shed listening idly to their talk or to the bursts of applause in the theatre. She was sitting there among the others perhaps waiting for him to appear. He tried to recall her appearance but could not. He could remember only that she had worn a shawl about her head like a cowl and that her dark eyes had invited and unnerved him. He wondered had he been in her thoughts as she had been in his. Then in the dark and unseen by the other two he rested the tips of the fingers of one hand upon the palm of the other hand, scarcely touching it lightly. But the pressure of her fingers had been lighter and steadier: and suddenly the memory of their touch traversed his brain and body like an invisible wave.

A boy came towards them, running along under the shed. He was excited and breathless.

— O, Dedalus, he cried, Doyle is in a great bake about you. You're to go in at once and get dressed for the play. Hurry up, you better.

— He's coming now, said Heron to the messenger with a haughty drawl, when he wants to.

The boy turned to Heron and repeated:

— But Doyle is in an awful bake.

— Will you tell Doyle with my best compliments that I damned his eyes? answered Heron.

— Well, I must go now, said Stephen, who cared little for such points of honour.

— I wouldn't, said Heron, damn me if I would. That's no way to send for one of the senior boys. In a bake, indeed! I think it's quite enough that you're taking a part in his bally old play.

This spirit of quarrelsome comradeship which he had observed lately in his rival had not seduced Stephen from his habits of quiet obedience. He mistrusted the turbulence and doubted the sincerity of such comradeship which seemed to him a sorry anticipation of manhood. The question of honour here raised was, like all such questions, trivial to him. While his mind had been pursuing its intangible phantoms and turning in irresolution from such pursuit he had heard about him the constant voices of his father and of his masters, urging him to be a gentleman above all things and urging him to be a good catholic above all things. These voices had now come to be hollow sounding in his ears. When the gymnasium had been opened he had heard another voice urging him to be strong and manly and healthy and when the movement towards national revival had begun to be felt in the college yet another voice had bidden him be true to his country and help to raise up her language and tradition. In the profane world, as he foresaw, a worldly voice would bid him raise up his father's fallen state by his labours and, meanwhile, the voice of his school-comrades urged him to be a decent fellow, to shield others from blame or to beg them off and to do his best to get free days for the school. And it was the din of all these hollowsounding voices that made him halt irresolutely in the pursuit of phantoms. He gave them ear only for a time but he was happy only when he was far from them, beyond their call, alone or in the company of phantasmal comrades.

In the vestry a plump freshfaced jesuit and an elderly man, in shabby blue clothes, were dabbling in a case of paints and chalks. The boys who had been painted walked about or stood still awkwardly, touching their faces in a gingerly fashion with their furtive fingertips. In the middle of the vestry a young jesuit, who was then on a visit to the college, stood rocking himself rhythmically from the tips of his toes to his heels and back again, his hands thrust well forward into his side pockets. His small head set off with glossy red curls and his newly shaven face agreed well with the spotless decency of his soutane and with his spotless shoes.

As he watched this swaying form and tried to read for himself the legend of the priest's mocking smile there came into Stephen's memory a saying which he had heard from his father before he had been sent to Clongowes, that you could always tell a jesuit by the style of his clothes. At the same moment he thought he saw a likeness between his father's mind and that of this smiling welldressed priest: and he was aware of some desecration of the priest's office or of the vestry itself whose silence was now routed by loud talk and joking and its air pungent with the smells of the gasjets and the grease.

While his forehead was being wrinkled and his jaws painted black and blue by the elderly man he listened distractedly to the voice of the plump young jesuit which bade him speak up and make his points clearly. He could hear the band playing *The Lily of Killarney* and knew that in a few moments the curtain would go up. He felt no stage fright but the thought of the part he had to play humiliated him. A remembrance of some of his lines made a sudden flush rise to his painted cheeks. He saw her serious alluring eyes watching him from among the audience and their image at once swept away his scruples, leaving his will compact. Another nature seemed to have been lent him: the infection of the excitement and youth about him entered into and transformed his moody mistrustfulness. For one rare moment he seemed to be clothed in the real apparel of boyhood: and, as he stood in the wings among the other players, he shared the common mirth amid which the drop scene was hauled upwards by two ablebodied priests with violent jerks and all awry.

A few moments after he found himself on the stage amid the garish gas and the dim scenery, acting before the innumerable faces of the void. It surprised him to see that the play which he had known at rehearsals for a disjointed lifeless thing had suddenly assumed a life of its own. It seemed now to play itself, he and his fellow actors aiding it with their parts. When the curtain fell on the last scene he heard the void filled with applause and, through a rift in a side scene, saw the simple body before which he had acted magically deformed, the void of faces breaking at all points and falling asunder into busy groups.

He left the stage quickly and rid himself of his mummery and passed out through the chapel into the college garden. Now that the play was over his nerves cried for some further adventure. He hurried onwards as if to overtake it. The doors of the theatre were all open and the audience had emptied out. On the lines which he had fancied the moorings of an ark a few lanterns swung in the night breeze, flickering cheerlessly. He mounted the steps from the garden in haste, eager that some prey should not elude him, and forced his way through the crowd in the hall and past the two jesuits who stood watching the exodus and bowing and shaking hands with the visitors. He pushed onward nervously, feigning a still greater haste and faintly conscious of the smiles and stares and nudges which his powdered head left in its wake.

When he came out on the steps he saw his family waiting for him at the first lamp. In a glance he noted that every figure of the group was familiar and ran down the steps angrily.

— I have to leave a message down in George's Street, he said to his father quickly. I'll be home after you.

Without waiting for his father's questions he ran across the road and began to walk at breakneck speed down the hill. He hardly knew where he was walking. Pride and hope and desire like crushed herbs in his heart sent up vapours of maddening incense before the eyes of his mind. He strode down the hill amid the tumult of suddenrisen vapours of wounded pride and fallen hope and baffled desire. They streamed upwards before his anguished eyes in dense and maddening fumes and passed away above him till at last the air was clear and cold again.

A film still veiled his eyes but they burned no longer. A power, akin to that which had often made anger or resentment fall from him, brought his steps to rest. He stood still and gazed up at the sombre porch of the morgue and from that to the dark cobbled laneway at its side. He saw the word *Lotts* on the wall of the lane and breathed slowly the rank heavy air.

— That is horse piss and rotted straw, he thought. It is a good odour to breathe. It will calm my heart. My heart is quite calm now. I will go back.

*   *   *

Stephen was once again seated beside his father in the corner of a railway carriage at Kingsbridge. He was travelling with his father by the night mail to Cork. As the train steamed out of the station he recalled his childish wonder of years before and every event of his first day at Clongowes. But he felt no wonder now. He saw the darkening lands slipping away past him, the silent telegraphpoles passing his window swiftly every four seconds, the little glimmering stations, manned by a few silent sentries, flung by the mail behind her and twinkling for a moment in the darkness like fiery grains flung backwards by a runner.

He listened without sympathy to his father's evocation of Cork and of scenes of his youth — a tale broken by sighs or draughts from his pocket flask whenever the image of some dead friend appeared in it, or whenever the evoker remembered suddenly the purpose of his actual visit. Stephen heard, but could feel no pity. The images of the dead were all strangers to him save that of Uncle Charles, an image which had lately been fading out of memory. He knew, however, that his father's property was going to be sold by auction and in the manner of his own dispossession he felt the world give the lie rudely to his phantasy.

At Maryborough he fell asleep. When he awoke the train had passed out of Mallow and his father was stretched asleep on the other seat. The cold light of the dawn lay over the country, over the unpeopled fields and the closed cottages. The terror of sleep fascinated his mind as he watched the silent country or heard from time to time his father's deep breath or sudden sleepy movement. The neighbourhood of unseen sleepers filled him with strange dread, as though they could harm him, and he prayed that the day might come quickly. His prayer, addressed neither to God nor saint, began with a shiver, as the chilly morning breeze crept through the chink of the carriage door to his feet, and ended in a trail of foolish words which he made to fit the insistent rhythm of the train; and silently, at intervals of four seconds, the telegraphpoles held the galloping notes of the music between punctual bars. This furious music allayed his dread and, leaning against the window ledge, he let his eyelids close again.

They drove in a jingle across Cork while it was still early morning and Stephen finished his sleep in a bedroom of the Victoria Hotel. The bright warm sunlight was streaming through the window and he could hear the din of traffic. His father was standing before the dressingtable, examining his hair and face and moustache with great care, craning his neck across the water jug and drawing it back sideways to see the better. While he did so he sang softly to himself with quaint accent and phrasing:

> " 'Tis youth and folly
> Makes young men marry,
> So here, my love, I'll
>   No longer stay.
> What can't be cured, sure,
> Must be injured, sure,
>   So I'll go to Amerikay.

> "My love she's handsome,
> My love she's bony:
> She's like good whisky
> When it is new;
> But when 'tis old
> And growing cold
> It fades and dies like
> The mountain dew."

The consciousness of the warm sunny city outside his window and the tender tremors with which his father's voice festooned the strange sad happy air, drove off all the mists of the night's ill humour from Stephen's brain. He got up quickly to dress and, when the song had ended, said:

— That's much prettier than any of your other *come-all-yous*.

— Do you think so? asked Mr Dedalus.

— I like it, said Stephen.

— It's a pretty old air, said Mr Dedalus, twirling the points of his moustache. Ah, but you should have heard Mick Lacy sing it! Poor Mick Lacy! He had little turns for it, grace notes he used to put in that I haven't got. That was the boy who could sing a *come-all-you*, if you like.

Mr Dedalus had ordered drisheens for breakfast and during the meal he cross-examined the waiter for local news. For the most part they spoke at cross purposes when a name was mentioned, the waiter having in mind the present holder and Mr Dedalus his father or perhaps his grandfather.

— Well, I hope they haven't moved the Queen's College anyhow, said Mr Dedalus, for I want to show it to this youngster of mine.

Along the Mardyke the trees were in bloom. They entered the grounds of the college and were led by the garrulous porter across the quadrangle. But their progress across the gravel was brought to a halt after every dozen or so paces by some reply of the porter's —

— Ah, do you tell me so? And is poor Pottlebelly dead?

— Yes, sir. Dead, sir.

During these halts Stephen stood awkwardly behind the two men, weary of the subject and waiting restlessly for the slow march to begin again. By the time they had crossed the quadrangle his restlessness had risen to fever. He wondered how his father, whom he knew for a shrewd suspicious man, could be duped by the servile manners of the porter; and the lively southern speech which had entertained him all the morning now irritated his ears.

They passed into the anatomy theatre where Mr Dedalus, the porter aiding him, searched the desks for his initials. Stephen remained in the background, depressed more than ever by the darkness and silence of the theatre and by the air it wore of jaded and formal study. On the desk he read the word *Fœtus* cut several times in the dark stained wood. The sudden legend startled his blood: he seemed to feel the absent students of the college about him and to shrink from their company. A vision of their life, which his father's words had been powerless to evoke, sprang up before him out of the word cut in the desk. A broad shouldered student with a moustache was cutting in the letters with a jack knife, seriously. Other students stood or sat near him laughing at his handi-work. One jogged his elbow. The big student turned on him, frowning. He was dressed in loose grey clothes and had tan boots.

Stephen's name was called. He hurried down the steps of the theatre so as to be as far away from the vision as he could be and, peering closely at his father's initials, hid his flushed face.

But the word and the vision capered before his eyes as he walked back across the quadrangle and towards the college gate. It shocked him to find in the outer world a trace of what he had deemed till then a brutish and individual malady of his own mind. His monstrous reveries came thronging into his memory. They too had sprung up before him, sud-denly and furiously, out of mere words. He had soon given in to them, and allowed them to sweep across and abase his intellect, wondering always where they came from, from what den of monstrous images, and always weak and humble towards others, restless and sickened of himself when they had swept over him.

— Ay, bedad! And there's the Groceries sure enough! cried Mr De-dalus. You often heard me speak of the Groceries, didn't you, Stephen. Many's the time we went down there when our names had been marked, a crowd of us, Harry Peard and little Jack Mountain and Bob Dyas and Maurice Moriarty, the Frenchman, and Tom O'Grady and Mick Lacy that I told you of this morning and Joey Corbet and poor little good hearted Johnny Keevers of the Tantiles.

The leaves of the trees along the Mardyke were astir and whispering in the sunlight. A team of cricketers passed, agile young men in flannels and blazers, one of them carrying the long green wicket bag. In a quiet by street a German band of five players in faded uniforms and with battered brass instruments was playing to an audience of street arabs and leisurely messenger boys. A maid in a white cap and apron was watering a box of plants on a sill which shone like a slab of limestone in the warm glare. From another window open to the air came the sound of a piano, scale after scale rising into the treble.

Stephen walked on at his father's side, listening to stories he had heard before, hearing again the names of the scattered and dead re-vellers who had been the companions of his father's youth. And a faint sickness sighed in his heart. He recalled his own equivocal position in

Belvedere, a free boy, a leader afraid of his own authority, proud and sensitive and suspicious, battling against the squalor of his life and against the riot of his mind. The letters cut in the stained wood of the desk stared upon him, mocking his bodily weakness and futile enthusiasms and making him loathe himself for his own mad and filthy orgies. The spittle in his throat grew bitter and foul to swallow and the faint sickness climbed to his brain so that for a moment he closed his eyes and walked on in darkness.

He could still hear his father's voice —

— When you kick out for yourself, Stephen — as I daresay you will one of these days — remember, whatever you do, to mix with gentlemen. When I was a young fellow I tell you I enjoyed myself. I mixed with fine decent fellows. Everyone of us could do something. One fellow had a good voice, another fellow was a good actor, another could sing a good comic song, another was a good oarsman or a good racket player, another could tell a good story and so on. We kept the ball rolling anyhow and enjoyed ourselves and saw a bit of life and we were none the worse of it either. But we were all gentlemen, Stephen — at least I hope we were — and bloody good honest Irishmen too. That's the kind of fellows I want you to associate with, fellows of the right kidney. I'm talking to you as a friend, Stephen. I don't believe a son should be afraid of his father. No, I treat you as your grandfather treated me when I was a young chap. We were more like brothers than father and son. I'll never forget the first day he caught me smoking. I was standing at the end of the South Terrace one day with some maneens like myself and sure we thought we were grand fellows because we had pipes stuck in the corners of our mouths. Suddenly the governor passed. He didn't say a word, or stop even. But the next day, Sunday, we were out for a walk together and when we were coming home he took out his cigar case and said: — By the by, Simon, I didn't know you smoked, or something like that. Of course I tried to carry it off as best I could. — If you want a good smoke, he said, try one of these cigars. An American captain made me a present of them last night in Queenstown.

Stephen heard his father's voice break into a laugh which was almost a sob.

— He was the handsomest man in Cork at that time, by God he was! The women used to stand to look after him in the street.

He heard the sob passing loudly down his father's throat and opened his eyes with a nervous impulse. The sunlight breaking suddenly on his sight turned the sky and clouds into a fantastic world of sombre masses with lakelike spaces of dark rosy light. His very brain was sick and powerless. He could scarcely interpret the letters of the signboards of the shops. By his monstrous way of life he seemed to have put himself beyond the limits of reality. Nothing moved him or spoke to him from the real world unless he heard in it an echo of the infuriated cries within him. He could respond to no earthly or human appeal, dumb and insensible to the call of summer and gladness and companionship, wearied and dejected by his father's voice. He could scarcely recognise as his his own thoughts, and repeated slowly to himself:

— I am Stephen Dedalus. I am walking beside my father whose name is Simon Dedalus. We are in Cork, in Ireland. Cork is a city. Our room is in the Victoria Hotel. Victoria and Stephen and Simon. Simon and Stephen and Victoria. Names.

The memory of his childhood suddenly grew dim. He tried to call forth some of its vivid moments but could not. He recalled only names. Dante, Parnell, Clane, Clongowes. A little boy had been taught geography by an old woman who kept two brushes in her wardrobe. Then he had been sent away from home to a college, he had made his first communion and eaten slim jim out of his cricket cap and watched the firelight leaping and dancing on the wall of a little bedroom in the infirmary and dreamed of being dead, of mass being said for him by the rector in a black and gold cope, of being buried then in the little graveyard of the community off the main avenue of lines. But he had not died then. Parnell had died. There had been no mass for the dead in the chapel, and no procession. He had not died but he had faded out like a film in the sun. He had been lost or had wandered out of existence for he no longer existed. How strange to think of him passing out of existence in such a way, not by death, but by fading out in the sun or by being lost and forgotten somewhere in the universe! It was strange to see his small body appear again for a moment: a little boy in a grey belted suit. His hands were in his side pockets and his trousers were tucked in at the knees by elastic bands.

On the evening of the day on which the property was sold Stephen followed his father meekly about the city from bar to bar. To the sellers in the market, to the barmen and barmaids, to the beggars who importuned him for a lob Mr Dedalus told the same tale, that he was an old Corkonian, that he had been trying for thirty years to get rid of his Cork accent up in Dublin and that Peter Pickackafax beside him was his eldest son but that he was only a Dublin jackeen.

They had set out early in the morning from Newcombe's coffeehouse, where Mr Dedalus' cup had rattled noisily against its saucer, and Stephen had tried to cover that shameful sign of his father's drinkingbout of the night before by moving his chair and coughing. One humiliation had succeeded another — the false smiles of the market sellers, the curvetings and oglings of the barmaids with whom his father flirted, the compliments and encouraging words of his father's friends.

They had told him that he had a great look of his grandfather and Mr Dedalus had agreed that he was an ugly likeness. They had unearthed traces of a Cork accent in his speech and made him admit that the Lee was a much finer river than the Liffey. One of them, in order to put his Latin to the proof, had made him translate short passages from Dilectus, and asked him whether it was correct to say: *Tempora mutantur nos et mutamur in illis*, or *Tempora mutantur et nos mutamur in illis*.[1] Another, a brisk old man, whom Mr Dedalus called Johnny Cashman, had covered him with confusion by asking him to say which were prettier, the Dublin girls or the Cork girls.

— He's not that way built, said Mr Dedalus. Leave him alone. He's a levelheaded thinking boy who doesn't bother his head about that kind of nonsense.

— Then he's not his father's son, said the little old man.

— I don't know, I'm sure, said Mr Dedalus, smiling complacently.

— Your father, said the little old man to Stephen, was the boldest flirt in the city of Cork in his day. Do you know that?

Stephen looked down and studied the tiled floor of the bar into which they had drifted.

— Now don't be putting ideas into his head, said Mr Dedalus. Leave him to his Maker.

— Yerra, sure I wouldn't put any ideas into his head. I'm old enough to be his grandfather. And I am a grandfather, said the little old man to Stephen. Do you know that?

— Are you? asked Stephen.

— Bedad I am, said the little old man. I have two bouncing grandchildren out at Sunday's Well. Now, then! What age do you think I am! And I remember seeing your grandfather in his red coat riding out to hounds. That was before you were born.

— Ay, or thought of, said Mr Dedalus.

— Bedad I did, repeated the little old man. And, more than that, I can remember even your great grandfather, old John Stephen Dedalus, and a fierce old fireeater he was. Now, then! There's a memory for you!

— That's three generations — four generations, said another of the company. Why, Johnny Cashman, you must be nearing the century.

— Well, I'll tell you the truth, said the little old man. I'm just twentyseven years of age.

— We're as old as we feel, Johnny, said Mr Dedalus. — And just finish what you have there, and we'll have another. Here, Tim or Tom or whatever your name is, give us the same again here. By God, I don't

---

[1] [Both mean *Circumstances change and we change with them*. The difference is one of poetic word order.]

feel more than eighteen myself. There's that son of mine there not half my age and I'm a better man than he is any day of the week.

— Draw it mild now, Dedalus. I think it's time for you to take a back seat, said the gentleman who had spoken before.

— No, by God! asserted Mr Dedalus. I'll sing a tenor song against him or I'll vault a fire-barred gate against him or I'll run with him after the hounds across the country as I did thirty years ago along with the Kerry Boy and the best man for it.

— But he'll beat you here, said the little old man, tapping his forehead and raising his glass to drain it.

— Well, I hope he'll be as good a man as his father. That's all I can say, said Mr Dedalus.

— If he is, he'll do, said the little old man.

— And thanks be to God, Johnny, said Mr Dedalus, that we lived so long and did so little harm.

— But did so much good, Simon, said the little old man gravely. Thanks be to God we lived so long and did so much good.

Stephen watched the three glasses being raised from the counter as his father and his two cronies drank to the memory of their past. An abyss of fortune or of temperament sundered him from them. His mind seemed older than theirs: it shone coldly on their strifes and happiness and regrets like a moon upon a younger earth. No life or youth stirred in him as it had stirred in them. He had known neither the pleasure of companionship with others nor the vigour of rude male health nor filial piety. Nothing stirred within his soul but a cold and cruel and loveless lust. His childhood was dead or lost and with it his soul capable of simple joys and he was drifting amid life like the barren shell of the moon.

> "Art thou pale for weariness
> Of climbing heaven and gazing on the earth,
> Wandering companionless? . . ."

He repeated to himself the lines of Shelley's fragment. Its alternation of sad human ineffectualness with vast inhuman cycles of activity chilled him, and he forgot his own human and ineffectual grieving.

*   *   *   *

Stephen's mother and his brother and one of his cousins waited at the corner of quiet Foster Place while he and his father went up the steps and along the colonnade where the Highland sentry was parading. When they had passed into the great hall and stood at the counter Stephen drew forth his orders on the governor of the bank of Ireland for thirty and three pounds; and these sums, the moneys of his exhibition and essay prize, were paid over to him rapidly by the teller in notes and in coin respectively. He bestowed them in his pockets with feigned composure and suffered the friendly teller, to whom his father chatted, to take his hand across the broad counter and wish him a brilliant career in after life. He was impatient of their voices and could not keep his feet at rest. But the teller still deferred the serving of others to say he was living in changed times and that there was nothing like giving a boy the best education that money could buy. Mr Dedalus lingered in the hall gazing about him and up at the roof and telling Stephen, who urged him to come out, that they were standing in the house of commons of the old Irish parliament.

— God help us! he said piously, to think of the men of those times, Stephen, Hely Hutchinson and Flood and Henry Grattan and Charles Kendal Bushe, and the noblemen we have now, leaders of the Irish people at home and abroad. Why, by God, they wouldn't be seen dead in a ten acre field with them. No, Stephen, old chap, I'm sorry to say that they are only as I roved out one fine May morning in the merry month of sweet July.

A keen October wind was blowing round the bank. The three figures standing at the edge of the muddy path had pinched cheeks and watery eyes. Stephen looked at his thinly clad mother and remembered that a few days before he had seen a mantle priced at twenty guineas in the windows of Barnardo's.

— Well that's done, said Mr Dedalus.

— We had better go to dinner, said Stephen. Where?

— Dinner? said Mr Dedalus. Well, I suppose we had better, what?

— Some place that's not too dear, said Mrs Dedalus.

— Underdone's?

— Yes. Some quiet place.

— Come along, said Stephen quickly. It doesn't matter about the dearness.

He walked on before them with short nervous steps, smiling. They tried to keep up with him, smiling also at his eagerness.

— Take it easy like a good young fellow, said his father. We're not out for the half mile, are we?

For a swift season of merrymaking the money of his prizes ran through Stephen's fingers. Great parcels of groceries and delicacies and dried fruits arrived from the city. Every day he drew up a bill of fare for the family and every night led a party of three or four to the theatre to see *Ingomar* or *The Lady of Lyons*. In his coat pockets he carried squares of Vienna chocolate for his guests while his trousers' pockets bulged with masses of silver and copper coins. He bought presents for everyone, overhauled his room, wrote out resolutions, marshalled his books up and down their shelves, pored upon all kinds of price lists, drew up a form of commonwealth for the household by which every member of it held some office, opened a loan bank for his family and pressed loans on willing borrowers so that he might have the pleasure of making out receipts and reckoning the interests on the sums lent. When he could do no more he drove up and down the city in trams. Then the season of pleasure came to an end. The pot of pink enamel paint gave out and the wainscot of his bedroom remained with its unfinished and ill plastered coat.

His household returned to its usual way of life. His mother had no further occasion to upbraid him for squandering his money. He, too, returned to his old life at school and all his novel enterprises fell to pieces. The commonwealth fell, the loan bank closed its coffers and its books on a sensible loss, the rules of life which he had drawn about himself fell into desuetude.

How foolish his aim had been! He had tried to build a breakwater of order and elegance against the sordid tide of life without him and to dam up, by rules of conduct and active interests and new filial relations, the powerful recurrence of the tide within him. Useless. From without as from within the water had flowed over his barriers: their tides began once more to jostle fiercely above the crumbled mole.

He saw clearly, too, his own futile isolation. He had not gone one step nearer the lives he had sought to approach nor bridged the restless shame and rancour that had divided him from mother and brother and sister. He felt that he was hardly of the one blood with them but stood to them rather in the mystical kinship of fosterage, foster child and foster brother.

He turned to appease the fierce longings of his heart before which everything else was idle and alien. He cared little that he was in mortal sin, that his life had grown to be a tissue of subterfuge and falsehood. Beside the savage desire within him to realise the enormities which he brooded on nothing was sacred. He bore cynically with the shameful details of his secret riots in which he exulted to defile with patience whatever image had attracted his eyes. By day and by night he moved among distorted images of the outer world. A figure that had seemed to him by day demure and innocent came towards him by night through the winding darkness of sleep, her face transfigured by a lecherous cunning, her eyes bright with brutish joy. Only the morning pained him with its dim memory of dark orgiastic riot, its keen and humiliating sense of transgression.

He returned to his wanderings. The veiled autumnal evenings led him from street to street as they had led him years before along the quiet avenues of Blackrock. But no vision of trim front gardens or of kindly lights in the windows poured a tender influence upon him now. Only at times, in the pauses of his desire, when the luxury that was wasting him gave room to a softer languor, the image of Mercedes traversed the background of his memory. He saw again the small white house and the garden of rosebushes on the road that led to the mountains and he remembered the sadly proud gesture of refusal which he was to make there, standing with her in the moonlit garden after years of estrangement and adventure. At those moments the soft speeches of Claude Melnotte rose to his lips and eased his unrest. A tender premonition touched him of the tryst he had then looked forward to and, in spite of the horrible reality which lay between his hope of then and now, of the holy encounter he had then imagined at which weakness and timidity and inexperience were to fall from him.

Such moments passed and the wasting fires of lust sprang up again. The verses passed from his lips and the inarticulate cries and the unspoken brutal words rushed forth from his brain to force a passage. His blood was in revolt. He wandered up and down the dark slimy streets peering into the gloom of lanes and doorways, listening eagerly for any sound. He moaned to himself like some baffled prowling beast. He wanted to sin with another of his kind, to force another being to sin with him and to exult with her in sin. He felt some dark presence moving irresistibly upon him from the darkness, a presence subtle and murmurous as a flood filling him wholly with itself. Its murmur besieged his ears like the murmur of some multitude in sleep; its subtle streams penetrated his being. His hands clenched convulsively and his teeth set together as he suffered the agony of its penetration. He stretched out his arms in the street to hold fast the frail swooning form that eluded him and incited him: and the cry that he had strangled for so long in his throat issued from his lips. It broke from him like a wail of despair from a hell of sufferers and died in a wail of furious entreaty, a cry for an iniquitous abandonment, a cry which was but the echo of an obscene scrawl which he had read on the oozing wall of a urinal.

He had wandered into a maze of narrow and dirty streets. From the foul laneways he heard bursts of hoarse riot and wrangling and the drawling of drunken singers. He walked onward, undismayed, wondering whether he had strayed into the quarter of the Jews. Women and girls dressed in long vivid gowns traversed the street from house to house. They were leisurely and perfumed. A trembling seized him and his eyes grew dim. The yellow gasflames arose before his troubled vision against the vapoury sky, burning as if before an altar. Before the doors and in the lighted halls groups were gathered arrayed as for some rite. He was in another world: he had awakened from a slumber of centuries.

He stood still in the middle of the roadway, his heart clamouring against his bosom in a tumult. A young woman dressed in a long pink gown laid her hand on his arm to detain him and gazed into his face. She said gaily:

— Good night, Willie dear!

Her room was warm and lightsome. A huge doll sat with her legs apart in the copious easychair beside the bed. He tried to bid his tongue speak that he might seem at ease, watching her as she undid her gown, noting the proud conscious movements of her perfumed head.

As he stood silent in the middle of the room she came over to him and embraced him gaily and gravely. Her round arms held him firmly to her and he, seeing her face lifted to him in serious calm and feeling the warm calm rise and fall of her breast, all but burst into hysterical weeping. Tears of joy and relief shone in his delighted eyes and his lips parted though they would not speak.

She passed her tinkling hand through his hair, calling him a little rascal.

— Give me a kiss, she said.

His lips would not bend to kiss her. He wanted to be held firmly in her arms, to be caressed slowly, slowly, slowly. In her arms he felt that he had suddenly become strong and fearless and sure of himself. But his lips would not bend to kiss her.

With a sudden movement she bowed his head and joined her lips to his and he read the meaning of her movements in her frank uplifted eyes. It was too much for him. He closed his eyes, surrendering himself to her, body and mind, conscious of nothing in the world but the dark pressure of her softly parting lips. They pressed upon his brain as upon his lips as though they were the vehicle of a vague speech; and between them he felt an unknown and timid pressure, darker than the swoon of sin, softer than sound or odour.

Chapter III

THE swift December dusk had come tumbling clownishly after its dull day and as he stared through the dull square of the window of the schoolroom he felt his belly crave for its food. He hoped there would be stew for dinner, turnips and carrots and bruised potatoes and fat mutton pieces to be ladled out in thick peppered flour-fattened sauce. Stuff it into you, his belly counselled him.

It would be a gloomy secret night. After early nightfall the yellow lamps would light up, here and there, the squalid quarter of the brothels. He would follow a devious course up and down the streets, circling always nearer and nearer in a tremor of fear and joy, until his feet led him suddenly round a dark corner. The whores would be just coming out of their houses making ready for the night, yawning lazily after their sleep and settling the hairpins in their clusters of hair. He would pass by them calmly waiting for a sudden movement of his own will or a sudden call to his sin-loving soul from their soft perfumed flesh. Yet as he prowled in quest of that call, his senses, stultified only by his desire, would note keenly all that wounded or shamed them; his eyes, a ring of porter froth on a clothless table or a photograph of two soldiers standing to attention on a gaudy playbill; his ears, the drawling jargon of greeting:

— Hello, Bertie, any good in your mind?
— Is that you, pigeon?
— Number ten. Fresh Nelly is waiting on you.
— Good night, husband! Coming in to have a short time?

The equation on the page of his scribbler began to spread out a widening tail, eyed and starred like a peacock's; and, when the eyes and stars of its indices had been eliminated, began slowly to fold itself together again. The indices appearing and disappearing were eyes opening and closing; the eyes opening and closing were stars being born and being quenched. The vast cycle of starry life bore his weary mind outward to its verge and inward to its centre, a distant music accompany-

ing him outward and inward. What music? The music came nearer and
he recalled the words, the words of Shelley's fragment upon the moon
wandering companionless, pale for weariness. The stars began to crumble and a cloud of fine star-dust fell through space.

The dull light fell more faintly upon the page whereon another
equation began to unfold itself slowly and to spread abroad its widening
tail. It was his own soul going forth to experience, unfolding itself sin by
sin, spreading abroad the balefire of its burning stars and folding back
upon itself, fading slowly, quenching its own lights and fires. They were
quenched: and the cold darkness filled chaos.

A cold lucid indifference reigned in his soul. At his first violent sin he
had felt a wave of vitality pass out of him and had feared to find his body
or his soul maimed by the excess. Instead the vital wave had carried him
on its bosom out of himself and back again when it receded: and no part
of body or soul had been maimed, but a dark peace had been estab-
lished between them. The chaos in which his ardour extinguished itself
was a cold indifferent knowledge of himself. He had sinned mortally not
once but many times and he knew that, while he stood in danger of
eternal damnation for the first sin alone, by every succeeding sin he
multiplied his guilt and his punishment. His days and works and
thoughts could make no atonement for him, the fountains of sanctifying
grace having ceased to refresh his soul. At most, by an alms given to a
beggar whose blessing he fled from, he might hope wearily to win for
himself some measure of actual grace. Devotion had gone by the board.
What did it avail to pray when he knew that his soul lusted after its own
destruction? A certain pride, a certain awe, withheld him from offering
to God even one prayer at night though he knew it was in God's power to
take away his life while he slept and hurl his soul hellward ere he could
beg for mercy. His pride in his own sin, his loveless awe of God, told him
that his offence was too grievous to be atoned for in whole or in part by a
false homage to the Allseeing and Allknowing.

— Well now, Ennis, I declare you have a head and so has my stick!
Do you mean to say that you are not able to tell me what a surd is?

The blundering answer stirred the embers of his contempt of his
fellows. Towards others he felt neither shame nor fear. On Sunday
mornings as he passed the church door he glanced coldly at the worshippers who stood bareheaded, four deep, outside the church, morally
present at the mass which they could neither see nor hear. Their dull
piety and the sickly smell of the cheap hair oil with which they had
anointed their heads repelled him from the altar they prayed at. He
stooped to the evil of hypocrisy with others, sceptical of their innocence
which he could cajole so easily.

On the wall of his bedroom hung an illuminated scroll, the certificate of his prefecture in the college of the sodality of the Blessed Virgin Mary. On Saturday mornings when the sodality met in the chapel to recite the little office his place was a cushioned kneeling-desk at the right of the altar from which he led his wing of boys through the responses. The falsehood of his position did not pain him. If at moments he felt an impulse to rise from his post of honour and, confessing before them all his unworthiness, to leave the chapel, a glance at their faces restrained him. The imagery of the psalms of prophecy soothed his barren pride. The glories of Mary held his soul captive: spikenard and myrrh and frankincense, symbolising her royal lineage, her emblems, the late-flowering plant and late-blossoming tree, symbolising the agelong gradual growth of her cultus among men. When it fell to him to read the lesson towards the close of the office he read it in a veiled voice, lulling his conscience to its music.

Quasi cedrus exaltata sum in Libanon et quasi cupressus in monte Sion. Quasi palma exaltata sum in Gades et quasi plantatio rosae in Jericho. Quasi uliva speciosa in campis et quasi platanus exaltata sum juxta aquam in plateis. Sicut cinnamomum et balsamum aromatizans odorem dedi et quasi myrrha electa dedi suavitatem odoris.[1]

His sin, which had covered him from the sight of God, had led him nearer to the refuge of sinners. Her eyes seemed to regard him with mild pity; her holiness, a strange light glowing faintly upon her frail flesh, did not humiliate the sinner who approached her. If ever he was impelled to cast sin from him and to repent, the impulse that moved him was the wish to be her knight. If ever his soul, re-entering her dwelling shyly after the frenzy of his body's lust had spent itself, was turned towards her whose emblem is the morning star, "bright and musical, telling of heaven and infusing peace," it was when her names were murmured softly by lips whereon there still lingered foul and shameful words, the savour itself of a lewd kiss.

That was strange. He tried to think how it could be but the dusk, deepening in the schoolroom, covered over his thoughts. The bell rang. The master marked the sums and cuts to be done for the next lesson and went out. Heron, beside Stephen, began to hum tunelessly.

My excellent friend Bombados.

---

[1] [*I have been exalted like a cedar in Lebanon and like a cypress on Mount Zion. I have been exalted like a palm tree in Gades and like a planting of roses in Jericho. I have been exalted like a beautiful olive tree in the fields and like a plane tree beside the water in the squares. I have emitted fragrance like cinnamon and aromatic balsam and I have furnished sweet smells like choice myrrh.* (from Ecclesiasticus 24).]

Ennis, who had gone to the yard, came back, saying:

— The boy from the house is coming up for the rector.

A tall boy behind Stephen rubbed his hands and said:

— That's game ball. We can scut the whole hour. He won't be in till after half two. Then you can ask him questions on the catechism, Dedalus.

Stephen, leaning back and drawing idly on his scribbler, listened to the talk about him which Heron checked from time to time by saying:

— Shut up, will you. Don't make such a bally racket!

It was strange too that he found an arid pleasure in following up to the end the rigid lines of the doctrines of the church and penetrating into obscure silences only to hear and feel the more deeply his own condemnation. The sentence of Saint James which says that he who offends against one commandment becomes guilty of all had seemed to him first a swollen phrase until he had begun to grope in the darkness of his own state. From the evil seed of lust all other deadly sins had sprung forth: pride in himself and contempt of others, covetousness in using money for the purchase of unlawful pleasures, envy of those whose vices he could not reach to and calumnious murmuring against the pious, gluttonous enjoyment of food, the dull glowering anger amid which he brooded upon his longing, the swamp of spiritual and bodily sloth in which his whole being had sunk.

As he sat in his bench gazing calmly at the rector's shrewd harsh face his mind wound itself in and out of the curious questions proposed to it. If a man had stolen a pound in his youth and had used that pound to amass a huge fortune how much was he obliged to give back, the pound he had stolen only or the pound together with the compound interest accruing upon it or all his huge fortune? If a layman in giving baptism pour the water before saying the words is the child baptised? Is baptism with a mineral water valid? How comes it that while the first beatitude promises the kingdom of heaven to the poor of heart, the second beatitude promises also to the meek that they shall possess the land? Why was the sacrament of the eucharist instituted under the two species of bread and wine if Jesus Christ be present body and blood, soul and divinity, in the bread alone and in the wine alone? Does a tiny particle of the consecrated bread contain all the body and blood of Jesus Christ or a part only of the body and blood? If the wine change into vinegar and the host crumble into corruption after they have been consecrated, is Jesus Christ still present under their species as God and as man?

— Here he is! Here he is!

A boy from his post at the window had seen the rector come from the house. All the catechisms were opened and all heads bent upon them silently. The rector entered and took his seat on the dais. A gentle kick from the tall boy in the bench behind urged Stephen to ask a difficult question.

The rector did not ask for a catechism to hear the lesson from. He clasped his hands on the desk and said:

— The retreat will begin on Wednesday afternoon in honour of Saint Francis Xavier whose feast day is Saturday. The retreat will go on from Wednesday to Friday. On Friday confession will be heard all the afternoon after beads. If any boys have special confessors perhaps it will be better for them not to change. Mass will be on Saturday morning at nine o'clock and general communion for the whole college. Saturday will be a free day. But Saturday and Sunday being free days some boys might be inclined to think that Monday is a free day also. Beware of making that mistake. I think you, Lawless, are likely to make that mistake.

— I, sir? Why, sir?

A little wave of quiet mirth broke forth over the class of boys from the rector's grim smile. Stephen's heart began slowly to fold and fade with fear like a withering flower.

The rector went on gravely:

— You are all familiar with the story of the life of Saint Francis Xavier, I suppose, the patron of your college. He came of an old and illustrious Spanish family and you remember that he was one of the first followers of Saint Ignatius. They met in Paris where Francis Xavier was professor of philosophy at the university. This young and brilliant nobleman and man of letters entered heart and soul into the ideas of our glorious founder, and you know that he, at his own desire, was sent by Saint Ignatius to preach to the Indians. He is called, as you know, the apostle of the Indies. He went from country to country in the east, from Africa to India, from India to Japan, baptising the people. He is said to have baptised as many as ten thousand idolators in one month. It is said that his right arm had grown powerless from having been raised so often over the heads of those whom he baptised. He wished then to go to China to win still more souls for God but he died of fever on the island of Sancian. A great saint, Saint Francis Xavier! A great soldier of God!

The rector paused and then, shaking his clasped hands before him, went on:

— He had the faith in him that moves mountains. Ten thousand souls won for God in a single month! That is a true conqueror, true to the motto of our order: *ad majorem Dei gloriam!* A saint who has great power in heaven, remember: power to intercede for us in our grief, power to obtain whatever we pray for if it be for the good of our souls, power above all to obtain for us the grace to repent if we be in sin. A great saint, Saint Francis Xavier! A great fisher of souls!

He ceased to shake his clasped hands and, resting them against his forehead, looked right and left of them keenly at his listeners out of his dark stern eyes.

In the silence their dark fire kindled the dusk into a tawny glow. Stephen's heart had withered up like a flower of the desert that feels the simoom coming from afar.

* * * *

— *Remember only thy last things and thou shalt not sin for ever* — words taken, my dear little brothers in Christ, from the book of Ecclesiastes, seventh chapter, fortieth verse.[1] In the name of the Father and of the Son and of the Holy Ghost. Amen.

Stephen sat in the front bench of the chapel. Father Arnall sat at a table to the left of the altar. He wore about his shoulders a heavy cloak; his pale face was drawn and his voice broken with rheum. The figure of his old master, so strangely rearisen, brought back to Stephen's mind his life at Clongowes: the wide playgrounds, swarming with boys, the square ditch, the little cemetery off the main avenue of limes where he had dreamed of being buried, the firelight on the wall of the infirmary where he lay sick, the sorrowful face of Brother Michael. His soul, as these memories came back to him, became again a child's soul.

— We are assembled here today, my dear little brothers in Christ, for one brief moment far away from the busy bustle of the outer world to celebrate and to honour one of the greatest of saints, the apostle of the Indies, the patron saint also of your college, Saint Francis Xavier. Year after year for much longer than any of you, my dear little boys, can remember or than I can remember the boys of this college have met in this very chapel to make their annual retreat before the feast day of their patron saint. Time has gone on and brought with it its changes. Even in the last few years what changes can most of you not remember? Many of the boys who sat in those front benches a few years ago are perhaps now in distant lands, in the burning tropics or immersed in professional duties or in seminaries or voyaging over the vast expanse of the deep or, it may be, already called by the great God to another life and to the rendering up of their stewardship. And still as the years roll by, bringing with them changes for good and bad, the memory of the great saint is honoured by the boys of his college who make every year their annual retreat on the days preceding the feast day set apart by our Holy Mother the Church to transmit to all the ages the name and fame of one of the greatest sons of catholic Spain.

— Now what is the meaning of this word *retreat* and why is it allowed on all hands to be a most salutory practise for all who desire to lead

---

[1] [Actually from the Apocryphal book Ecclesiasticus.]

before God and in the eyes of men a truly Christian life? A retreat, my dear boys, signifies a withdrawal for a while from the cares of our life, the cares of this workaday world, in order to examine the state of our conscience, to reflect on the mysteries of holy religion and to understand better why we are here in this world. During these few days I intend to put before you some thoughts concerning the four last things. They are, as you know from your catechism, death, judgment, hell and heaven. We shall try to understand them fully during these few days so that we may derive from the understanding of them a lasting benefit to our souls. And remember, my dear boys, that we have been sent into this world for one thing and for one thing alone: to do God's holy will and to save our immortal souls. All else is worthless. One thing alone is needful, the salvation of one's soul. What doth it profit a man to gain the whole world if he suffer the loss of his immortal soul? Ah, my dear boys, believe me there is nothing in this wretched world that can make up for such a loss.

— I will ask you therefore, my dear boys, to put away from your minds during these few days all worldly thoughts, whether of study or pleasure or ambition, and to give all your attention to the state of your souls. I need hardly remind you that during the days of the retreat all boys are expected to preserve a quiet and pious demeanour and to shun all loud unseemly pleasure. The elder boys, of course, will see that this custom is not infringed and I look especially to the prefects and officers of the sodality of Our Blessed Lady and of the sodality of the Holy Angels to set a good example to their fellow-students.

— Let us try, therefore, to make this retreat in honour of Saint Francis with our whole heart and our whole mind. God's blessing will then be upon all your year's studies. But, above and beyond all, let this retreat be one to which you can look back in after years when, may be, you are far from this college and among very different surroundings, to which you can look back with joy and thankfulness and give thanks to God for having granted you this occasion of laying the first foundation of a pious honourable zealous Christian life. And if, as may so happen, there be at this moment in these benches any poor soul who has had the unutterable misfortune to lose God's holy grace and to fall into grievous sin, I fervently trust and pray that this retreat may be the turning-point in the life of that soul. I pray to God through the merits of His zealous servant Francis Xavier that such a soul may be led to sincere repentance and that the holy communion on Saint Francis' day of this year may be a lasting covenant between God and that soul. For just and unjust, for saint and sinner alike, may this retreat be a memorable one.

— Help me, my dear little brothers in Christ. Help me by your pious attention, by your own devotion, by your outward demeanour. Banish from your minds all worldly thoughts, and think only of the last things, death, judgment, hell and heaven. He who remembers these things, says Ecclesiastes, shall not sin for ever. He who remembers the last things will act and think with them always before his eyes. He will live a good life and die a good death, believing and knowing that, if he has sacrificed much in this earthly life, it will be given to him a hundredfold and a thousandfold more in the life to come, in the kingdom without end — a blessing, my dear boys, which I wish you from my heart, one and all, in the name of the Father and of the Son and of the Holy Ghost. Amen!

As he walked home with silent companions a thick fog seemed to compass his mind. He waited in stupor of mind till it should lift and reveal what it had hidden. He ate his dinner with surly appetite and when the meal was over and the grease-strewn plates lay abandoned on the table, he rose and went to the window, clearing the thick scum from his mouth with his tongue and licking it from his lips. So he had sunk to the state of a beast that licks his chaps after meat. This was the end; and a faint glimmer of fear began to pierce the fog of his mind. He pressed his face against the pane of the window and gazed out into the darkening street. Forms passed this way and that through the dull light. And that was life. The letters of the name of Dublin lay heavily upon his mind, pushing one another surlily hither and thither with slow boorish insistence. His soul was fattening and congealing into a gross grease, plunging ever deeper in its dull fear into a sombre threatening dusk, while the body that was his stood, listless and dishonoured, gazing out of darkened eyes, helpless, perturbed and human for a bovine god to stare upon.

The next day brought death and judgment, stirring his soul slowly from its listless despair. The faint glimmer of fear became a terror of spirit as the hoarse voice of the preacher blew death into his soul. He suffered its agony. He felt the death-chill touch the extremities and creep onward towards the heart, the film of death veiling the eyes, the bright centres of the brain extinguished one by one like lamps, the last sweat oozing upon the skin, the powerlessness of the dying limbs, the speech thickening and wandering and failing, the heart throbbing faintly and more faintly, all but vanquished, the breath, the poor helpless human spirit, sobbing and sighing, gurgling and rattling in the throat. No help! No help! He — he himself — his body to which he had yielded was dying. Into the grave with it. Nail it down into a wooden box, the corpse. Carry it out of the house on the shoulders of hirelings. Thrust it out of men's sight into a long hole in the ground, into the grave, to rot, to feed the mass of its creeping worms and to be devoured by scuttling plump-bellied rats.

And while the friends were still standing in tears by the bedside the soul of the sinner was judged. At the last moment of consciousness the whole earthly life passed before the vision of the soul and, ere it had time to reflect; the body had died and the soul stood terrified before the judgment seat. God, who had long been merciful, would then be just. He had long been patient, pleading with the sinful soul, giving it time to repent, sparing it yet awhile. But that time had gone. Time was to sin and to enjoy, time was to scoff at God and at the warnings of His holy church, time was to defy His majesty, to disobey His commands, to hoodwink one's fellow men, to commit sin after sin and to hide one's corruption from the sight of men. But that time was over. Now it was God's turn: and He was not to be hoodwinked or deceived. Every sin would then come forth from its lurking-place, the most rebellious against the divine will and the most degrading to our poor corrupt nature, the tiniest imperfection and the most heinous atrocity. What did it avail then to have been a great emperor, a great general, a marvellous inventor, the most learned of the learned? All were as one before the judgment seat of God. He would reward the good and punish the wicked. One single instant was enough for the trial of a man's soul. One single instant after the body's death, the soul had been weighed in the balance. The particular judgment was over and the soul had passed to the abode of bliss or to the prison of purgatory or had been hurled howling into hell.

Nor was that all. God's justice had still to be vindicated before men: after the particular there still remained the general judgment. The last day had come. The doomsday was at hand. The stars of heaven were falling upon the earth like the figs cast by the figtree which the wind has shaken. The sun, the great luminary of the universe, had become as sackcloth of hair. The moon was blood red. The firmament was as a scroll rolled away. The archangel Michael, the prince of the heavenly host, appeared glorious and terrible against the sky. With one foot on the sea and one foot on the land he blew from the archangelical trumpet the brazen death of time. The three blasts of the angel filled all the universe. Time is, time was, but time shall be no more. At the last blast the souls of universal humanity throng towards the valley of Jehosaphat, rich and poor, gentle and simple, wise and foolish, good and wicked. The soul of every human being that has ever existed, the souls of all those who shall yet be born, all the sons and daughters of Adam, all are assembled on that supreme day. And lo, the supreme judge is coming! No longer the lowly Lamb of God, no longer the meek Jesus of Nazareth, no longer the Man of Sorrows, no longer the Good Shepherd, He is seen now coming upon the clouds, in great power and majesty, attended by nine choirs of angels, angels and archangels, principalities, powers and virtues, thrones and dominations, cherubim and seraphim, God Omnipotent, God everlasting. He speaks: and His voice is heard even at the farthest limits of space, even in the bottomless abyss. Supreme Judge, from His sentence there will be and can be no appeal. He calls the just to His side, bidding them enter into the Kingdom, the eternity of bliss, prepared for them. The unjust He casts from Him, crying in His offended majesty: *Depart from me, ye cursed, into everlasting fire which was prepared for the devil and his angels.* O, what agony then for the miserable sinners! Friend is torn apart from friend, children are torn from their parents, husbands from their wives. The poor sinner holds out his arms to those who were dear to him in this earthly world, to those whose simple piety perhaps he made a mock of, to those who counselled him and tried to lead him on the right path, to a kind brother, to a loving sister, to the mother and father who loved him so dearly. But it is too late: the just turn away from the wretched damned souls which now appear before the eyes of all in their hideous and evil character. O you hypocrites, O you whited sepulchres, O you who present a smooth smiling face to the world while your soul within is a foul swamp of sin, how will it fare with you in that terrible day?

And this day will come, shall come, must come; the day of death and the day of judgment. It is appointed unto man to die, and after death the judgment. Death is certain. The time and manner are uncertain, whether from long disease or from some unexpected accident; the Son of God cometh at an hour when you little expect Him. Be therefore ready every moment, seeing that you may die at any moment. Death is the end of us all. Death and judgment, brought into the world by the sin of our first parents, are the dark portals that close our earthly existence, the portals that open into the unknown and the unseen, portals through which every soul must pass, alone, unaided save by its good works, without friend or brother or parent or master to help it, alone and trembling. Let that thought be ever before our minds and then we cannot sin. Death, a cause of terror to the sinner, is a blessed moment for him who has walked in the right path, fulfilling the duties of his station in life, attending to his morning and evening prayers, approaching the holy sacrament frequently and performing good and merciful works. For the pious and believing catholic, for the just man, death is no cause of terror. Was it not Addison, the great English writer, who, when on his deathbed, sent for the wicked young earl of Warwick to let him see how a christian can meet his end. He it is and he alone, the pious and believing christian, who can say in his heart:

> O grave, where is thy victory?
> O death, where is thy sting?

Every word of it was for him. Against his sin, foul and secret, the whole wrath of God was aimed. The preacher's knife had probed deeply into his disclosed conscience and he felt now that his soul was festering in sin. Yes, the preacher was right. God's turn had come. Like a beast in its lair his soul had lain down in its own filth but the blasts of the angel's trumpet had driven him forth from the darkness of sin into the light. The words of doom cried by the angel shattered in an instant his presumptuous peace. The wind of the last day blew through his mind; his sins, the jeweleyed harlots of his imagination, fled before the hurricane, squeaking like mice in their terror and huddled under a mane of hair.

As he crossed the square, walking homeward, the light laughter of a girl reached his burning ear. The frail, gay sound smote his heart more strongly than a trumpetblast, and, not daring to lift his eyes, he turned aside and gazed, as he walked, into the shadow of the tangled shrubs. Shame rose from his smitten heart and flooded his whole being. The image of Emma appeared before him and under her eyes the flood of shame rushed forth anew from his heart. If she knew to what his mind had subjected her or how his brute-like lust had torn and trampled upon her innocence! Was that boyish love? Was that chivalry? Was that poetry? The sordid details of his orgies stank under his very nostrils. The sootcoated packet of pictures which he had hidden in the flue of the fireplace and in the presence of whose shameless or bashful wantonness he lay for hours sinning in thought and deed; his monstrous dreams, peopled by apelike creatures and by harlots with gleaming jewel eyes; the foul long letters he had written in the joy of guilty confession and carried secretly for days and days only to throw them under cover of night among the grass in the corner of a field or beneath some hingeless door or in some niche in the hedges where a girl might come upon them as she walked by and read them secretly. Mad! Mad! Was it possible he had done these things? A cold sweat broke out upon his forehead as the foul memories condensed within his brain.

When the agony of shame had passed from him he tried to raise his soul from its abject powerlessness. God and the Blessed Virgin were too far from him: God was too great and stern and the Blessed Virgin too pure and holy. But he imagined that he stood near Emma in a wide land and, humbly and in tears, bent and kissed the elbow of her sleeve.

In the wide land under a tender lucid evening sky, a cloud drifting westward amid a pale green sea of heaven, they stood together, children that had erred. Their error had offended deeply God's majesty though it was the error of two children; but it had not offended her whose beauty "is not like earthly beauty, dangerous to look upon, but like the morning star which is its emblem, bright and musical." The eyes were not offended which she turned upon him nor reproachful. She placed their hands together, hand in hand, and said, speaking to their hearts.

— Take hands, Stephen and Emma. It is a beautiful evening now in heaven. You have erred but you are always my children. It is one heart that loves another heart. Take hands together, my dear children, and you will be happy together and your hearts will love each other.

The chapel was flooded by the dull scarlet light that filtered through the lowered blinds; and through the fissure between the last blind and the sash a shaft of wan light entered like a spear and touched the embossed brasses of the candlesticks upon the altar that gleamed like the battle-worn mail armour of angels.

Rain was falling on the chapel, on the garden, on the college. It would rain for ever, noiselessly. The water would rise inch by inch, covering the grass and shrubs, covering the trees and houses, covering the monuments and the mountain tops. All life would be choked off, noiselessly: birds, men, elephants, pigs, children: noiselessly floating corpses amid the litter of the wreckage of the world. Forty days and forty nights the rain would fall till the waters covered the face of the earth.

It might be. Why not?

— *Hell has enlarged its soul and opened its mouth without any limits* — words taken, my dear little brothers in Christ Jesus, from the book of Isaias, fifth chapter, fourteenth verse. In the name of the Father and of the Son and of the Holy Ghost. Amen.

The preacher took a chainless watch from a pocket within his soutane and, having considered its dial for a moment in silence, placed it silently before him on the table.

He began to speak in a quiet tone.

— Adam and Eve, my dear boys, were, as you know, our first parents, and you will remember that they were created by God in order that the seats in heaven left vacant by the fall of Lucifer and his rebellious angels might be filled again. Lucifer, we are told, was a son of the morning, a radiant and mighty angel; yet he fell: he fell and there fell with him a third part of the host of heaven: he fell and was hurled with his rebellious angels into hell. What his sin was we cannot say. Theologians consider that it was the sin of pride, the sinful thought conceived in an instant: *non serviam: I will not serve*. That instant was his ruin. He offended the majesty of God by the sinful thought of one instant and God cast him out of heaven into hell for ever.

— Adam and Eve were then created by God and placed in Eden, in the plain of Damascus, that lovely garden resplendent with sunlight and colour, teeming with luxuriant vegetation. The fruitful earth gave them her bounty: beasts and birds were their willing servants: they knew not the ills our flesh is heir to, disease and poverty and death: all that a great and generous God could do for them was done. But there was one condition imposed on them by God: obedience to His word. They were not to eat of the fruit of the forbidden tree.

— Alas, my dear little boys, they too fell. The devil, once a shining angel, a son of the morning, now a foul fiend came in the shape of a serpent, the subtlest of all the beasts of the field. He envied them. He, the fallen great one, could not bear to think that man, a being of clay, should possess the inheritance which he by his sin had forfeited for ever. He came to the woman, the weaker vessel, and poured the poison of his eloquence into her ear, promising her — O, the blasphemy of that promise! — that if she and Adam ate of the forbidden fruit they would become as gods, nay as God Himself. Eve yielded to the wiles of the arch tempter. She ate the apple and gave it also to Adam who had not the moral courage to resist her. The poison tongue of Satan had done its work. They fell.

— And then the voice of God was heard in that garden, calling His creature man to account: and Michael, prince of the heavenly host, with a sword of flame in his hand, appeared before the guilty pair and drove them forth from Eden into the world, the world of sickness and striving, of cruelty and disappointment, of labour and hardship, to earn their bread in the sweat of their brow. But even then how merciful was God! He took pity on our poor degraded parents and promised that in the fulness of time He would send down from heaven One who would redeem them, make them once more children of God and heirs to the kingdom of heaven: and that One, that Redeemer of fallen man, was to be God's only begotten Son, the Second Person of the Most Blessed Trinity, the Eternal Word.

— He came. He was born of a virgin pure, Mary the virgin mother. He was born in a poor cowhouse in Judea and lived as a humble carpenter for thirty years until the hour of his mission had come. And then, filled with love for men, He went forth and called to men to hear the new gospel.

— Did they listen? Yes, they listened but would not hear. He was seized and bound like a common criminal, mocked at as a fool, set aside to give place to a public robber, scourged with five thousand lashes, crowned with a crown of thorns, hustled through the streets by the Jewish rabble and the Roman soldiery, stripped of his garments and hanged upon a gibbet and His side was pierced with a lance and from the wounded body of our Lord water and blood issued continually.

— Yet even then, in that hour of supreme agony, Our Merciful Redeemer had pity for mankind. Yet even there, on the hill of Calvary, He founded the Holy Catholic Church against which, it is promised, the gates of hell shall not prevail. He founded it upon the rock of ages and endowed it with His grace, with sacraments and sacrifice, and promised that if men would obey the word of His Church they would still enter into eternal life, but if, after all that had been done for them, they still persisted in their wickedness there remained for them an eternity of torment: hell.

The preacher's voice sank. He paused, joined his palms for an instant, parted them. Then he resumed:

— Now let us try for a moment to realise, as far as we can, the nature of that abode of the damned which the justice of an offended God has called into existence for the eternal punishment of sinners. Hell is a strait and dark and foul smelling prison, an abode of demons and lost souls, filled with fire and smoke. The straitness of this prison house is expressly designed by God to punish those who refused to be bound by His laws. In earthly prisons the poor captive has at least some liberty of movement, were it only within the four walls of his cell or in the gloomy yard of his prison. Not so in hell. There, by reason of the great number of the damned, the prisoners are heaped together in their awful prison, the walls of which are said to be four thousand miles thick: and the damned are so utterly bound and helpless that, as a blessed saint, Saint Anselm, writes in his book on Similitudes, they are not even able to remove from the eye a worm that gnaws it.

— They lie in exterior darkness. For, remember, the fire of hell gives forth no light. As, at the command of God, the fire of the Babylonian furnace lost its heat but not its light so, at the command of God, the fire of hell, while retaining the intensity of its heat, burns eternally in darkness. It is a neverending storm of darkness, dark flames and dark smoke of burning brimstone, amid which the bodies are heaped one upon another without even a glimpse of air. Of all the plagues with which the land of the Pharaohs was smitten one plague alone, that of darkness, was called horrible. What name, then, shall we give to the darkness of hell which is to last not for three days alone but for all eternity?

— The horror of this strait and dark prison is increased by its awful stench. All the filth of the world, all the offal and scum of the world, we are told, shall run there as to a vast reeking sewer when the terrible conflagration of the last day has purged the world. The brimstone, too, which burns there in such prodigious quantity fills all hell with its intolerable stench; and the bodies of the damned themselves exhale such a pestilential odour that as Saint Bonaventure says, one of them alone would suffice to infect the whole world. The very air of this world, that pure element, becomes foul and unbreathable when it has been long enclosed. Consider then what must be the foulness of the air of hell. Imagine some foul and putrid corpse that has lain rotting and decomposing in the grave, a jellylike mass of liquid corruption. Imagine such a corpse a prey to flames, devoured by the fire of burning brimstone and giving off dense choking fumes of nauseous loathsome decomposition. And then imagine this sickening stench, multiplied a millionfold and a millionfold again from the millions upon millions of fetid carcasses massed together in the reeking darkness, a huge and rotting human fungus. Imagine all this and you will have some idea of the horror of the stench of hell.

— But this stench is not, horrible though it is, the greatest physical torment to which the damned are subjected. The torment of fire is the greatest torment to which the tyrant has ever subjected his fellow creatures. Place your finger for a moment in the flame of a candle and you will feel the pain of fire. But our earthly fire was created by God for the benefit of man, to maintain in him the spark of life and to help him in the useful arts whereas the fire of hell is of another quality and was created by God to torture and punish the unrepentant sinner. Our earthly fire also consumes more or less rapidly according as the object which it attacks is more or less combustible so that human ingenuity has even succeeded in inventing chemical preparations to check or frustrate its action. But the sulphurous brimstone which burns in hell is a substance which is specially designed to burn for ever and for ever with unspeakable fury. Moreover our earthly fire destroys at the same time as it burns so that the more intense it is the shorter is its duration: but the fire of hell has this property that it preserves that which it burns and though it rages with incredible intensity it rages for ever.

— Our earthly fire again, no matter how fierce or widespread it may be, is always of a limited extent: but the lake of fire in hell is boundless, shoreless and bottomless. It is on record that the devil himself, when asked the question by a certain soldier, was obliged to confess that if a whole mountain were thrown into the burning ocean of hell it would be burned up in an instant like a piece of wax. And this terrible fire will not afflict the bodies of the damned only from without but each lost soul will be a hell unto itself, the boundless fire raging in its very vitals. O, how terrible is the lot of those wretched beings! The blood seethes and boils in the veins, the brains are boiling in the skull, the heart in the breast glowing and bursting, the bowels a redhot mass of burning pulp, the tender eyes flaming like molten balls.

— And yet what I have said as to the strength and quality and boundlessness of this fire is as nothing when compared to its intensity, an intensity which it has as being the instrument chosen by divine design for the punishment of soul and body alike. It is a fire which proceeds directly from the ire of God, working not of its own activity but as an instrument of divine vengeance. As the waters of baptism cleanse the soul with the body so do the fires of punishment torture the spirit with the flesh. Every sense of the flesh is tortured and every faculty of the soul therewith: the eyes with impenetrable utter darkness, the nose with noisome odours, the ears with yells and howls and execrations, the taste with foul matter, leprous corruption, nameless suffocating filth, the touch with redhot goads and spikes, with cruel tongues of flame. And through the several torments of the senses the immortal soul is tortured eternally in its very essence amid the leagues upon leagues of glowing fires kindled in the abyss by the offended majesty of the Omnipotent God and fanned into everlasting and ever increasing fury by the breath of the anger of the Godhead.

— Consider finally that the torment of this infernal prison is increased by the company of the damned themselves. Evil company on earth is so noxious that the plants, as if by instinct, withdraw from the company of whatsoever is deadly or hurtful to them. In hell all laws are overturned — there is no thought of family or country, of ties, of relationships. The damned howl and scream at one another, their torture and rage intensified by the presence of beings tortured and raging like themselves. All sense of humanity is forgotten. The yells of the suffering sinners fill the remotest corners of the vast abyss. The mouths of the damned are full of blasphemies against God and of hatred for their fellow sufferers and of curses against those souls which were their accomplices in sin. In olden times it was the custom to punish the parricide, the man who had raised his murderous hand against his father, by casting him into the depths of the sea in a sack in which were placed a cock, a monkey and a serpent. The intention of those law-givers who framed such a law, which seems cruel in our times, was to punish the criminal by the company of hurtful and hateful beasts. But what is the fury of those dumb beasts compared with the fury of execration which bursts from the parched lips and aching throats of the damned in hell when they behold in their companions in misery those who aided and abetted them in sin, those whose words sowed the first seeds of evil thinking and evil living in their minds, those whose immodest suggestions led them on to sin, those whose eyes tempted and allured them from the path of virtue. They turn upon those accomplices and upbraid them and curse them. But they are helpless and hopeless: it is too late now for repentance.

— Last of all consider the frightful torment to those damned souls, tempters and tempted alike, of the company of the devils. These devils will afflict the damned in two ways, by their presence and by their reproaches. We can have no idea of how horrible these devils are. Saint Catherine of Siena once saw a devil, and she has written that, rather than look again for one single instant on such a frightful monster, she would prefer to walk until the end of her life along a track of red coals. These devils, who were once beautiful angels, have become as hideous and ugly as they once were beautiful. They mock and jeer at the lost souls whom they dragged down to ruin. It is they, the foul demons, who are made in hell the voices of conscience. Why did you sin? Why did you lend an ear to the temptings of friends? Why did you turn aside from your pious practices and good works? Why did you not shun the occasions of sin? Why did you not leave that evil companion? Why did you not give up that lewd habit, that impure habit? Why did you not listen to the counsels of your confessor? Why did you not, even after you had fallen the first or the second or the third or the fourth or the hundredth time, repent of your evil ways and turn to God who only waited for your repentance to absolve you of your sins? Now the time for repentance has gone by. Time is, time was, but time shall be no more! Time was to sin in secrecy, to indulge in that sloth and pride, to covet the unlawful, to yield to the promptings of your lower nature, to live like the beasts of the field, nay worse than the beasts of the field for they, at least, are but brutes and have not reason to guide them: time was but time shall be no more. God spoke to you by so many voices but you would not hear. You would not crush out that pride and anger in your heart, you would not restore those ill-gotten goods, you would not obey the precepts of your holy church nor attend to your religious duties, you would not abandon tho·e wicked companions, you would not avoid those dangerous temptations. Such is the language of those fiendish tormentors, words of taunting and of reproach, of hatred and of disgust. Of disgust, Yes! For even they, the very devils, when they sinned, sinned by such a sin as alone was compatible with such angelical natures, a rebellion of the intellect: and they, even they, the foul devils must turn away, revolted and disgusted, from the contemplation of those unspeakable sins by which degraded man outrages and defiles the temple of the Holy Ghost, defiles and pollutes himself.

— O, my dear little brothers in Christ, may it never be our lot to hear that language! May it never be our lot, I say! In the last day of terrible reckoning I pray fervently to God that not a single soul of those who are in this chapel today may be found among those miserable beings whom the Great Judge shall command to depart for ever from His sight, that not one of us may ever hear ringing in his ears the awful sentence of rejection: *Depart from me, ye cursed, into everlasting fire which was prepared for the devil and his angels!* —

He came down the aisle of the chapel, his legs shaking and the scalp of his head trembling as though it had been touched by ghostly fingers. He passed up the staircase and into the corridor along the walls of which the overcoats and waterproofs hung like gibbeted malefactors, headless and dripping and shapeless. And at every step he feared that he had already died, that his soul had been wrenched forth of the sheath of his body, that he was plunging headlong through space.

He could not grip the floor with his feet and sat heavily at his desk, opening one of his books at random and poring over it. Every word for

him! It was true. God was almighty. God could call him now, call him as
he sat at his desk, before he had time to be conscious of the summons.
God had called him. Yes? What? Yes? His flesh shrank together as it felt
the approach of the ravenous tongues of flames, dried up as it felt about
it the swirl of stifling air. He had died. Yes. He was judged. A wave of fire
swept through his body: the first. Again a wave. His brain began to glow.
Another. His brain was simmering and bubbling within the cracking
tenement of the skull. Flames burst forth from his skull like a corolla,
shrieking like voices:

— Hell! Hell! Hell! Hell! Hell! —

Voices spoke near him:

— On hell. —

— I suppose he rubbed it into you well. —

— You bet he did. He put us all into a blue funk. —

— That's what you fellows want: and plenty of it to make you work. —

He leaned back weakly in his desk. He had not died. God had spared
him still. He was still in the familiar world of the school. Mr Tate and
Vincent Heron stood at the window, talking, jesting, gazing out at the
bleak rain, moving their heads.

— I wish it would clear up. I had arranged to go for a spin on the bike
with some fellows out by Malahide. But the roads must be kneedeep. —

— It might clear up, sir. —

The voices that he knew so well; the common words, the quiet of the
classroom when the voices paused and the silence was filled by the
sound of softly browsing cattle as the other boys munched their lunches
tranquilly lulled his aching soul.

There was still time. O Mary, refuge of sinners, intercede for him! O
Virgin Undefiled, save him from the gulf of death!

The English lesson began with the hearing of the history. Royal
persons, favorites, intriguers, bishops, passed like mute phantoms behind their veil of names. All had died: all had been judged. What did it
profit a man to gain the whole world if he lost his soul? At last he had
understood: and human life lay around him, a plain of peace whereon
antlike men laboured in brotherhood, their dead sleeping under quiet
mounds. The elbow of his companion touched him and his heart was
touched: and when he spoke to answer a question of his master he heard
his own voice full of the quietude of humility and contrition.

His soul sank back deeper into depths of contrite peace, no longer
able to suffer the pain of dread, and sending forth, as she sank, a faint
prayer. Ah yes, he would still be spared; he would repent in his heart and
be forgiven; and then those above, those in heaven, would see what he
would do to make up for the past: a whole life, every hour of life. Only
wait.

— All, God! All, all! —

A messenger came to the door to say that confessions were being heard in the chapel. Four boys left the room; and he heard others passing down the corridor. A tremulous chill blew round his heart, no stronger than a little wind, and yet, listening and suffering silently, he seemed to have laid an ear against the muscle of his own heart, feeling it close and quail, listening to the flutter of its ventricles.

No escape. He had to confess, to speak out in words what he had done and thought, sin after sin. How? How?

— Father, I . . . —

The thought slid like a cold shining rapier into his tender flesh: confession. But not there in the chapel of the college. He would confess all, every sin of deed and thought, sincerely: but not there among his school companions. Far away from there in some dark place he would murmur out his own shame: and he besought God humbly not to be offended with him if he did not dare to confess in the college chapel: and in utter abjection of spirit he craved forgiveness mutely of the boyish hearts about him.

Time passed.

He sat again in the front bench of the chapel. The daylight without was already failing and, as it fell slowly through the dull red blinds, it seemed that the sun of the last day was going down and that all souls were being gathered for the judgment.

— *I am cast away from the sight of Thine eyes:* words taken, my dear little brothers in Christ, from the Book of Psalms, thirtieth chapter, twenty-third verse. In the name of the Father and of the Son and of the Holy Ghost. Amen.

The preacher began to speak in a quiet friendly tone. His face was kind and he joined gently the fingers of each hand, forming a frail cage by the union of their tips.

— This morning we endeavoured, in our reflection upon hell, to make what our holy founder calls in his book of spiritual exercises, the composition of place. We endeavoured, that is, to imagine with the senses of the mind, in our imagination, the material character of that awful place and of the physical torments which all who are in hell endure. This evening we shall consider for a few moments the nature of the spiritual torments of hell.

— Sin, remember, is a twofold enormity. It is a base consent to the promptings of our corrupt nature to the lower instincts, to that which is gross and beastlike; and it is also a turning away from the counsel of our higher nature, from all that is pure and holy, from the Holy God Himself. For this reason mortal sin is punished in hell by two different forms of punishment, physical and spiritual.

Now of all these spiritual pains by far the greatest is the pain of loss, so great, in fact, that in itself it is a torment greater than all the others. Saint Thomas, the greatest doctor of the Church, the angelic doctor, as he is called, says that the worst damnation consists in this, that the understanding of man is totally deprived of Divine light and his affection obstinately turned away from the goodness of God. God, remember, is a being infinitely good and therefore the loss of such a being must be a loss infinitely painful. In this life we have not a very clear idea of what such a loss must be but the damned in hell, for their greater torment, have a full understanding of that which they have lost and understand that they have lost it through their own sins and have lost it for ever. At the very instant of death the bonds of the flesh are broken asunder and the soul at once flies towards God as towards the centre of her existence. Remember, my dear little boys, our souls long to be with God. We come from God, we live by God, we belong to God: we are His, inalienably His. God loves with a divine love every human soul and every human soul lives in that love. How could it be otherwise? Every breath that we draw, every thought of our brain, every instant of life proceeds from God's inexhaustible goodness. And if it be pain for a mother to be parted from her child, for a man to be exiled from hearth and home, for friend to be sundered from friend, O think what pain, what anguish, it must be for the poor soul to be spurned from the presence of the supremely good and loving Creator Who has called that soul into existence from nothingness and sustained it in life and loved it with an immeasurable love. This, then, to be separated for ever from its greatest good, from God, and to feel the anguish of that separation, knowing full well that it is unchangeable, this is the greatest torment which the created soul is capable of bearing, *poena damni*, the pain of loss.

The second pain which will afflict the souls of the damned in hell is the pain of conscience. Just as in dead bodies worms are engendered by putrefaction so in the souls of the lost there arises a perpetual remorse from the putrefaction of sin, the sting of conscience, the worm, as Pope Innocent the Third calls it, of the triple sting. The first sting inflicted by this cruel worm will be the memory of past pleasures. O what a dreadful memory will that be! In the lake of alldevouring flame the proud king will remember the pomps of his court, the wise but wicked man his libraries and instruments of research, the lover of artistic pleasures his marbles and pictures and other art treasures, he who delighted in the pleasures of the table his gorgeous feasts, his dishes prepared with such delicacy, his choice wines, the miser will remember his hoard of gold, the robber his illgotten wealth, the angry and revengeful and merciless murderers their deeds of blood and violence in which they revelled, the impure and adulterous the unspeakable and filthy pleasures in which they delighted. They will remember all this and loathe themselves and their sins. For how miserable will all those pleasures seem to the soul condemned to suffer in hell-fire for ages and ages. How they will rage and fume to think that they have lost the bliss of heaven for the dross of earth, for a few pieces of metal, for vain honours, for bodily comforts, for a tingling of the nerves. They will repent indeed: and this is the second sting of the worm of conscience, a late and fruitless sorrow for sins committed. Divine justice insists that the understanding of those miserable wretches be fixed continually on the sins of which they were guilty and moreover, as Saint Augustine points out, God will impart to them His own knowledge of sin so that sin will appear to them in all its hideous malice as it appears to the eyes of God Himself. They will behold their sins in all their foulness and repent but it will be too late and then they will bewail the good occasions which they neglected. This is the last and deepest and most cruel sting of the worm of conscience. The conscience will say: You had time and opportunity to repent and would not. You were brought up religiously by your parents. You had the sacraments and graces and indulgences of the church to aid you. You had the minister of God to preach to you to call you back when you had strayed, to forgive you your sins, no matter how many, how abominable, if only you had confessed and repented. No. You would not. You flouted the ministers of holy religion, you turned your back on the confessional, you wallowed deeper and deeper in the mire of sin. God appealed to you, threatened you, entreated you to return to him. O, what shame, what misery! The Ruler of the universe entreated you, a creature of clay, to love Him Who made you and to keep His law. No. You would not. And now, though you were to flood all hell with your tears if you could still weep, all that sea of repentance would not gain for you what a single tear of true repentance shed during your mortal life would have gained for you. You implore now a moment of earthly life wherein to repent: in vain. That time is gone: gone for ever.

— Such is the threefold sting of conscience, the viper which gnaws the very heart's core of the wretches in hell so that filled with hellish fury they curse themselves for their folly and curse the evil companions who have brought them to such ruin and curse the devils who tempted them in life and now mock them in eternity and even revile and curse the Supreme Being Whose goodness and patience they scorned and slighted but Whose justice and power they cannot evade.

— The next spiritual pain to which the damned are subjected is the pain of extension. Man, in this earthly life, though he be capable of many evils, is not capable of them all at once inasmuch as one evil corrects and counteracts another, just as one poison frequently corrects another. In hell, on the contrary, one torment, instead of counteracting another, lends it still greater force: and, moreover, as the internal faculties are more perfect than the external senses, so are they more capable of suffering. Just as every sense is afflicted with a fitting torment so is every spiritual faculty; the fancy with horrible images, the sensitive faculty with alternate longing and rage, the mind and understanding with an interior darkness more terrible even than the exterior darkness which reigns in that dreadful prison. The malice, impotent though it be, which possesses these demon souls is an evil of boundless extension, of limitless duration, a frightful state of wickedness which we can scarcely realise unless we bear in mind the enormity of sin and the hatred God bears to it.

— Opposed to this pain of extension and yet co-existent with it we have the pain of intensity. Hell is the centre of evils and, as you know, things are more intense at their centres than at their remotest points. There are no contraries or admixtures of any kind to temper or soften in the least the pains of hell. Nay, things which are good in themselves become evil in hell. Company, elsewhere a source of comfort to the afflicted, will be there a continual torment: knowledge, so much longed for as the chief good of the intellect, will there be hated worse than ignorance: light, so much coveted by all creatures from the lord of creation down to the humblest plant in the forest, will be loathed intensely. In this life our sorrows are either not very long or not very great because nature either overcomes them by habits or puts an end to them by sinking under their weight. But in hell the torments cannot be overcome by habit, for while they are of terrible intensity they are at the same time of continual variety, each pain, so to speak, taking fire from another and re-endowing that which has enkindled it with a still fiercer flame. Nor can nature escape from these intense and various tortures by succumbing to them for the soul is sustained and maintained in evil so that its suffering may be the greater. Boundless extension of torment, incredible intensity of suffering, unceasing variety of torture — this is what the divine majesty, so outraged by sinners, demands, this is what the holiness of heaven, slighted and set aside for the lustful and low pleasures of the corrupt flesh, requires, this is what the blood of the innocent Lamb of God, shed for the redemption of sinners, trampled upon by the vilest of the vile, insists upon.

— Last and crowning torture of all the tortures of that awful place is the eternity of hell. Eternity! O, dread and dire word. Eternity! What mind of man can understand it? And remember, it is an eternity of pain. Even though the pains of hell were not so terrible as they are yet they would become infinite as they are destined to last for ever. But while they are everlasting they are at the same time, as you know, intolerably intense, unbearably extensive. To bear even the sting of an insect for all eternity would be a dreadful torment. What must it be, then, to bear the manifold tortures of hell for ever? For ever! For all eternity! Not for a year or for an age but for ever. Try to imagine the awful meaning of this. You have often seen the sand on the seashore. How fine are its tiny grains! And how many of those tiny little grains go to make up the small handful which a child grasps in its play. Now imagine a mountain of that sand, a million miles high, reaching from the earth to the farthest heavens, and a million miles broad, extending to remotest space, and a million miles in thickness: and imagine such an enormous mass of countless particles of sand multiplied as often as there are leaves in the forest, drops of water in the mighty ocean, feathers on birds, scales on fish, hairs on animals, atoms in the vast expanse of the air: and imagine that at the end of every million years a little bird came to that mountain and carried away in its beak a tiny grain of that sand. How many millions upon millions of centuries would pass before that bird had carried away even a square foot of that mountain, how many eons upon eons of ages before it had carried away all. Yet at the end of that immense stretch of time not even one instant of eternity could be said to have ended. At the end of all those billions and trillions of years eternity would have scarcely begun. And if that mountain rose again after it had been all carried away and if the bird came again and carried it all away again grain by grain: and if it so rose and sank as many times as there are stars in the sky, atoms in the air, drops of water in the sea, leaves on the trees, feathers upon birds, scales upon fish, hairs upon animals, at the end of all those innumerable risings and sinkings of that immeasurably vast mountain not one single instant of eternity could be said to have ended; even then, at the end of such a period, after that eon of time the mere thought of which makes our very brain reel dizzily, eternity would have scarcely begun.

— A holy saint (one of our own fathers I believe it was) was once vouchsafed a vision of hell. It seemed to him that he stood in the midst of a great hall, dark and silent save for the ticking of a great clock. The ticking went on unceasingly; and it seemed to this saint that the sound of the ticking was the ceaseless repetition of the words: ever, never; ever, never. Ever to be in hell, never to be in heaven; ever to be shut off from the presence of God, never to enjoy the beatific vision; ever to be eaten with flames, gnawed by vermin, goaded with burning spikes, never to be free from those pains; ever to have the conscience upbraid one, the memory enrage, the mind filled with darkness and despair, never to escape; ever to curse and revile the foul demons who gloat fiendishly over the misery of their dupes, never to behold the shining raiment of the blessed spirits; ever to cry out of the abyss of fire to God for an instant, a single instant, of respite from such awful agony, never to receive, even for an instant, God's pardon; ever to suffer, never to enjoy; ever to be damned, never to be saved; ever, never; ever, never. O, what a dreadful punishment! An eternity of endless agony, of endless bodily and spiritual torment, without one ray of hope, without one moment of cessation, of agony limitless in intensity, of torment infinitely varied, of torture that sustains eternally that which it eternally devours, of anguish that everlastingly preys upon the spirit while it racks the flesh, an eternity, every instant of which is itself an eternity of woe. Such is the terrible punishment decreed for those who die in mortal sin by an almighty and a just God.

— Yes, a just God! Men, reasoning always as men, are astonished that God should mete out an everlasting and infinite punishment in the fires of hell for a single grievous sin. They reason thus because, blinded by the gross illusion of the flesh and the darkness of human understanding they are unable to comprehend the hideous malice of mortal sin. They reason thus because they are unable to comprehend that even venial sin is of such a foul and hideous nature that even if the omnipotent Creator could end all the evil and misery in the world, the wars, the diseases, the robberies, the crime, the deaths, the murders, on condition that he allowed a single venial sin to pass unpunished, a single venial sin, a lie, an angry look, a moment of wilful sloth, He, the great omnipotent God could not do so because sin, be it in thought or deed, is a transgression of His law and God would not be God if He did not punish the transgressor.

— A sin, an instant of rebellious pride of the intellect, made Lucifer and a third part of the cohorts of angels fall from their glory. A sin, an instant of folly and weakness, drove Adam and Eve out of Eden and brought death and suffering into the world. To retrieve the consequences of that sin the Only Begotten Son of God came down to earth, lived and suffered and died a most painful death, hanging for three hours on the cross.

— O, my dear little brethren in Christ Jesus, will we then offend that good Redeemer and provoke His anger? Will we trample again upon that torn and mangled corpse? Will we spit upon that face so full of sorrow and love? Will we too, like the cruel Jews and the brutal soldiers, mock that gentle and compassionate Saviour Who trod alone for our sake the awful winepress of sorrow? Every word of sin is a wound in His tender side. Every sinful act is a thorn piercing His head. Every impure thought, deliberately yielded to, is a keen lance transfixing that sacred and loving heart. No, no. It is impossible for any human being to do that which offends so deeply the divine Majesty, that which is punished by an eternity of agony, that which crucifies again the Son of God and makes a mockery of Him.

— I pray to God that my poor words may have availed today to confirm in holiness those who are in a state of grace, to strengthen the wavering, to lead back to the state of grace the poor soul that has strayed if any such be among you. I pray to God, and do you pray with me, that we may repent of our sins. I will ask you now, all of you, to repeat after me the act of contrition, kneeling here in this humble chapel in the presence of God. He is there in the tabernacle burning with love for mankind, ready to comfort the afflicted. Be not afraid. No matter how many or how foul the sins if only you repent of them they will be forgiven you. Let no worldly shame hold you back. God is still the merciful Lord who wishes not the eternal death of the sinner but rather that he be converted and live.

— He calls you to Him. You are His. He made you out of nothing. He loved you as only a God can love. His arms are open to receive you even though you have sinned against Him. Come to Him, poor sinner, poor vain and erring sinner. Now is the acceptable time. Now is the hour.

The priest rose and turning towards the altar knelt upon the step before the tabernacle in the fallen gloom. He waited till all in the chapel had knelt and every least noise was still. Then, raising his head, he repeated the act of contrition, phrase by phrase, with fervour. The boys answered him phrase by phrase. Stephen, his tongue cleaving to his palate, bowed his head, praying with his heart.

> — *O my God!* —
> — *O my God!* —
> — *I am heartily sorry* —
> — *I am heartily sorry* —
> — *for having offended Thee* —
> — *for having offended Thee* —
> — *and I detest my sins* —
> — *and I detest my sins* —
> — *above every other evil* —
> — *above every other evil* —
> — *because they displease Thee, my God* —
> — *because they displease Thee, my God* —
> — *Who art so deserving* —
> — *Who art so deserving* —
> — *of all my love* —
> — *of all my love* —
> — *and I firmly purpose* —
> — *and I firmly purpose* —
> — *by Thy Holy grace* —
> — *by Thy Holy grace* —
> — *never more to offend Thee* —
> — *never more to offend Thee* —
> — *and to amend my life* —
> — *and to amend my life* —

*   *   *   *

He went up to his room after dinner in order to be alone with his soul: and at every step his soul seemed to sigh: at every step his soul mounted with his feet, sighing in the ascent, through a region of viscid gloom.

He halted on the landing before the door and then, grasping the porcelain knob, opened the door quickly. He waited in fear, his soul pining within him, praying silently that death might not touch his brow as he passed over the threshold, that the fiends that inhabit darkness might not be given power over him. He waited still at the threshold as at the entrance to some dark cave. Faces were there; eyes: they waited and watched.

— We knew perfectly well of course that although it was bound to come to the light he would find considerable difficulty in endeavouring to try to induce himself to try to endeavour to ascertain the spiritual plenipotentiary and so we knew of course perfectly well —

Murmuring faces waited and watched; murmurous voices filled the dark shell of the cave. He feared intensely in spirit and in flesh but, raising his head bravely, he strode into the room firmly. A doorway, a room, the same room, same window. He told himself calmly that those words had absolutely no sense which had seemed to rise murmurously from the dark. He told himself that it was simply his room with the door open.

He closed the door and, walking swiftly to the bed, knelt beside it and covered his face with his hands. His hands were cold and damp and his limbs ached with chill. Bodily unrest and chill and weariness beset him, routing his thoughts. Why was he kneeling there like a child saying his evening prayers? To be alone with his soul, to examine his conscience, to meet his sins face to face, to recall their times and manners and circumstances, to weep over them. He could not weep. He could not summon them to his memory. He felt only an ache of soul and body, his whole being, memory, will, understanding, flesh, benumbed and weary.

That was the work of devils, to scatter his thoughts and overcloud his conscience, assailing him at the gates of the cowardly and sin-corrupted flesh: and, praying God timidly to forgive him his weakness, he crawled up on to the bed and, wrapping the blankets closely about him, covered his face again with his hands. He had sinned. He had sinned so deeply against heaven and before God that he was not worthy to be called God's child.

Could it be that he, Stephen Dedalus, had done those things? His conscience sighed in answer. Yes, he had done them, secretly, filthily, time after time and, hardened in sinful impenitence, he had dared to wear the mask of holiness before the tabernacle itself while his soul within was a living mass of corruption. How came it that God had not struck him dead? The leprous company of his sins closed about him, breathing upon him, bending over him from all sides. He strove to forget them in an act of prayer, huddling his limbs closer together and binding down his eyelids: but the senses of his soul would not be bound and, though his eyes were shut fast, he saw the places where he had sinned and, though his ears were tightly covered, he heard. He desired with all his will not to hear nor see. He desired till his frame shook under the strain of his desire and until the senses of his soul closed. They closed for an instant and then opened. He saw.

A field of stiff weeds and thistles and tufted nettlebunches. Thick among the tufts of rank stiff growth lay battered canisters and clots and coils of solid excrement. A faint marsh light struggling upwards from all the ordure through the bristling grey green weeds. An evil smell, faint and foul as the light, curled upwards sluggishly out of the canisters and from the stale crusted dung.

Creatures were in the field; one, three, six: creatures were moving in the field, hither and thither. Goatish creatures with human faces, horny browed, lightly bearded and grey as indiarubber. The malice of evil glittered in their hard eyes, as they moved hither and thither, trailing their long tails behind them. A rictus of cruel malignity lit up greyly their old bony faces. One was clasping about his ribs a torn flannel waistcoat, another complained monotonously as his beard stuck in the tufted weeds. Soft language issued from their spittleless lips as they swished in slow circles round and round the field, winding hither and thither through the weeds, dragging their long tails amid the rattling canisters. They moved in slow circles, circling closer and closer to enclose, to enclose, soft language issuing from their lips, their long swishing tails besmeared with stale shite, thrusting upwards their terrific faces . . .

Help!

He flung the blankets from him madly to free his face and neck. That was his hell. God had allowed him to see the hell reserved for his sins: stinking, bestial, malignant, a hell of lecherous goatish fiends. For him! For him!

He sprang from the bed, the reeking odour pouring down his throat, clogging and revolting his entrails. Air! The air of heaven! He stumbled towards the window, groaning and almost fainting with sickness. At the washstand a convulsion seized him within; and, clasping his cold forehead wildly, he vomited profusely in agony.

When the fit had spent itself he walked weakly to the window and lifting the sash, sat in a corner of the embrasure and leaned his elbow upon the sill. The rain had drawn off; and amid the moving vapours from point to point of light the city was spinning about herself a soft cocoon of yellowish haze. Heaven was still and faintly luminous and the air sweet to breathe, as in a thicket drenched with showers: and amid

peace and shimmering lights and quiet fragrance he made a covenant
with his heart.

He prayed:

— *He once had meant to come on earth in heavenly glory but we
sinned: and then He could not safely visit us but with a shrouded majesty
and a bedimmed radiance for He was God. So He came Himself in
weakness not in power and He sent thee, a creature in His stead, with a
creature's comeliness and lustre suited to our state. And now thy very face
and form, dear mother, speak to us of the Eternal; not like earthly beauty,
dangerous to look upon, but like the morning star which is thy emblem,
bright and musical, breathing purity, telling of heaven and infusing
peace. O harbinger of day! O light of the pilgrim! Lead us still as thou
hast led. In the dark night, across the bleak wilderness guide us on to our
Lord Jesus, guide us home. —*

His eyes were dimmed with tears and, looking humbly up to heaven,
he wept for the innocence he had lost.

When evening had fallen he left the house and the first touch of the
damp dark air and the noise of the door as it closed behind him made
ache again his conscience, lulled by prayer and tears. Confess! Confess!
It was not enough to lull the conscience with a tear and a prayer. He had
to kneel before the minister of the Holy Ghost and tell over his hidden
sins truly and repentantly. Before he heard again the footboard of the
housedoor trail over the threshold as it opened to let him in, before he
saw again the table in the kitchen set for supper he would have knelt and
confessed. It was quite simple.

The ache of conscience ceased and he walked onward swiftly through
the dark streets. There were so many flagstones on the footpath of that
street and so many streets in that city and so many cities in the world. Yet
eternity had no end. He was in mortal sin. Even once was a mortal sin. It
could happen in an instant. But how so quickly? By seeing or by
thinking of seeing. The eyes see the thing, without having wished first to
see. Then in an instant it happens. But does that part of the body
understand or what? The serpent, the most subtle beast of the field. It
must understand when it desires in one instant and then prolongs its
own desire instant after instant, sinfully. It feels and understands and
desires. What a horrible thing! Who made it to be like that, a bestial part
of the body able to understand bestially and desire bestially? Was that
then he or an inhuman thing moved by a lower soul? His soul sickened
at the thought of a torpid snaky life feeding itself out of the tender
marrow of his life and fattening upon the slime of lust. O why was that
so? O why?

He cowered in the shadow of the thought abasing himself in the awe of God Who had made all things and all men. Madness. Who could think such a thought? And, cowering in darkness and abject, he prayed mutely to his angel guardian to drive away with his sword the demon that was whispering to his brain.

The whisper ceased and he knew then clearly that his own soul had sinned in thought and word and deed wilfully through his own body. Confess! He had to confess every sin. How could he utter in words to the priest what he had done? Must, must. Or how could he explain without dying of shame? Or how could he have done such things without shame? A madman! Confess! O he would indeed to be free and sinless again! Perhaps the priest would know. O dear God!

He walked on and on through ill-lit streets, fearing to stand still for a moment lest it might seem that he held back from what awaited him, fearing to arrive at that towards which he still turned with longing. How beautiful must be a soul in the state of grace when God looked upon it with love!

Frowsy girls sat along the curbstones before their baskets. Their dank hair hung trailed over their brows. They were not beautiful to see as they crouched in the mire. But their souls were seen by God; and if their souls were in a state of grace they were radiant to see: and God loved them, seeing them.

A wasting breath of humiliation blew bleakly over his soul to think of how he had fallen, to feel that those souls were dearer to God than his. The wind blew over him and passed on to the myriads and myriads of other souls, on whom God's favour shone now more and now less, stars now brighter and now dimmer, sustained and failing. And the glimmering souls passed away, sustained and failing, merged in a moving breath. One soul was lost; a tiny soul: his. It flickered once and went out, forgotten, lost. The end: black cold void waste.

Consciousness of place came ebbing back to him slowly over a vast tract of time unlit, unfelt, unlived. The squalid scene composed itself around him; the common accents, the burning gasjets in the shops, odours of fish and spirits and wet sawdust, moving men and women. An old woman was about to cross the street, an oilcan in her hand. He bent down and asked her was there a chapel near.

— A chapel, sir? Yes, sir. Church Street chapel. —
— Church? —
She shifted the can to her other hand and directed him: and, as she held out her reeking withered right hand under its fringe of shawl, he bent lower towards her, saddened and soothed by her voice.

— Thank you. —
— You are quite welcome, sir. —
The candles on the high altar had been extinguished but the fra-

grance of incense still floated down the dim nave. Bearded workmen
with pious faces were guiding a canopy out through a side door, the
sacristan aiding them with quiet gestures and words. A few of the faithful
still lingered praying before one of the sidealtars or kneeling in the
benches near the confessionals. He approached timidly and knelt at the
last bench in the body, thankful for the peace and silence and fragrant
shadow of the church. The board on which he knelt was narrow and
worn and those who knelt near him were humble followers of Jesus.
Jesus too had been born in poverty and had worked in the shop of a
carpenter, cutting boards and planing them, and had first spoken of the
kingdom of God to poor fishermen, teaching all men to be meek and
humble of heart.

He bowed his head upon his hands, bidding his heart be meek and
humble that he might be like those who knelt beside him and his prayer
as acceptable as theirs. He prayed beside them but it was hard. His soul
was foul with sin and he dared not ask forgiveness with the simple trust
of those whom Jesus, in the mysterious ways of God, had called first to
His side, the carpenters, the fishermen, poor and simple people following a lowly trade, handling and shaping the wood of trees, mending
their nets with patience.

A tall figure came down the aisle and the penitents stirred: and, at the
last moment glancing up swiftly, he saw a long grey beard and the brown
habit of a capuchin. The priest entered the box and was hidden. Two
penitents rose and entered the confessional at either side. The wooden
slide was drawn back and the faint murmur of a voice troubled the
silence.

His blood began to murmur in his veins, murmuring like a sinful city
summoned from its sleep to bear its doom. Little flakes of fire fell and
powdery ashes fell softly, alighting on the houses of men. They stirred,
waking from sleep, troubled by the heated air.

The slide was shot back. The penitent emerged from the side of the
box. The farther side was drawn. A woman entered quietly and deftly
where the first penitent had knelt. The faint murmur began again.

He could still leave the chapel. He could stand up, put one foot
before the other and walk out softly and then run, run, run swiftly
through the dark streets. He could still escape from the shame. Had it
been any terrible crime but that one sin! Had it been murder! Little fiery
flakes fell and touched him at all points, shameful thoughts, shameful
words, shameful acts. Shame covered him wholly like fine glowing
ashes falling continually. To say it in words! His soul, stifling and
helpless, would cease to be.

The slide was shot back. A penitent emerged from the farther side of
the box. The near slide was drawn. A penitent entered where the other

penitent had come out. A soft whispering noise floated in vaporous cloudlets out of the box. It was the woman: soft whispering cloudlets, soft whispering vapour, whispering and vanishing.

He beat his breast with his fist humbly, secretly under cover of the wooden armrest. He would be at one with others and with God. He would love his neighbour. He would love God Who had made and loved him. He would kneel and pray with others and be happy. God would look down on him and on them and would love them all.

It was easy to be good. God's yoke was sweet and light. It was better never to have sinned, to have remained always a child, for God loved little children and suffered them to come to Him. It was a terrible and a sad thing to sin. But God was merciful to poor sinners who were truly sorry. How true that was! That was indeed goodness.

The slide was shot to suddenly. The penitent came out. He was next. He stood up in terror and walked blindly into the box.

At last it had come. He knelt in the silent gloom and raised his eyes to the white crucifix suspended above him. God could see that he was sorry. He would tell all his sins. His confession would be long, long. Everybody in the chapel would know then what a sinner he had been. Let them know. It was true. But God had promised to forgive him if he was sorry. He was sorry. He clasped his hands and raised them towards the white form, praying with his darkened eyes, praying with all his trembling body, swaying his head to and fro like a lost creature, praying with whimpering lips.

— Sorry! Sorry! O sorry! —

The slide clicked back and his heart bounded in his breast. The face of an old priest was at the grating, averted from him, leaning upon a hand. He made the sign of the cross and prayed of the priest to bless him for he had sinned. Then, bowing his head, he repeated the *Confiteor* in fright. At the words *my most grievous fault* he ceased, breathless.

— How long is it since your last confession, my child? —

— A long time, father. —

— A month, my child? —

— Longer, father. —

— Three months, my child? —

— Longer, father. —

— Six months? —

— Eight months, father. —

He had begun. The priest asked:

— And what do you remember since that time? —

He began to confess his sins: masses missed, prayers not said, lies.

— Anything else, my child? —

Sins of anger, envy of others, gluttony, vanity, disobedience.

— Anything else, my child? —

There was no help. He murmured:

— I . . . committed sins of impurity, father. —

The priest did not turn his head.

— With yourself, my child? —

— And . . . with others. —

— With women, my child? —

— Yes, father. —

— Were they married women, my child? —

He did not know. His sins trickled from his lips, one by one, trickled in shameful drops from his soul festering and oozing like a sore, a squalid stream of vice. The last sins oozed forth, sluggish, filthy. There was no more to tell. He bowed his head, overcome.

The priest was silent. Then he asked:

— How old are you, my child? —

— Sixteen, father. —

The priest passed his hand several times over his face. Then, resting his forehead against his hand, he leaned towards the grating and, with eyes still averted, spoke slowly. His voice was weary and old.

— You are very young, my child — he said, — and let me implore of you to give up that sin. It is a terrible sin. It kills the body and it kills the soul. It is the cause of many crimes and misfortunes. Give it up, my child, for God's sake. It is dishonourable and unmanly. You cannot know where that wretched habit will lead you or where it will come against you. As long as you commit that sin, my poor child, you will never be worth one farthing to God. Pray to our mother Mary to help you. She will help you, my child. Pray to Our Blessed Lady when that sin comes into your mind. I am sure you will do that, will you not? You repent of all those sins. I am sure you do. And you will promise God now that by His holy grace you will never offend Him any more by that wicked sin. You will make that solemn promise to God, will you not? —

— Yes, father. —

The old and weary voice fell like sweet rain upon his quaking parching heart. How sweet and sad!

— Do so, my poor child. The devil has led you astray. Drive him back to hell when he tempts you to dishonour your body in that way — the foul spirit who hates Our Lord. Promise God now that you will give up that sin, that wretched wretched sin. —

Blinded by his tears and by the light of God's mercifulness he bent his head and heard the grave words of absolution spoken and saw the priest's hand raised above him in token of forgiveness.

— God bless you, my child. Pray for me. —

He knelt to say his penance, praying in a corner of the dark nave: and his prayers ascended to heaven from his purified heart like perfume streaming upwards from a heart of white rose.

The muddy streets were gay. He strode homeward, conscious of an invisible grace pervading and making light his limbs. In spite of all he had done it. He had confessed and God had pardoned him. His soul was made fair and holy once more, holy and happy.

It would be beautiful to die if God so willed. It was beautiful to live in grace a life of peace and virtue and forbearance with others.

He sat by the fire in the kitchen, not daring to speak for happiness. Till that moment he had not known how beautiful and peaceful life could be. The green square of paper pinned round the lamp cast down a tender shade. On the dresser was a plate of sausages and white pudding and on the shelf there were eggs. They would be for the breakfast in the morning after the communion in the college chapel. White pudding and eggs and sausages and cups of tea. How simple and beautiful was life after all! And life lay all before him.

In a dream he fell asleep. In a dream he rose and saw that it was morning. In a waking dream he went through the quiet morning towards the college.

The boys were all there, kneeling in their places. He knelt among them, happy and shy. The altar was heaped with fragrant masses of white flowers: and in the morning light the pale flames of the candles among the white flowers were clear and silent as his own soul.

He knelt before the altar with his classmates, holding the altar cloth with them over a living rail of hands. His hands were trembling and his soul trembled as he heard the priest pass with the ciborium from communicant to communicant.

— *Corpus Domini nostri.* —[1]

Could it be? He knelt there sinless and timid: and he would hold upon his tongue the host and God would enter his purified body.

— *In vitam eternam.*[2] *Amen.* —

Another life! A life of grace and virtue and happiness! It was true. It was not a dream from which he would wake. The past was past.

— *Corpus Domini nostri.* —

The ciborium had come to him.

---

[1] [*The body of our Lord.*]
[2] [*To everlasting life.*]

Chapter IV

SUNDAY was dedicated to the mystery of the Holy Trinity, Monday to the Holy Ghost, Tuesday to the Guardian Angels, Wednesday to Saint Joseph, Thursday to the Most Blessed Sacrament of the Altar, Friday to the Suffering Jesus, Saturday to the Blessed Virgin Mary.

Every morning he hallowed himself anew in the presence of some holy image or mystery. His day began with an heroic offering of its every moment of thought or action for the intentions of the sovereign pontiff and with an early mass. The raw morning air whetted his resolute piety; and often as he knelt among the few worshippers at the side altar, following with his interleaved prayer book the murmur of the priest, he glanced up for an instant towards the vested figure standing in the gloom between the two candles, which were the old and the new testaments, and imagined that he was kneeling at mass in the catacombs.

His daily life was laid out in devotional areas. By means of ejaculations and prayers he stored up ungrudgingly for the souls in purgatory centuries of days and quarantines and years; yet the spiritual triumph which he felt in achieving with ease so many fabulous ages of canonical penances did not wholly reward his zeal of prayer since he could never know how much temporal punishment he had remitted by way of suffrage for the agonising souls: and, fearful lest in the midst of the purgatorial fire, which differed from the infernal only in that it was not everlasting, his penance might avail no more than a drop of moisture he drove his soul daily through an increasing circle of works of supererogation.

Every part of his day, divided by what he regarded now as the duties of his station in life, circled about its own centre of spiritual energy. His life seemed to have drawn near to eternity; every thought, word and deed, every instance of consciousness could be made to revibrate radiantly in heaven: and at times his sense of such immediate repercussion was so lively that he seemed to feel his soul in devotion pressing like

105

fingers the keyboard of a great cash register and to see the amount of his purchase start forth immediately in heaven, not as a number but as a frail column of incense or as a slender flower.

The rosaries, too, which he said constantly — for he carried his beads loose in his trousers' pockets that he might tell them as he walked the streets — transformed themselves into coronals of flowers of such vague unearthly texture that they seemed to him as hueless and odourless as they were nameless. He offered up each of his three daily chaplets that his soul might grow strong in each of the three theological virtues, in faith in the Father Who had created him, in hope in the Son Who had redeemed him, and in love of the Holy Ghost Who had sanctified him; and this thrice triple prayer he offered to the Three Persons through Mary in the name of her joyful and sorrowful and glorious mysteries.

On each of the seven days of the week he further prayed that one of the seven gifts of the Holy Ghost might descend upon his soul and drive out of it day by day the seven deadly sins which had defiled it in the past; and he prayed for each gift on its appointed day, confident that it would descend upon him, though it seemed strange to him at times that wisdom and understanding and knowledge were so distinct in their nature that each should be prayed for apart from the others. Yet he believed that at some future stage of his spiritual progress this difficulty would be removed when his sinful soul had been raised up from its weakness and enlightened by the Third Person of the Most Blessed Trinity. He believed this all the more, and with trepidation, because of the divine gloom and silence wherein dwelt the unseen Paraclete, Whose symbols were a dove and a mighty wind, to sin against Whom was a sin beyond forgiveness, the eternal, mysterious secret Being to Whom, as God, the priests offered up mass once a year, orbed in the scarlet of the tongues of fire.

The imagery through which the nature and kinship of the Three Persons of the Trinity were darkly shadowed forth in the books of devotion which he read — the Father contemplating from all eternity as in a mirror His Divine Perfections and thereby begetting eternally the Eternal Son and the Holy Spirit proceeding out of Father and Son from all eternity — were easier of acceptance by his mind by reason of their august incomprehensibility than was the simple fact that God had loved his soul from all eternity, for ages before he had been born into the world, for ages before the world itself had existed.

He had heard the names of the passions of love and hate pronounced solemnly on the stage and in the pulpit, had found them set forth solemnly in books, and had wondered why his soul was unable to harbour them for any time or to force his lips to utter their names with conviction. A brief anger had often invested him, but he had never been able to make it an abiding passion and had always felt himself passing out of it as if his very body were being divested with ease of some outer skin or peel. He had felt a subtle, dark and murmurous presence penetrate his being and fire him with a brief iniquitous lust: it, too, had slipped beyond his grasp leaving his mind lucid and indifferent. This, it seemed, was the only love and that the only hate his soul would harbour.

But he could no longer disbelieve in the reality of love since God himself had loved his individual soul with divine love from all eternity. Gradually, as his soul was enriched with spiritual knowledge, he saw the whole world forming one vast symmetrical expression of God's power and love. Life became a divine gift for every moment and sensation of which, were it even the sight of a single leaf hanging on the twig of a tree, his soul should praise and thank the giver. The world for all its solid substance and complexity no longer existed for his soul save as a theorem of divine power and love and universality. So entire and unquestionable was this sense of the divine meaning in all nature granted to his soul that he could scarcely understand why it was in any way necessary that he should continue to live. Yet that was part of the divine purpose and he dared not question its use, he above all others who had sinned so deeply and so foully against the divine purpose. Meek and abased by this consciousness of the one eternal omnipresent perfect reality his soul took up again her burden of pieties, masses and prayers and sacraments and mortifications, and only then for the first time since he had brooded on the great mystery of love did he feel within him a warm movement like that of some newly born life or virtue of the soul itself. The attitude of rapture in sacred art, the raised and parted hands, the parted lips and eyes as of one about to swoon, became for him an image of the soul in prayer, humiliated and faint before her Creator.

But he had been forewarned of the dangers of spiritual exaltation and did not allow himself to desist from even the least or lowliest devotion, striving also by constant mortification to undo the sinful past rather than to achieve a saintliness fraught with peril. Each of his senses was brought under a rigorous discipline. In order to mortify the sense of sight he made it his rule to walk in the street with downcast eyes, glancing neither to right nor left and never behind him. His eyes shunned every encounter with the eyes of women. From time to time also he balked them by a sudden effort of the will, as by lifting them suddenly in the middle of an unfinished sentence and closing the book. To mortify his hearing he exerted no control over his voice which was then breaking, neither sang nor whistled and made no attempt to flee from noise which caused him painful nervous irritation such as the sharpening of knives on the knifeboard, the gathering of cinders on the fireshovel and the twigging of the carpet. To mortify his smell was more difficult as he found in himself no instinctive repugnance to bad odours, whether they were the odours of the outdoor world such as those of dung or tar or the odours of his own person among which he had made many curious comparisons and experiments. He found in the end that the only odour against which his sense of smell revolted was a certain stale fishy stink like that of longstanding urine: and whenever it was possible he subjected himself to this unpleasant odour. To mortify the taste he practised strict habits at table, observed to the letter all the fasts of the church and sought by distraction to divert his mind from the savours of different foods. But it was to the mortification of touch that he brought the most assiduous ingenuity of inventiveness. He never consciously changed his position in bed, sat in the most uncomfortable positions, suffered patiently every itch and pain, kept away from the fire, remained on his knees all through the mass except at the gospels, left parts of his neck and face undried so that air might sting them and, whenever he was not saying his beads, carried his arms stiffly at his sides like a runner and never in his pockets or clasped behind him.

He had no temptations to sin mortally. It surprised him, however, to find that at the end of his course of intricate piety and selfrestraint he was so easily at the mercy of childish and unworthy imperfections. His prayers and fasts availed him little for the suppression of anger at hearing his mother sneeze or at being disturbed in his devotions. It needed an immense effort of his will to master the impulse which urged him to give outlet to such irritation. Images of the outbursts of trivial anger which he had often noted among his masters, their twitching mouths, closeshut lips and flushed cheeks, recurred to his memory, discouraging him, for all his practice of humility, by the comparison. To merge his life in the common tide of other lives was harder for him than any fasting or prayer, and it was his constant failure to do this to his own satisfaction which caused in his soul at last a sensation of spiritual dryness together with a growth of doubts and scruples. His soul traversed a period of desolation in which the sacraments themselves seemed to have turned into dried up sources. His confession became a channel for the escape of scrupulous and unrepented imperfections. His actual reception of the eucharist did not bring him the same dissolving moments of virginal selfsurrender as did those spiritual communions made by him sometimes at the close of some visit to the Blessed Sacrament. The book which he used for these visits was an old neglected book written by Saint Alphonsus Liguori, with fading characters and sere foxpapered leaves. A faded world of fervent love and virginal responses seemed to be evoked for his soul by the reading of its pages in which the imagery of the canticles was interwoven with the communicant's prayers. An inaudible voice seemed to caress the soul, telling her names and glories, bidding her arise as for espousal and come away, bidding her look forth, a spouse, from Amana and from the mountains of the leopards; and the soul seemed to answer with the same inaudible voice, surrendering herself: *Inter ubera mea commorabitur.*[1]

This idea of surrender had a perilous attraction for his mind now that he felt his soul beset once again by the insistent voices of the flesh which began to murmur to him again during his prayers and meditations. It gave him an intense sense of power to know that he could by a single act of consent, in a moment of thought, undo all that he had done. He seemed to feel a flood slowly advancing towards his naked feet and to be waiting for the first faint timid noiseless wavelet to touch his fevered skin. Then, almost at the instant of that touch, almost at the verge of sinful consent, he found himself standing far away from the flood upon a dry shore, saved by a sudden act of the will or a sudden ejaculation: and, seeing the silver line of the floor far away and beginning again its slow advance towards his feet, a new thrill of power and satisfaction shook his soul to know that he had not yielded nor undone all.

When he had eluded the flood of temptation many times in this way he grew troubled and wondered whether the grace which he had refused to lose was not being filched from him little by little. The clear certitude of his own immunity grew dim and to it succeeded a vague fear that his soul had really fallen unawares. It was with difficulty that he won back his old consciousness of his state of grace by telling himself that he had prayed to God at every temptation and that the grace which he had prayed for must have been given to him inasmuch as God was obliged to give it. The very frequency and violence of temptations showed him at last the truth of what he had heard about the trials of the saints. Frequent and violent temptations were a proof that the citadel of the soul had not fallen and that the devil raged to make it fall.

Often when he had confessed his doubts and scruples, some momentary inattention at prayer, a movement of trivial anger in his soul or a subtle wilfulness in speech or act, he was bidden by his confessor to name some sin of his past life before absolution was given him. He named it with humility and shame and repented of it once more. It humiliated and shamed him to think that he would never be freed from it wholly, however holily he might live or whatever virtues or perfections he might attain. A restless feeling of guilt would always be present with him: he would confess and repent and be absolved, confess and repent again and be absolved again, fruitlessly. Perhaps that first hasty confession wrung from him by the fear of hell had not been good? Perhaps, concerned only for his imminent doom, he had not had sincere sorrow

---

[1] [*He shall lie between my breasts.*]

for his sin? But the surest sign that his confession had been good and that he had had sincere sorrow for his sin was, he knew, the amendment of his life.

— I have amended my life, have I not? he asked himself. —

     *　　　*　　　*　　　*

The director stood in the embrasure of the window, his back to the light, leaning an elbow on the brown crossblind, and, as he spoke and smiled, slowly dangling and looping the cord of the other blind, Stephen stood before him, following for a moment with his eyes the waning of the long summer daylight above the roofs or the slow deft movements of the priestly fingers. The priest's face was in total shadow, but the waning daylight from behind him touched the deeply grooved temples and the curves of the skull. Stephen followed also with his ears the accents and intervals of the priest's voice as he spoke gravely and cordially of indifferent themes, the vacation which had just ended, the colleges of the order abroad, the transference of masters. The grave and cordial voice went on easily with its tale, and in the pauses Stephen felt bound to set it on again with respectful questions. He knew that the tale was a prelude and his mind waited for the sequel. Ever since the message of summons had come for him from the director his mind had struggled to find the meaning of the message; and during the long restless time he had sat in the college parlour waiting for the director to come in his eyes had wandered from one sober picture to another around the walls and his mind wandered from one guess to another until the meaning of the summons had almost become clear. Then, just as he was wishing that some unforeseen cause might prevent the director from coming, he had heard the handle of the door turning and the swish of a soutane.

The director had begun to speak of the Dominican and Franciscan orders and of the friendship between Saint Thomas and Saint Bonaventure. The Capuchin dress, he thought, was rather too. . . .

Stephen's face gave back the priest's indulgent smile and, not being anxious to give an opinion, he made a slight dubitative movement with his lips.

— I believe, — continued the director, — that there is some talk now among the Capuchins themselves of doing away with it and following the example of the other Franciscans. —

— I suppose they would retain it in the cloisters? — said Stephen.

— O, certainly, — said the director. — For the cloister it is all right, but for the street I really think it would be better to do away with, don't you? —

— It must be troublesome, I imagine? —

— Of course it is, of course. Just imagine when I was in Belgium I used to see them out cycling in all kinds of weather with this thing up about their knees! It was really ridiculous. *Les jupes*,[1] they call them in Belgium. —

The vowel was so modified as to be indistinct.

— What do they call them? —

— *Les jupes*. —

— O! —

Stephen smiled again in answer to the smile which he could not see on the priest's shadowed face, its image or spectre only passing rapidly across his mind as the low discreet accent fell upon his ear. He gazed calmly before him at the waning sky, glad of the cool of the evening and the faint yellow glow which hid the tiny flame kindling upon his cheek.

The names of articles of dress worn by women or of certain soft and delicate stuffs used in their making brought always to his mind a delicate and sinful perfume. As a boy he had imagined the reins by which horses are driven as slender silken bands and it shocked him to feel at Stradbrooke the greasy leather of harness. It had shocked him, too, when he had felt for the first time beneath his tremulous fingers the brittle texture of a woman's stocking for, retaining nothing of all he read save that which seemed to him an echo or a prophecy of his own state, it was only amid softworded phrases or within rosesoft stuffs that he dared to conceive of the soul or body of a woman moving with tender life.

But the phrase on the priest's lips was disingenuous for he knew that a priest should not speak lightly on that theme. The phrase had been spoken lightly with design and he felt that his face was being searched by the eyes in the shadow. Whatever he had heard or read of the craft of jesuits he had put aside frankly as not borne out by his own experience. His masters, even when they had not attracted him, had seemed to him always intelligent and serious priests, athletic and highspirited prefects. He thought of them as men who washed their bodies briskly with cold water and wore clean cold linen. During all the years he had lived among them in Clongowes and in Belvedere he had received only two pandies and, though these had been dealt him in the wrong, he knew that he had often escaped punishment. During all those years he had never heard from any of his masters a flippant word: it was they who had taught him christian doctrine and urged him to live a good life and, when he had fallen into grievous sin, it was they who had led him back to grace. Their presence had made him diffident of himself when he was

---

[1] [The skirts.]

a muff in Clongowes and it had made him diffident of himself also while he had held his equivocal position in Belvedere. A constant sense of this had remained with him up to the last year of his school life. He had never once disobeyed or allowed turbulent companions to seduce him from his habit of quiet obedience: and, even when he doubted some statement of a master, he had never presumed to doubt openly. Lately some of their judgments had sounded a little childish in his ears and had made him feel a regret and pity as though he were slowly passing out of an accustomed world and were hearing its language for the last time. One day when some boys had gathered round a priest under the shed near the chapel, he heard the priest say:

— I believe that Lord Macaulay was a man who probably never committed a mortal sin in his life, that is to say, a deliberate mortal sin. —

Some of the boys had then asked the priest if Victor Hugo were not the greatest French writer. The priest had answered that Victor Hugo had never written half so well when he had turned against the church as he had written when he was a catholic.

— But there are many eminent French critics, — said the priest, — who consider that even Victor Hugo, great as he certainly was, had not so pure a French style as Louis Veuillot. —

The tiny flame which the priest's allusion had kindled upon Stephen's cheek had sunk down again and his eyes were still fixed calmly on the colourless sky. But an unresting doubt flew hither and thither before his mind. Masked memories passed quickly before him: he recognised scenes and persons yet he was conscious that he had failed to perceive some vital circumstance in them. He saw himself walking about the grounds watching the sports in Clongowes and eating chocolate out of his cricketcap. Some jesuits were walking round the cycletrack in the company of ladies. The echoes of certain expressions used in Clongowes sounded in remote caves of his mind.

His ears were listening to these distant echoes amid the silence of the parlour when he became aware that the priest was addressing him in a different voice.

— I sent for you today, Stephen, because I wished to speak to you on a very important subject. —

— Yes, sir. —

— Have you ever felt that you had a vocation? —

Stephen parted his lips to answer yes and then withheld the word suddenly. The priest waited for the answer and added:

— I mean have you ever felt within yourself, in your soul, a desire to join the order. Think. —

— I have sometimes thought of it, — said Stephen.

The priest let the blindcord fall to one side and, uniting his hands, leaned his chin gravely upon them, communing with himself.

— In a college like this, — he said at length, — there is one boy or perhaps two or three boys whom God calls to the religious life. Such a boy is marked off from his companions by his piety, by the good example he shows to others. He is looked up to by them; he is chosen perhaps as prefect by his fellow sodalists. And you, Stephen, have been such a boy in this college, prefect of Our Blessed Lady's sodality. Perhaps you are the boy in this college whom God designs to call to Himself. —

A strong note of pride reinforcing the gravity of the priest's voice made Stephen's heart quicken in response.

— To receive that call, Stephen, — said the priest, — is the greatest honour that the Almighty God can bestow upon a man. No king or emperor on this earth has the power of the priest of God. No angel or archangel in heaven, no saint, not even the Blessed Virgin herself has the power of a priest of God: the power of the keys, the power to bind and to loose from sin, the power of exorcism, the power to cast out from the creatures of God the evil spirits that have power over them, the power, the authority, to make the great God of Heaven come down upon the altar and take the form of bread and wine. What an awful power, Stephen! —

A flame began to flutter again on Stephen's cheek as he heard in this proud address an echo of his own proud musings. How often had he seen himself as a priest wielding calmly and humbly the awful power of which angels and saints stood in reverence! His soul had loved to muse in secret on this desire. He had seen himself, a young and silentmannered priest, entering a confessional swiftly, ascending the altarsteps, incensing, genuflecting, accomplishing the vague acts of the priesthood which pleased him by reason of their semblance of reality and of their distance from it. In that dim life which he had lived through in his musings he had assumed the voices and gestures which he had noted with various priests. He had bent his knee sideways like such a one, he had shaken the thurible only slightly like such a one, his chasuble had swung open like that of such another as he turned to the altar again after having blessed the people. And above all it had pleased him to fill the second place in those dim scenes of his imagining. He shrank from the dignity of celebrant because it displeased him to imagine that all the vague pomp should end in his own person or that the ritual should assign to him so clear and final an office. He longed for the minor sacred offices, to be vested with the tunicle of subdeacon at high mass, to stand aloof from the altar, forgotten by the people, his shoulders covered with a humeral veil, holding the paten within its folds or, when the sacrifice had been accomplished, to stand as deacon in a dalmatic cloth of gold on the step below the celebrant, his hands joined and his face towards the people, and sing the chant, *Ite missa est*.[1] If ever he had seen himself celebrant it was as in the pictures of the mass in his child's massbook, in a church without worshippers, save for the angel of the sacrifice, at a bare altar and served by an acolyte scarcely more boyish than himself. In vague sacrificial or sacramental acts alone his will seemed drawn to go forth to encounter reality: and it was partly the absence of an appointed rite which had always constrained him to inaction whether he had allowed silence to cover his anger or pride or had suffered only an embrace he longed to give.

He listened in reverent silence now to the priest's appeal and through the words he heard even more distinctly a voice bidding him approach, offering him secret knowledge and secret power. He would know then what was the sin of Simon Magus and what the sin against the Holy Ghost for which there was no forgiveness. He would know obscure things, hidden from others, from those who were conceived and born children of wrath. He would know the sins, the sinful longings and sinful thoughts and sinful acts, of others, hearing them murmured into his ears in the confessional under the shame of a darkened chapel by the lips of women and of girls: but rendered immune mysteriously at his ordination by the imposition of hands his soul would pass again uncontaminated to the white peace of the altar. No touch of sin would linger upon the hands with which he would elevate and break the host; no touch of sin would linger on his lips in prayer to make him eat and drink damnation to himself not discerning the body of the Lord. He would hold his secret knowledge and secret power, being as sinless as the innocent: and he would be a priest for ever according to the order of Melchisedec.

— I will offer up my mass tomorrow morning, said the director, that Almighty God may reveal to you His holy will. And let you, Stephen, make a novena to your holy patron saint, the first martyr who is very powerful with God, that God may enlighten your mind. But you must be quite sure, Stephen, that you have a vocation because it would be terrible if you found afterwards that you had none. Once a priest always a priest, remember. Your catechism tells you that the sacrament of Holy Orders is one of those which can be received only once because it imprints on the soul an indelible spiritual mark which can never be effaced. It is before you must weigh well, not after. It is a solemn question, Stephen, because on it may depend the salvation of your eternal soul. But we will pray to God together. —

He held open the heavy hall door and gave his hand as if already to a companion in the spiritual life. Stephen passed out on to the wide

---

[1] [*Go, the Mass is ended.*]

platform above the steps and was conscious of the caress of mild evening air. Towards Findlater's church a quartette of young men were striding along with linked arms, swaying their heads and stepping to the agile melody of their leader's concertina. The music passed in an instant, as the first bars of sudden music always did, over the fantastic fabrics of his mind, dissolving them painlessly and noiselessly as a sudden wave dissolves the sandbuilt turrets of children. Smiling at the trivial air he raised his eyes to the priest's face and, seeing in it a mirthless reflection of the sunken day, detached his hand slowly which had acquiesced faintly in that companionship.

As he descended the steps the impression which effaced his troubled selfcommunion was that of a mirthless mask reflecting a sunken day from the threshold of the college. The shadow, then, of the life of the college passed gravely over his consciousness. It was a grave and ordered and passionless life that awaited him, a life without material cares. He wondered how he would pass the first night in the novitiate and with what dismay he would wake the first morning in the dormitory. The troubling odour of the long corridors of Clongowes came back to him and he heard the discreet murmur of the burning gas flames. At once from every part of his being unrest began to irradiate. A feverish quickening of his pulses followed and a din of meaningless words drove his reasoned thoughts hither and thither confusedly. His lungs dilated and sank as if he were inhaling a warm moist unsustaining air, and he smelt again the moist warm air which hung in the bath in Clongowes above the sluggish turfcoloured water.

Some instinct, waking at these memories, stronger than education or piety quickened within him at every near approach to that life, an instinct subtle and hostile, and armed him against acquiescence. The chill and order of the life repelled him. He saw himself rising in the cold of the morning and filing down with the others to early mass and trying vainly to struggle with his prayers against the fainting sickness of his stomach. He saw himself sitting at dinner with the community of a college. What, then, had become of that deeprooted shyness of his which had made him loth to eat or drink under a strange roof? What had come of the pride of his spirit which had always made him conceive himself as a being apart in every order?

The Reverend Stephen Dedalus, S. J.

His name in that new life leaped into characters before his eyes and to it there followed a mental sensation of an undefined face or colour of a face. The colour faded and became strong like a changing glow of pallid brick red. Was it the raw reddish glow he had so often seen on wintry mornings on the shaven gills of the priests? The face was eyeless and sourfavoured and devout, shot with pink tinges of suffocated anger. Was it not a mental spectre of the face of one of the jesuits whom some of the boys called Lantern Jaws and others Foxy Campbell?

He was passing at that moment before the jesuit house in Gardiner Street, and wondered vaguely which window would be his if he ever joined the order. Then he wondered at the vagueness of his wonder, at the remoteness of his own soul from what he had hitherto imagined her sanctuary, at the frail hold which so many years of order and obedience had of him when once a definite and irrevocable act of his threatened to end for ever, in time and in eternity, his freedom. The voice of the director urging upon him the proud claims of the church and the mystery and power of the priestly office repeated itself idly in his memory. His soul was not there to hear and greet it and he knew now that the exhortation he had listened to had already fallen into an idle formal tale. He would never swing the thurible before the tabernacle as priest. His destiny was to be elusive of social or religious orders. The wisdom of the priest's appeal did not touch him to the quick. He was destined to learn his own wisdom apart from others or to learn the wisdom of others himself wandering among the snares of the world.

The snares of the world were its ways of sin. He would fall. He had not yet fallen but he would fall silently, in an instant. Not to fall was too hard, too hard: and he felt the silent lapse of his soul, as it would be at some instant to come, falling, falling, but not yet fallen, still unfallen, but about to fall.

He crossed the bridge over the stream of the Tolka, and turned his eyes coldly for an instant towards the faded blue shrine of the Blessed Virgin which stood fowlwise on a pole in the middle of a hamshaped encampment of poor cottages. Then, bending to the left, he followed the lane which led up to his house. The faint sour stink of rotted cabbages came towards him from the kitchen gardens on the rising ground above the river. He smiled to think that it was this disorder, the misrule and confusion of his father's house and the stagnation of vegetable life, which was to win the day in his soul. Then a short laugh broke from his lips as he thought of that solitary farmhand in the kitchen gardens behind their house whom they had nicknamed The Man with the Hat. A second laugh, taking rise from the first after a pause, broke from him involuntarily as he thought of how The Man with the Hat worked, considering in turn the four points of the sky and then regretfully plunging his spade in the earth.

He pushed open the latchless door of the porch and passed through the naked hallway into the kitchen. A group of his brothers and sisters was sitting round the table. Tea was nearly over and only the last of the second watered tea remained in the bottoms of the small glass jars and jampots which did service for teacups. Discarded crusts and lumps of sugared bread, turned brown by the tea which had been poured over them, lay scattered on the table. Little wells of tea lay here and there on the board and a knife with a broken ivory handle was stuck through the pith of a ravaged turnover.

The sad quiet greyblue glow of the dying day came through the window and the open door, covering over and allaying quietly a sudden instinct of remorse in Stephen's heart. All that had been denied them had been freely given to him, the eldest: but the quiet glow of evening showed him in their faces no sign of rancour.

He sat near them at the table and asked where his father and mother were. One answered:

— Goneboro toboro lookboro atboro aboro houseboro. —

Still another removal! A boy named Fallon, in Belvedere, had often asked him with a silly laugh why they moved so often. A frown of scorn darkened quickly his forehead as he heard again the silly laugh of the questioner.

He asked:

— Why are we on the move again, if it's a fair question? —

— Becauseboro theboro landboro lordboro willboro putboro usboro outboro. —

The voice of his youngest brother from the farther side of the fireplace began to sing the air "Oft in the Stilly Night." One by one the others took up the air until a full choir of voices was singing. They would sing so for hours, melody after melody, glee after glee, till the last pale light died down on the horizon, till the first dark nightclouds came forth and night fell.

He waited for some moments, listening, before he too took up the air with them. He was listening with pain of spirit to the overtone of weariness behind their frail fresh innocent voices. Even before they set out on life's journey they seemed weary already of the way.

He heard the choir of voices in the kitchen echoed and multiplied through an endless reverberation of the choirs of endless generations of children: and heard in all the echoes an echo also of the recurring note of weariness and pain. All seemed weary of life even before entering upon it. And he remembered that Newman had heard this note also in the broken lines of Virgil "giving utterance, like the voice of Nature herself, to that pain and weariness yet hope of better things which has been the experience of her children in every time."

*   *   *   *

He could wait no longer.

From the door of Byron's public-house to the gate of Clontarf Chapel, from the gate of Clontarf Chapel to the door of Byron's public-house, and then back again to the chapel and then back again to the public-house he had paced slowly at first, planting his steps scrupulously in the spaces of the patchwork of the footpath, then timing their fall to the fall of verses. A full hour had passed since his father had gone in with Dan Crosby, the tutor, to find out for him something about the university. For a full hour he had paced up and down, waiting: but he could wait no longer.

He set off abruptly for the Bull, walking rapidly lest his father's shrill whistle might call him back; and in a few moments he had rounded the curve at the police barrack and was safe.

Yes, his mother was hostile to the idea, as he had read from her listless silence. Yet her mistrust pricked him more keenly than his father's pride and he thought coldly how he had watched the faith which was fading down in his soul ageing and strengthening in her eyes. A dim antago-nism gathered force within him and darkened his mind as a cloud against her disloyalty: and when it passed, cloudlike, leaving his mind serene and dutiful towards her again, he was made aware dimly and without regret of a first noiseless sundering of their lives.

The university! So he had passed beyond the challenge of the sentries who had stood as guardians of his boyhood and had sought to keep him among them that he might be subject to them and serve their ends. Pride after satisfaction uplifted him like long slow waves. The end he had been born to serve yet did not see had led him to escape by an unseen path: and now it beckoned to him once more and a new adventure was about to be opened to him. It seemed to him that he heard notes of fitful music leaping upwards a tone and downwards a diminishing fourth, upwards a tone and downwards a major third, like triple-branching flames leaping fitfully, flame after flame, out of a midnight wood. It was an elfin prelude, endless and formless; and, as it grew wilder and faster, the flames leaping out of time, he seemed to hear from under the boughs and grasses wild creatures racing, their feet pattering like rain upon the leaves. Their feet passed in pattering tumult over his mind, the feet of hares and rabbits, the feet of harts and hinds and antelopes, until he heard them no more and remembered only a proud cadence from Newman: —

— Whose feet are as the feet of harts and underneath the everlasting arms. —

The pride of that dim image brought back to his mind the dignity of the office he had refused. All through his boyhood he had mused upon that which he had so often thought to be his destiny and when the moment had come for him to obey the call he had turned aside, obeying a wayward instinct. Now time lay between: the oils of ordination would never anoint his body. He had refused. Why?

He turned seaward from the road at Dollymount and as he passed on to the thin wooden bridge he felt the planks shaking with the tramp of heavily shod feet. A squad of Christian Brothers was on its way back from the Bull and had begun to pass, two by two, across the bridge. Soon the whole bridge was trembling and resounding. The uncouth faces passed him two by two, stained yellow or red or livid by the sea, and as he strove to look at them with ease and indifference, a faint stain of personal shame and commiseration rose to his own face. Angry with himself he tried to hide his face from their eyes by gazing down sideways into the shallow swirling water under the bridge but he still saw a reflection therein of their topheavy silk hats, and humble tapelike collars and loosely hanging clerical clothes.

— Brother Hickey.

Brother Quaid.

Brother MacArdle.

Brother Keogh. —

Their piety would be like their names, like their faces, like their clothes; and it was idle for him to tell himself that their humble and contrite hearts, it might be, paid a far richer tribute of devotion than his had ever been, a gift tenfold more acceptable than his elaborate adoration. It was idle for him to move himself to be generous towards them, to tell himself that if he ever came to their gates, stripped of his pride, beaten and in beggar's weeds, that they would be generous towards him, loving him as themselves. Idle and embittering, finally, to argue, against his own dispassionate certitude, that the commandment of love bade us not to love our neighbours as ourselves with the same amount and intensity of love but to love him as ourselves with the same kind of love.

He drew forth a phrase from his treasure and spoke it softly to himself:

— A day of dappled seaborne clouds. —

The phrase and the day and the scene harmonised in a chord. Words. Was it their colours? He allowed them to glow and fade, hue after hue: sunrise gold, the russet and green of apple orchards, azure of waves, the greyfringed fleece of clouds. No, it was not their colours: it was the poise and balance of the period itself. Did he then love the rhythmic rise and fall of words better than their associations of legend and colour? Or was it that, being as weak of sight as he was shy of mind, he drew less pleasure from the reflection of the glowing sensible world through the prism of a language manycoloured and richly storied than from the contemplation of an inner world of individual emotions mirrored perfectly in a lucid supple periodic prose.

He passed from the trembling bridge on to firm land again. At that instant, as it seemed to him, the air was chilled; and looking askance towards the water he saw a flying squall darkening and crisping suddenly the tide. A faint click at his heart, a faint throb in his throat told him once more of how his flesh dreaded the cold infrahuman odour of the sea: yet he did not strike across the downs on his left but held straight on along the spine of rocks that pointed against the river's mouth.

A veiled sunlight lit up faintly the grey sheet of water where the river was embayed. In the distance along the course of the slowflowing Liffey slender masts flecked the sky and, more distant still, the dim fabric of the city lay prone in haze. Like a scene on some vague arras, old as man's weariness, the image of the seventh city of christendom was visible to him across the timeless air, no older nor more weary nor less patient of subjection than in the days of the thingmote.

Disheartened, he raised his eyes towards the slow drifting clouds, dappled and seaborne. They were voyaging across the deserts of the sky, a host of nomads on the march, voyaging high over Ireland, westward bound. The Europe they had come from lay out there beyond the Irish Sea, Europe of strange tongues and valleyed and woodbegirt and citadelled and of entrenched and marshalled races. He heard a confused music within him as of memories and names which he was almost conscious of but could not capture even for an instant; then the music seemed to recede, to recede, to recede: and from each receding trail of nebulous music there fell always one long-drawn calling note, piercing like a star the dusk of silence. Again! Again! Again! A voice from beyond the world was calling.

— Hello, Stephanos! —

— Here comes The Dedalus! —

— Ao! . . . Eh, give it over, Dwyer, I'm telling you or I'll give you a stuff in the kisser for yourself. . . . Ao! —

— Good man, Towser! Duck him! —

— Come along, Dedalus! Bous Stephanoumenos! Bous Stephaneforos![1] —

— Duck him! Guzzle him now, Towser! —

— Help! Help! . . . Ao! —

He recognised their speech collectively before he distinguished their faces. The mere sight of that medley of wet nakedness chilled him to the bone. Their bodies, corpsewhite or suffused with a pallid golden light or rawly tanned by the sun, gleamed with the wet of the sea. Their divingstone, poised on its rude supports and rocking under their plunges, and the rough-hewn stones of the sloping breakwater over which they scrambled in their horseplay, gleamed with cold wet lustre. The towels

---

[1] [Garlanded ox! Garland-bearing ox!]

with which they smacked their bodies were heavy with cold seawater: and drenched with cold brine was their matted hair.

He stood still in deference to their calls and parried their banter with easy words. How characterless they looked: Shuley without his deep unbuttoned collar, Ennis without his scarlet belt with the snaky clasp, and Connolly without his Norfolk coat with the flapless sidepockets! It was a pain to see them and a sword-like pain to see the signs of adolescence that made repellent their pitiable nakedness. Perhaps they had taken refuge in number and noise from the secret dread in their souls. But he, apart from them and in silence, remembered in what dread he stood of the mystery of his own body.

— Stephanos Dedalos! Bous Stephanoumenos! Bous Stephaneforos! —

Their banter was not new to him and now it flattered his mild proud sovereignty. Now, as never before, his strange name seemed to him a prophecy. So timeless seemed the grey warm air, so fluid and impersonal his own mood, that all ages were as one to him. A moment before the ghost of the ancient kingdom of the Danes had looked forth through the vesture of the hazewrapped city. Now, at the name of the fabulous artificer, he seemed to hear the noise of dim waves and to see a winged form flying above the waves and slowly climbing the air. What did it mean? Was it a quaint device opening a page of some medieval book of prophecies and symbols, a hawklike man flying sunward above the sea, a prophecy of the end he had been born to serve and had been following through the mists of childhood and boyhood, a symbol of the artist forging anew in his workshop out of the sluggish matter of the earth a new soaring impalpable imperishable being?

His heart trembled; his breath came faster and a wild spirit passed over his limbs as though he were soaring sunward. His heart trembled in an ecstasy of fear and his soul was in flight. His soul was soaring in an air beyond the world and the body he knew was purified in a breath and delivered of incertitude and made radiant and commingled with the element of the spirit. An ecstasy of flight made radiant his eyes and wild his breath and tremulous and wild and radiant his windswept limbs.

— One! Two! . . . Look out! —

— O, Cripes, I'm drownded! —

— One! Two! Three and away! —

— The next! The next! —

— One! . . . Uk! —

— Stephaneforos! —

His throat ached with a desire to cry aloud, the cry of a hawk or eagle on high, to cry piercingly of his deliverance to the winds. This was the call of life to his soul not the dull gross voice of the world of duties and despair, not the inhuman voice that had called him to the pale service of the altar. An instant of wild flight had delivered him and the cry of triumph which his lips withheld cleft his brain.

— Stephaneforos! —

What were they now but the cerements shaken from the body of death — the fear he had walked in night and day, the incertitude that had ringed him round, the shame that had abased him within and without — cerements, the linens of the grave?

His soul had arisen from the grave of boyhood, spurning her grave-clothes. Yes! Yes! Yes! He would create proudly out of the freedom and power of his soul, as the great artificer whose name he bore, a living thing, new and soaring and beautiful, impalpable, imperishable.

He started up nervously from the stoneblock for he could no longer quench the flame in his blood. He felt his cheeks aflame and his throat throbbing with song. There was a lust of wandering in his feet that burned to set out for the ends of the earth. On! On! his heart seemed to cry. Evening would deepen above the sea, night fall upon the plains, dawn glimmer before the wanderer and show him strange fields and hills and faces. Where?

He looked northward towards Howth. The sea had fallen below the line of seawrack on the shallow side of the breakwater and already the tide was running out fast along the foreshore. Already one long oval bank of sand lay warm and dry amid the wavelets. Here and there warm isles of sand gleamed above the shallow tide: and about the isles and around the long bank and amid the shallow currents of the beach were lightclad figures, wading and delving.

In a few moments he was barefoot, his stockings folded in his pockets, and his canvas shoes dangling by their knotted laces over his shoulders: and, picking a pointed salteaten stick out of the jetsam among the rocks, he clambered down the slope of the breakwater.

There was a long rivulet in the strand: and, as he waded slowly up its course, he wondered at the endless drift of seaweed. Emerald and black and russet and olive, it moved beneath the current, swaying and turning. The water of the rivulet was dark with endless drift and mirrored the highdrifting clouds. The clouds were drifting above him silently and silently the seatangle was drifting below him; and the grey warm air was still: and a new wild life was singing in his veins.

Where was his boyhood now? Where was the soul that had hung back from her destiny, to brood alone upon the shame of her wounds and in her house of squalor and subterfuge to queen it in faded cerements and in wreaths that withered at the touch? Or, where was he.

He was alone. He was unheeded, happy, and near to the wild heart of life. He was alone and young and wilful and wildhearted, alone amid a waste of wild air and brackish waters and the seaharvest of shells and tangle and veiled grey sunlight and gayclad lightclad figures of children and girls and voices childish and girlish in the air.

A girl stood before him in midstream: alone and still, gazing out to sea. She seemed like one whom magic had changed into the likeness of a strange and beautiful seabird. Her long slender bare legs were delicate as a crane's and pure save where an emerald trail of seaweed had fashioned itself as a sign upon the flesh. Her thighs, fuller and softhued as ivory, were bared almost to the hips where the white fringes of her drawers were like feathering of soft white down. Her slate-blue skirts were kilted boldly about her waist and dovetailed behind her. Her bosom was as a bird's, soft and slight, slight and soft as the breast of some dark-plumaged dove. But her long fair hair was girlish: and girlish, and touched with the wonder of mortal beauty, her face.

She was alone and still, gazing out to sea; and when she felt his presence and the worship of his eyes her eyes turned to him in quiet sufferance of his gaze, without shame or wantonness. Long, long she suffered his gaze and then quietly withdrew her eyes from his and bent them towards the stream, gently stirring the water with her foot hither and thither. The first faint noise of gently moving water broke the silence, low and faint and whispering, faint as the bells of sleep; hither and thither, hither and thither: and a faint flame trembled on her cheek.

— Heavenly God! cried Stephen's soul, in an outburst of profane joy. —

He turned away from her suddenly and set off across the strand. His cheeks were aflame; his body was aglow; his limbs were trembling. On and on and on and on he strode, far out over the sands, singing wildly to the sea, crying to greet the advent of the life that had cried to him.

Her image had passed into his soul for ever and no word had broken the holy silence of his ecstasy. Her eyes had called him and his soul had leaped at the call. To live, to err, to fall, to triumph, to recreate life out of life! A wild angel had appeared to him, the angel of mortal youth and beauty, an envoy from the fair courts of life, to throw open before him in an instant of ecstasy the gates of all the ways of error and glory. On and on and on and on!

He halted suddenly and heard his heart in the silence. How far had he walked? What hour was it?

There was no human figure near him nor any sound borne to him over the air. But the tide was near the turn and already the day was on the wane. He turned landward and ran towards the shore and, running up the sloping beach, reckless of the sharp shingle, found a sandy nook amid a ring of tufted sand knolls and lay down there that the peace and silence of the evening might still the riot of his blood.

He felt above him the vast indifferent dome and the calm processes of the heavenly bodies: and the earth beneath him, the earth that had borne him, had taken him to her breast.

He closed his eyes in the languor of sleep. His eyelids trembled as if they felt the vast cyclic movement of the earth and her watchers, trembled as if they felt the strange light of some new world. His soul was swooning into some new world, fantastic, dim, uncertain as under sea, traversed by cloudy shapes and beings. A world, a glimmer, or a flower? Glimmering and trembling, trembling and unfolding, a breaking light, an opening flower, it spread in endless succession to itself, breaking in full crimson and unfolding and fading to palest rose, leaf by leaf and wave of light by wave of light, every flush deeper than the other.

Evening had fallen when he woke and the sand and arid grasses of his bed glowed no longer. He rose slowly and, recalling the rapture of his sleep, sighed at its joy.

He climbed to the crest of the sandhill and gazed about him. Evening had fallen. A rim of the young moon cleft the pale waste of sky line, the rim of a silver hoop embedded in grey sand: and the tide was flowing in fast to the land with a low whisper of her waves, islanding a few last figures in distant pools.

Chapter V

HE drained his third cup of watery tea to the dregs and set to chewing the crusts of fried bread that were scattered near him, staring into the dark pool of the jar. The yellow dripping had been scooped out like a boghole, and the pool under it brought back to his memory the dark turfcoloured water of the bath in Clongowes. The box of pawn tickets at his elbow had just been rifled and he took up idly one after another in his greasy fingers the blue and white dockets, scrawled and sanded and creased and bearing the name of the pledger as Daly or MacEvoy.

1 Pair Buskins.
1 D. Coat.
3 Articles and White.
1 Man's Pants.

Then he put them aside and gazed thoughtfully at the lid of the box, speckled with louse marks, and asked vaguely:

— How much is the clock fast now?

His mother straightened the battered alarm clock that was lying on its side in the middle of the mantelpiece until its dial showed a quarter to twelve and then laid it once more on its side.

— An hour and twenty five minutes, she said. The right time now is twenty past ten. The dear knows you might try to be in time for your lectures.

— Fill out the place for me to wash, said Stephen.

— Katey, fill out the place for Stephen to wash.

— Booty, fill out the place for Stephen to wash.

— I can't, I'm going for blue. Fill it out, you, Maggie.

When the enamelled basin had been fitted into the well of the sink and the old washing glove flung on the side of it, he allowed his mother to scrub his neck and root into the folds of his ears and into the interstices at the wings of his nose.

125

— Well, it's a poor case, she said, when a university student is so dirty that his mother has to wash him.

— But it gives you pleasure, said Stephen calmly.

An ear splitting whistle was heard from upstairs and his mother thrust a damp overall into his hands, saying:

— Dry yourself and hurry out for the love of goodness.

A second shrill whistle, prolonged angrily, brought one of the girls to the foot of the staircase.

— Yes, father?

— Is your lazy bitch of a brother gone out yet?

— Yes, father.

— Sure?

— Hm!

The girl came back, making signs to him to be quick and go out quietly by the back. Stephen laughed and said:

— He has a curious idea of genders if he thinks a bitch is masculine.

— Ah, it's a scandalous shame for you, Stephen, said his mother, and you'll live to rue the day you set your foot in that place. I know how it has changed you.

— Good morning, everybody, said Stephen, smiling and kissing the tips of his fingers in adieu.

The lane behind the terrace was waterlogged and as he went down it slowly, choosing his steps amid heaps of wet rubbish, he heard a mad nun screeching in the nun's madhouse beyond the wall.

— Jesus! O Jesus! Jesus!

He shook the sound out of his ears by an angry toss of his head and hurried on, stumbling through the mouldering offal, his heart already bitten by an ache of loathing and bitterness. His father's whistle, his mother's mutterings, the screech of an unseen maniac were to him now so many voices offending and threatening to humble the pride of his youth. He drove their echoes even out of his heart with an execration: but, as he walked down the avenue and felt the grey morning light falling about him through the dripping trees and smelt the strange wild smell of the wet leaves and bark, his soul was loosed of her miseries.

The rain laden trees of the avenue evoked in him, as always, memories of the girls and women in the plays of Gerhart Hauptmann; and the memory of their pale sorrows and the fragrance falling from the wet branches mingled in a mood of quiet joy. His morning walk across the city had begun; and he foreknew that as he passed the sloblands of Fairview he would think of the cloistral silverveined prose of Newman; that as he walked along the North Strand Road, glancing idly at the windows of the provision shops, he would recall the dark humour of Guido Cavalcanti and smile; that as he went by Baird's stone cutting works in Talbot Place the spirit of Ibsen would blow through him like a keen wind, a spirit of wayward boyish beauty; and that passing a grimy marine dealer's shop beyond the Liffey he would repeat the song by Ben Jonson which begins:

I was not wearier where I lay.

His mind when wearied of its search for the essence of beauty amid the spectral words of Aristotle or Aquinas turned often for its pleasure to the dainty songs of the Elizabethans. His mind, in the vesture of a doubting monk, stood often in shadow under the windows of that age, to hear the grave and mocking music of the lutenists or the frank laughter of waistcoateers until a laugh too low, a phrase, tarnished by time, of chambering and false honour, stung his monkish pride and drove him on from his lurking-place.

The lore which he was believed to pass his days brooding upon so that it had rapt him from the companionship of youth was only a garner of slender sentences from Aristotle's Poetics and Psychology and a *Synopsis Philosophiæ Scholasticæ ad mentem divi Thomæ*.[1] His thinking was a dusk of doubt and selfmistrust, lit up at moments by the lightnings of intuition, but lightnings of so clear a splendour that in those moments the world perished about his feet as if it had been fire-consumed: and thereafter his tongue grew heavy and he met the eyes of others with unanswering eyes for he felt that the spirit of beauty had folded him round like a mantle and that in reverie at least he had been acquainted with nobility. But, when this brief pride of silence upheld him no longer, he was glad to find himself still in the midst of common lives, passing on his way amid the squalor and noise and sloth of the city fearlessly and with a light heart.

Near the hoardings on the canal he met the consumptive man with the doll's face and the brimless hat coming towards him down the slope of the bridge with little steps, tightly buttoned into his chocolate overcoat, and holding his furled umbrella a span or two from him like a divining road. It must be eleven, he thought, and peered into a dairy to see the time. The clock in the dairy told him that it was five minutes to five but, as he turned away, he heard a clock somewhere near him, but unseen, beating eleven strokes in swift precision. He laughed as he heard it for it made him think of McCann; and he saw him a squat figure in a shooting jacket and breeches and with a fair goatee, standing in the wind at Hopkins' corner, and heard him say:

— Dedalus, you're an anti-social being, wrapped up in yourself. I'm not. I'm a democrat: and I'll work and act for social liberty and equality

---

[1] [*Synopsis of Scholastic Philosophy for the Understanding of St. Thomas.*]

among all classes and sexes in the United States of the Europe of the future.

Eleven! Then he was late for that lecture too. What day of the week was it? He stopped at a newsagent's to read the headline of a placard. Thursday. Ten to eleven, English; eleven to twelve, French; twelve to one, Physics. He fancied to himself the English lecture and felt, even at that distance, restless and helpless. He saw the heads of his classmates meekly bent as they wrote in their notebooks the points they were bidden to note, nominal definitions, essential definitions and examples or dates of birth or death, chief works, a favourable and an unfavourable criticism side by side. His own head was unbent for his thoughts wandered abroad and whether he looked around the little class of students or out of the window across the desolate gardens of the Green an odour assailed him of cheerless cellar damp and decay. Another head than his, right before him in the first benches, was poised squarely above its bending fellows like the head of a priest appealing without humility to the tabernacle for the humble worshippers about him. Why was it that when he thought of Cranly he could never raise before his mind the entire image of his body but only the image of the head and face? Even now against the grey curtain of the morning he saw it before him like the phantom of a dream, the face of a severed head or death-mask, crowned on the brows by its stiff black upright hair as by an iron crown. It was a priestlike face, priestlike in its pallor, in the wide winged nose, in the shadowings below the eyes and along the jaws, priestlike in the lips that were long and bloodless and faintly smiling: and Stephen, remembering swiftly how he had told Cranly of all the tumults and unrest and longings in his soul, day after day and night by night, only to be answered by his friend's listening silence, would have told himself that it was the face of a guilty priest who heard confessions of those whom he had not power to absolve but that he felt again in memory the gaze of its dark womanish eyes.

Through this image he had a glimpse of a strange dark cavern of speculation but at once turned away from it, feeling that it was not yet the hour to enter it. But the night shade of his friend's listlessness seemed to be diffusing in the air around him a tenuous and deadly exhalation; and he found himself glancing from one casual word to another on his right or left in stolid wonder that they had been so silently emptied of instantaneous sense until every mean shop legend bound his mind like the words of a spell and his soul shrivelled up sighing with age as he walked on in a lane among heaps of dead language. His own consciousness of language was ebbing from his brain and trickling into the very words themselves which set to band and disband themselves in wayward rhythms:

The ivy whines upon the wall,
And whines and twines upon the wall,
The yellow ivy upon the wall,
Ivy, ivy up the wall.

Did any one ever hear such drivel? Lord Almighty! Who ever heard of ivy whining on a wall? Yellow ivy: that was all right. Yellow ivory also. And what about ivory ivy?

The word now shone in his brain, clearer and brighter than any ivory sawn from the mottled tusks of elephants. *Ivory, ivoire, avorio, ebur.* One of the first examples that he had learnt in Latin had run: *India mittit ebur;*[1] and he recalled the shrewd northern face of the rector who had taught him to construe the Metamorphoses of Ovid in a courtly English, made whimsical by the mention of porkers and potshreds and chines of bacon. He had learnt what little he knew of the laws of Latin verse from a ragged book written by a Portuguese priest.

Contrahit orator, variant in carmine vates.[2]

The crises and victories and secessions in Roman history were handed on to him in the trite words *in tanto discrimine*[3] and he had tried to peer into the social life of the city of cities through the words *implere ollam denariorum*[4] which the rector had rendered sonorously as the filling of a pot with denaries. The pages of his timeworn Horace never felt cold to the touch even when his own fingers were cold: they were human pages: and fifty years before they had been turned by the human fingers of John Duncan Inverarity and by his brother, William Malcolm Inverarity. Yes, those were noble names on the dusky flyleaf and, even for so poor a Latinist as he, the dusky verses were as fragrant as though they had lain all those years in myrtle and lavender and vervain; but yet it wounded him to think that he would never be but a shy guest at the feast of the world's culture and that the monkish learning, in terms of which he was striving to forge out an esthetic philosophy, was held no higher by the age he lived in than the subtle and curious jargons of heraldry and falconry.

The grey block of Trinity on his left, set heavily in the city's ignorance like a dull stone set in a cumbrous ring, pulled his mind downward; and while he was striving this way and that to free his feet from the fetters of the reformed conscience he came upon the droll statue of the national poet of Ireland.

---

[1] [*India exports ivory.*]
[2] [*Speakers summarize, poets transform in their verses.*]
[3] [*In such a great crisis.*]
[4] [*To fill a jar with coins.*]

He looked at it without anger: for, though sloth of the body and of the soul crept over it like unseen vermin, over the shuffling feet and up the folds of the cloak and around the servile head, it seemed humbly conscious of its indignity. It was a Firbolg in the borrowed cloak of a Milesian; and he thought of his friend Davin, the peasant student. It was a jesting name between them, but the young peasant bore with it lightly:

— Go on, Stevie, I have a hard head, you tell me. Call me what you will.

The homely version of his christian name on the lips of his friend had touched Stephen pleasantly when first heard for he was as formal in speech with others as they were with him. Often, as he sat in Davin's rooms in Grantham Street, wondering at his friend's well made boots that flanked the wall pair by pair and repeating for his friend's simple ear the verses and cadences of others which were the veils of his own longing and dejection, the rude Firbolg mind of his listener had drawn his mind towards it and flung it back again, drawing it by a quiet inbred courtesy of attention or by a quaint turn of old English speech or by the force of its delight in rude bodily skill — for Davin had sat at the feet of Michael Cusack, the Gael — repelling swiftly and suddenly by a grossness of intelligence or by a bluntness of feeling or by a dull stare of terror in the eyes, the terror of soul of a starving Irish village in which the curfew was still a nightly fear.

Side by side with his memory of the deeds of prowess of his uncle Mat Davin, the athlete, the young peasant worshipped the sorrowful legend of Ireland. The gossip of his fellow students which strove to render the flat life of the college significant at any cost loved to think of him as a young fenian. His nurse had taught him Irish and shaped his rude imagination by the broken lights of Irish myth. He stood towards the myth upon which no individual mind had ever drawn out a line of beauty and to its unwieldy tales that divided themselves as they moved down the cycles in the same attitude as towards the Roman catholic religion, the attitude of a dull witted loyal serf. Whatsoever of thought or of feeling came to him from England or by way of English culture his mind stood armed against in obedience to a password: and of the world that lay beyond England he knew only the foreign legion of France in which he spoke of serving.

Coupling this ambition with the young man's humour Stephen had often called him one of the tame geese: and there was even a point of irritation in the name pointed against that very reluctance of speech and deed in his friend which seemed so often to stand between Stephen's mind, eager of speculation, and the hidden ways of Irish life.

One night the young peasant, his spirit stung by the violent or luxurious language in which Stephen escaped from the cold silence of intellectual revolt, had called up before Stephen's mind a strange vision. The two were walking slowly towards Davin's rooms through the dark narrow streets of the poorer jews.

— A thing happened to myself, Stevie, last autumn, coming on winter, and I never told it to a living soul and you are the first person now I ever told it to. I disremember if it was October or November. It was October because it was before I came up here to join the matriculation class.

Stephen had turned his smiling eyes towards his friend's face, flattered by his confidence and won over to sympathy by the speaker's simple accent.

— I was away all that day from my own place over in Buttevant — I don't know if you know where that is — at a hurling match between the Croke's Own Boys and the Fearless Thurles and by God, Stevie, that was the hard fight. My first cousin, Fonsy Davin, was stripped to his buff that day minding cool for the Limericks but he was up with the forwards half the time and shouting like mad. I never will forget that day. One of the Crokes made a woeful wipe at him one time with his caman and I declare to God he was within an aim's ace of getting it at the side of his temple. Oh, honest to God, if the crook of it caught him that time he was done for.

— I am glad he escaped, Stephen had said with a laugh, but surely that's not the strange thing that happened you?

— Well, I suppose that doesn't interest you but leastways there was such noise after the match that I missed the train home and I couldn't get any kind of a yoke to give me a lift for, as luck would have it, there was a mass meeting that same day over in Castletownroche and all the cars in the country were there. So there was nothing for it only to stay the night or to foot it out. Well, I started to walk and on I went and it was coming on night when I got into the Ballyhoura Hills, that's better than ten miles from Kilmallock and there's a long lonely road after that. You wouldn't see the sign of a christian house along the road or hear a sound. It was pitch dark almost. Once or twice I stopped by the way under a bush to redden my pipe and only for the dew was thick I'd have stretched out there and slept. At last, after a bend of the road, I spied a little cottage with a light in the window. I went up and knocked at the door. A voice asked who was there and I answered I was over at the match in Buttevant and was walking back and that I'd be thankful for a glass of water. After a while a young woman opened the door and brought me out a big mug of milk. She was half undressed as if she was going to bed when I knocked and she had her hair hanging; and I thought by her figure and by something in the look of her eyes that she must be carrying a child. She kept me in talk a long while at the door and I thought it strange because her breast and her shoulders were bare. She asked me was I tired and would I like to stop the night there. She said she was all alone in the house and that her husband had gone that morning to Queenstown with his sister to see her off. And all the time she was talking, Stevie, she had her eyes fixed on my face and she stood so close to me I could hear her breathing. When I handed her back the mug at last she took my hand to draw me in over the threshold and said: *'Come in and stay the night here. You've no call to be frightened. There's no one in but ourselves. . . .'* I didn't go in, Stevie. I thanked her and went on my way again, all in a fever. At the first bend of the road I looked back and she was standing at the door.

The last words of Davin's story sang in his memory and the figure of the woman in the story stood forth, reflected in other figures of the peasant women whom he had seen standing in the doorways at Clane as the college cars drove by, as a type of her race and of his own, a batlike soul waking to the consciousness of itself in darkness and secrecy and loneliness and, through the eyes and voice and gesture of a woman without guile, calling the stranger to her bed.

A hand was laid on his arm and a young voice cried:

— Ah, gentleman, your own girl, sir! The first handsel today, gentleman. Buy that lovely bunch. Will you, gentleman?

The blue flowers which she lifted towards him and her young blue eyes seemed to him at that instant images of guilelessness; and he halted till the image had vanished and he saw only her ragged dress and damp coarse hair and hoydenish face.

— Do, gentlemen! Don't forget your own girl, sir!

— I have no money, said Stephen.

— Buy them lovely ones, will you, sir? Only a penny.

— Did you hear what I said? asked Stephen, bending towards her. I told you I had no money. I tell you again now.

— Well, sure, you will some day, sir, please God, the girl answered after an instant.

— Possibly, said Stephen, but I don't think it likely.

He left her quickly, fearing that her intimacy might turn to gibing and wishing to be out of the way before she offered her ware to another, a tourist from England or a student of Trinity. Grafton Street, along which he walked, prolonged that moment of discouraged poverty. In the roadway at the head of the street a slab was set to the memory of Wolfe Tone and he remembered having been present with his father at its laying. He remembered with bitterness that scene of tawdry tribute. There were four French delegates in a brake and one, a plump smiling young man, held, wedged on a stick, a card on which were printed the words: *Vive l'Irlande!*[1]

----

[1] [*Long live Ireland!*]

But the trees in Stephen's Green were fragrant of rain and the rainsodden earth gave forth its mortal odour, a faint incense rising upward through the mould from many hearts. The soul of the gallant venal city which his elders had told him of had shrunk with time to a faint mortal odour rising from the earth and he knew that in a moment when he entered the sombre college he would be conscious of a corruption other than that of Buck Egan and Burnchapel Whaley.

It was too late to go upstairs to the French class. He crossed the hall and took the corridor to the left which led to the physics theatre. The corridor was dark and silent but not unwatchful. Why did he feel that it was not unwatchful? Was it because he had heard that in Buck Whaley's time there was a secret staircase there? Or was the jesuit house extra-territorial and was he walking among aliens? The Ireland of Tone and of Parnell seemed to have receded in space.

He opened the door of the theatre and halted in the chilly grey light that struggled through the dusty windows. A figure was crouching before the large grate and by its leanness and greyness he knew that it was the dean of studies lighting the fire. Stephen closed the door quietly and approached the fireplace.

— Good morning, sir! Can I help you? —

The priest looked up quickly and said:

— One moment now, Mr. Dedalus, and you will see. There is an art in lighting a fire. We have the liberal arts and we have the useful arts. This is one of the useful arts. —

— I will try to learn it — said Stephen.

— Not too much coal — said the dean — working briskly at his task — that is one of the secrets. —

He produced four candle butts from the side pockets of his soutane and placed them deftly among the coals and twisted papers. Stephen watched him in silence. Kneeling thus on the flagstone to kindle the fire and busied with the disposition of his wisps of paper and candle butts he seemed more than ever a humble server making ready the place of sacrifice in an empty temple, a levite of the Lord. Like a levite's robe of plain linen the faded worn soutane draped the kneeling figure of one whom the canonicals or the bellybordered ephod would irk and trouble. His very body had waxed old in lowly service of the Lord — in tending the fire upon the altar, in bearing tidings secretly, in waiting upon worldlings, in striking swiftly when bidden — and yet had remained ungraced by aught of saintly or of prelatic beauty. Nay, his very soul had waxed old in that service without growing towards light and beauty or spreading abroad a sweet odour of her sanctity — a mortified will no more responsive to the thrill of its obedience than was to the thrill of love or combat his ageing body, spare and sinewy, greyed with a silver-pointed down.

The dean rested back on his hunkers and watched the sticks catch. Stephen, to fill the silence, said:

— I am sure I could not light a fire. —

— You are an artist, are you not, Mr Dedalus? — said the dean, glancing up and blinking his pale eyes. — The object of the artist is the creation of the beautiful. What the beautiful is is another question. —

He rubbed his hands slowly and drily over the difficulty.

— Can you solve that question now? — he asked.

— Aquinas — answered Stephen — says *pulcra sunt quæ visa placent.* — [1]

— This fire before us — said the dean — will be pleasing to the eye. Will it therefore be beautiful? —

— In so far as it is apprehended by the sight, which I suppose means here esthetic intellection, it will be beautiful. But Aquinas also says *Bonum est in quod tendit appetitus.*[2] In so far as it satisfies the animal craving for warmth fire is a good. In hell, however, it is an evil. —

— Quite so — said the dean — you have certainly hit the nail on the head. —

He rose nimbly and went towards the door, set it ajar and said:

— A draught is said to be a help in these matters. —

As he came back to the hearth, limping slightly but with a brisk step, Stephen saw the silent soul of a jesuit look out at him from the pale loveless eyes. Like Ignatius he was lame but in his eyes burned no spark of Ignatius' enthusiasm. Even the legendary craft of the company, a craft subtler and more secret than its fabled books of secret subtle wisdom, had not fired his soul with the energy of apostleship. It seemed as if he used the shifts and lore and cunning of the world, as bidden to do, for the greater glory of God, without joy in their handling or hatred of that in them which was evil but turning them, with a firm gesture of obedience, back upon themselves: and for all this silent service it seemed as if he loved not at all the master and little, if at all, the ends he served. *Similiter atque senis baculus,* he was, as the founder would have had him, like a staff in an old man's hand, to be leaned on in the road at nightfall or in stress of weather, to lie with a lady's nosegay on a garden seat, to be raised in menace.

The dean returned to the hearth and began to stroke his chin.

— When may we expect to have something from you on the esthetic question? — he asked.

---

[1] [*Beauty is that which gives pleasure to the eye.*]
[2] [*The good is that which our instincts crave.*]

— From me! — said Stephen in astonishment. — I stumble on an idea once a fortnight if I am lucky. —

— These questions are very profound, Mr Dedalus — said the dean. — It is like looking down from the cliffs of Moher into the depths. Many go down into the depths and never come up. Only the trained diver can go down into those depths and explore them and come to the surface again. —

— If you mean speculation, sir — said Stephen — I also am sure that there is no such thing as free thinking inasmuch as all thinking must be bound by its own laws. —

— Ha! —

— For my purpose I can work on at present by the light of one or two ideas of Aristotle and Aquinas. —

— I see. I quite see your point. —

— I need them only for my own use and guidance until I have done something for myself by their light. If the lamp smokes or smells I shall try to trim it. If it does not give light enough I shall sell it and buy another. —

— Epictetus also had a lamp — said the dean — which was sold for a fancy price after his death. It was the lamp he wrote his philosophical dissertations by. You know Epictetus? —

— An old gentleman — said Stephen coarsely — who said that the soul is very like a bucketful of water. —

— He tells us in his homely way — the dean went on — that he put an iron lamp before a statue of one of the gods and that a thief stole the lamp. What did the philosopher do? He reflected that it was in the character of a thief to steal and determined to buy an earthen lamp next day instead of the iron lamp. —

A smell of molten tallow came up from the dean's candle butts and fused itself in Stephen's consciousness with the jingle of the words, bucket and lamp and lamp and bucket. The priest's voice, too, had a hard jingling tone. Stephen's mind halted by instinct, checked by the strange tone and the imagery and by the priest's face which seemed like an unlit lamp or a reflector hung in a false focus. What lay behind it or within it? A dull torpor of the soul or the dullness of the thundercloud, charged with intellection and capable of the gloom of God?

— I meant a different kind of lamp, sir — said Stephen.

— Undoubtedly — said the dean.

— One difficulty — said Stephen — in esthetic discussion is to know whether words are being used according to the literary tradition or according to the tradition of the marketplace. I remember a sentence of Newman's, in which he says of the Blessed Virgin that she was detained in the full company of the saints. The use of the word in the marketplace is quite different. *I hope I am not detaining you.* —

— Not in the least — said the dean politely.

— No, no — said Stephen, smiling — I mean . . . —

— Yes, yes: I see — said the dean quickly — I quite catch the point: *detain.* —

He thrust forward his under jaw and uttered a dry short cough.

— To return to the lamp — he said — the feeding of it is also a nice problem. You must choose the pure oil and you must be careful when you pour it in not to overflow it, not to pour in more than the funnel can hold. —

— What funnel? — asked Stephen.

— The funnel through which you pour the oil into your lamp. —

— That? — said Stephen. — Is that called a funnel? Is it not a tundish? —

— What is a tundish? —

— That. The . . . the funnel. —

— Is that called a tundish in Ireland? — asked the dean. — I never heard the word in my life. —

— It is called a tundish in Lower Drumcondra — said Stephen, laughing — where they speak the best English. —

— A tundish — said the dean reflectively. — That is a most interesting word. I must look that word up. Upon my word I must. —

His courtesy of manner rang a little false, and Stephen looked at the English convert with the same eyes as the elder brother in the parable may have turned on the prodigal. A humble follower in the wake of clamorous conversions, a poor Englishman in Ireland, he seemed to have entered on the stage of jesuit history when that strange play of intrigue and suffering and envy and struggle and indignity had been all but given through — a late comer, a tardy spirit. From what had he set out? Perhaps he had been born and bred among serious dissenters, seeing salvation in Jesus only and abhoring the vain pomps of the establishment. Had he felt the need of an implicit faith amid the welter of sectarianism and the jargon of its turbulent schisms, six principal men, peculiar people, seed and snake baptists, supralapsarian dogmatists? Had he found the true church all of a sudden in winding up to the end like a reel of cotton some finespun line of reasoning upon insufflation on the imposition of hands or the procession of the Holy Ghost? Or had Lord Christ touched him and bidden him follow, like that disciple who had sat at the receipt of custom, as he sat by the door of some zinc roofed chapel, yawning and telling over his church pence?

The dean repeated the word yet again.

— Tundish! Well now, that is interesting! —

— The question you asked me a moment ago seems to me more interesting. What is that beauty which the artist struggles to express from lumps of earth — said Stephen coldly.

The little word seemed to have turned a rapier point of his sensitiveness against this courteous and vigilant foe. He felt with a smart of dejection that the man to whom he was speaking was a countryman of Ben Jonson. He thought:

— The language in which we are speaking is his before it is mine. How different are the words *home*, *Christ*, *ale*, *master*, on his lips and on mine! I cannot speak or write these words without unrest of spirit. His language, so familiar and so foreign, will always be for me an acquired speech. I have not made or accepted its words. My voice holds them at bay. My soul frets in the shadow of his language. —

— And to distinguish between the beautiful and the sublime — the dean added — to distinguish between moral beauty and material beauty. And to inquire what kind of beauty is proper to each of the various arts. These are some interesting points we might take up. —

Stephen, disheartened suddenly by the dean's firm dry tone, was silent: and through the silence a distant noise of many boots and confused voices came up the staircase.

— In pursuing these speculations — said the dean conclusively — there is, however, the danger of perishing of inanition. First you must take your degree. Set that before you as your first aim. Then, little by little, you will see your way. I mean in every sense, your way in life and in thinking. It may be uphill pedalling at first. Take Mr Moonan. He was a long time before he got to the top. But he got there. —

— I may not have his talent — said Stephen quietly.

— You never know — said the dean brightly. — We never can say what is in us. I most certainly should not be despondent. *Per aspera ad astra.* — [1]

He left the hearth quickly and went towards the landing to oversee the arrival of the first arts' class.

Leaning against the fireplace Stephen heard him greet briskly and impartially every student of the class and could almost see the frank smiles of the coarser students. A desolating pity began to fall like dew upon his easily embittered heart for this faithful servingman of the knightly Loyola, for this half brother of the clergy, more venal than they in speech, more steadfast of soul than they, one whom he would never call his ghostly father: and he thought how this man and his companions had earned the name of worldlings at the hands not of the unworldly only but of the worldly also for having pleaded, during all

---

[1] [*Through adversity, to the stars.*]

their history, at the bar of God's justice for the souls of the lax and the lukewarm and the prudent.

The entry of the professor was signalled by a few rounds of Kentish fire from the heavy boots of those students who sat on the highest tier of the gloomy theatre under the grey cobwebbed windows. The calling of the roll began, and the responses to the names were given out in all tones until the name of Peter Byrne was reached.

— Here! —

A deep base note in response came from the upper tier, followed by coughs of protest along the other benches.

The professor paused in his reading and called the next name:

— Cranly! —

No answer.

— Mr Cranly! —

A smile flew across Stephen's face as he thought of his friend's studies.

— Try Leopardstown! — said a voice from the bench behind.

Stephen glanced up quickly but Moynihan's snoutish face, outlined on the grey light, was impassive. A formula was given out. Amid the rustling of the notebooks Stephen turned back again and said:

— Give me some paper for God's sake. —

— Are you as bad as that? — asked Moynihan with a broad grin.

He tore a sheet from his scribbler and passed it down, whispering:

— In case of necessity any layman or woman can do it. —

The formula which he wrote obediently on the sheet of paper, the coiling and uncoiling calculations of the professor, the spectrelike symbols of force and velocity fascinated and jaded Stephen's mind. He had heard some say that the old professor was an atheist freemason. Oh, the grey dull day! It seemed a limbo of painless patient consciousness through which souls of mathematicians might wander, projecting long slender fabrics from plane to plane of ever rarer and paler twilight, radiating swift eddies to the last verges of a universe ever vaster, farther and more impalpable.

— So we must distinguish between elliptical and ellipsoidal. Perhaps some of you gentlemen may be familiar with the works of Mr W.S. Gilbert. In one of his songs he speaks of the billiard sharp who is condemned to play:

> *On a cloth untrue*
> *With a twisted cue*
> *And elliptical billiard balls.*

— He means a ball having the form of the ellipsoid of the principal axes of which I spoke a moment ago. —

Moynihan leaned down towards Stephen's ear and murmured:

— What price ellipsoidal balls! chase me, ladies, I'm in the cavalry! —

His fellow student's rude humour ran like a gust through the clositer of Stephen's mind, shaking into gay life limp priestly vestments that hung upon the walls, setting them to sway and caper in a sabbath of misrule. The forms of the community emerged from the gust blown vestments, the dean of studies, the portly florid bursar with his cap of grey hair, the president, the little priest with feathery hair who wrote devout verses, the squat peasant form of the professor of economics, the tall form of the young professor of mental science discussing on the landing a case of conscience with his class like a giraffe cropping high leafage among a herd of antelopes, the grave troubled prefect of the sodality, the plump round headed professor of Italian with his rogue's eyes. They came ambling and stumbling, tumbling and capering, kilting their gowns for leap frog, holding one another back, shaken with deep false laughter, smacking one another behind and laughing at their rude malice, calling to one another by familiar nicknames, protesting with sudden dignity at some rough usage, whispering two and two behind their hands.

The professor had gone to the glass cases on the sidewall, from a shelf of which he took down a set of coils, blew away the dust from many points and, bearing it carefully to the table, held a finger on it while he proceeded with his lecture. He explained that the wires in modern coils were of a compound called platinoid lately discovered by F. W. Martino.

He spoke clearly the initials and surname of the discoverer. Moynihan whispered from behind:

— Good old Fresh Water Martin! —

— Ask him — Stephen whispered back with weary humour — if he wants a subject for electrocution. He can have me. —

Moynihan, seeing the professor bend over the coils, rose in his bench and, clacking noiselessly the fingers of his right hand, began to call with the voice of a slobbering urchin:

— Please, teacher! This boy is after saying a bad word, teacher. —

— Platinoid — the professor said solemnly — is preferred to German silver because it has a lower coefficient of resistance by changes of temperature. The platinoid wire is insulated and the covering of silk that insulates it is wound on the ebonite bobbins just where my finger is. If it were wound single an extra current would be induced in the coils. The bobbins are saturated in hot paraffin-wax . . . —

A sharp Ulster voice said from the bench below Stephen:

— Are we likely to be asked questions on applied science? —

The professor began to juggle gravely with the terms pure science and applied science. A heavybuilt student, wearing gold spectacles, stared

with some wonder at the questioner. Moynihan murmured from behind
in his natural voice:

— Isn't MacAlister a devil for his pound of flesh? —

Stephen looked down coldly on the oblong skull beneath him over-
grown with tangled twinecoloured hair. The voice, the accent, the mind
of the questioner offended him and he allowed the offence to carry him
towards wilful unkindness, bidding his mind think that the student's
father would have done better had he sent his son to Belfast to study and
have saved something on the train fare by so doing.

The oblong skull beneath did not turn to meet this shaft of thought
and yet the shaft came back to its bowstring: for he saw in a moment the
student's whey pale face.

— That thought is not mine — he said to himself quickly. — It came
from the comic Irishman in the bench behind. Patience. Can you say
with certitude by whom the soul of your race was bartered and its elect
betrayed — by the questioner or by the mocker? Patience. Remember
Epictetus. It is probably in his character to ask such a question at such a
moment in such a tone and to pronounce the word *science* as a mono-
syllable. —

The droning voice of the professor continued to wind itself slowly
round and round the coils it spoke of, doubling, trebling, quadrupling its
somnolent energy as the coil multiplied its ohms of resistance.

Moynihan's voice called from behind in echo to a distant bell:

— Closing time, gents! —

The entrance hall was crowded and loud with talk. On a table near
the door were two photographs in frames and between them a long roll
of paper bearing an irregular tail of signatures. MacCann went briskly to
and fro among the students, talking rapidly, answering rebuffs and
leading one after another to the table. In the inner hall the dean of
studies stood talking to a young professor, stroking his chin gravely and
nodding his head.

Stephen, checked by the crowd at the door, halted irresolutely. From
under the wide falling leaf of a soft hat Cranly's dark eyes were watching
him.

— Have you signed? — Stephen asked.

Cranly closed his long thinlipped mouth, communed with himself an
instant and answered:

— *Ego habeo.* —[1]
— What is it for? —
— *Quod?* —[2]

---

[1] [*I have.*]
[2] [*What?*]

— What is it for? —

Cranly turned his pale face to Stephen and said blandly and bitterly:

— *Per pax universalis.* — [1]

Stephen pointed to the Tsar's photograph and said:

— He has the face of a besotted Christ. —

The scorn and anger in his voice brought Cranly's eyes back from a calm survey of the walls of the hall.

— Are you annoyed? — he asked.

— No — answered Stephen.

— Are you in bad humour? —

— No. —

— *Credo ut vos sanguinarius mendax estis* — said Cranly — *quia facies vostra monstrat ut vos in damno malo humore estis.* — [2]

Moynihan, on his way to the table, said in Stephen's ear:

— MacCann is in tiptop form. Ready to shed the last drop. Brand new world. No stimulants and votes for the bitches. —

Stephen smiled at the manner of this confidence and, when Moynihan had passed, turned again to meet Cranly's eyes.

— Perhaps you can tell me — he said — why he pours his soul so freely into my ear. Can you? —

A dull scowl appeared on Cranly's forehead. He stared at the table where Moynihan had bent to write his name on the roll; and then said flatly:

— A sugar! —

— *Quis est in malo humore* — said Stephen — *ego aut vos?* — [3]

Cranly did not take up the taunt. He brooded sourly on his judgment and repeated with the same flat force:

— A flaming bloody sugar, that's what he is! —

It was his epitaph for all dead friendships and Stephen wondered whether it would ever be spoken in the same tone over his memory. The heavy lumpish phrase sank slowly out of hearing like a stone through a quagmire. Stephen saw it sink as he had seen many another, feeling its heaviness depress his heart. Cranly's speech, unlike that of Davin, had neither rare phrases of Elizabethan English nor quaintly turned versions of Irish idioms. Its drawl was an echo of the quays of Dublin given back by a bleak decaying seaport, its energy an echo of the sacred eloquence of Dublin given back flatly by a Wicklow pulpit.

---

[1] [*For universal peace.*]

[2] [*I believe you are a bloody liar because your face shows you are in a damned bad humor.*]

[3] [*Who is in a bad humor — me or you?*]

The heavy scowl faded from Cranly's face as MacCann marched briskly towards them from the other side of the hall.

— Here you are! — said MacCann cheerily.

— Here I am! — said Stephen.

— Late as usual. Can you not combine the progressive tendency with a respect for punctuality? —

— That question is out of order — said Stephen. — Next business. —

His smiling eyes were fixed on a silver wrapped tablet of milk chocolate which peeped out of the propagandist's breast-pocket. A little ring of listeners closed round to hear the war of wits. A lean student with olive skin and lank black hair thrust his face between the two, glancing from one to the other at each phrase and seeming to try to catch each flying phrase in his open moist mouth. Cranly took a small grey handball from his pocket and began to examine it closely, turning it over and over.

— Next business? — said MacCann. — Hom! —

He gave a loud cough of laughter, smiled broadly, and tugged twice at the strawcoloured goatee which hung from his blunt chin.

— The next business is to sign the testimonial. —

— Will you pay me anything if I sign? — asked Stephen.

— I thought you were an idealist — said MacCann.

The gipsylike student looked about him and addressed the onlookers in an indistinct bleating voice.

— By hell, that's a queer notion. I consider that notion to be a mercenary notion. —

His voice faded into silence. No heed was paid to his words. He turned his olive face, equine in expression, towards Stephen, inviting him to speak again.

MacCann began to speak with fluent energy of the Tsar's rescript, of Stead, of general disarmament, arbitration in cases of international disputes, of the signs of the times, of the new humanity and the new gospel of life which would make it the business of the community to secure as cheaply as possible the greatest possible happiness of the greatest possible number.

The gipsy student responded to the close of the period by crying:

— Three cheers for universal brotherhood! —

— Go on, Temple — said a stout ruddy student near him. — I'll stand you a pint after. —

— I'm a believer in universal brotherhood — said Temple, glancing about him out of his dark, oval eyes. — Marx is only a bloody cod. —

Cranly gripped his arm tightly to check his tongue, smiling uneasily, and repeated:

— Easy, easy, easy! —

Temple struggled to free his arm but continued, his mouth flecked by a thin foam:

— Socialism was founded by an Irishman and the first man in Europe who preached the freedom of thought was Collins. Two hundred years ago. He denounced priestcraft, the philosopher of Middlesex. Three cheers for John Anthony Collins! —

A thin voice from the verge of the ring replied:

— Pip! pip! —

Moynihan murmured beside Stephen's ear:

— And what about John Anthony's poor little sister:

> *Lottie Collins lost her drawers;*
> *Won't you kindly lend her yours?*

Stephen laughed and Moynihan, pleased with the result, murmured again:

— We'll have five bob each way on John Anthony Collins. —

— I am waiting for your answer — said MacCann briefly.

— The affair doesn't interest me in the least — said Stephen wearily. — You know that well. Why do you make a scene about it? —

— Good! — said MacCann, smacking his lips. — You are a reactionary, then? —

— Do you think you impress me — Stephen asked — when you flourish your wooden sword? —

— Metaphors! — said MacCann bluntly. — Come to facts. —

Stephen blushed and turned aside. MacCann stood his ground and said with hostile humour:

— Minor poets, I suppose, are above such trivial questions as the question of universal peace. —

Cranly raised his head and held the handball between the two students by way of a peaceoffering, saying:

— *Pax super totum sanguinarium globum.* — [1]

Stephen, moving away the bystanders, jerked his shoulder angrily in the direction of the Tsar's image, saying:

— Keep your icon. If you must have a Jesus, let us have a legitimate Jesus. —

— By hell, that's a good one! — said the gipsy student to those about him — that's a fine expression. I like that expression immensely. —

He gulped down the spittle in his throat as if he were gulping down the phrase and, fumbling at the peak of his tweed cap, turned to Stephen, saying:

---

[1] [*Peace over all this bloody globe.*]

— Excuse me, sir, what do you mean by that expression you uttered just now? —

Feeling himself jostled by the students near him, he said to them:

— I am curious to know now what he meant by that expression. —

He turned again to Stephen and said in a whisper:

— Do you believe in Jesus? I believe in man. Of course, I don't know if you believe in man. I admire you, sir. I admire the mind of man independent of all religions. Is that your opinion about the mind of Jesus? —

— Go on, Temple — said the stout ruddy student, returning, as was his wont, to his first idea — that pint is waiting for you. —

— He thinks I'm an imbecile — Temple explained to Stephen — because I'm a believer in the power of mind. —

Cranly linked his arms into those of Stephen and his admirer and said:

— *Nos ad manum ballum jocabimus.* — [1]

Stephen, in the act of being led away, caught sight of MacCann's flushed bluntfeatured face.

— My signature is of no account — he said politely. — You are right to go your way. Leave me to go mine. —

— Dedalus — said MacCann crisply — I believe you're a good fellow but you have yet to learn the dignity of altruism and the responsibility of the human individual. —

A voice said:

— Intellectual crankery is better out of this movement than in it. —

Stephen, recognising the harsh tone of MacAlister's voice, did not turn in the direction of the voice. Cranly pushed solemnly through the throng of students, linking Stephen and Temple like a celebrant attended by his ministers on his way to the altar.

Temple bent eagerly across Cranly's breast and said:

— Did you hear MacAlister what he said? That youth is jealous of you. Did you see that? I bet Cranly didn't see that. By hell, I saw that at once. —

As they crossed the inner hall the dean of studies was in the act of escaping from the student with whom he had been conversing. He stood at the foot of the staircase, a foot on the lowest step, his threadbare soutane gathered about him for the ascent with womanish care, nodding his head often and repeating:

— Not a doubt of it, Mr. Hackett! Very fine! Not a doubt of it!

In the middle of the hall the prefect of the college sodality was speaking earnestly, in a soft querulous voice, with a boarder. As he spoke

---

[1] [*Let's go play handball.*]

he wrinkled a little his freckled brow, and bit, between his phrases, at a tiny bone pencil.

— I hope the matric men will all come. The first arts men are pretty sure. Second arts, too. We must make sure of the newcomers. —

Temple bent again across Cranly, as they were passing through the doorway, and said in a swift whisper:

— Do you know that he is a married man? He was a married man before they converted him. He has a wife and children somewhere. By hell, I think that's the queerest notion I ever heard! Eh? —

His whisper trailed off into sly cackling laughter. The moment they were through the doorway Cranly seized him rudely by the neck and shook him, saying:

— You flaming floundering fool! I'll take my dying bible there isn't a bigger bloody ape, do you know, than you in the whole flaming bloody world! —

Temple wriggled in his grip, laughing still with sly content, while Cranly repeated flatly at every rude shake:

— A flaming flaring bloody idiot! —

They crossed the weedy garden together. The president, wrapped in a heavy loose cloak, was coming towards them along one of the walks, reading his office. At the end of the walk he halted before turning and raised his eyes. The students saluted, Temple fumbling as before at the peak of his cap. They walked forward in silence. As they neared the alley Stephen could hear the thuds of the players' hands and the wet smacks of the ball and Davin's voice crying out excitedly at each stroke.

The three students halted round the box on which Davin sat to follow the game. Temple, after a few moments, sidled across to Stephen and said:

— Excuse me, I wanted to ask you do you believe that Jean Jacques Rousseau was a sincere man? —

Stephen laughed outright. Cranly, picking up the broken stave of a cask from the grass at his feet, turned swiftly and said sternly:

— Temple, I declare to the living God if you say another word, do you know, to anybody on any subject I'll kill you *super spottum*. — [1]

— He was like you, I fancy — said Stephen — an emotional man. —

— Blast him, curse him! — said Cranly broadly. — Don't talk to him at all. Sure, you might as well be talking, do you know, to a flaming chamberpot as talking to Temple. Go home, Temple. For God's sake, go home. —

— I don't care a damn about you, Cranly — answered Temple, moving out of reach of the uplifted stave and pointing at Stephen. — He's

---

[1] [*On the spot.*]

the only man I see in this institution that has an individual mind. —

— Institution! Individual! — cried Cranly. — Go home, blast you, for you're a hopeless bloody man. —

— I'm an emotional man — said Temple. — That's quite rightly expressed. And I'm proud that I'm an emotionalist. —

He sidled out of the alley, smiling slyly. Cranly watched him with a blank expressionless face.

— Look at him! — he said. — Did you ever see such a go-by-the-wall? —

His phrase was greeted by a strange laugh from a student who lounged against the wall, his peaked cap down on his eyes. The laugh, pitched in a high key and coming from a so muscular frame, seemed like the whinny of an elephant. The student's body shook all over and, to ease his mirth, he rubbed both his hands delightedly, over his groins.

— Lynch is awake — said Cranly.

Lynch, for answer, straightened himself and thrust forward his chest.

— Lynch puts out his chest — said Stephen — as a criticism of life. —

Lynch smote himself sonorously on the chest and said:

— Who has anything to say about my girth? —

Cranly took him at the word and the two began to tussle. When their faces had flushed with the struggle they drew apart, panting. Stephen bent down towards Davin who, intent on the game, had paid no heed to the talk of the others.

— And how is my little tame goose? — he asked. — Did he sign, too? —

Davin nodded and said:

— And you, Stevie? —

Stephen shook his head.

— You're a terrible man, Stevie — said Davin, taking the short pipe from his mouth — always alone. —

— Now that you have signed the petition for universal peace — said Stephen — I suppose you will burn that little copybook I saw in your room. —

As Davin did not answer Stephen began to quote:

— Long pace, fianna! Right incline, fianna! Fianna, by numbers, salute, one, two! —

— That's a different question — said Davin. — I'm an Irish nationalist, first and foremost. But that's you all out. You're a born sneerer, Stevie. —

— When you make the next rebellion with hurleysticks — said Stephen — and want the indispensable informer, tell me. I can find you a few in this college. —

— I can't understand you — said Davin. — One time I hear you talk against English literature. Now you talk against the Irish informers. What with your name and your ideas . . . are you Irish at all? —

— Come with me now to the office of arms and I will show you the tree of my family — said Stephen.

— Then be one of us — said Davin. — Why don't you learn Irish? Why did you drop out of the league class after the first lesson? —

— You know one reason why — answered Stephen.

Davin tossed his head and laughed.

— Oh, come now — he said. — Is it on account of that certain young lady and Father Moran? But that's all in your own mind, Stevie. They were only talking and laughing. —

Stephen paused and laid a friendly hand upon Davin's shoulder.

— Do you remember — he said — when we knew each other first? The first morning we met you asked me to show you the way to the matriculation class, putting a very strong stress on the first syllable. You remember? Then you used to address the jesuits as father, you remember? I ask myself about you: *Is he as innocent as his speech?* —

— I'm a simple person — said Davin. — You know that. When you told me that night in Harcourt Street those things about your private life, honest to God, Stevie, I was not able to eat my dinner. I was quite bad. I was awake a long time that night. Why did you tell me those things? —

— Thanks — said Stephen. — You mean I am a monster. —

— No — said Davin — but I wish you had not told me. —

A tide began to surge beneath the calm surface of Stephen's friendliness.

— This race and this country and this life produced me — he said. — I shall express myself as I am. —

— Try to be one of us — repeated Davin. — In your heart you are an Irishman but your pride is too powerful. —

— My ancestors threw off their language and took another — Stephen said. — They allowed a handful of foreigners to subject them. Do you fancy I am going to pay in my own life and person debts they made? What for? —

— For our freedom — said Davin.

— No honourable and sincere man — said Stephen — has given up to you his life and his youth and his affections from the days of Tone to those of Parnell but you sold him to the enemy or failed him in need or reviled him and left him for another. And you invite me to be one of you. I'd see you damned first. —

— They died for their ideals, Stevie — said Davin. — Our day will come yet, believe me. —

Stephen, following his own thought, was silent for an instant.

— The soul is born — he said vaguely — first in those moments I told you of. It has a slow and dark birth, more mysterious than the birth of the body. When the soul of a man is born in this country there are nets flung at it to hold it back from flight. You talk to me of nationality, language, religion. I shall try to fly by those nets. —

Davin knocked the ashes from his pipe.

— Too deep for me, Stevie — he said. — But a man's country comes first. Ireland first, Stevie. You can be a poet or mystic after. —

— Do you know what Ireland is? — asked Stephen with cold violence. — Ireland is the old sow that eats her farrow. —

Davin rose from his box and went towards the players, shaking his head sadly. But in a moment his sadness left him and he was hotly disputing with Cranly and the two players who had finished their game. A match of four was arranged, Cranly insisting, however, that his ball should be used. He let it rebound twice or thrice to his hand and struck it strongly and swiftly towards the base of the alley, exclaiming in answer to its thud:

— Your soul! —

Stephen stood with Lynch till the score began to rise. Then he plucked him by the sleeve to come away. Lynch obeyed, saying:

— Let us eke go, as Cranly has it. —

Stephen smiled at this sidethrust.

They passed back through the garden and out through the hall where the doddering porter was pinning up a notice in the frame. At the foot of the steps they halted and Stephen took a packet of cigarettes from his pocket and offered it to his companion.

— I know you are poor — he said.

— Damn your yellow insolence — answered Lynch.

This second proof of Lynch's culture made Stephen smile again.

— It was a great day for European culture — he said — when you made up your mind to swear in yellow. —

They lit their cigarettes and turned to the right. After a pause Stephen began:

— Aristotle has not defined pity and terror. I have. I say . . . —

Lynch halted and said bluntly:

— Stop! I won't listen! I am sick. I was out last night on a yellow drunk with Horan and Goggins. —

Stephen went on:

— Pity is the feeling which arrests the mind in the presence of whatsoever is grave and constant in human sufferings and unites it with the human sufferer. Terror is the feeling which arrests the mind in the presence of whatsoever is grave and constant in human sufferings and unites it with the secret cause. —

— Repeat — said Lynch.

Stephen repeated the definitions slowly.

— A girl got into a hansom a few days ago — he went on — in London. She was on her way to meet her mother whom she had not seen for many years. At the corner of a street the shaft of a lorry shivered the window of the hansom in the shape of a star. A long fine needle of the shivered glass pierced her heart. She died on the instant. The reporter called it a tragic death. It is not. It is remote from terror and pity according to the terms of my definitions.

— The tragic emotion, in fact, is a face looking two ways, towards terror and towards pity, both of which are phases of it. You see I use the word *arrest*. I mean that the tragic emotion is static. Or rather the dramatic emotion is. The feelings excited by improper art are kinetic, desire or loathing. Desire urges us to possess, to go to something; loathing urges us to abandon, to go from something. The arts which excite them, pornographical or didactic, are therefore improper arts. The esthetic emotion (I used the general term) is therefore static. The mind is arrested and raised above desire and loathing. —

— You say that art must not excite desire — said Lynch — I told you that one day I wrote my name in pencil on the backside of the Venus of Praxiteles in the Museum. Was that not desire? —

— I speak of normal natures — said Stephen. — You also told me that when you were a boy in that charming carmelite school you ate pieces of dried cowdung. —

Lynch broke again into a whinny of laughter and again rubbed both his hands over his groins but without taking them from his pockets.

— O, I did! I did! — he cried.

Stephen turned towards his companion and looked at him for a moment boldly in the eyes. Lynch, recovering from his laughter, answered his look from his humbled eyes. The long slender flattened skull beneath the long pointed cap brought before Stephen's mind the image of a hooded reptile. The eyes, too, were reptilelike in glint and gaze. Yet at that instant, humbled and alert in their look, they were lit by one tiny human point, the window of a shrivelled soul, poignant and selfembittered.

— As for that — Stephen said in polite parenthesis — we are all animals. I also am an animal. —

— You are — said Lynch.

— But we are just now in a mental world — Stephen continued. — The desire and loathing excited by improper esthetic means are really not esthetic emotions not only because they are kinetic in character but also because they are not more than physical. Our flesh shrinks from what it dreads and responds to the stimulus of what it desires by a purely reflex action of the nervous system. Our eyelid closes before we are aware that the fly is about to enter our eye. —

— Not always — said Lynch critically.

— In the same way — said Stephen — your flesh responded to the stimulus of a naked statue but it was, I say, simply a reflex action of the nerves. Beauty expressed by the artist cannot awaken in us an emotion which is kinetic or a sensation which is purely physical. It awakens, or ought to awaken, or induces, or ought to induce, an esthetic stasis, an ideal pity or an ideal terror, a stasis called forth, prolonged and at last dissolved by what I call the rhythm of beauty. —

— What is that exactly? — asked Lynch.

— Rhythm — said Stephen — is the first formal esthetic relation of part to part in any esthetic whole or of an esthetic whole to its part or parts or of any part to the esthetic whole of which it is a part. —

— If that is rhythm — said Lynch — let me hear what you call beauty: and, please remember, though I did eat a cake of cowdung once, that I admire only beauty. —

Stephen raised his cap as if in greeting. Then, blushing slightly, he laid his hand on Lynch's thick tweed sleeve.

— We are right — he said — and the others are wrong. To speak of these things and to try to understand their nature and, having understood it, to try slowly and humbly and constantly to express, to press out again, from the gross earth or what it brings forth, from sound and shape and colour which are the prison gates of our soul, an image of the beauty we have come to understand — that is art. —

They had reached the canal bridge and, turning from their course, went on by the trees. A crude grey light, mirrored in the sluggish water, and a smell of wet branches over their heads seemed to war against the course of Stephen's thought.

— But you have not answered my question — said Lynch — What is art? What is the beauty it expresses? —

— That was the first definition I gave you, you sleepyheaded wretch — said Stephen — when I began to try to think out the matter for myself. Do you remember the night? Cranly lost his temper and began to talk about Wicklow bacon. —

— I remember — said Lynch. — He told us about them flaming fat devils of pigs. —

— Art — said Stephen — is the human disposition of sensible or intelligible matter for an esthetic end. You remember the pigs and forgot that. You are a distressing pair, you and Cranly. —

Lynch made a grimace at the raw grey sky and said:

— If I am to listen to your esthetic philosophy give me at least another cigarette. I don't care about it. I don't even care about women. Damn you and damn everything. I want a job of five hundred a year. You can't get me one. —

Stephen handed him the packet of cigarettes. Lynch took the last one that remained, saying simply:

— Proceed! —

— Aquinas — said Stephen — says that is beautiful the apprehension of which pleases. —

Lynch nodded.

— I remember that — he said — *Pulcra sunt quæ visa placent.* —

— He uses the word *visa* — said Stephen — to cover esthetic apprehensions of all kinds, whether through sight or hearing or through any other avenue of apprehension. This word, though it is vague, is clear enough to keep away good and evil, which excite desire and loathing. It means certainly a stasis and not a kinesis. How about the true? It produces also a stasis of the mind. You would not write your name in pencil across the hypotenuse of a rightangled triangle. —

— No, — said Lynch — give me the hypotenuse of the Venus of Praxiteles. —

— Static therefore — said Stephen — Plato, I believe, said that beauty is the splendour of truth. I don't think that it has a meaning but the true and the beautiful are akin. Truth is beheld by the intellect which is appeased by the most satisfying relations of the intelligible: beauty is beheld by the imagination which is appeased by the most satisfying relations of the sensible. The first step in the direction of truth is to understand the frame and scope of the intellect itself, to comprehend the act itself of intellection. Aristotle's entire system of philosophy rests upon his book of psychology and that, I think, rests on his statement that the same attribute cannot at the same time and in the same connexion belong to and not belong to the same subject. The first step in the direction of beauty is to understand the frame and scope of the imagination, to comprehend the act itself of esthetic apprehension. Is that clear? —

— But what is beauty? — asked Lynch impatiently. — Out with another definition. Something we see and like! Is that the best you and Aquinas can do? —

— Let us take woman — said Stephen. —

— Let us take her! — said Lynch fervently. —

— The Greek, the Turk, the Chinese, the Copt, the Hottentot — said Stephen — all admire a different type of female beauty. That seems to be a maze out of which we cannot escape. I see, however, two ways out. One is this hypothesis: that every physical quality admired by men in women is in direct connexion with the manifold functions of women for the propagation of the species. It may be so. The world, it seems, is drearier than even you, Lynch, imagined. For my part I dislike that way out. It leads to eugenics rather than to esthetic. It leads you out of the maze into a new gaudy lecture room where MacCann, with one hand on *The Origin of Species* and the other hand on the new testament, tells you that you admired the great flanks of Venus because you felt that she would bear you burly offspring and admired her great breasts because you felt that she would give good milk to her children and yours. —

— Then MacCann is a sulphuryellow liar — said Lynch energetically.

— There remains another way out — said Stephen, laughing.

— To wit? — said Lynch.

— This hypothesis — Stephen began.

A long dray laden with old iron came round the corner of Sir Patrick Dun's hospital covering the end of Stephen's speech with the harsh roar of jangled and rattling metal. Lynch closed his ears and gave out oath after oath till the dray had passed. Then he turned on his heel rudely. Stephen turned also and waited for a few moments till his companion's ill-humour had had its vent.

— This hypothesis — Stephen repeated — is the other way out: that, though the same object may not seem beautiful to all people, all people who admire a beautiful object find in it certain relations which satisfy and coincide with the stages themselves of all esthetic apprehension. These relations of the sensible, visible to you through one form and to me through another, must be therefore the necessary qualities of beauty. Now, we can return to our old friend Saint Thomas for another pennyworth of wisdom. —

Lynch laughed.

— It amuses me vastly — he said — to hear you quoting him time after time like a jolly round friar. Are you laughing in your sleeve? —

— MacAlister — answered Stephen — would call my esthetic theory applied Aquinas. So far as this side of esthetic philosophy extends Aquinas will carry me all along the line. When we come to the phenomena of artistic conception, artistic gestation and artistic reproduction, I require a new terminology and a new personal experience. —

— Of course — said Lynch. — After all Aquinas, in spite of his intellect, was exactly a good round friar. But you will tell me about the new personal experience and new terminology some other day. Hurry up and finish the first part. —

— Who knows? — said Stephen, smiling. — Perhaps Aquinas would understand me better than you. He was a poet himself. He wrote a hymn for Maundy Thursday. It begins with the words *Pange lingua gloriosi*.[1]

---

[1] [*Tell, my tongue, the glories.*]

They say it is the highest glory of the hymnal. It is an intricate and soothing hymn. I like it: but there is no hymn that can be put beside that mournful and majestic processional song, the *Vexilla Regis*[1] of Venantius Fortunatus. —

Lynch began to sing softly and solemnly in a deep bass voice:

> *Inpleta sunt quæ concinit*
> *David fideli carmine*
> *Dicendo nationibus*
> *Regnavit a ligno Deus.*[2]

— That's great! — he said, well pleased. — Great music! —

They turned into Lower Mount Street. A few steps from the corner a fat young man, wearing a silk neckcloth, saluted them and stopped.

— Did you hear the results of the exams ? — he asked. — Griffin was plucked. Halpin and O'Flynn are through the home civil. Moonan got fifth place in the Indian. O'Shaughnessy got fourteenth. The Irish fellows in Clark's gave them a feed last night. They all ate curry. —

His pallid bloated face expressed benevolent malice and, as he had advanced through his tidings of success, his small fat encircled eyes vanished out of sight and his weak wheezing voice out of hearing.

In reply to a question of Stephen's his eyes and his voice came forth again from their lurking places.

— Yes, MacCullagh and I — he said. — He's taking pure mathematics and I'm taking constitutional history. There are twenty subjects. I'm taking botany too. You know I'm a member of the field club. —

He drew back from the other two in a stately fashion and placed a plump woollen gloved hand on his breast, from which muttered wheezing laughter at once broke forth.

— Bring us a few turnips and onions the next time you go out — said Stephen drily — to make a stew. —

The fat student laughed indulgently and said:

— We are all highly respectable people in the field club. Last Saturday we went out to Glenmalure, seven of us. —

— With women, Donovan? — said Lynch.

Donovan again laid his hand on his chest and said:

— Our end is the acquisition of knowledge. —

Then he said quickly:

— I hear you are writing some essay about esthetics. —

— Stephen made a vague gesture of denial.

---

[1] [*Banners of the King.*]
[2] [*Fulfilled are those promises David sang in a faithful song, telling the nations God has reigned from the cross.*]

— Goethe and Lessing — said Donovan — have written a lot on that subject, the classical school and the romantic school and all that. The Laocoon interested me very much when I read it. Of course it is idealistic, German, ultra profound. —

Neither of the others spoke. Donovan took leave of them urbanely.

— I must go — he said softly and benevolently — I have a strong suspicion, amounting almost to a conviction, that my sister intended to make pancakes today for the dinner of the Donovan family. —

— Goodbye — Stephen said in his wake. — Don't forget the turnips for me and my mate. —

Lynch gazed after him, his lip curling in slow scorn till his face resembled a devil's mask:

— To think that that yellow pancake eating excrement can get a good job — he said at length — and I have to smoke cheap cigarettes! —

They turned their faces towards Merrion Square and went on for a little in silence.

— To finish what I was saying about beauty — said Stephen — the most satisfying relations of the sensible must therefore correspond to the necessary phases of artistic apprehension. Find these and you find the qualities of universal beauty. Aquinas says: *Ad pulcritudinem tria requiruntur integritas, consonantia, claritas*. I translate it so: *Three things are needed for beauty, wholeness, harmony and radiance*. Do these correspond to the phases of apprehension? Are you following? —

— Of course, I am — said Lynch. — If you think I have an excrementitious intelligence run after Donovan and ask him to listen to you. —

Stephen pointed to a basket which a butcher's boy had slung inverted on his head.

— Look at that basket — he said.

— I see it — said Lynch.

— In order to see that basket — said Stephen — your mind first of all separates the basket from the rest of the visible universe which is not the basket. The first phase of apprehension is a bounding line drawn about the object to be apprehended. An esthetic image is presented to us either in space or in time. What is audible is presented in time, what is visible is presented in space. But temporal or spatial, the esthetic image is first luminously apprehended as selfbounded and selfcontained upon the immeasurable background of space or time which is not it. You apprehended it as *one* thing. You see it as one whole. You apprehend its wholeness. That is *integritas*. —

— Bull's eye! — said Lynch, laughing — Go on. —

— Then — said Stephen — you pass from point to point, led by its formal lines; you apprehend it as balanced part against part within its limits; you feel the rhythm of its structure. In other words, the synthesis of immediate perception is followed by the analysis of apprehension. Having first felt that it is *one* thing you feel now that it is a *thing*. You apprehend it as complex, multiple, divisible, separable, made up of its parts, the result of its parts and their sum, harmonious. That is *consonantia*. —

— Bull's eye again! — said Lynch wittily. — Tell me now what is claritas and you win the cigar. —

— The connotation of the word — Stephen said — is rather vague. Aquinas uses a term which seems to be inexact. It baffled me for a long time. It would lead you to believe that he had in mind symbolism or idealism, the supreme quality of beauty being a light from some other world, the idea of which the matter was but the shadow, the reality of which it was but the symbol. I thought he might mean that *claritas* was the artistic discovery and representation of the divine purpose in anything or a force of generalization which would make the esthetic image a universal one, make it outshine its proper conditions. But that is literary talk. I understand it so. When you have apprehended that basket as one thing and have then analysed it according to its form and apprehended it as a thing you make the only synthesis which is logically and esthetically permissible. You see that it is that thing which it is and no other thing. The radiance of which he speaks in the scholastic *quidditas*, the *whatness* of a thing. This supreme quality is felt by the artist when the esthetic image is first conceived in his imagination. The mind in that mysterious instant Shelley likened beautifully to a fading coal. The instant wherein that supreme quality of beauty, the clear radiance of the esthetic image, is apprehended luminously by the mind which has been arrested by its wholeness and fascinated by its harmony is the luminous silent stasis of esthetic pleasure, a spiritual state very like to that cardiac condition which the Italian physiologist Luigi Galvani, using a phrase almost as beautiful as Shelley's, called the enchantment of the heart. —

Stephen paused and, though his companion did not speak, felt that his words had called up around them a thought enchanted silence.

— What I have said — he began again — refers to beauty in the wider sense of the word, in the sense which the word has in the literary tradition. In the market place it has another sense. When we speak of beauty in the second sense of the term our judgment is influenced in the first place by the art itself and by the form of that art. The image, it is clear, must be set between the mind or senses of the artist himself and the mind or senses of others. If you bear this in memory you will see that art necessarily divides itself into three forms progressing from one to the next. These forms are: the lyrical form, the form wherein the artist presents his image in immediate relation to himself; the epical form, the form wherein he presents his image in mediate relation to himself and to others; the dramatic form, the form wherein he presents his image in immediate relation to others. —

— That you told me a few nights ago — said Lynch — and we began the famous discussion. —

— I have a book at home — said Stephen — in which I have written down questions which are more amusing than yours were. In finding the answers to them I found the theory of the esthetic which I am trying to explain. Here are some questions I set myself: *Is a chair finely made tragic or comic? Is the portrait of Mona Lisa good if I desire to see it? Is the bust of Sir Philip Crampton lyrical, epical or dramatic? If not, why not?* —

— Why not, indeed? — said Lynch, laughing.

— *If a man hacking in fury at a block of wood* — Stephen continued — *make there an image of a cow, is that image a work of art? If not, why not?* —

— That's a lovely one — said Lynch, laughing again. — That has the true scholastic stink. —

— Lessing — said Stephen — should not have taken a group of statues to write of. The art, being inferior, does not present the forms I spoke of distinguished clearly one from another. Even in literature, the highest and most spiritual art, the forms are often confused. The lyrical form is in fact the simplest verbal vesture of an instant of emotion, a rhythmical cry such as ages ago cheered on the man who pulled at the oar or dragged stones up a slope. He who utters it is more conscious of the instant of emotion than of himself as feeling emotion. The simplest epical form is seen emerging out of lyrical literature when the artist prolongs and broods upon himself as the centre of an epical event and this form progresses till the centre of emotional gravity is equidistant from the artist himself and from others. The narrative is no longer purely personal. The personality of the artist passes into the narration itself, flowing round and round the persons and the action like a vital sea. This progress you will see easily in that old English ballad *Turpin Hero*, which begins in the first person and ends in the third person. The dramatic form is reached when the vitality which has flowed and eddied round each person fills every person with such vital force that he or she assumes a proper and intangible esthetic life. The personality of the artist, at first a cry or a cadence or a mood and then a fluid and lambent narrative, finally refines itself out of existence, impersonalizes itself, so to speak. The esthetic image in the dramatic form is life purified in and reprojected from the human imagination. The mystery of esthetic like that of material creation is accomplished. The artist, like the God of the creation, remains within or behind or beyond or above his handiwork, invisible, refined out of existence, indifferent, paring his fingernails. —

— Trying to refine them also out of existence — said Lynch.

A fine rain began to fall from the high veiled sky and they turned into the duke's lawn, to reach the national library before the shower came.

— What do you mean — Lynch asked surlily — by prating about beauty and the imagination in this miserable God forsaken island? No wonder the artist retired within or behind his handiwork after having perpetrated this country. —

The rain fell faster. When they passed through the passage beside the royal Irish academy they found many students sheltering under the arcade of the library. Cranly, leaning against a pillar, was picking his teeth with a sharpened match, listening to some companions. Some girls stood near the entrance door. Lynch whispered to Stephen:

— Your beloved is here. —

Stephen took his place silently on the step below the group of students, heedless of the rain which fell fast, turning his eyes towards her from time to time. She too stood silently among her companions. She has no priest to flirt with, he thought with conscious bitterness, remembering how he had seen her last. Lynch was right. His mind, emptied of theory and courage, lapsed back into a listless peace.

He heard the students talking among themselves. They spoke of two friends who had passed the final medical examination, of the chances of getting places on ocean liners, of poor and rich practices.

— That's all a bubble. An Irish country practice is better. —

— Hynes was two years in Liverpool and he says the same. A frightful hole he said it was. Nothing but midwifery cases. —

— Do you mean to say it is better to have a job here in the country than in a rich city like that? I know a fellow . . . —

— Hynes has no brains. He got through by stewing, pure stewing. —

— Don't mind him. There's plenty of money to be made in a big commercial city. —

— Depends on the practice. —

— *Ego credo ut vita pauperum est simpliciter atrox, simpliciter sanguinarius atrox, in Liverpoolio.* — [1]

Their voices reached his ears as if from a distance in interrupted pulsation. She was preparing to go away with her companions.

The quick light shower had drawn off, tarrying in clusters of diamonds among the shrubs of the quadrangle where an exhalation was breathed forth by the blackened earth. Their trim boots prattled as they

---

[1] [*I believe the life of the poor is simply frightful, simply bloody frightful, in Liverpool.*]

stood on the steps of the colonnade, talking quietly and gaily, glancing at the clouds, holding their umbrellas at cunning angles against the few last raindrops, closing them again, holding their skirts demurely.

And if he had judged her harshly? If her life were a simple rosary of hours, her life simple and strange as a bird's life, gay in the morning, restless all day, tired at sundown? Her heart simple and wilful as a bird's heart?

*   *   *   *

Towards dawn he awoke. O what sweet music! His soul was all dewy wet. Over his limbs in sleep pale cool waves of light had passed. He lay still, as if his soul lay amid cool waters, conscious of faint sweet music. His mind was waking slowly to a tremulous morning knowledge, a morning inspiration. A spirit filled him, pure as the purest water, sweet as dew, moving as music. But how faintly it was inbreathed, how passionlessly, as if the seraphim themselves were breathing upon him! His soul was waking slowly, fearing to awake wholly. It was that windless hour of dawn when madness wakes and strange plants open to the light and the moth flies forth silently.

An enchantment of the heart! The night had been enchanted. In a dream or vision he had known the ecstasy of seraphic life. Was it an instant of enchantment only or long hours and years and ages?

The instant of inspiration seemed now to be reflected from all sides at once from a multitude of cloudy circumstances of what had happened or of what might have happened. The instant flashed forth like a point of light and now from cloud on cloud of vague circumstance confused form was veiling softly its afterglow. O! In the virgin womb of the imagination the word was made flesh. Gabriel the seraph had come to the virgin's chamber. An afterglow deepened within his spirit, whence the white flame had passed, deepening to a rose and ardent light. That rose and ardent light was her strange wilful heart, strange that no man had known or would know, wilful from before the beginning of the world: and lured by that ardent roselike glow the choirs of the seraphim were falling from heaven.

> *Are you not weary of ardent ways,*
> *Lure of the fallen seraphim?*
> *Tell no more of enchanted days.*

The verses passed from his mind to his lips and, murmuring them over, he felt the rhythmic movement of a villanelle pass through them. The roselike glow sent forth its rays of rhyme; ways, days, blaze, praise, raise. Its rays burned up the world, consumed the hearts of men and angels: the rays from the rose that was her wilful heart.

Your eyes have set man's heart ablaze
And you have had your will of him.
Are you not weary of ardent ways?

And then? The rhythm died away, ceased, began again to move and beat. And then? Smoke, incense ascending from the altar of the world.

Above the flame the smoke of praise
Goes up from ocean rim to rim
Tell no more of enchanted days.

Smoke went up from the whole earth, from the vapoury oceans, smoke of her praise. The earth was like a swinging swaying censer, a ball of incense, an ellipsoidal ball. The rhythm died out at once; the cry of his heart was broken. His lips began to murmur the first verses over and over; then went on stumbling through half verses, stammering and baffled; then stopped. The heart's cry was broken.

The veiled windless hour had passed and behind the panes of the naked window the morning light was gathering. A bell beat faintly very far away. A bird twittered; two birds, three. The bell and the bird ceased: and the dull white light spread itself east and west, covering the world, covering the roselight in his heart.

Fearing to lose all, he raised himself suddenly on his elbow to look for paper and pencil. There was neither on the table; only the soup plate he had eaten the rice from for supper and the candlestick with its tendrils of tallow and its paper socket, singed by the last flame. He stretched his arm wearily towards the foot of the bed, groping with his hand in the pockets of the coat that hung there. His fingers found a pencil and then a cigarette packet. He lay back and, tearing open the packet, placed the last cigarette on the window ledge and began to write out the stanzas of the villanelle in small neat letters on the rough cardboard surface.

Having written them out he lay back on the lumpy pillow, murmuring them again. The lumps of knotted flock under his head reminded him of the lumps of knotted horsehair in the sofa of her parlour on which he used to sit, smiling or serious, asking himself why he had come, displeased with her and with himself, confounded by the print of the Sacred Heart above the untenanted sideboard. He saw her approach him in a lull of the talk and beg him to sing one of his curious songs. Then he saw himself sitting at the old piano, striking chords softly from its speckled keys and singing, amid the talk which had risen again in the room, to her who leaned beside the mantelpiece a dainty song of the Elizabethans, a sad and sweet loth to depart, the victory chant of Agincourt, the happy air of Greensleeves. While he sang and she listened, or feigned to listen, his heart was at rest but when the quaint old songs had ended and he heard again the voices in the room he remembered his own sarcasm: the house where young men are called by their christian names a little too soon.

At certain instants her eyes seemed about to trust him but he had waited in vain. She passed now dancing lightly across his memory as she had been that night at the carnival ball, her white dress a little lifted, a white spray nodding in her hair. She danced lightly in the round. She was dancing towards him and, as she came, her eyes were a little averted and a faint glow was on her cheek. At the pause in the chain of hands her hand had lain in his an instant, a soft merchandise.

— You are a great stranger now. —

— Yes. I was born to be a monk. —

— I am afraid you are a heretic. —

— Are you much afraid? —

For answer she had danced away from him along the chain of hands, dancing lightly and discreetly, giving herself to none. The white spray nodded to her dancing and when she was in shadow the glow was deeper on her cheek.

A monk! His own image started forth a profaner of the cloister, a heretic Franciscan, willing and willing not to serve, spinning like Gherardino da Borgo San Donnino, a lithe web of sophistry and whispering in her ear.

No, it was not his image. It was like the image of the young priest in whose company he had seen her last, looking at him out of dove's eyes, toying with the pages of her Irish phrasebook.

— Yes, yes, the ladies are coming round to us. I can see it every day. The ladies are with us. The best helpers the language has. —

— And the church, Father Moran? —

— The church too. Coming round too. The work is going ahead there too. Don't fret about the church. —

Bah! he had done well to leave the room in disdain. He had done well not to salute her on the steps of the library. He had done well to leave her to flirt with her priest, to toy with a church which was the scullery-maid of christendom.

Rude brutal anger routed the last lingering instant of ecstasy from his soul. It broke up violently her fair image and flung the fragments on all sides. On all sides distorted reflections of her image started from his memory: the flower girl in the ragged dress with damp coarse hair and a hoyden's face who had called herself his own girl and begged his handsel, the kitchen-girl in the next house who sang over the clatter of her plates, with the drawl of a country singer, the first bars of *By Killarney's Lakes and Fells*, a girl who had laughed gaily to see him stumble when the iron grating in the footpath near Cork Hill had caught the broken sole of his shoe, a girl he had glanced at, attracted by her small ripe mouth as she passed out of Jacob's biscuit factory, who had cried to him over her shoulder:

— Do you like what you seen of me, straight hair and curly eyebrows? —

And yet he felt that, however he might revile and mock her image, his anger was also a form of homage. He had left the classroom in disdain that was not wholly sincere, feeling that perhaps the secret of her race lay behind those dark eyes upon which her long lashes flung a quick shadow. He had told himself bitterly as he walked through the streets that she was a figure of the womanhood of her country, a batlike soul waking to the consciousness of itself in darkness and secrecy and loneliness, tarrying awhile, loveless and sinless, with her mild lover and leaving him to whisper of innocent transgressions in the latticed ear of a priest. His anger against her found vent in coarse railing at her paramour, whose name and voice and features offended his baffled pride: a priested peasant, with a brother a policeman in Dublin and a brother a potboy in Moycullen. To him she would unveil her soul's shy nakedness, to one who was but schooled in the discharging of a formal rite rather than to him, a priest of the eternal imagination, transmuting the daily bread of experience into the radiant body of everliving life.

The radiant image of the eucharist united again in an instant his bitter and despairing thoughts, their cries arising unbroken in a hymn of thanksgiving.

> *Our broken cries and mournful lays*
> *Rise in one eucharistic hymn*
> *Are you not weary of ardent ways?*
> *While sacrificing hands upraise*
> *The chalice flowing to the brim*
> *Tell no more of enchanted days.*

He spoke the verses aloud from the first lines till the music and rhythm suffused his mind, turning it to quiet indulgence; then copied them painfully to feel them the better by seeing them; then lay back on his bolster.

The full morning light had come. No sound was to be heard: but he knew that all around him life was about to awaken in common noises, hoarse voices, sleepy prayers. Shrinking from that life he turned towards the wall, making a cowl of the blanket and staring at the great overblown scarlet flowers of the tattered wallpaper. He tried to warm his perishing joy in their scarlet glow, imagining a roseway from where he lay upwards to heaven all strewn with scarlet flowers. Weary! Weary! He too was weary of ardent ways.

A gradual warmth, a languorous weariness passed over him, descending along his spine from his closely cowled head. He felt it descend and, seeing himself as he lay, smiled. Soon he would sleep.

He had written verses for her again after ten years. Ten years before she had worn her shawl cowlwise about her head, sending sprays of her warm breath into the night air, tapping her foot upon the glassy road. It was the last tram; the lank brown horses knew it and shook their bells to the clear night in admonition. The conductor talked with the driver, both nodding often in the green light of the lamp. They stood on the steps of the tram, he on the upper, she on the lower. She came up to his step many times between their phrases and went down again and once or twice remained beside him forgetting to go down and then went down. Let be! Let be!

Ten years from that wisdom of children to his folly. If he sent her the verses? They would be read out at breakfast amid the tapping of egg-shells. Folly indeed! Her brothers would laugh and try to wrest the page from each other with their strong hard fingers. The suave priest, her uncle, seated in his armchair would hold the page at arm's length, read it smiling and approve of the literary form.

No, no: that was folly. Even if he sent her the verses she would not show them to others. No, no: she could not.

He began to feel that he had wronged her. A sense of her innocence moved him almost to pity her, an innocence he had never understood till he had come to the knowledge of it through sin, an innocence which she too had not understood while she was innocent or before the strange humiliation of her nature had first come upon her. Then first her soul had begun to live as his soul had when he had first sinned: and a tender compassion filled his heart as he remembered her frail pallor and her eyes, humbled and saddened by the dark shame of womanhood.

While his soul had passed from ecstasy to languor where had she been? Might it be, in the mysterious ways of spiritual life, that her soul at those same moments had been conscious of his homage? It might be.

A glow of desire kindled again his soul and fired and fulfilled all his body. Conscious of his desire she was waking from odorous sleep, the temptress of his villanelle. Her eyes, dark and with a look of languor, were opening to his eyes. Her nakedness yielded to him, radiant, warm odorous and lavish limbed, enfolded him like a shining cloud, enfolded him like water with a liquid life: and like a cloud of vapour or like waters circumfluent in space the liquid letters of speech, symbols of the element of mystery, flowed forth over his brain.

Are you not weary of ardent ways,
Lure of the fallen seraphim?
Tell no more of enchanted days.

Your eyes have set man's heart ablaze
And you have had your will of him.
Are you not weary of ardent ways?

Above the flame the smoke of praise
Goes up from ocean rim to rim.
Tell no more of enchanted days.

Our broken cries and mournful lays
Rise in one eucharistic hymn.
Are you not weary of ardent ways?

While sacrificing hands upraise
The chalice flowing to the brim.
Tell no more of enchanted days.

And still you hold our longing gaze
With languorous look and lavish limb!
Are you not weary of ardent ways?
Tell no more of enchanted days.

*   *   *   *

What birds were they? He stood on the steps of the library to look at
them, leaning wearily on his ashplant. They flew round and round the
jutting shoulder of a house in Molesworth Street. The air of the late
March evening made clear their flight, their dark darting quivering
bodies flying clearly against the sky as against a limp hung cloth of
smoky tenuous blue.

He watched their flight; bird after bird: a dark flash, a swerve, a flutter
of wings. He tried to count them before all their darting quivering bodies
passed: Six, ten, eleven: and wondered were they odd or even in number. Twelve, thirteen: for two came wheeling down from the upper sky.
They were flying high and low but ever round and round in straight and
curving lines and ever flying from left to right, circling about a temple
of air.

He listened to the cries: like the squeak of mice behind the wainscot:
a shrill twofold note. But the notes were long and shrill and whirring,
unlike the cry of vermin, falling a third or a fourth and trilled as the
flying beaks clove the air. Their cry was shrill and clear and fine and
falling like threads of silken light unwound from whirring spools.

The inhuman clamour soothed his ears in which his mother's sobs and reproaches murmured insistently and the dark frail quivering bodies wheeling and fluttering and swerving round an airy temple of the tenuous sky soothed his eyes which still saw the image of his mother's face.

Why was he gazing upwards from the steps of the porch, hearing their shrill twofold cry, watching their flight? For an augury of good or evil? A phrase of Cornelius Agrippa flew through his mind and then there flew hither and thither shapeless thoughts from Swedenborg on the correspondence of birds to things of the intellect and of how the creatures of the air have their knowledge and know their times and seasons because they, unlike man, are in the order of their life and have not perverted that order by reason.

And for ages men had gazed upward as he was gazing at birds in flight. The colonnade above him made him think vaguely of an ancient temple and the ashplant on which he leaned wearily of the curved stick of an augur. A sense of fear of the unknown moved in the heart of his weariness, a fear of symbols and portents, of the hawklike man whose name he bore soaring out of his captivity on osier woven wings, of Thoth, the god of writers, writing with a reed upon a tablet and bearing on his narrow ibis head the cusped moon.

He smiled as he thought of the god's image, for it made him think of a bottle-nosed judge in a wig, putting commas into a document which he held at arm's length and he knew that he would not have remembered the god's name but that it was like an Irish oath. It was folly. But was it for this folly that he was about to leave for ever the house of prayer and prudence into which he had been born and the order of life out of which he had come?

They came back with shrill cries over the jutting shoulder of the house, flying darkly against the fading air. What birds were they? He thought that they must be swallows who had come back from the south. Then he was to go away? For they were birds ever going and coming, building ever an unlasting home under the eaves of men's houses and ever leaving the homes they had built to wander.

> *Bend down your faces, Oona and Aleel,*
> *I gaze upon them as the swallow gazes*
> *Upon the nest under the eave before*
> *He wander the loud waters.*

A soft liquid joy like the noise of many waters flowed over his memory and he felt in his heart the soft peace of silent spaces of fading tenuous sky above the waters, of oceanic silence, of swallows flying through the seadusk over the flowing waters.

A soft liquid joy flowed through the words where the soft long vowels hurtled noiselessly and fell away, lapping and flowing back and ever shaking the white bells of their waves in mute chime and mute peal and soft low swooning cry; and he felt that the augury he had sought in the wheeling darting birds and in the pale space of sky above him had come forth from his heart like a bird from a turret quietly and swiftly.

Symbol of departure or of loneliness? The verses crooned in the ear of his memory composed slowly before his remembering eyes the scene of the hall on the night of the opening of the national theatre. He was alone at the side of the balcony, looking out of jaded eyes at the culture of Dublin in the stalls and at the tawdry scenecloths and human dolls framed by the garish lamps of the stage. A burly policeman sweated behind him and seemed at every moment about to act. The catcalls and hisses and mocking cries ran in rude gusts round the hall from his scattered fellow students.

— A libel on Ireland! —
— Made in Germany —
— Blasphemy! —
— We never sold our faith! —
— We want no amateur atheist. —
— We want no budding buddhists. —

A sudden swift hiss fell from the windows above him and he knew that the electric lamps had been switched on in the reader's room. He turned into the pillared hall, now calmly lit, went up the staircase and passed in through the clicking turnstile.

Cranly was sitting over near the dictionaries. A thick book, opened at the frontispiece, lay before him on the wooden rest. He leaned back in his chair, inclining his ear like that of a confessor to the face of the medical student who was reading to him a problem from the chess page of a journal. Stephen sat down at his right and the priest at the other side of the table closed his copy of *The Tablet* with an angry snap and stood up.

Cranly gazed after him blandly and vaguely. The medical student went on in a softer voice:

— Pawn to king's fourth. —
— We had better go, Dixon — said Stephen in warning. — He has gone to complain. —

Dixon folded the journal and rose with dignity, saying:

— Our men retired in good order. —
— With guns and cattle — added Stephen, pointing to the titlepage of Cranly's book on which was written *Diseases of the Ox*.

As they passed through a lane of the tables Stephen said:

— Cranly, I want to speak to you. —

Cranly did not answer or turn. He laid his book on the counter and passed out, his well shod feet sounding flatly on the floor. On the staircase he paused and gazing absently at Dixon repeated:

— Pawn to king's bloody fourth. —

— Put it that way if you like — Dixon said.

He had a quiet toneless voice and urbane manners and on a finger of his plump clean hand he displayed at moments a signet ring.

As they crossed the hall a dwarfish stature came towards them. Under the dome of his tiny hat his unshaven face began to smile with pleasure and he was heard to murmur. The eyes were melancholy as those of a monkey.

— Good evening, gentlemen — said the stubble-grown monkeyish face.

— Warm weather for March — said Cranly. — They have the windows open upstairs. —

Dixon smiled and turned his ring. The blackish monkey-puckered face pursed its human mouth with gentle pleasure and its voice purred:

— Delightful weather for March. Simply delightful. —

— There are two nice young ladies upstairs, captain, tired of waiting — Dixon said.

Cranly smiled and said kindly:

— The captain has only one love: Sir Walter Scott. Isn't that so, captain? —

— What are you reading now, captain? — Dixon asked. — *The Bride of Lammermoor?* —

— I love old Scott — the flexible lips said — I think he writes something lovely. There is no writer can touch Sir Walter Scott. —

He moved a thin shrunken brown hand gently in the air in time to his praise and his thin quick eyelids beat often over his sad eyes.

Sadder to Stephen's ear was his speech: a genteel accent, low and moist, marred by errors: and, listening to it, he wondered was the story true and was the thin blood that flowed in his shrunken frame noble and come of an incestuous love?

The park trees were heavy with rain and rain fell still and ever in the lake, lying grey like a shield. A game of swans flew there and the water and the shore beneath were fouled with their greenwhite slime. They embraced softly, impelled by the grey rainy light, the wet silent trees, the shield like witnessing lake, the swans. They embraced without joy or passion, his arm about his sister's neck. A grey woollen cloak was wrapped athwart her from her shoulder to her waist: and her fair head was bent in willing shame. He had loose redbrown hair and tender shapely strong freckled hands. Face? There was no face seen. The brother's face was bent upon her fair rain fragrant hair. The hand freckled and strong and shapely and caressing was Davin's hand.

He frowned angrily upon his thought and on the shrivelled mannikin who had called it forth. His father's gibes at the Bantry gang leaped out of his memory. He held them at a distance and brooded uneasily on his own thought again. Why were they not Cranly's hands? Had Davin's simplicity and innocence stung him more secretly?

He walked on across the hall with Dixon, leaving Cranly to take leave elaborately of the dwarf.

Under the colonnade Temple was standing in the midst of a little group of students. One of them cried:

— Dixon, come over till you hear. Temple is in grand form. —

Temple turned on him his dark gipsy eyes.

— You're a hypocrite, O'Keeffe — he said. — And Dixon is a smiler. By hell, I think that's a good literary expression. —

He laughed slily, looking in Stephen's face, repeating:

— By hell, I'm delighted with that name. A smiler. —

A stout student who stood below them on the steps said:

— Come back to the mistress, Temple. We want to hear about that. —

— He had, faith — Temple said. — And he was a married man too. And all the priests used to be dining there. By hell, I think they all had a touch. —

— We shall call it riding a hack to spare the hunter — said Dixon.

— Tell us, Temple — O'Keeffe said — how many quarts of porter have you in you? —

— All your intellectual soul is in that phrase, O'Keeffe — said Temple with open scorn.

He moved with a shambling gait round the group and spoke to Stephen.

— Did you know that the Forsters are the kings of Belgium? — he asked.

Cranly came out through the door of the entrance hall, his hat thrust back on the nape of his neck and picking his teeth with care.

— And here's the wiseacre — said Temple. — Do you know that about the Forsters? —

He paused for an answer. Cranly dislodged a fig seed from his teeth on the point of his rude toothpick and gazed at it intently.

— The Forster family — Temple said — is descended from Baldwin the First, king of Flanders. He was called the Forester. Forester and Forster, are the same name. A descendant of Baldwin the First, captain Francis Forster, settled in Ireland and married the daughter of the last chieftain of Clanbrassil. Then there are the Blake Forsters. That's a different branch. —

— From Baldhead, king of Flanders. — Cranly repeated, rooting again deliberately at his gleaming uncovered teeth.

— Where did you pick up all that history? — O'Keeffe asked.

— I know all the history of your family too — Temple said, turning to Stephen. — Do you know what Giraldus Cambrensis says about your family? —

— Is he descended from Baldwin too? — asked a tall consumptive student with dark eyes.

— Baldhead — Cranly repeated, sucking at a crevice in his teeth.

— *Pernobilis et pervetusta familia*[1] — Temple said to Stephen.

The stout student who stood below them on the steps farted briefly. Dixon turned towards him saying in a soft voice:

— Did an angel speak?

Cranly turned also and said vehemently but without anger:

— Goggins, you're the flamingest dirty devil I ever met, do you know. —

— I had it on my mind to say that — Goggins answered firmly. — It did no one any harm, did it? —

— We hope — Dixon said suavely — that it was not of the kind known to science as a *paulo post futurum*. — [2]

— Didn't I tell you he was a smiler? — said Temple, turning right and left. — Didn't I give him that name? —

— You did. We're not deaf — said the tall consumptive.

Cranly still frowned at the stout student below him. Then, with a snort of disgust, he shoved him violently down the steps.

— Go away from here — he said rudely. — Go away, you stinkpot. And you are a stinkpot. —

Goggins skipped down on to the gravel and at once returned to his place with good humour. Temple turned back to Stephen and asked:

— Do you believe in the law of heredity? —

— Are you drunk or what are you or what are you trying to say? — asked Cranly, facing round on him with an expression of wonder.

— The most profound sentence ever written — Temple said with enthusiasm — is the sentence at the end of the zoology. Reproduction is the beginning of death. —

He touched Stephen timidly at the elbow and said eagerly:

— Do you feel how profound that is because you are a poet? —

Cranly pointed his long forefinger.

— Look at him! — he said with scorn to the others — Look at Ireland's hope! —

They laughed at his words and gesture. Temple turned on him bravely, saying:

— Cranly, you're always sneering at me. I can seen that. But I am as

---

[1] [A *very noble and ancient family.*]

[2] [A Latin phrase signifying the future perfect tense in Greek.]

good as you any day. Do you know what I think about you now as
compared with myself? —

— My dear man — said Cranly urbanely — you are incapable, do
you know, absolutely incapable of thinking. —

— But do you know — Temple went on — what I think of you and of
myself compared together? —

— Out with it, Temple! — the stout student cried from the steps. —
Get it out in bits! —

Temple turned right and left, making sudden feeble gestures as he
spoke.

— I'm a ballocks — he said, shaking his head in despair — I am and I
know am. And I admit it that I am. —

Dixon patted him lightly on the shoulder and said mildly:

— And it does you every credit, Temple. —

— But he — Temple said, pointing to Cranly — he is a ballocks, too,
like me. Only he doesn't know it. And that's the only difference, I see. —

A burst of laughter covered his words. But he turned again to Stephen
and said with a sudden eagerness:

— That word is a most interesting word. That's the only English dual
number. Did you know? —

— Is it? — Stephen said vaguely.

He was watching Cranly's firm featured suffering face, lit up now by a
smile of false patience. The gross name had passed over it like foul water
poured over an old stone image, patient of injuries: and, as he watched
him, he saw him raise his hat in salute and uncover the black hair that
stood up stiffly from his forehead like an iron crown.

She passed out from the porch of the library and bowed across
Stephen in reply to Cranly's greeting. He also? Was there not a slight
flush on Cranly's cheek? Or had it come forth at Temple's words? The
light had waned. He could not see.

Did that explain his friend's listless silence, his harsh comments, the
sudden intrusions of rude speech with which he had shattered so often
Stephen's ardent wayward confessions? Stephen had forgiven freely for
he had found this rudeness also in himself. And he remembered an
evening when he had dismounted from a borrowed creaking bicycle to
pray to God in a wood near Malahide. He had lifted up his arms and
spoken in ecstasy to the sombre nave of the trees, knowing that he stood
on holy ground and in a holy hour. And when two constabulary men
had come into sight round a bend in the gloomy road he had broken off
his prayer to whistle loudly an air from the last pantomime.

He began to beat the frayed end of his ashplant against the base of a
pillar. Had Cranly not heard him? Yet he could wait. The talk about him
ceased for a moment: and a soft hiss fell again from a window above. But

no other sound was in the air and the swallows whose flight had followed with idle eyes were sleeping.

She had passed through the dusk. And therefore the air was silent save for one soft hiss that fell. And therefore the tongues about him had ceased their babble. Darkness was falling.

Darkness falls from the air.

A trembling joy, lambent as a faint light, played like a fairy host around him. But why? Her passage through the darkening air or the verse with its black vowels and its opening sound, rich and lutelike?

He walked away slowly towards the deeper shadows at the end of the colonnade, beating the stone softly with his stick to hide his revery from the students whom he had left: and allowed his mind to summon back to itself the age of Dowland and Byrd and Nash.

Eyes, opening from the darkness of desire, eyes that dimmed the breaking east. What was their languid grace but the softness of chambering? And what was their shimmer but the shimmer of the scum that mantled the cesspool of the court of a slobbering Stuart. And he tasted in the language of memory ambered wines, dying fallings of sweet airs, the proud pavan: and saw with the eyes of memory kind gentlewomen in Covent Garden wooing from their balconies with sucking mouths and the pox fouled wenches of the taverns and young wives that, gaily yielding to their ravishers, clipped and clipped again.

The images he had summoned gave him no pleasure. They were secret and enflaming but her image was not entangled by them. That was not the way to think of her. It was not even the way in which he thought of her. Could his mind then not trust itself? Old phrases, sweet only with a disinterred sweetness like the fig seeds Cranly rooted out of his gleaming teeth.

It was not thought nor vision, though he knew vaguely that her figure was passing homeward through the city. Vaguely first and then more sharply he smelt her body. A conscious unrest seethed in his blood. Yes, it was her body he smelt: a wild and languid smell: the tepid limbs over which his music had flowed desirously and the secret soft linen upon which her flesh distilled odour and a dew.

A louse crawled over the nape of his neck and, putting his thumb and forefinger deftly beneath his loose collar, he caught it. He rolled its body, tender yet brittle as a grain of rice, between thumb and finger for an instant before he let it fall from him and wondered would it live or die. There came to his mind a curious phrase from Cornelius a Lapide which said that the lice born of human sweat were not created by God with the other animals on the sixth day. But the tickling of the skin of his neck made his mind raw and red. The life of his body, ill clad, ill fed, louse eaten, made him close his eyelids in a sudden spasm of despair: and in the darkness he saw the brittle bright bodies of lice falling from the air and turning often as they fell. Yes; and it was not darkness that fell from the air. It was brightness.

Brightness falls from the air.

He had not even remembered rightly Nash's line. All the images it had awakened were false. His mind bred vermin. His thoughts were lice born of the sweat of sloth.

He came back quickly along the colonnade towards the group of students. Well then let her go and be damned to her! She could love some clean athlete who washed himself every morning to the waist and had black hair on his chest. Let her.

Cranly had taken another dried fig from the supply in his pocket and was eating it slowly and noisily. Temple sat on the pediment of a pillar, leaning back, his cap pulled down on his sleepy eyes. A squat young man came out of the porch, a leather portfolio tucked under his armpit. He marched towards the group, striking the flags with the heels of his boots and with the ferrule of his heavy umbrella. Then, raising the umbrella in salute, he said to all:

— Good evening, sirs. —

He stuck the flags again and tittered while his head trembled with a slight nervous movement. The tall consumptive student and Dixon and O'Keeffe were speaking in Irish and did not answer him. Then, turning to Cranly, he said:

— Good evening, particularly to you. —

He moved the umbrella in indication and tittered again. Cranly, who was still chewing the fig, answered with loud movements of his jaws.

— Good? Yes. It is a good evening. —

The squat student looked at him seriously and shook his umbrella gently and reprovingly.

— I can see — he said — that you are about to make obvious remarks. —

— Um — Cranly answered, holding out what remained of the half chewed fig and jerking it towards the squat student's mouth in sign that he should eat.

The squat student did not eat it but, indulging his special humour, said gravely, still tittering and prodding his phrase with his umbrella:

— Do you intend that . . . —

He broke off, pointed bluntly to the munched pulp of the fig and said loudly:

— I allude to that. —

— Um — Cranly said as before.

— Do you intend that now — the squat student said — as *ipso facto* or, let us say, as so to speak? —

Dixon turned aside from his group, saying:

— Goggins was waiting for you, Glynn. He has gone round to the Adelphi to look for you and Moynihan. What have you there? — he asked, tapping the portfolio under Glynn's arm.

— Examination papers — Glynn answered. — I give them monthly examinations to see that they are profiting by my tuition. —

He also tapped the portfolio and coughed gently and smiled.

— Tuition! — said Cranly rudely. — I suppose you mean the bare-footed children that are taught by a bloody ape like you. God help them! —

He bit off the rest of the fig and flung away the butt.

— I suffer little children to come unto me — Glynn said amiably.

— A bloody ape — Cranly repeated with emphasis — and a blasphemous bloody ape! —

Temple stood up and, pushing past Cranly addressed Glynn:

— That phrase you said now — he said — is from the new testament about suffer the children to come to me. —

— Go to sleep again, Temple — said O'Keeffe.

— Very well, then — Temple continued, still addressing Glynn — and if Jesus suffered the children to come why does the church send them all to hell if they die unbaptised? Why is that? —

— Were you baptised yourself, Temple? — the consumptive student asked.

— But why are they sent to hell if Jesus said they were all to come? — Temple said, his eyes searching Glynn's eyes.

Glynn coughed and said gently, holding back with difficulty the nervous titter in his voice and moving his umbrella at every word:

— And, as you remark, if it is thus I ask emphatically whence comes this thusness. —

— Because the church is cruel like all old sinners — Temple said.

— Are you quite orthodox on that point, Temple? — Dixon said suavely.

— Saint Augustine says that about unbaptised children going to hell — Temple answered — because he was a cruel old sinner too. —

— I bow to you — Dixon said — but I had the impression that limbo existed for such cases. —

— Don't argue with him, Dixon — Cranly said brutally. — Don't talk to him or look at him. Lead him home with a sugan the way you'd lead a bleating goat. —

— Limbo! — Temple cried. — That's a fine invention too. Like hell. —

— But with the unpleasantness left out — Dixon said.

He turned smiling to the others and said:

— I think I am voicing the opinions of all present in saying so much. —

— You are — Glynn said in a firm tone. — On that point Ireland is united. —

He struck the ferrule of his umbrella on the stone floor of the colonnade.

— Hell — Temple said. — I can respect that invention of the grey spouse of Satan. Hell is Roman, like the walls of the Romans, strong and ugly. But what is limbo? —

— Put him back into the perambulator, Cranly — O'Keeffe called out.

Cranly made a swift step towards Temple, halted, stamping his foot, crying as if to a fowl:

— Hoosh! —

Temple moved away nimbly.

— Do you know what limbo is? — he cried. — Do you know what we call a notion like that in Roscommon? —

— Hoosh! Blast you! — Cranly cried, clapping his hands.

— Neither my arse nor my elbow! — Temple cried out scornfully. — And that's what I call limbo. —

— Give us that stick here — Cranly said.

He snatched the ashplant roughly from Stephen's hand and sprang down the steps: but Temple, hearing him move in pursuit, fled through the dusk like a wild creature, nimble and fleet footed. Cranly's heavy boots were heard loudly charging across the quadrangle and then returning heavily, foiled and spurning the gavel at each step.

His step was angry and with an angry abrupt gesture he thrust the stick back into Stephen's hand. Stephen felt that his anger had another cause, but feigning patience, touched his arm slightly and said quietly:

— Cranly, I told you I wanted to speak to you. Come away. —

Cranly looked at him for a few moments and asked:

— Now? —

— Yes, now — Stephen said — We can't speak here. Come away. —

They crossed the quadrangle together without speaking. The bird call from Siegfried whistled softly followed them from the steps of the porch. Cranly turned: and Dixon, who had whistled, called out:

— Where are you fellows off to? What about that game, Cranly? —

They parleyed in shouts across the still air about a game of billiards to be played in the Adelphi hotel. Stephen walked on alone and out into the quiet of Kildare Street opposite Maple's hotel he stood to wait, patient again. The name of the hotel, a colourless polished wood, and its colourless front stung him like a glance of polite disdain. He stared angrily back at the softly lit drawingroom of the hotel in which he imagined the sleek lives of the patricians of Ireland housed in calm. They thought of army commissions and land agents: peasants greeted them along the roads in the country: they knew the names of certain French dishes and gave orders to jarvies in highpitched provincial voices which pierced through their skintight accents.

How could he hit their conscience or how cast his shadow over the imaginations of their daughters, before their squires begat upon them, that they might breed a race less ignoble than their own? And under the deepened dusk he felt the thoughts and desires of the race to which he belonged flitting like bats, across the dark country lanes, under trees by the edges of streams and near the pool mottled bogs. A woman had waited in the doorway as Davin had passed by at night and, offering him a cup of milk, had all but wooed him to her bed: for Davin had the mild eyes of one who could be secret. But him no woman's eyes had wooed.

His arm was taken in a strong grip and Cranly's voice said:

— Let us eke go. —

They walked southward in silence. Then Cranly said:

— That blithering idiot, Temple! I swear to Moses, do you know, that I'll be the death of that fellow one time. —

But his voice was no longer angry and Stephen wondered was he thinking of her greeting to him under the porch.

They turned to the left and walked on as before. When they had gone on so far for some time Stephen said:

— Cranly, I had an unpleasant quarrel this evening. —

— With your people? — Cranly asked.

— With my mother. —

— About religion? —

— Yes — Stephen answered.

After a pause Cranly asked:

— What age is your mother? —

— Not old — Stephen said. — She wishes me to make my easter duty. —

— And will you? —

— I will not — Stephen said.

— Why not? — Cranly said.

— I will not serve — answered Stephen.

— That remark was made before — Cranly said calmly.

— It is made behind now — said Stephen hotly.

Cranly pressed Stephen's arm, saying:

— Go easy, my dear man. You're an excitable bloody man, do you know. —

He laughed nervously as he spoke and, looking up into Stephen's face with moved and friendly eyes, said:

— Do you know that you are an excitable man? —

— I daresay I am — said Stephen, laughing also.

Their minds, lately estranged, seemed suddenly to have been drawn closer, one to the other.

— Do you believe in the eucharist? — Cranly asked.

— I do not — Stephen said.

— Do you disbelieve then? —

— I neither believe in it nor disbelieve in it — Stephen answered.

— Many persons have doubts, even religious persons, yet they overcome them or put them aside — Cranly said. — Are your doubts on that point too strong? —

— I do not wish to overcome them — Stephen answered.

Cranly, embarrassed for a moment, took another fig from his pocket and was about to eat it when Stephen said:

— Don't, please. You cannot discuss this question with your mouth full of chewed fig. —

Cranly examined the fig by the light of a lamp under which he halted. Then he smelt it with both nostrils, bit a tiny piece, spat it out and threw the fig rudely into the gutter. Addressing it as it lay, he said:

— Depart from me, ye cursed, into everlasting fire! —

Taking Stephen's arm, he went on again and said:

— Do you not fear that those words may be spoken to you on the day of judgment? —

— What is offered me on the other hand? — Stephen asked. — An eternity of bliss in the company of the dean of studies? —

— Remember — Cranly said — that he would be glorified. —

— Ay — Stephen said somewhat bitterly — bright agile, impassible and, above all, subtle. —

— It is a curious thing, do you know — Cranly said dispassionately — how your mind is supersaturated with the religion in which you say you disbelieve. Did you believe in it when you were at school? I bet you did. —

— I did — Stephen answered.

— And were you happier then? — Cranly asked softly — happier than you are now, for instance? —

— Often happy — Stephen said — and often unhappy. I was someone else then. —

— How someone else? What do you mean by that statement? —

— I mean — said Stephen — that I was not myself as I am now, as I had to become. —

— Not as you are now, not as you had to become — Cranly repeated. — Let me ask you a question. Do you love your mother? —

Stephen shook his head slowly.

— I don't know what your words mean — he said simply.

— Have you never loved anyone? — Cranly asked.

— Do you mean women? —

— I am not speaking of that — Cranly said in a colder tone. — I ask you if you ever felt love towards anyone or anything. —

Stephen walked on beside his friend, staring gloomily at the footpath.

— I tried to love God — he said at length. — It seems now I failed. It is very difficult. I tried to unite my will with the will of God instant by instant. In that I did not always fail. I could perhaps do that still . . . —

Cranly cut him short by asking:

— Has your mother had a happy life? —

— How do I know? — Stephen said.

— How many children had she? —

— Nine or ten — Stephen answered. — Some died. —

— Was your father . . .

— Cranly interrupted himself for an instant: and then said:

— I don't want to pry into your family affairs. But was your father what is called well-to-do? I mean when you were growing up? —

— Yes — Stephen said.

— What was he? — Cranly asked after a pause.

Stephen began to enumerate glibly his father's attributes.

— A medical student, an oarsman, a tenor, an amateur actor, a shouting politician, a small landlord, a small investor, a drinker, a good fellow, a storyteller, somebody's secretary, something in a distillery, a taxgatherer, a bankrupt and at present a praiser of his own past. —

Cranly laughed, tightening his grip on Stephen's arm, and said:

— The distillery is damn good. —

— Is there anything else you want to know? — Stephen asked.

— Are you in good circumstances at present? —

— Do I look it? — Stephen asked bluntly.

— So then — Cranly went on musingly — you were born in the lap of luxury. —

He used the phrase broadly and loudly as he often used technical expressions as if he wished his hearer to understand that they were used by him without conviction.

— Your mother must have gone through a good deal of suffering — he said then. — Would you not try to save her from suffering more even if . . . or would you? —

— If I could — Stephen said — that would cost me very little. —

— Then do so — Cranly said. — Do as she wishes you to do. What is it for you? You disbelieve in it. It is a form: nothing else. And you will set her mind at rest. —

He ceased and, as Stephen did not reply, remained silent. Then, as if giving utterance to the process of his own thought, he said:

— Whatever else is unsure in this stinking dunghill of a world a mother's love is not. Your mother brings you into the world, carries you first in her body. What do we know about what she feels? But whatever she feels, it, at least, must be real. It must be. What are our ideas or ambitions? Play. Ideas! Why, that bloody bleating goat Temple has ideas. MacCann has ideas too. Every jackass going the roads thinks he has ideas. —

Stephen, who had been listening to the unspoken speech behind the words, said with assumed carelessness:

— Pascal, if I remember rightly, would not suffer his mother to kiss him as he feared the contact of her sex. —

— Pascal was a pig — said Cranly.

— Aloysius Gonzaga, I think, was of the same mind — Stephen said.

— And he was another pig then — said Cranly.

— The church calls him a saint — Stephen objected.

— I don't care a flaming damn what anyone calls him — Cranly said rudely and flatly. — I call him a pig. —

Stephen, preparing the words neatly in his mind, continued:

— Jesus, too, seems to have treated his mother with scant courtesy in public but Suarez a jesuit theologian and Spanish gentleman, has apologised for him. —

— Did the idea ever occur to you — Cranly asked — that Jesus was not what he pretended to be? —

— The first person to whom that idea occurred — Stephen answered — was Jesus himself. —

— I mean — Cranly said, hardening in his speech — did the idea ever occur to you that he was himself a conscious hypocrite, what he called the jews of his time, a white sepulchre? Or, to put it more plainly, that he was a blackguard? —

— That idea never occurred to me — Stephen answered. — But I am curious to know are you trying to make a convert of me or a pervert of yourself? —

He turned towards his friend's face and saw there a raw smile which some force of will strove to make finely significant. —

Cranly asked suddenly in a plain sensible tone:

— Tell me the truth. Were you at all shocked by what I said? —

— Somewhat — Stephen said.

— And why were you shocked — Cranly pressed on in the same

tone — if you feel sure that our religion is false and that Jesus was not the son of God? —

— I am not at all sure of it — Stephen said. — He is more like a son of God than a son of Mary. —

— And is that why you will not communicate — Cranly asked — because you are not sure of that too, because you feel that the host, too, may be the body and blood of the son of God and not a wafer of bread? And because you fear that it may be? —

— Yes — Stephen said quietly — I feel that and I also fear it. —

— I see. — Cranly said.

Stephen, struck by his tone of closure, reopened the discussion at once by saying:

— I fear many things: dogs, horses, firearms, the sea, thunderstorms, machinery, the country roads at night. —

— But why do you fear a bit of bread? —

— I imagine — Stephen said — that there is a malevolent reality behind those things I say I fear. —

— Do you fear then — Cranly asked — that the God of the Roman catholics would strike you dead and damn you if you made a sacrilegious communion? —

— The God of the Roman catholics could do that now — Stephen said. — I fear more than that the chemical action which would be set up in my soul by a false homage to a symbol behind which are massed twenty centuries of authority and veneration. —

— Would you — Cranly asked — in extreme danger commit that particular sacrilege? For instance, if you lived in the penal days? —

— I cannot answer for the past — Stephen replied. — Possibly not. —

— Then — said Cranly — you do not intend to become a protestant? —

— I said that I had lost the faith — Stephen answered — but not that I had lost selfrespect. What kind of liberation would that be to forsake an absurdity which is logical and coherent and to embrace one which is illogical and incoherent? —

They had walked on towards the township of Pembroke and now, as they went on slowly along the avenues, the trees and the scattered lights in the villas soothed their minds. The air of wealth and repose diffused about them seemed to comfort their neediness. Behind a hedge of laurel a light glimmered in the window of a kitchen and the voice of a servant was heard singing as she sharpened knives. She sang, in short broken bars,

Rosie O'Grady —

Cranly stopped to listen, saying:

— *Mulier cantat.* — [1]

The soft beauty of the Latin word touched with an enchanting touch the dark of the evening, with a touch fainter and more persuading than the touch of music or of a woman's hand. The strife of their minds was quelled. The figure of woman as she appears in the liturgy of the church passed silently through the darkness: a white robed figure, small and slender as a boy, and with a falling girdle. Her voice, frail and high as a boy's, was heard intoning from a distant choir the first words of a woman which pierce the gloom and clamour of the first chanting of the passion:

— *Et tu cum Jesu Galilæo eras.* — [2]

And all hearts were touched and turned to her voice, shining like a young star, shining clearer as the voice intoned the proparoxyton and more faintly as the cadence died.

The singing ceased. They went on together, Cranly repeating in strongly stressed rhythm the end of the refrain:

> *And when we are married,*
> *O, how happy we'll be*
> *For I love sweet Rosie O'Grady*
> *And Rosie O'Grady loves me.*

— There's real poetry for you — he said. — There's real love. —

He glanced sideways at Stephen with a strange smile and said:

— Do you consider that poetry? Or do you know what the words mean? —

— I want to see Rosie first — said Stephen.

— She's easy to find — Cranly said.

His hat had come down on his forehead. He shoved it back: and in the shadow of the trees Stephen saw his pale face, framed by the dark, and his large dark eyes. Yes. His face was handsome: and his body was strong and hard. He had spoken of a mother's love. He felt then the sufferings of women, the weaknesses of their bodies and souls: and would shield them with a strong and resolute arm and bow his mind to them.

Away then: it is time to go. A voice spoke softly to Stephen's lonely heart, bidding him go and telling him that his friendship was coming to an end. Yes; he would go. He could not strive against another. He knew his part.

— Probably I shall go away — he said.

— Where? — Cranly asked.

— Where I can — Stephen said.

---

[1] [*A woman sings.*]

[2] [*And you too were with Jesus of Galilee* (Matthew 26:69).]

— Yes — Cranly said. — It might be difficult for you to live here now. But is it that makes you go? —

— I have to go — Stephen answered.

— Because — Cranly continued — you need not look upon yourself as driven away if you do not wish to go or as a heretic or an outlaw. There are many good believers who think as you do. Would that surprise you? The church is not the stone building nor even the clergy and their dogmas. It is the whole mass of those born into it. I don't know what you wish to do in life. Is it what you told me the night we were standing outside Harcourt Street station? —

— Yes — Stephen said, smiling in spite of himself at Cranly's way of remembering thoughts in connexion with places. — The night you spent half an hour wrangling with Doherty about the shortest way from Sallygap to Larras. —

— Pothead! — Cranly said with calm contempt. — What does he know about the way from Sallygap to Larras? Or what does he know about anything for that matter? And the big slobbering washingpot head of him! —

He broke out into a loud long laugh.

— Well? — Stephen said. — Do you remember the rest? —

— What you said, is it? — Cranly asked. — Yes, I remember it. To discover the mode of life or of art whereby your spirit could express itself in unfettered freedom. —

Stephen raised his hat in acknowledgment.

— Freedom! — Cranly repeated. — But you are not free enough yet to commit a sacrilege. Tell me would you rob? —

— I would beg first — Stephen said.

— And if you got nothing, would you rob? —

— You wish me to say — Stephen answered — that the rights of property are provisional and that in certain circumstances it is not unlawful to rob. Everyone would act in that belief. So I will not make you that answer. Apply to the jesuit theologian Juan Mariana de Talavera who will also explain to you in what circumstances you may lawfully kill your king and whether you had better hand him his poison in a goblet or smear it for him upon his robe or his saddlebow. Ask me rather would I suffer others to rob me or, if they did, would I call down upon them what I believe is called the chastisement of the secular arm? —

— And would you? —

— I think — Stephen said — it would pain me as much to do as to be robbed. —

— I see — Cranly said.

He produced his match and began to clean the crevice between two teeth. Then he said carelessly:

— Tell me, for example, would you deflower a virgin? —

— Excuse me — Stephen said politely — is that not the ambition of most young gentlemen? —

— What then is your point of view? — Cranly asked.

His last phrase, sour smelling as the smoke of charcoal and disheartening, excited Stephen's brain, over which its fumes seemed to brood.

— Look here, Cranly — he said. — You have asked me what I would do and what I would not do. I will tell you what I will do and what I will not do. I will not serve that in which I no longer believe, whether it call itself my home, my fatherland or my church: and I will try to express myself in some mode of life or art as freely as I can and as wholly as I can, using for my defence the only arms I allow myself to use, silence, exile and cunning. —

Cranly seized his arm and steered him round so as to lead back towards Leeson Park. He laughed almost slyly and pressed Stephen's arm with an elder's affection.

— Cunning indeed! — he said. — Is it you? You poor poet, you! —

— And you made me confess to you — Stephen said, thrilled by his touch — as I have confessed to you so many other things, have I not? —

— Yes, my child — Cranly said, still gaily.

— You made me confess the fears that I have. But I will tell you also what I do not fear. I do not fear to be alone or to be spurned for another or to leave whatever I have to leave. And I am not afraid to make a mistake, even a great mistake, a lifelong mistake and perhaps as long as eternity too. —

Cranly, now grave again, slowed his pace and said:

— Alone, quite alone. You have no fear of that. And you know what that word means? Not only to be separate from all others but to have not even one friend. —

— I will take the risk — said Stephen.

— And not to have any one person — Cranly said — who would be more than a friend, more even than the noblest and truest friend a man ever had.

His words seemed to have struck some deep chord in his own nature. Had he spoken of himself, of himself as he was or wished to be? Stephen watched his face for some moments in silence. A cold sadness was there. He had spoken of himself, of his own loneliness which he feared.

— Of whom are you speaking? — Stephen asked at length. —

Cranly did not answer.

*   *   *   *

March 20. Long talk with Cranly on the subject of my revolt.

He had his grand manner on. I supple and suave. Attacked me on the score of love for one's mother. Tried to imagine his mother: cannot. Told me once, in a moment of thoughtlessness, his father was sixty-one when he was born. Can see him. Strong farmer type. Pepper and salt suit. Square feet. Unkempt grizzled beard. Probably attends coursing matches. Pays his dues regularly but not plentifully to Father Dwyer of Larras. Sometimes talks to girls after nightfall. But his mother? Very young or very old? Hardly the first. If so, Cranly would not have spoken as he did. Old then. Probably, and neglected. Hence Cranly's despair of soul: the child of exhausted loins.

March 21. *morning.* Thought this in bed last night but was too lazy and free to add it. Free, yes. The exhausted loins are those of Elizabeth and Zacchary. Then he is the precursor. Item: he eats chiefly belly bacon and dried figs. Read locusts and wild honey. Also, when thinking of him, saw always a stern severed head or death mask as if outlined on a grey curtain or veronica. Decollation they call it in the fold. Puzzled for the moment by saint John at the Latin gate. What do I see? A decollated precursor trying to pick the lock.

March 21. *night.* Free. Soul free and fancy free. Let the dead bury the dead. Ay. And let the dead marry the dead.

March 22. In company with Lynch followed a sizable hospital nurse. Lynch's idea. Dislike it. Two lean hungry greyhounds walking after a heifer.

March 23. Have not seen her since that night. Unwell? Sits at the fire perhaps with mamma's shawl on her shoulders. But not peevish. A nice bowl of gruel? Won't you now?

March 24. Began with a discussion with my mother. Subject: B.V.M. Handicapped by my sex and youth. To escape held up relations between Jesus and Papa against those between Mary and her son. Said religion was not a lying-in hospital. Mother indulgent. Said I have a queer mind and have read too much. Not true. Have read little and understood less. Then she said I would come back to faith because I had a restless mind. This means to leave church by backdoor of sin and reenter through the skylight of repentance. Cannot repent. Told her so and asked for sixpence. Got threepence.

Then went to college. Other wrangle with little round head rogue's eye Ghezzi. This time about Bruno the Nolan. Began in Italian and ended in pidgin English. He said Bruno was a terrible heretic. I said he was terribly burned. He agreed to this with some sorrow. Then gave me recipe for what he calls *risotto alla bergamasca.*[1] When he pronounces a soft *o* he protrudes his full carnal lips as if he kissed the vowel. Has he? And could he repent? Yes, he could: and cry two round rogue's tears, one from each eye.

---

[1] [Rice prepared in the manner of the town of Bergamo, Italy.]

Crossing Stephen's, that is, my Green, remembered that his country-men and not mine had invented what Cranly the other night called our religion. A quartet of them, soldiers of the ninetyseventh infantry regi-ment, sat at the foot of the cross and tossed up dice for the overcoat of the crucified.

Went to library. Tried to read three reviews. Useless. She is not out yet. Am I alarmed? About what? That she will never be out again.

Blake wrote:

> *I wonder if William Bond will die,*
> *For assuredly he is very ill.*

Alas, poor William!

I was once at a diorama in Rotunda. At the end were pictures of big nobs. Among them William Ewart Gladstone, just then dead. Orchestra played *O, Willie, we have missed you.*

A race of clodhoppers!

March 25, morning. A troubled night of dreams. Want to get them off my chest.

A long curving gallery. From the floor ascend pillars of dark vapours. It is peopled by the images of fabulous kings, set in stone. Their hands are folded upon their knees in token of weariness and their eyes are darkened for the errors of men go up before them for ever as dark vapours.

Strange figures advance as from a cave. They are not as tall as men. One does not seem to stand quite apart from another. Their faces are phosphorescent, with darker streaks. They peer at me and their eyes seem to ask me something. They do not speak.

March 30. This evening Cranly was in the porch of the library, proposing a problem to Dixon and her brother. A mother let her child fall into the Nile. Still harping on the mother. A crocodile seized the child. Mother asked it back. Crocodile said all right if she told him what he was going to do with the child, eat it or not eat it.

This mentality, Lepidus would say, is indeed bred out of your mud by the operation of your sun.

And mine? Is it not too? Then into Nile mud with it!

April 1. Disapprove of this last phrase.

April 2. Saw her drinking tea and eating cakes in Johnston's, Mooney and O'Brien's. Rather, lynx eyed Lynch saw her as we passed. He tells me Cranly was invited there by brother. Did he bring his crocodile? Is he the shining light now? Well, I discovered him. I protest I did. Shining quietly behind a bushel of Wicklow bran.

April 3. Met Davin at the cigar shop opposite Findlater's church. He was in a black sweater and had a hurley stick. Asked me was it true I was going away and why. Told him the shortest way to Tara was *via* Holyhead. Just then my father came up. Introduction. Father, polite and observant. Asked Davin if he might offer him some refreshment. Davin could not, was going to a meeting. When we came away father told me he had a good honest eye. Asked me why I did not join a rowing club. I pretended to think it over. Told me then how he broke Pennyfeather's heart. Wants me to read law. Says I was cut out for that. More mud, more crocodiles.

April 5. Wild spring. Scudding clouds. O life! Dark stream of swirling bogwater on which apple trees have cast down their delicate flowers. Eyes of girls among the leaves. Girls demure and romping. All fair or auburn: no dark ones. They blush better. Houp-la!

April 6. Certainly she remembers the past. Lynch says all women do. Then she remembers the time of her childhood — and mine if I was ever a child. The past is consumed in the present and the present is living only because it brings forth the future. Statues of women, if Lynch be right, should always be fully draped, one hand of the woman feeling regretfully her own hinder parts.

April 6, *later*. Michael Robartes remembers forgotten beauty and, when his arms wrap her round, he presses in his arms the loveliness which has long faded from the world. Not this. Not at all. I desire to press in my arms the loveliness which has not yet come into the world.

April 10. Faintly, under the heavy night, through the silence of the city which has turned from dreams to dreamless sleep as a weary lover whom no caresses move, the sound of hoofs upon the road. Not so faintly now as they come near the bridge: and in a movement as they pass the darkened windows the silence is cloven by alarm as by an arrow. They are heard now far away, hoofs that shine amid the heavy night as gems, hurrying beyond the sleeping fields to what journey's end — what heart? — bearing what tidings?

April 11. Read what I wrote last night. Vague words for a vague emotion. Would she like it? I think so. Then I should have to like it also.

April 13. That tundish has been on my mind for a long time. I looked it up and find it English and good old blunt English too. Damn the dean of studies and his funnel! What did he come here for to teach us his own language or to learn it from us. Damn him one way or the other!

April 14. John Alphonsus Mulrennan has just returned from the west of Ireland. European and Asiatic papers please copy. He told us he met an old man there in a mountain cabin. Old man had red eyes and short pipe. Old man spoke Irish. Mulrennan spoke Irish. Then old man and Mulrennan spoke English. Mulrennan spoke to him about universe and stars. Old man sat, listened, smoked, spat. Then said:

— Ah, there must be terrible queer creatures at the latter end of the world. —

I fear him. I fear his redrimmed horny eyes. It is with him I must struggle all through this night till day come, till he or I lie dead, gripping him by the sinewy throat till . . . Till what? Till he yield to me? No. I mean him no harm.

April 15. Met her today point blank in Grafton Street. The crowd brought us together. We both stopped. She asked me why I never came, said she had heard all sorts of stories about me. This was only to gain time. Asked me, was I writing poems? About whom? I asked her. This confused her more and I felt sorry and mean. Turned off that valve at once and opened the spiritual-heroic refrigerating apparatus, invented and patented in all countries by Dante Alighieri. Talked rapidly of myself and my plans. In the midst of it unluckily I made a sudden gesture of a revolutionary nature. I must have looked like a fellow throwing a handful of peas up into the air. People began to look at us. She shook hands a moment after and, in going away, said she hoped I would do what I said.

Now I call that friendly, don't you?

Yes, I liked her today. A little or much? Don't know. I liked her and it seems a new feeling to me. Then, in that case, all the rest, all that I thought I thought and all that I felt I felt, all the rest before now, in fact . . . O, give it up, old chap! Sleep it off!

April 16. Away! Away!

The spell of arms and voices: the white arms of roads, their promise of close embraces and the black arms of tall ships that stand against the moon, their tale of distant nations. They are held out to say: We are alone — come. And the voices say with them: We are your kinsmen. And the air is thick with their company as they call to me, their kinsman, making ready to go, shaking the wings of their exultant and terrible youth.

April 26. Mother is putting my new secondhand clothes in order. She prays now, she says, that I may learn in my own life and away from home and friends what the heart is and what it feels. Amen. So be it. Welcome, O life! I go to encounter for the millionth time the reality of experience and to forge in the smithy of my soul the uncreated conscience of my race.

April 27. Old father, old artificer, stand me now and ever in good stead.

THE END

Dublin, 1904.
Trieste, 1914.

Study Guide

Text by

Matthew Mitchell

(B.A., Rutgers University)

Department of English
University of Illinois of Urbana-Champaign
Urbana, Illinois

Contents

> **Each Chapter includes List of Characters,
> Summary, Analysis, Study Questions and
> Answers, and Suggested Essay Topics.**

SECTION ONE

Introduction

The Life and Work of James Joyce

James Joyce was born in Dublin, Ireland, on February 2, 1882. He was the oldest of ten children, and was born into a comfortable and, by some standards, wealthy home. However, while Joyce was growing up, his family's economic situation became progressively worse.

He was able to attend Clongowes Wood College, an exclusive Jesuit boarding school, from age six to nine, but was forced to leave in 1891 when his father, John Stanislaus Joyce, lost his position as collector of rates in Dublin and could no longer afford to send James to school. After a brief stint at the Christian Brothers' School, James was allowed to attend the Jesuit Belvedere College, thanks to a special arrangement by a former rector at Clongowes, Father John Conmee. Father Conmee had become prefect of studies at Belvedere and, remembering James' ability as a student, arranged for him and his brothers to attend Belvedere without fees.

Joyce was a distinguished student at Belvedere, winning several exhibitions (cash prizes for scholarship in national competitions), and being elected, two years in a row, to the office of prefect of the Sodality of the Blessed Virgin Mary, the highest honor at Belvedere. He became interested in poetry, drama, philosophy and languages, and upon graduation in 1898, entered University College, Dublin at age 16.

Joyce gained a reputation as a radical thinker by reading a paper entitled "Drama and Life" before the Literary and Historical Society. He published an essay in the *Fortnightly Review* entitled "Ibsen's New Drama," defending the controversial play-wright. In these and other essays and reviews he wrote during this period, Joyce defended a realistic representation of life on stage, as opposed to what he took to be a sentimental and moral-istic nationalism. The trouble he faced getting permission from the president of the university to read "Drama and Life" was the first of many struggles with censorship in Joyce's career. He grad-uated in 1902, with a degree in modern languages, having studied Italian, French, German, and literary Norwegian as well as Latin.

The Joyce family during this time had been getting both larger and poorer—they had to move around frequently, setting up temporary residences, and were forced to sell many of their possessions to keep creditors at bay. Anxious to escape what he saw as a confining and restrictive environment in Dublin, Joyce left in 1902 to live in self-imposed "exile" in Paris. He had to return, however, in April 1903, as his mother was dying. Mary Jane Joyce died in August of that year, and James Joyce remained in Dublin for over a year, during which time he wrote and pub-lished poetry, worked on short stories (some of which were eventually published in the *Dubliners* collection), and began the initial draft of *A Portrait of the Artist as a Young Man*, then entitled *Stephen Hero*.

He left Dublin again in October 1904, with Nora Barnacle. Joyce never returned to Dublin, except for a few brief visits (the last of which was in 1912), though his home city and country continued to dominate his imagination. He lived and taught in Trieste and Rome until World War I, then moved with Nora, their son Giorgio and daughter Lucia to neutral Zurich, where they stayed until 1920. The Joyces then moved to Paris, where they lived until 1940. James and Nora then returned to Zurich, where James Joyce died on January 13, 1941.

A Portrait of the Artist as a Young Man was published in 1916, but the story of its composition covers a ten-year span in Joyce's life. At the end of the novel, we see the words "Dublin 1904—Trieste 1914." This does not mean, as we might expect, that Joyce spent these ten years working on the text as we have it. In 1904, he wrote a combination short story and autobiographi-cal essay entitled "A Portrait of the Artist." When he could not get it published, he began to rewrite it as a novel with the working title *Stephen Hero*. Joyce worked on *Stephen Hero* intermittently for four years, but became ultimately dissatisfied with his lengthy and cumbersome method. He decided to rewrite the unfinished *Stephen Hero* in five long chapters, selecting and condensing only the most significant episodes in Stephen Dedalus' development. This novel, *A Portrait of the Artist as a Young Man*, was finished in 1914, published serially in *The Egoist* during 1914 and 1915, and finally published by B. W. Huebsch in New York in 1916. As with his other work, Joyce had considerable trouble getting *Portrait* published, both because of the obscenity laws and because of his unconventional literary form.

James Joyce's literary reputation is remarkable when we consider his relatively scant output. Aside from his play, *Exiles*, and a few books of poetry, which have not earned much attention, Joyce's canon consists of a collection of stories, *Dubliners* (1914), and three novels—besides *Portrait*, the mammoth *Ulysses* (1922) and the even more mammoth *Finnegans Wake* (1939). Each of these represents a cornerstone of modernist fiction, and in each work Joyce extends his innovative and experimental style to further limits, leaving a permanent mark on the development of twentieth- century literature. His reputation and influence are as strong today as ever—from high school classrooms to graduate seminars and international professional conferences, Joyce's work continues to generate a staggering degree of critical interest. As Richard Ellmann wrote, "We are still learning to be James Joyce's contemporaries."

Perhaps the first thing that will strike a first-time reader of *A Portrait of the Artist as a Young Man* is the initial strangeness of the language. Joyce's technique is to have the language of the narration try to mirror the linguistic and intellectual development of Stephen Dedalus—therefore, in the first chapter, the vocabulary and sentence structure are more simplistic, limited, and childlike. The narrative is closely aligned with Stephen's consciousness and perspective—therefore, the narrative style could be said to mature along with young Stephen. As the novel progresses, and Stephen becomes better acclimatized to his world, the language expands and develops accordingly.

Whereas in the *Stephen Hero* stage of the novel's composition Joyce was trying to cram every detail about Stephen's life into the narrative, in *A Portrait of the Artist as a Young Man* he exercises much more selectivity. The novel presents only the most important events in Stephen's life, without as much attention to chronological and temporal sequence as we would find in a traditional novel. The subject of the novel is Stephen's internal intellectual and artistic development, so the conflicts and climaxes which would motivate a traditionally plotted novel are in this case a matter of internal relations. A conflict is important because it is so for Stephen; a climax is such because of its importance in Stephen's ultimate spiritual development Each scene or episode in the novel, then, will be loaded with significance on a number of levels.

Fundamental to the technique and structure of this novel is Joyce's conception of *epiphany*. An epiphany, as Joyce conceives it, is a moment of intense perception, or a feeling of total understanding; one's life is punctuated by such moments. In *Stephen Hero*, Joyce defines his (and Stephen's) conception of epiphany thus:

> By an epiphany he meant a sudden spiritual manifestation, whether in the vulgarity of speech or of gesture or in a memorable phase of the mind itself. He believed that it was for the man of letters to record these epiphanies with extreme care, seeing that they themselves are the most delicate and evanescent of moments.

The epiphany is a moment of extreme significance for the subject, or the beholder, and for the object which he or she observes—the epiphany reveals something essential about the person or thing that is observed. Stephen and Joyce understand that the purpose of the artist is to record and present these moments of privileged spiritual insight. The religious source of Joyce's conception (the feast day celebrating the revelation of the infant Christ to the Magi) indicates that this is a spiritual, non-rational conception of knowledge.

A Portrait of the Artist as a Young Man represents the growth and development of Stephen's soul, and the novel is structured around the epiphanies Stephen experiences while growing up. Thus, the narrator is less concerned with dates, ages, time, and a clear chronological sequence. Joyce's conception of epiphany allows us to view time in the novel as a coalescence of past, present, and future. This means, then, for our reading and interpretation of the novel, that each scene will be dense with significance, shedding light on past events in the narrative as well as looking forward to future developments. Joyce is extremely selective—there are many gaps in the story of Stephen's life we must fill in while reading. But this means that we must pay extra attention to the episodes we are given, and the language in which they are told.

Historical Background

A Portrait of the Artist as a Young Man is an autobiographical novel—Stephen Dedalus is Joyce's fictional figure for himself in the early years of his life, and the events in the novel closely parallel those of Joyce's own life. We should be careful not to push this identification of Stephen with young Joyce too far, for the author of a novel is certainly free to take creative liberties that the author of a strict biography would not take. The novel should and does stand as an autonomous artifact in its own right. It is clear, however, that the historical and cultural context of Dublin in the 1890s is as crucial toward our understanding of Stephen Dedalus and his world as it is toward our understanding of Joyce and his world.

Though the novel is ambiguous when it comes to precise dates, the events in *A Portrait of the Artist as a Young Man* cover the period from roughly 1890 through the end of the century. Ireland was then, as it indeed is now, a country torn apart by politics and religion. The Republic of Ireland had not yet won its independence from the British crown, though the liberation movement was fervent. Battle lines were drawn between Protestants and Catholics. Institutionalized religious discrimination had long been used by the Protestant British government as a means of division and control of the Irish-Catholic population, and this naturally trickled down into day-to-day hostility and resentment between Protestant and Catholic people in Ireland. The lines were not always quite this clear, however; there were many among the liberationists who criticized the Catholic church for hindering the anti-British cause.

This anti-Catholic sentiment—which we hear voiced in the novel by Stephen's father and Mr. Casey at Christmas dinner in Chapter 1—is due in large degree to the downfall of Charles Stewart Parnell. Parnell was a liberation leader who was extremely popular, powerful and influential; he was seen by many as the savior of Ireland. However, a scandal erupted in 1889 and 1890, when Captain William Henry O'Shea filed for divorce from his wife, Kitty, on grounds of her adultery with Parnell. The controversy surrounding this affair led directly to the dissolution of Parnell's party, and he died within a year. Parnell's devotees then saw him as a kind of tragic hero, and criticized the Catholic church for their role in condemning the Irish Nationalist leader. They would argue that Parnell's "sin" was a personal matter that should not have jeopardized what they saw as their greatest hope for independence. Joyce, in particular, saw Parnell's case as an apt illustration of what was wrong with Ireland: he was persecuted and discredited, on moralistic grounds, by the same people he had spent his life trying to liberate.

As the largest and most cosmopolitan city in Ireland, Dublin was a hotbed of political and religious conflict in the 1890s. In the arts, too, there was fierce debate as to what direction Ireland should take. The poet and playwright William Butler Yeats was instrumental in working toward an Irish literature, in English, that could become a recognized and appreciated part of European culture. At the same time, however, a more conservative nationalist element called for, along with a renewed interest in Irish folklore and a Gaelic language, positive or "pure" representations of Irish culture in the arts. Therefore, much of the groundbreaking dramatic work of Yeats and J. M. Synge was condemned loudly by many critics, reviewers, and audiences. Joyce associated this kind of attitude with a puritanical orthodoxy which he dislikes intensely. His personal literary development tended to move apart from the Irish literary revival.

It stands to reason, then, that Joyce would feel a need to "escape" from Ireland. He was more interested in studying Italian or German than Gaelic, and was more interested in reading

European literature than Irish folktales. However, it is equally clear that the end of the nineteenth century in Dublin, and the political and cultural conflicts which dominated the world into which Joyce grew, continued to have a profound grip on his imagination. Dublin is the setting for all of his literary work, even though he was living in Europe while most of it was written. These formative years, which are detailed in *A Portrait of the Artist as a Young Man*, are the only time Joyce really lived in Ireland. His self-imposed "exile," however, should not be seen as a total rejection of Ireland. He retained a profoundly ambivalent attitude toward his home city for the rest of his life; he despised aspects of it, but remained fascinated by it.

The publication of Joyce's work caused something of a scandal in Dublin. His portrayal of the city is not always flattering, and he frequently incorporates real people from the city into his work. It is obvious why a nationalistic reader, who thinks that Irish literature should be primarily concerned with representing Ireland in a positive light, would think Joyce something of a national embarrassment. Initial reviews a *A Portrait of the Artist as a Young Man*, both in Ireland and abroad, often alternated between recognition and praise of the artistic skill of the novel, while balking at some of the offensive and crude realism in the novel.

For a first novel, Joyce's *Portrait* got a substantial critical response, gaining the attention of contemporary literary figures such as Ezra Pound, W. B. Yeats, H. G. Wells, and Wyndham Lewis. He did not gain his full reputation as an avant-garde innovator in the art of prose, however, until the publication of *Ulysses*, which is more radical in its formal departures from literary conventions.

A Portrait of the Artist as a Young Man will obviously have a strong appeal to young adults with a Catholic upbringing or an artistic disposition. Such students will surely identify specifically with much of Stephen's experience. However, the more general theme of a young person coming of age, and the complex interplay of rebellion and conformity which this involves— growing away from the world of parents and the church as well as growing within it—has had and will continue to have a more universal appeal to younger readers from various backgrounds.

Master List of Characters

Simon Dedalus—*Stephen's father, originally from the city of Cork, a friendly and humorous man, a strong and vocal supporter of Parnell; his wealth declines throughout the novel.*

Mary Dedalus—*Stephen's mother, a quiet, religious woman, who wants Stephen to observe his Easter duties at the end of the novel.*

Stephen Dedalus—*The protagonist and focal character of the narrative; it is essentially "his" story we are reading, following him from about age six until age eighteen, as he grows through and past the Catholic church, deciding finally to leave Dublin for Europe to become an artist.*

Uncle Charles—*Simon's uncle, Stephen's granduncle, who lives with the Dedalus family in the early stage of the novel; trying to preserve calm with Mrs. Dedalus, he remains noncommittal through the Christmas dinner argument.*

Dante—*Stephen's governess, a nickname for "aunt." A well-read and intelligent woman who teaches Stephen geography. She is vehement in her devotion to the Catholic church, and joins it in condemning Parnell despite her desire for liberation.*

Brigid—*The Dedalus' maid; she only appears in the first chapter, and stands as an indication of their relative wealth as the novel begins.*

Mr. Casey—*A close friend of the Dedalus family, who attends Christmas dinner, and is instrumental in provoking the argument with Dante. Mr. Casey, like Mr. Dedalus, is a devout supporter of Parnell.*

Rody Kickham—*A student at Clongowes, a good football player and, according to young Stephen, a "descent fellow."*

Nasty Roche—*A student at Clongowes, whose father is a magistrate. He questions Stephen about his own father, and teases him about his unusual name. Stephen considers him a "stink."*

Wells—*The student at Clongowes who pushes Stephen into the square ditch (the drainage for the outhouse). He teases and intimidates Stephen, but when it is clear that he has made*

Stephen ill by pushing him into the ditch, Wells begs him not to tell the rector.

Jack Lawton—*Classmate of Stephen's at Clongowes; he is Stephen's "rival" in academic classroom competitions.*

Simon Moonan and Tusker Boyle—*Students at Clongowes, in Stephen's class, who were allegedly caught "smugging" (a mild form of homosexual petting) with three older students. Stephen and the others discuss how Moonan and Boyle will be flogged.*

Father Arnall—*Stephen's math and Latin teacher at Clongowes; he excuses Stephen from his lesson since he broke his glasses. He reappears in Chapter Three, and leads the retreat of St. Francis Xavier.*

Fleming—*A student at Clongowes, who is friendly and sympathetic to Stephen. He asks if Stephen is okay when he wakes up ill, then urges him to stay in bed.*

Father Dolan—*The prefect of studies and disciplinarian at Clongowes, who comes in and interrupts Latin class.*

Brother Michael—*The medical attendant at the infirmary when Stephen is ill.*

Athy—*The older student (in the third of grammar) who Stephen meets in the infirmary. He is friendly and tells Stephen riddles.*

Eileen—*A friend of Stephen's at home. She is a Protestant, and Stephen associates her white hands with the tower of Ivory.*

Cecil Thunder—*A classmate of Stephen's at Clongowes.*

Corrigan—*One of the older students involved in the smugging incident with Moonan and Boyle; given the choice between expulsion and flogging, Athy claims that Corrigan opted for flogging by Mr. Gleeson.*

Mr. Harford—*Stephen's writing teacher at Clongowes.*

Father Conmee—*The rector at Clongowes; Stephen goes to speak to him about Father Dolan; Father Conmee is sympathetic and promises to speak to the prefect.*

Mike Flynn—*An old friend of Simon Dedalus, who is Stephen's running trainer.*

Aubrey Mills—*Stephen's childhood friend at home after Stephen leaves Clongowes; the two boys play adventure games together.*

Maurice—*Stephen's younger brother, who is sent with Stephen to Belvedere College.*

Vincent Heron—*Stephen's friend, antagonist, and "rival" at Belvedere; he delights in Stephen's acts of "heresy," yet condemns Byron, Stephen's favorite poet, as a heretic.*

Wallis—*Heron's sidekick; Stephen sees them together smoking outside of the play, and they, jokingly, make him recite the* Confiteor.

Mr. Tate—*Stephen's English teacher at Belvedere, who accuses Stephen of heresy in an essay.*

Boland and Nash—*Heron's two friends; the "dunce" and "idler" of the class, respectively. They try to argue with Stephen about poetry, mostly aping Heron's opinion that Tennyson is the "best poet." They condemn Stephen's favorite, Byron, as a heretic.*

Doyle—*The director of the play Stephen is in at Belvedere.*

Johnny Cashman—*An old man to whom Stephen and his father speak while visiting Cork; Johnny claims to know many of Stephen's ancestors.*

E--- C--- / Emma—*The girl to whom Stephen addresses his poems; she doesn't actually appear in the novel, except through Stephen's memories (the "her" throughout Chapter V).*

Ennis—*A classmate of Stephen's at Belvedere.*

Old Woman—*Stephen meets her in the street. She directs him to the Church Street chapel.*

Priest—*The priest at the Church Street chapel to whom Stephen confesses, rather than the priest at the retreat.*

The Director—*At Belvedere College, he asks Stephen if he has considered joining the priesthood.*

Dan Crosby—*A tutor; goes with Simon Dedalus to find out about the university for Stephen.*

Dwyer, Towser, Shuley, Ennis, Connolly—*Acquaintances of Stephen; he sees them swimming as he walks along the strand. They seem to him grotesque and immature.*

Katey, Boody, Maggie—*Stephen's younger sisters.*

Cranly—*Stephen's friend and confidant at the university; Stephen speaks to him about his plans to leave Ireland, and Cranly urges Stephen to appease him mother and observe his Easter duties.*

Davin—*A friend of Stephen's at the university; he is from a rural area of Ireland, a "peasant student," the other students tend to romanticize his accent and his "simple" ways.*

Dean of Studies—*An Englishman who talks with Stephen about his developing theory of aesthetics.*

Moynihan—*A fellow university student who tells ribald jokes during lecture.*

Professor of Physics—*Stephen attends his lecture, but is not engaged.*

MacAlister—*A fellow student from the north of Ireland whom Stephen dislikes intensely.*

MacCann—*A student at the university, a socialist and political activist who engages Stephen in a brief public debate outside of the physics lecture.*

Temple—*A student at the university, a gypsy and a socialist, he admires Stephen immensely, much to the chagrin of Cranly, who finds Temple repulsive.*

Lynch—*A student at the university, to whom Stephen talks about his theory of aesthetics and morality.*

Donovan—*A student who Stephen and Lynch encounter during their walk; Stephen dislikes him.*

Father Moran—*A priest with whom Stephen thinks Emma has been flirting.*

Dixon—*The medical student at the library with Cranly.*

The Captain—*A dwarfish old man who Stephen, Dixon, and Cranly see at the library.*

O'Keefe—*A student who riles Temple outside the library.*

Goggins—*A stout student, part of the crowd outside the library.*

Glynn—*A young man at the library.*

Summary of the Novel

A Portrait of the Artist as a Young Man covers the child-hood and adolescence of Stephen Dedalus. We see him, over the course of the novel, grow from a little boy to a young man of eighteen who has decided to leave his country for Europe, in order to be an artist.

At the start of the novel, Stephen is a young boy, probably about five-years-old. He is one of the younger students at Clongowes Wood College for boys (a Jesuit elementary school, not a "college" in the American sense). He had been pushed into an outhouse drainage ditch by a student named Wells a few days earlier, and he wakes up ill. While in the infirmary, Stephen dreams of going home for the Christmas holidays. We then see the Dedalus family at Christmas dinner, and a heated argument erupts between Stephen's father and Dante, Stephen's governess, about Parnell and the Catholic church. Back at school, Stephen has broken his glasses and has been excused from classwork by his teacher, Father Arnall. The prefect of studies, Father Dolan, comes into class to discipline the students, and singles out Stephen as a "lazy idle little loafer." Stephen is pandied (his knuckles beaten with a bat) in front of the class, and feels the injustice of his punishment deeply. The other students urge him to speak to the rector of the college. He gets up the courage to do so, and the rector promises to speak to Father Dolan. Stephen is cheered by the other students.

In the second chapter, Stephen is a few years older. He is no longer at Clongowes but at Belvedere College. He has started to become interested in literature, and tends to romanticize his life based on what he reads. He tries to write a poem to the girl he loves, but cannot. He is in a play at Belvedere, and outside of the theater he sees two other students, Heron and Wallis, who tease him about the play, and jokingly make him recite the *Confiteor*. Stephen, while doing so, remembers a recent incident when his English teacher suspected him of heresy. Stephen takes a trip to Cork with his father, and his father shows him the town where he was born and raised, and the school he attended when he was Stephen's age. Back in Dublin, Stephen wins a sum of money for an essay competition, and, for a brief time, treats himself and his family to a "season of pleasure." When the money runs out, we can see him wandering the red light districts of Dublin, fantasizing about the prostitutes. As the chapter ends, Stephen has his first experience with a prostitute.

In Chapter III, it is apparent that Stephen has made a habit of soliciting prostitutes. He goes through the motions in school and at church, and is not bothered by the duplicity of his life. He goes on a religious retreat with his class, and the priest's sermon about sin and damnation affects Stephen deeply. He repents, goes to confession at the chapel across town, and takes communion.

Stephen has now dedicated his life to God. He prays constantly, and goes about mortifying his senses. He has completely renounced his sinful relations with the prostitutes, and the director at Belvedere speaks to him about becoming a priest. The idea first seems to appeal to Stephen, but he ultimately decides that he could not become a priest.

His father is making plans for Stephen, now 16, to enter the university. Walking along the seashore one afternoon, thinking about poetry, Stephen sees a young woman bathing. They stare at each other, but do not speak. Stephen takes this as a spiritual sign, and he excitedly decides to dedicate his life to art.

In the final chapter, Stephen is at the university. He is lazy about his classes but vehement about his developing theory of aesthetics. He refuses to sign a political petition, trying to set himself apart from the concerns of his country's politics or religion. Talking to his close friend, Cranly, Stephen announces that he has decided to leave Ireland for Europe to pursue his artistic vocation. The novel closes with a few pages out of Stephen's diary, as he makes plans to leave for the continent.

Estimated Reading Time

A Portrait of the Artist as a Young Man is broken up into five chapters—the first four are about equal in length; the fifth is about twice as long as the others. Each chapter should take about an hour to read, though the language and unconventional narration style may take some getting used to. Spending two separate hour-long sittings on the fifth chapter, a student should be able to read the novel in six one-hour sittings.

SECTION TWO

Chapter I
(pages 1–40)

New Characters:

Mr. Dedalus: *Stephen's father*

Mrs. Dedalus: *Stephen's mother*

Stephen Dedalus: *the protagonist and focal character of the narrative*

Uncle Charles: *Stephen's granduncle*

Dante: *Stephen's governess*

Brigid: *the Dedalus' maid*

Rody Kickham: *student at Clongowes*

Nasty Roche: *student at Clongowes*

Wells: *student at Clongowes who pushed Stephen into the ditch*

Simon Moonan: *student at Clongowes, caught "smugging"*

Tusker Boyle: *student at Clongowes, caught "smugging" with Simon*

Jack Lawton: *Stephen's competitor in class*

Father Arnall: *Stephen's math and Latin teacher*

Fleming: *student at Clongowes; Stephen's friend*

Father Dolan: *prefect of studies at Clongowes*

Brother Michael: *medical attendant in the infirmary*

Athy: *student at Clongowes*

Mr. Casey: *friend of the Dedalus family*

Eileen: *Stephen's friend, a Protestant*

Cecil Thunder: *student at Clongowes*

Corrigan: *older student at Clongowes*

Mr. Gleeson: *teacher at Clongowes, will flog Corrigan*

Mr. Harford: *Stephen's writing teacher at Clongowes*

Father Conmee: *the rector at Clongowes*

Summary

In the first brief section of the chapter, Stephen is very young. He remembers a story his father told him, and a song he likes to sing. He thinks about Dante, and her brushes (maroon for Michael Davitt, green for Parnell—both Irish nationalist leaders), and about their neighbors, the Vances.

Next, Stephen is at Clongowes Wood College. Stephen is playing football (soccer) with the others, but stays outside of the action because he is younger, smaller, and weaker. He remembers another student, Nasty Roche, questioning him about his name and his father. He remembers being left at school by his mother and father, his mother crying, and his father telling him to write if he wanted anything, and "never to peach on a fellow." He remembers being pushed into a drainage ditch by a student named Wells. Stephen is cold and obviously homesick, and is counting the days until Christmas break.

The boys go inside, into a math class. The teacher, Father Arnall, has a game where the students are divided into teams, York and Lancaster (after the English War of the Roses), and Stephen is struggling with the difficult math. He and another student, Jack Lawton, are constantly competing for first place in these classroom games.

At dinner, Stephen is not hungry and only drinks tea. He feels ill, and thinks about being home. Later, in the playroom, he is teased by Wells about whether or not he kisses his mother before going to bed. In study hall, he changes the number on his desk from 27 to 26 days until the Christmas holiday. He tries to study geography but cannot concentrate. His mind wanders, and he thinks about his father, Dante, and Mr. Casey arguing about politics—Stephen does not understand politics, but wishes he did.

They go to chapel for night prayers, and then go to be. In bed, Stephen fantasizes about traveling home for the holidays. When he wakes up, he feels even more ill, and his friend Fleming tells him to stay in bed. Wells, worried that he has made Stephen ill by pushing him into the ditch, begs Stephen not to tell on him. The prefect comes, and, convinced that Stephen is really ill, tells him to go to the infirmary. In the infirmary, Stephen meets Brother Michael, and thinks once again of home and his parents. He is afraid he might die before he sees them again. He talks to an older boy, Athy, who tells him riddles. In the infirmary, Stephen thinks about his father and his grandfather, and about the death of Parnell.

In the next section, Stephen is home for Christmas dinner. His family, Dante, and Mr. Casey are there. The meal is lavish, prepared and served by servants. An argument erupts at the table between Mr. Dedalus, Mr. Casey, and Dante about the Catholic church and its role in political matters. Stephen's mother and Uncle Charles try to end it, not taking sides and pleading that they not discuss politics at Christmas. The discussion continues, and moves to the more specific and recent issue of Parnell and the role of the church in his downfall. Despite the urgings of Mrs. Dedalus and Uncle Charles, the conflict continues on a subtler level, as Mr. Casey tells an "instructive" anecdote aimed to provoke Dante, about spitting in the eye of a woman who was taunting him about Parnell. This brings the conflict to a boil, and the section ends with Mr. Casey and Dante shouting at each other across the table, Mr. Casey saying "no God for Ireland," and Dante calling him a blasphemer. As Dante storms out of the room, Stephen notices that Mr. Casey and his father are crying for Parnell.

In the next section, Stephen is back at Clongowes. He and the other students are talking about some boys who were in trouble at the school—some say they stole cash, others that they drank the altar wine, and Athy says they are all wrong, that the boys were caught "smugging," a mild form of homosexual petting. The conversation then moves to the question of what punishment the boys will receive. The younger of the five, Simon

Moonan and Tusker Boyle, will be flogged, while the three older boys can choose between expulsion and flogging.

They are called in from the playground, and in writing class Stephen has trouble because he has broken his glasses on the cinderpath. In Latin class, Father Arnall has exempted Stephen from work. The prefect of studies comes in to intimidate and discipline the students. First, he punishes Fleming, who Father Arnall had made kneel in the aisle for writing a bad theme and missing a question in grammar. He then singles out Stephen, and punishes him for not working, thinking that Stephen has tricked Father Arnall. When he is gone, Father Arnall lets them return to their seats, and Stephen is bewildered and upset at his unfair punishment.

Outside of the class, the other boys sympathize with Stephen, and urge him to go tell the rector. At lunch, Stephen decides that he will go and speak to the rector, though he remains hesitant and unsure until the last minute. As he leaves the refectory, he gets up the courage to turn and climb the stairs to the rector's office.

After Stephen explains his case, the rector says that he is sure that Father Dolan made a mistake, and that he will speak to him. Stephen hurries out to the other students, who loudly cheer his success, lifting him onto their shoulders. The crowd dissipates, and at the end of the chapter Stephen is standing alone as the other students play cricket.

Analysis

The novel begins with a cliched storytelling device: "Once upon a time...," be we soon learn that this is not a conventional narrative. The initially confusing and opaque first paragraph represents a story Mr. Dedalus had told Stephen, who is very young in this first short section of the novel. Stephen is identified with the subject of the story ("He was baby tuckoo"), and it quickly becomes clear that the narrative is closely aligned with his perspective. The narrative is thus purposely limited by his immature vocabulary. For example, when we read, "his father looked at him through a glass: he had a hair face," we are to understand that Stephen does not yet know the word "beard." Stephen remembers a song he likes to sing, "O, the wild rose blossoms /

On the little green place," but the narrator shows us that he is not yet old enough to pronounce it correctly: "O, the green wothe botheth." These first two pages are fragmentary and scattered, in order to represent the associative and impressionistic mind of a young child. Even in these seemingly random and incoherent fragments of his consciousness, the greater themes of the novel and the motivating forces of Stephen's world are represented in microcosm. The political world is represented by Dante's two brushes. The world of his family is shown to us. Sexuality is hinted at: ("when he was grown up he was going to marry Eileen"). Art is represented through his father's story and Stephen's song.

In these early pages of the novel, we are being introduced to the world of the protagonist, Stephen Dedalus, as well as being shown Joyce's original and unusual narrative style. Although it is not a first-person narrative, the narrator is intimately engaged with Stephen's consciousness throughout. This method has been called "free indirect discourse," a third-person narrator, with many first-person characteristics. The narrator does not have a voice that is clearly distinct from Stephen's, and he does not comment explicitly on the action. It is not a detached or conventionally omniscient storyteller, but is rather closely aligned with Stephen's consciousness, mirroring his intellectual and linguistic development. It is not clear that the narrator knows more than Stephen does. Can the narrator, then, like the young man, be mistaken or deluded? Throughout the novel, there is the persistent possibility that we should not take the narrator's words at face value, and that Stephen is being treated by the author with a subtle irony.

Throughout the first chapter, Joyce is trying to recreate the impressionistic world of a young child. After the first brief section, Stephen is older—probably about five or six years old. The novel is not always clear about dates, ages, and chronological time. Months and years will pass without mention, and we must infer Stephen's age and maturity from various clues in the narration. A person's life, as Joyce conceives it, is not significant because of its events or the order and circumstances in which they occur. Rather, memories are always colored by the present moment and expectations for the future; likewise, the present is always colored by memories and past experiences. Joyce's narrative tries to capture this more fluid conception of the protagonist's life, and is thus not concerned with establishing clear dates and times.

The narrative in the first chapter is highly impressionistic. Stephen's senses are active—sight, smell, sound, and touch are all emphasized throughout. He is sensitive to color, and especially to hot and cold. His experience of being at school at Clongowes is characteristically cold and damp; his memories of home are characteristically warm and dry. This betrays both a childlike sensitivity to simple sense perception, as well as suggesting the early stages of Stephen's developing artistic disposition. Stephen's young imagination is especially vivid, and his sense perceptions are often, in this chapter, closely associated with an imaginative flight (such as when he dreams of going home).

Stephen's reactions to his world are colored heavily by the influence of others—Dante, his father, and the older students. When Wells is questioning Stephen about whether or not he kisses his mother before going to bed, and then teases him when he says yes and when he says no, Stephen despairs: "What was the right answer to the question? He had given two and still Wells laughed." It is not that Stephen is concerned with the true answer, but with the *right* one, the one that will allow him to fit into the social situation at hand. Stephen is, throughout the first chapter, trying to acclimatize himself to the existing social, political, and familial structures of his world. He is younger and smaller than the other students, and not at all self-confident.

Another aspect of the older students' influence on young Stephen is his tendency to use their slang to explain things. When Stephen encounters some strange and ambiguous graffiti in the square, he confidently asserts, "Some fellows had drawn it there for a cod." He is using his classmates' slang, but it is not clear that he is at home with their language, that he either understands the joke itself, or even what a "cod" is at all. The words seem somewhat uncomfortable to him, as if he is quoting someone else. He will use this, throughout the chapter, as a way of "understanding" what is going on around him, but it is as if we don't quite believe that he does in fact understand.

It is important to recognize that Stephen's way of making sense involves a particular specific concern with language, here in the first chapter as throughout the novel. He is fascinated by words as names—his own name, as well as others:

> God was God's name just as his name was Stephen. *Dieu* was the French for God and that was God's name too; and when anyone prayed to God and said *Dieu* then God knew at once that it was a French person that was praying.

This passage represents an interesting and illustrative combination of Stephen's early capacity for abstract, complex, metaphysical thought, as well as the comically childlike simplicity of his understanding of language and religion. Stephen is fascinated by language, by the very fact that a word can represent a person, or even God.

Stephen is also intrigued by meaning, especially cases of double meaning: "He kept his hands in the sidepockets of his belted grey suit. That was a belt round his pocket. And belt was also to give a fellow a belt." Note the confident simplicity of Stephen's tone. Recognizing a new aspect of language is, for Stephen, to have gained a new level of understanding.

Stephen's life at Clongowes is presented as alternating between a hostile and unpleasant present and a more desirable alternative. The strength of his young imagination contributes greatly to this—he is constantly imagining, in vivid detail, his impending journey home for the holidays. While his impression of Clongowes is constantly couched in terms of coldness and wetness, unfriendliness and unfamiliarity, he imagines his home as warm, dry, familiar, and friendly. So it is appropriate that the next section, as Stephen is home at Christmas, begins with this description:

> A great fire, banked high and red, flamed in the grate and under the ivytwined branches of the chandelier the Christmas table was spread.

The narrator, assuming Stephen's level of associations, sets up the scene at home using language of warmth, comfort, and tranquility. Stephen is more at ease there, though he is still an outsider.

This is the first year he is old enough to sit with the adults, so he feels a distance and alienation from them similar to what he felt at Clongowes. He is a total stranger to the world of politics that dominates their discussion, and once again we see him sit silently, observing and reacting rather than acting and speaking himself.

Stephen's understanding of politics, as described in the earlier section, is typical in its binary construction:

> He wondered if they were arguing at home about that. That was called politics. There were two sides in it: Dante was on one side and his father and Mr. Casey were on the other side but his mother and Uncle Charles were on no side. Every day there was something in the paper about it. It pained him that he did not know well what politics meant...

The world which Stephen is growing into is highly politically charged—he is aware of this, but also aware that he does not understand it and must remain, for the time being, outside of this dynamic.

The argument at Christmas dinner both confirms and alters the conception of politics Stephen had. The "two sides," at his house anyway, are clear. Mr. Casey and his father are devout supporters of Parnell, and spare no words in their criticism and even condemnation of the Catholic church. Dante, though also a supporter of Irish liberation, is foremost a Catholic, and condemns Parnell for his adulterous affair. We hear Stephen remember her ripping the green velvet back from the Parnell brush when the scandal broke.

Stephen is, of course, silent during the argument, though Uncle Charles and Dante periodically refer to his presence, scolding Mr. Dedalus for his language in front of the child. Although he is silent and passive, we are aware that his mind, as ever, is active. As he tries to understand the conflict he has witnessed, he must complicate some of the categories and binaries he has constructed:

> Stephen looked with affection at Mr. Casey's face which stared across the table over his joined hands....But

why was he against the priests? Because Dante must be right then. But he had heard his father say that she was a spoiled nun and that she had come out of the convent in the Alleghanies when her brother had got the money from the savages for the trinkets and the chainies. Perhaps that made her severe against Parnell.

Stephen clearly does not understand the terms of the conflict, and in a sense the specifics are not what are important here. This is a significant, perhaps epiphanous, moment in Stephen's life—not because of what he learned about Irish politics at the dinner table, but because he is forced to consider his sources of authority. He likes his father, Dante and Mr. Casey equally, and must come to terms with their radical disagreement. This memory becomes significant for Stephen because of its more general implications for his understanding of national and religious politics, which he eventually seeks to escape altogether. The stable world of Stephen's binaries—right, wrong; good, bad—seems threatened here.

Mr. Dedalus' vocal and quite crass questioning of Catholic authority shocks Stephen, but influences him profoundly. His father's criticism of the church prefigures his own questioning of Jesuit authority at the end of this chapter, and ultimately his rejection of the church as a young adult.

If we understand Stephen as a figure for the young artist, then we can see Clongowes and the Jesuit authority as representing many of the forces active in Ireland that, in Joyce's conception, repressed the artist. First, the incident with Wells pushing him into the ditch places Stephen in the role of the righteous innocent victim, which the other boys seem to support by agreeing that "it was a mean thing to do." He comes to embrace this image as the novel progresses. His alienation from the other students and his existence along the margins of the social scene at the school prefigure his sense of the necessity of "exile" from his home country.

When Stephen, at the start of the final section of this chapter, hears the other students discussing Simon Moonan and Tusker Boyle, he is primarily trying to figure out what they did wrong; he does not think to question that they did wrong. It would never occur to him to question the school authorities here. It is clear that Stephen is convinced that the students must have been doing something wrong for them to be punished so severely.

When he is punished unjustly by Father Dolan, he seems immediately certain that the authority, in this case, has made a mistake. Stephen never wavers in his moral indignation—he is certain that the punishment was indeed "cruel and unfair." The pain of his punishment is moral rather than physical—his ego and his integrity are hurt more than his hand. Likewise, his hesitation when it comes to informing the rector is practical, not moral—he thinks the rector might not believe him, in which case the other students will laugh at him. That might just mean more pandying at the hands of Father Dolan. However, for the first time in the novel, Stephen decides to act of his own accord, and his certainty is rewarded. His "success" in going to speak to the rector is one of many "climaxes" in the novel. It represents an important moment in the development of Stephen's soul; this questioning of authority prefigures his later rebellions.

At the end of the chapter, the tone is triumphant. Stephen is cheered by his classmates, and carried on their shoulders—symbolically centralized among them, rather than marginalized. However, the crowd soon dissipates and Stephen is alone once again. He observes rather than participates in the cricket match, but this time his isolation and distance seem different. Rather than feeling uncomfortably alienated, he feels good to be alone—"He was happy and free." This kind of "happy exile," or willful alienation, will come to characterize Stephen's relationship with the politics and religion of his country as he gets older. He is still outside of the game as the chapter ends, but he has achieved an apparently significant moral victory for himself.

Study Questions

1. Through which characters' consciousness is the narrative focused?

2. Who is "baby tuckoo"?

3. What is the significance of Dante's maroon and green brushes?

4. What advice does Stephen's father give him as they leave him off at Clongowes?

5. Why did Wells push Stephen into the ditch?

6. How does Mrs. Dedalus respond to the argument at the Christmas dinner table?

7. What is the story Mr. Casey tells at dinner?

8. According to Athy, why are Simon Moonan and Tusker Boyle in trouble?

9. Why was Stephen exempt from classwork by Father Arnall?

10. What do Stephen's classmates encourage him to do after Father Conmee pandies him?

Answers

1. The narrative is focused, in the style of "free indirect discourse," through Stephen Dedalus' consciousness.

2. "Baby Tuckoo" is the "nicens little boy" in the story Stephen's father tells him when he is very young. It is a figure for Stephen himself.

3. The maroon brush stands for Michael Davitt, and the green brush stands for Parnell, the famous Irish nationalist leaders.

4. He tells him to write home if he wanted anything, and "whatever he did, never to peach on a fellow."

5. Wells pushed Stephen into the ditch because Stephen refused to swap his snuffbox for Wells' "seasoned hacking chestnut."

6. Mrs. Dedalus does not take sides in the debate. She wants them to refrain from discussing politics, if only on this one day of the year, Christmas.

7. Mr. Casey tells a story, designed to provoke Dante, about being harassed by a woman who was condemning Parnell's affair with Kitty O'Shea. He says that he heard her call Kitty O'Shea a name that he won't repeat, and so he spit his mouthful of tobacco juice in her face.

8. He says that they were caught in the square with three older students "smugging." Since homosexual activity is against the rules at Clongowes, they are to be flogged.

9. Stephen was exempted from classwork until his new glasses arrive; he accidentally broke them when he fell on the cinderpath, and cannot see well enough without them to participate.

10. Stephen's classmates urge him to go speak to the rector, since his punishment was cruel and unfair.

Suggested Essay Topics

1. Discuss Stephen's relationship with language in his chapter. Why is his interest in language significant at this early age? Does this make him more or less engaged with the other students his age? Are there any political implications, in light of the Irish nationalist movement, to his identification of English as "his" language?

2. At various points in this chapter, Stephen proposes a theory of language based upon onomatopoeia—the idea that a word's sound has a kind of concordance to its meaning. Examples of onamatopoeia would be "splat, bam, pow." In what ways does Joyce's narration in this chapter use the *sound* of language to achieve its effects? How would you characterize the tone of the narrator at the start of the chapter? At the end? Is there a thematic connection?

3. Stephen's senses are very acute, and throughout the first chapter Joyce makes us aware of the color, smell, temperature, and sound of Stephen's surroundings. Trace the language of the senses in this chapter. How does Joyce use repeating sense-images to characterize Clongowes or Stephen's home in Dublin?

SECTION THREE

Chapter II
(pages 41–71)

New Characters:

Mike Flynn: *Stephen's running coach*

Aubrey Mills: *Stephen's friend in Blackrock*

Maurice: *Stephen's younger brother*

Vincent Heron: *Stephen's friend and "rival" at Belvedere*

Wallis: *Heron's friend*

Mr. Tate: *Stephen's English teacher at Belvedere*

Boland and Nash: *Heron's two friends*

Doyle: *the director of the play Stephen is in at Belvedere*

Johnny Cashman: *an old friend of Simon Dedalus in Cork*

E--- C--- / Emma: *the girl Stephen secretly admires*

Summary

In the first section, the narrator says that Uncle Charles smokes his morning pipe in the outhouse, because Stephen's father finds the tobacco smell unbearable. The Dedalus family has now moved to Blackrock, a suburb of Dublin, and it is summer. Stephen is spending a lot of time with Uncle Charles, going around town doing errands, and practicing track running in the park with Mike Flynn, a friend of Stephen's father. After practice, they often go to chapel, where Charles prays piously, while Stephen sits respectfully. He would go on long walks every Sunday with his father and Uncle Charles, during which he would listen to them talk about politics and family history. At night, he would read a translation of *The Count of Monte Cristo*. The hero of this book, Edmond Dantes, appeals to Stephen, and he imagines his own life to be heroic and romantic. He has become friends with a boy named Aubrey Mills. They have formed a gang, and play adventure games together, in which Stephen, rather than dressing in a costume, makes a point of imitating Napoleon's plain style of dress.

In September, Stephen does not go back to Clongowes because his father cannot afford to send him. Mike Flynn is in the hospital, and Aubrey is at school, so Stephen starts driving around with the milkman on his route. His family's wealth is declining, and Stephen begins to imagine a female figure, such as Mercedes in *The Count of Monte Cristo*, who will transfigure and save him from the plainness of his life.

In the next section, the family has moved from Blackrock back to the city, and most of their furniture has just been repossessed by Mr. Dedalus' creditors. Stephen understands that his father is in trouble, but does not know the details. Uncle Charles has gotten too old to go outside, so Stephen explores Dublin on his own. He visits relatives with his mother, but continues to feel bitter and aloof. After a children's party, he takes the last tram home with the girl he admires. They stand near each other and, though they remain silent, Stephen feels a kind of connection with her. He thinks that she wants him to hold and kiss her, but he hesitates. The next day, he tries to write a poem to her. In the poem, he alters some of the details from the previous night— they are under trees rather than on a tram, and at the "moment of farewell," this time, they kiss.

One night, Stephen learns that his father has arranged for him and his brother, Maurice, to attend Belvedere College, another Jesuit school. His father then recounts, at dinner, how Father Conmee told him about Stephen going to speak to him about Father Dolan. Mr. Dedalus imitates Father Conmee saying they had a "hearty laugh together over it."

In the next section, Stephen is near the end of his second year at Belvedere. It is the night of the school play, and Stephen has the leading role in the second section, playing a comical teacher.

Stephen, impatient with the first act, goes out of the chapel where the play is being staged. He encounters two of his classmates—Heron and Wallis—smoking outside. Heron urges Stephen to imitate the rector of Belvedere in the play. Heron says that he saw Stephen's father going in, and teases him because Emma was with him. Their jesting makes Stephen angry and uncomfortable, but this mood soon passes. As they jokingly implore him to "admit" that he is "no saint," Stephen plays along, reciting the *Confiteor*.

While doing so, Stephen's mind wanders to a time, about a year back, when his writing teacher had found a mild example of heresy in one of his essays. Stephen does not argue, but corrects his error. A few days later, however, Heron and two others stop him and tease him about it, asking him who the "greatest writer" and "best poet" are. When Stephen says that Byron is the best poet, Heron mocks him, calling Byron a heretic. They hold Stephen and hit him with a cane and cabbage stump, telling him to "admit that Byron was no good."

Remembering the incident now, he is not angry. He is thinking of the fact that Emma will be in the audience, and he tries to remember what she looks like. A younger student comes up and tells Stephen he'd better hurry back and dress for the play.

He goes back in and gets his face painted for the part. He is not nervous, though he is humiliated by the silliness of the part he has to play. The play goes well, and Stephen leaves in a hurry as soon as it is over. Seeing his family outside, and noting that Emma is not with them, he leaves ahead of them—angry, frustrated, and restless.

In the next section, Stephen is on a train to Cork with his father. Cork is the city where Simon Dedalus grew up. They are traveling now because the Dedalus' properties are going to be sold. His father tells stories about his youth in Cork, but Stephen listens without sympathy or pity. In Cork, Mr. Dedalus asks just about everyone they meet about local news, and people he used to know, which makes Stephen restless and impatient. While visiting the Queen's College, Stephen becomes depressed looking at the carvings on the desks, imagining the lives of the students. His father finds his own initials, carved years ago, which only depresses Stephen further.

Hearing his father tell more stories, Stephen thinks of
his own position at Belvedere. His father gives him advice, to
"always mix with gentlemen," and reminisces about his own
father. Stephen is ashamed of his father, and thinks that the
people they meet are condescending and patronizing. He feels
distant from the world of his father, and the section ends with
Stephen repeating to himself lines from Shelley's poem, "To The
Moon."

In the final section, Stephen has won 33 pounds in an essay
competition. He takes his parents to dinner, telling his mother
not to worry about the cost. He orders fruits and groceries, takes
people to the theater, gives gifts, and spends his money generously, if unwisely. His "season of pleasure," however, doesn't last
long, and soon life returns to normal. He is dismayed that he was
unable to stop the family's decline, which causes him so much
shame.

He begins to wander the seedy parts of Dublin, this
time searching for a woman to sin with, rather than for the
Mercedes-figure from the start of the chapter. At the close of the
chapter, he has his first encounter with a prostitute. She seduces
him, and Stephen's reaction is passive and submissive.

Analysis

After the dramatic ending of the first chapter, which closes
with Stephen winning the approval of his classmates, the beginning of this chapter might be something of a let-down. Rather
than immediately continuing Stephen's story, the narrative
spends the first page or so describing seemingly banal, inciden-
tal, and trivial details about how Uncle Charles goes out to the
outhouse to smoke his tobacco, because Stephen's father can't
stand the smell. The tone of this chapter, as it begins, suggests
routinization, habit—rather than presenting singular events,
the narrator describes what Uncle Charles would do "every
morning," or what he and Stephen would do "on week days." The
long and ultimately circular walks Stephen takes, every Sunday,
with his father and Uncle Charles, suggest how much his life has
become a progression of routines, and how much his freedom
is limited by the adult world once again, Though he is no longer

at Clongowes, he is still, to some degree, at the disposal of adult authority. His literal, physical freedom is limited, and his means of escape, throughout this chapter, becomes imaginative.

This juxtaposition of a dramatic moment at the end of one chapter, and a tone of routinization which tends to deflate that climax at the start of the next chapter, initiates a pattern that will continue throughout the novel. Each chapter will character-istically end with an energetic climax, a moment of enlighten-ment for Stephen, while the next chapter, as it begins, will seem to show that this moment may not have been as significant as we had thought. This might suggest that the narrator, despite his close engagement with Stephen's perspective, has a tendency to ironize or parody aspects of his youthful triumphs. It may be that we feel that we can see or know more than Stephen, as Ste-phen is so young that he does not know all he thinks he does. This is the case throughout the novel, though it is perhaps less obvious as he gets older. The narrator always asks us to consider Stephen in a critical light, even when the language of the narra-tion seems to be wholeheartedly affirming him.

This point is made especially specific in the second chap-ter, as we (and Stephen) hear Mr. Dedalus recount, over dinner, an encounter with Father Conmee, the rector at Clongowes. He retells the story, which had seemed like such an unambiguous triumph for young Stephen at the end of the previous chapter, in a patronizing, almost ridiculing tone:

> . . . we were chatting away quite friendly and he asked
> me did our friend here wear glasses still and then he
> told me the whole story.
> —And was he annoyed, Simon?
> —Annoyed! Note he! *Manly little chap!* he said.
> Mr Dedalus imitated the mincing nasal tone of the
> provincial.
> —Father Dolan and I, when I told them all at dinner
> about it, Father Dolan and I had a great laugh over
> it. You *better mind yourself, Father Dolan,* said I, or
> *young Dedalus will send you up for twice nine.* We had a
> famous laugh together over it. Ha! Ha! Ha!

Stephen's great act of self-assertion, heroism and confi-dence is reduced here to a comic anecdote; the champion of justice and the Roman people and senate is here reduced to a "manly little chap." While this passage is on the one hand, evidence of his father's insensitivity to his son—we will tend to sympathize with Stephen here—it will also cause us to reconsider the dramatic ending of the previous chapter in a different light.

One important effect of this moment for Stephen, we imag-ine, is upon his trust in authority. The confidence which he thought he shared with Father Conmee has been betrayed. Rather than reprimanding Father Dolan for his unfair treat-ment, the two joked about Stephen together. Throughout the second chapter, Stephen becomes more suspicious of author-ity figures. He has matured in many ways from the naive young boy of the first chapter. He is older now, and living in a different place—Blackrock, a suburb of Dublin. The spatial and tempo-ral distance from Clongowes mirrors the other ways in which he has grown apart from his earlier life.

A telling example of this change in Stephen's attitude occurs early in the chapter, as he is training with Mike Flynn, an old friend of his father:

> Though he had heard his father say that Mike Flynn had put some of the best runners of modern times through his hands Stephen often glanced with mistrust at his trainer's flabby stubblecovered face, as it bent over the long stained fingers through which he rolled his cigarette, and with pity at the mild lusterless blue eyes which would look up suddenly from the task and gaze vaguely into the blue distance....

Contrast this mistrustful and suspicious attitude toward his father's recommended running trainer with the way Stephen asserts throughout the first chapter what "father said," or "Dante said," or "Uncle Charles said." There is a subtle sense of arro-gance in the way Stephen looks "with pity" upon the man who is his trainer, his elder, and a close friend of his father. However, we must remember that, despite these changes in Stephen's attitude, he is still at the disposal of adult authority—there is no indication that Stephen is enrolled in track training because he wants to be. Although Mike Flynn's style of running—"his head high lifted, his knees well lifted and his hands held straight down by his sides"—seems antiquated and absurd to Stephen, he complies nonetheless.

Stephen's attitude toward religion, which is of course closely related to his attitude toward adult authority in general, is also changing as he gets older. This too is evident early on in the chapter, as Stephen visits the chapel with Uncle Charles. While Charles prays habitually and piously, Stephen is respectful, "though he did not share [Charles'] piety":

> He often wondered what his granduncle prayed for so seriously. Perhaps he prayed for the souls of purgatory or for the grace of a happy death or perhaps he prayed that God might send him back a part of the big fortune he squandered in Cork.

Stephen not only does not understand his uncle's religious belief, the familiar questioning tone which we recognize from the first chapter has now a sharper, subtly sarcastic edge. By suggesting that Charles might be praying for God to "send him back" the fortune he "squandered," Stephen is not only making a critique of Charles' religious faith (equating the selfless prayers with the selfish), but expressing his dissatisfaction with the family's declining economic status. This suggests the extent to which he is beginning to blame his father and Charles for being careless.

Stephen's faith in authority has weakened. He assumes a highly critical, almost arrogant, attitude toward those in a position of authority. His father is in serious economic trouble. Father Conmee has betrayed his confidence. Stephen is at once betrayed by and disappointed in various figures of authority in his life, while at the same time he begins to assume such roles himself. He is the leader of the boys' gang in their adventure games, fashioning himself after Napoleon. He is the leader of his class. He has been elected secretary of the gymnasium. He even assumes the paternal role of economic provider when he distributes the prize money from the essay contest.

Stephen is quick to set himself apart from his peers and to assume responsibility himself. As the day-to-day circumstances of his life become more dreary, and as the family is continually forced to move and to sell its property, Stephen's hopes become pinned to some kind of deliverance. His attitude throughout the chapter is a kind of restless expectation, an impatience with his prosaic surroundings, and a reliance upon his increasingly poetic imagination. More than once we are told of his sense of destiny, how he feels greater things are in store for him, and that his hardship is only temporary. While he listens to his father and Uncle Charles talk about Irish politics, history, and folktales, Stephen is silent, but intrigued.

The life that has seemed so incomprehensible to him in the first chapter now seems like a world of not-too-distant potential. However, it soon becomes clear that this is not a matter of following in his father's and Charles' footsteps; Stephen's sense of uniqueness and potential moves him away from his family's plight, and into the "intangible fantasies" of his own mind.

Stephen's increasingly critical attitude toward authority does not lead to a spirit of conflict. Rather, he assumes a pose of detachment. As when Uncle Charles was praying, and Stephen has an air of what we could call "respectful" silence, he feels a disengaged dissatisfac-tion with his family's declining wealth. When he feels that his father expects his support, that he "was being enlisted for the fight" his family was going to have with its creditors, Stephen's reaction is to remain as detached as possible, to think again of the future.

The change in the family's situation has clearly changed Stephen's perception of the world: "For some time he had felt the slight changes in his house; and those changes in what he had deemed unchangeable were so many slight shocks to his boyish conception of the world." This shaking of his faith in his father's stability results, in part, in a suspicion of his father, and in a sense that he must try to become more independent. He begins to consciously assume and accept the role of the exile or pariah that he was uncomfortable with in the first chapter.

Stephen's pose of detachment, then, does not lead to any direct rebellion at this point. Unlike Heron, his classroom rival who delights in bullying younger students and disrespecting the teachers (at least behind their backs), Stephen does not sway from his "quiet obedience." Amidst all the worldly voices surrounding him at school and at home, Stephen pins his hopes on his imagination. He begins to look at his present surroundings as temporary—he is trapped by circumstance, but feels that he will be able to be free soon. His longings are of course heavily colored by the literature he reads. Literature, for Stephen, provides a means of escape from the reality of his surroundings. While reading *The Count of Monte Cristo*, he fancies himself the dark romantic hero, proud in his exile. He imagines his wanderings through the city as a "quest" for a figure like Mercedes, who would have the power to "transfigure" him, at which time "weakness and timidity and inexperience would fall from him."

This idealized Mercedes—which of course doesn't connect with anything in Stephen's experience—forms his attitude toward Emma, and women more generally, throughout the novel. Emma or "E--- C---," is rarely mentioned by name in the novel. She is most often referred to as "her" or "she," which is significant because it shows how Stephen reduces her to a symbolic, and highly literary, "woman-figure" rather than perceiving her as a thinking and feeling person in her own right. She functions for Stephen, throughout the novel, more as an idea than as an actual person. As he imagines her waiting in the audience at the play, and is anxious and apparently in love, it is telling that he cannot even recall what she looks like: "He tried to recall her appearance but could not. He could only remember that she had worn a shawl about her head like a cowl and that her dark eyes had invited and unnerved him." It is telling that, as Stephen tries to recall something about her appearance, his mind reverts immediately to the effect she had on him.

Our perspective, as with everywhere else in the novel, is limited to Stephen, and in the case of Emma we sense this acutely. How different, we imagine, would Emma's account of their ride on the tram be? Whenever Stephen is obsessing over her, we cannot but suspect that here, as elsewhere, his imagination is largely responsible. It is significant that Emma is hard to distinguish from other female figures in the novel, such as Eileen, his childhood friend, and Mercedes, for whom he searches the city. Stephen treats women as symbolic and abstract figures in his life, and not as actualities. Therefore, this "image" will always be in conflict with the actuality of her behavior. In the second chapter and throughout the novel, we suspect that Emma would be surprised by Stephen's descriptions and fantasies. We wonder, with him, whether he is present in her mind at all. However, we hesitate to assign to her any "unfaithfulness" for this as he does. Given the scarcity of their actual contact, it is quite reasonable that she doesn't think of him.

This situation is illustrated nowhere better than in the poem Stephen composes for her. This is our first glimpse at an attempt of artistic creation on Stephen's part. The narrator mentions an attempt, after the Christmas dinner in the first chapter, when Stephen tried to write a poem about Parnell, but couldn't because "his brain had then refused to grapple with the theme." This time, Stephen succeeds in composing a poem, though we do not get to see it. This suggests, given the selectivity of this narrative, that the circumstances surrounding the act of creation are more important than the product of its labors. He is inspired by the incident on the late night tram with Emma, and his poem is supposedly written for her.

Stephen's composition is highly formal—he seems more enamored of the idea of writing a poem than of the poem itself. He entitles it before he starts writing, and is sure to draw an "ornamental line" underneath the title. His paper is headed with the Jesuit motto, "A.M.D.G." *("Ad Majerum Dei Gloriam"),* and at the foot of the page he writes another motto, "L.D.S." *("Laus Deo Semper").* His title shows how much he sees himself as working within a tradition of English poetry. He titles it "To E--- C---," asserting that "He knew it was right to begin so for he had seen similar titles in the collected poems of Lord Byron." The influence of Byron, however, is as superficial as the Jesuit mottoes, which he includes "from force of habit." It is as if all these extraneous, decorative surroundings—the title, the ornamental line, the Jesuit mottoes, the new bottle of ink, new pen, and new notebook—all get in the way of his creation.

It is no surprise, then, that once he is able to compose his

poem (after a brief daydream), that it is as removed as possible
from the scene the night before which inspired it. Stephen uses
his art to transform and obscure reality, while improving on it.
If he hesitates to kiss her in life, he doesn't in the poem. Just as
his way of dealing with his family's financial trouble is to detach
himself, his way of escaping the "squalor" of his life is to engage
in imaginative fantasy. His poem serves just this purpose. Just
as his interest in Emma is more in the idea of a female-figure in
his life, his interest in poetry, at this point, is more in the idea of
being a poet. It is personal and private—he hides the book, and
as far as we know doesn't show anyone. Art for Stephen, at this
point, is another means of escape and detachment from reality.

Language, throughout this chapter, continues to be fasci-
nation for Stephen, and a key aspect of the way his mind works
(and, consequently, of the way this narrative works). Consider
how, when Heron and Wallis are harassing him, it is the word
"Admit!" which sets his mind off on the long digression about
the time his English teacher accused him of heresy. This memory is spurred by this "familiar word of admonition"—he recalls
how that time, too, Heron had tried to force him to "admit" that
Byron is a heretic. The logic of this narrative is associative, and
such transitions and digressions are justified by the associations
in Stephen's mind. As we noted in the previous chapter, these
are frequently linguistic.

This capacity for a word to spawn a virtual mental flood
for Stephen is not simply limited to cases of memory, however.
While visiting Queen's College in Cork with his father, he sees
the word *Foetus* carved into a desk. Its effect on Stephen is
instantaneous:

> The sudden legend startled his blood: he seemed to
> feel the absent students of the college about him and to
> shrink from their company. A vision of their life, which
> his father's words had been powerless to evoke, sprang
> up before him out of the word cut in the desk.

Words in their active application do not have this kind of
force for Stephen—his father's constant descriptions and anec-
dotes about his school days had bored and annoyed Stephen.

But this word, carved into a desk and removed from any active or purposeful use, brings the scene immediately to life. It is as if this potential resides somewhere in the word itself.

As we soon learn, the force of this experience is greater because this word and its associations—which for Stephen are primarily sexual—resonate with his own life. Stephen experiences normal, adolescent, sexual awakening as a profoundly singular, abnormal, "brutish and individual malady." We learn that the reason that the word *Foetus* has such an effect on him is because it shocks him that other boys would think about the same "monstrous" things as he does. Again, Stephen tends to see his own experience as unique—he shies from any deep connection with others, and thus assumes that he is the only one who feels as he does. We could also read Stephen's hyperbolic reaction as a critique of Catholic teaching on adolescent sexuality—despite his pose of singularity and uniqueness, we know that Stephen did not get the idea that this is "monstrous" on his own.

Stephen's somewhat excessive reaction here is typical, especially in this chapter. As we have noted, he tends to romanticize his life, and has begun to relish the role of the sensitive and misunderstood exile. If at times Stephen seems to overdramatize himself, the narrator certainly has a role in this. As we saw earlier, this narrator is trying to mirror, through language, aspects of Stephen's personality as it develops. Throughout Chapter Two, his language is often somewhat excessive and melodramatic, to mirror Stephen's tendencies to view himself in this light. The narrative participates, with a seemingly straight face, in Stephen's posturings, presenting them as it were at face value. But do we take Stephen seriously throughout this chapter? Or might the narrator, by choosing such extreme language, be subtly parodying him?

When the narrator describes Stephen as answering Heron "urbanely," "Might I ask what you are talking about?," are we to understand that 16-year-old Stephen was "really" more urbane and sophisticated than his rude classmate, or that he was *acting* this way, putting on airs? His pretentious, elevated style of speech is not lost on Heron, anyway, who responds, "Indeed you might." Throughout this chapter, it seems that the narrator will participate in Stephen's posturings, using excessive or melodramatic language to describe his stance or tone of voice, while subtly undercutting him, or inviting us to be critical of him.

Like Stephen's poem, the narrator's language, by "participating" in Stephen's state of mind to this degree, often renders it difficult to distinguish exactly what is happening. For example, near the end of the chapter, after Stephen had squandered his money and has taken to wandering the seedy areas of Dublin at night, the narrator tells of his "shameful" and "secret riots." Only after a very close reading does it become clear that these are only in his mind, and that his encounter with the prostitute at the close of the chapter is his first. The narrator distorts the actuality in a similar way as Stephen himself does—we are to understand, after the *Foetus* episode, that he experiences his sexuality and fantasies in this extreme manner. The narrator is attempting to replicate and reflect the state of Stephen's mind; by doing so, he often participates in the same kind of distortions as Stephen.

Throughout this chapter, Stephen sets himself as far apart as possible from his surroundings. His family and his city are a source of shame, and the binary between fantasy and reality is operative throughout the chapter. Stephen begins to assume the role of the exile, modeling himself after Lord Byron and Edmond Dantes from *The Count of Monte Cristo*. He has a vague sense of a "calling," some "special purpose" for his life, though it is not yet clear what this will be. He sets himself apart from the other students at the school, and from the members of his family; he is convinced that he is unique. However, in many ways the narrative seems to suggest that Stephen might not be as different as he thinks. The fact that other boys his age have and have always had sexual fantasies comes as an absolute shock to him. He characterizes his sexuality in extreme, abnormal terms but the narrator seems to suggest that it is not as strange as he might think. And, although he criticizes his father and Uncle Charles for their irresponsibility with money, Stephen's excess and carelessness with his prize money shows us that he might not be as far from his father's world as he would like to think. He assumes the role of paternal provider, to try "to build a breakwater of order and elegance against the sordid tide of life," but realizes, of course, that he cannot sustain it. Alongside all of Stephen's assertions that he is a unique figure, the narrative continues to suggest ways he is not.

Study Questions

1. Where is the Dedalus family living at the start of the chapter?

2. What does Stephen read alone in his room at night?

3. Why does Stephen not return to Clongowes in September?

4. When the family has moved back to Dublin, why does Stephen spend so much time alone?

5. Why does Stephen feel it is appropriate to entitle his poem, "To E--- C---"?

6. Where does Stephen go to school after Clongowes?

7. Why does Heron mock Byron, who Stephen says is "the best poet"?

8. What word does Stephen see carved on a desk at Queen's College in Cork?

9. Where does Stephen get the money for his "season of pleasure"?

10. How does Stephen react to the prostitute at the end of the chapter?

Answers

1. The family has moved to Blackrock, a suburb on the coast southeast of Dublin.

2. Stephen reads a translation of *The Count of Monte Cristo* by Alexandre Dumas.

3. Stephen is unable to return to Clongowes because his father can no longer afford to send him.

4. Stephen spends so much time alone in Dublin because he has few friends, and his Uncle Charles has gotten too old to go outside.

5. Stephen imitates the titles of some poems he has seen in the collected works of Lord Byron, the English Romantic poet.

6. Stephen is sent to Belvedere College by special arrangement by Father Conmee, Stephen's former rector at Clongowes. Conmee is now at Belvedere, and arranges for Stephen and his brother Maurice to attend the Jesuit academy.

7. Heron says that Byron was a heretic.

8. Stephen sees the word *"Foetus"* carved in the desk in the lecture hall at Queen's College.

9. Stephen wins 33 pounds in an essay competition, which he spends lavishly and generously, if quickly and irresponsibly.

10. Stephen's reaction to the prostitute is passive and submissive.

Suggested Essay Topics

1. Stephen's attitude toward authority and authority figures undergoes some important changes in Chapter II. Discuss some ways in which Stephen's behavior in this chapter contrasts with his behavior in the first chapter. Examine specific scenes and passages where this contrast is evident.

2. Throughout Chapter II, we learn much about Stephen's attitude toward women. From the Mercedes-figure in the early pages to the prostitute at the end, we see his idea and ideal of women develop. Compare and contrast the female-figures in the novel (Mercedes, Emma, the prostitutes) and the place they hold in Stephen's imaginative life.

3. In what ways does this narrator seem to undercut Stephen's sense of uniqueness and singularity? Examine some scenes where it seems that the narrator takes an ironic view toward Stephen.

SECTION FOUR

Chapter III

(pages 72–104)

New Characters:

Ennis: *a classmate of Stephen's at Belvedere*

Old Woman: *in the street, who directs Stephen to the chapel*

Priest: *at the Church Street chapel where Stephen confesses*

Summary

Stephen has now made a habit of visiting brothels. In school, he is bored and uninspired, and the narrative details the wanderings of his mind while he sits in class. He is not plagued by guilt for his sins, but rather feels a "cold lucid indifference." He feels that he is beyond salvation, and can do nothing to control his lust. He has begun to despise his fellow students, in part because of what he sees as an empty and hypocritical piety on their part. He serves as prefecture of the sodality of the Blessed Virgin Mary—a highly esteemed religious organization at Belvedere—but feels no guilt at the "falsehood of his position." He sometimes considers confessing to the members of the sodality, but feels such contempt for them that he does not.

After the math class is over, the other students urge Stephen to try and stall the teacher of the next class by asking difficult questions about the catechism. Before the religion class, Stephen enjoys contemplating the theological dilemmas. When the rector comes in, he announces that a religious retreat in honor of St. Francis Xavier will begin on Wednesday afternoon. He tells the class about Francis Xavier's life—he was one of the first followers of Ignatius, the Founder of the Jesuit order. He spends his career converting pagans in the Indies, Africa and Asia, and is known for the great number of converts he amassed. Stephen anticipates the coming retreat with anxiety and fear.

In the next section, Stephen is at the retreat. Father Arnall is giving an introductory sermon, which causes Stephen to remember his days at Clongowes. Father Arnall welcomes the boys, and speaks of the tradition of this retreat. He talks of the boys who have done it in years past, and wonders where they are now. He explains the significance and importance of a periodic retreat from ordinary life, and says that during the retreat they will be taught about the "four last things": death, judgment, hell, and heaven. He encourages them to clear their minds of worldly thoughts, and to attend to their souls. Father Arnall claims that this retreat will have a profound impact on their lives.

After dinner, it is clear that the promise of the next four days has already had an effect on Stephen—he perceives himself as a "beast," and begins to feel fear.

This fear becomes "a terror of spirit" as the sermon makes Stephen think of his own death and judgment in morbid detail. This leads him to consider Doomsday, the final judgment. The sermon affects Stephen deeply and personally, and he feels how his "soul was festering in sin."

Walking home, he hears a girl laughing, which causes him intense shame. He thinks of Emma, and is ashamed as he imagines how she would react to his lifestyle. He imagines repenting, and her forgiving him, and he imagines the Virgin Mary simultaneously marrying and forgiving the both of them. It is raining, and Stephen thinks of the biblical flood.

Next, we hear a sermon which solidifies Stephen's conviction that he must repent. Beginning with Creation and Original Sin, the sermon reaches the story of Jesus and the importance of repentance and God's forgiveness. Then follows a lengthy and detailed description of the torments of hell and damnation—it is a physical and geographical account of hell, and a graphic depiction of the bodily and psychological torments hell inflicts on the damned.

As he leaves the chapel, Stephen is greatly upset by the sermon. He fears hell and death, and decides that there is still time to change his life. In class, Stephen's thoughts are saturated with the language of the sermon. When confessions are being heard, Stephen feels that he must confess, but wonders if he can. He decides that he cannot confess in the college chapel, but must go elsewhere.

That night, the sermon focuses upon the spiritual torments of hell. It details how the damned have a full awareness of what they have lost, and that their conscience will continue to plague them with guilt. He reminds the boys of the eternity of hell, and describes how the awareness of this would torment the damned. He describes sin as a personal affront to Jesus, and the sermon ends with a prayer of repentance, which Stephen takes to heart.

After dinner, Stephen goes up to his room to pray, still feeling the effects of the sermon. He thinks about his sins, and feels surprised that God has allowed him to live this long. With his eyes closed, he has a vision of hell—Stephen's hell is a land of dry thistle and weed, solid excrement, dim light, and goat-like, half-human creatures who mumble and circle around him. His vision of hell sickens and frightens him. He almost faints, then vomits, and, weakened, he prays.

In the evening, he leaves the house, looking to confess his sins, but is scared that he won't be able to. Seeing some poor girls sitting on the side of the street, Stephen is ashamed at the thought that their souls are dearer to God than his. He asks an old woman where the nearest chapel is, and she directs him.

Inside the Church St. Chapel, he kneels at the last bench. Once the priest arrives and the other people in the chapel begin going in for confession, Stephen has second thoughts. When his turn comes, however, he goes in almost automatically. Inside the confessional, he recites the *Confiteor,* and tells the priest that it has been eight months since his last confession. First he confesses more minor sins—masses he missed, prayers not said—then gradually reaches his "sins of impurity." He tells the priest all the details. When the priest asks how old he is, Stephen answers, "sixteen." The priest implores Stephen to repent and to change his lifestyle, suggesting that he pray to the Virgin Mary when he is tempted. The priest blesses him, and Stephen prays fervently.

On his way home, Stephen is ecstatic, feeling an inner peace

in his life. In the morning, he takes communion with his classmates. The ritual affects Stephen deeply, and he feels that a new
life has begun for him.

Analysis

Once again, the chapter begins with a sense of dull routine.
The excitement of his transgression, which had ended Chapter
Two is here deflated—there is no indication of any sense of thrill
or danger in Stephen's now frequent visits to the brothels. Instead,
they have become as dull and ordinary for him as the rest of the
Dublin society from which he seeks to distance himself. Stephen's attempts to set himself apart from his surroundings seem
frustrated—the narrator is showing us, at the start of this chapter,
that perhaps Stephen's experience with the prostitute was not the
significant transformative experience that he had thought.

The verb tense throughout the opening paragraphs, as Stephen is in class thinking of the night to come, suggests just how
much of a habit this has become for him:

> It would be a gloomy secret night. After early nightfall
> the yellow lamps would light up, here and there, the
> squalid quarter of the brothels. He would follow a
> devious course up and down the streets....

Clearly, this "gloomy secret night" will not differ greatly
from any other night of the week for Stephen. Visiting the brothels seems to have become as much a part of his daily routine as
school.

However, the fact that this habit has lost its charge of excitement for Stephen is made clear by the narrator's use of light
imagery, which characterizes Stephen's present life as dull,
dusky, and dim:

> The swift December dusk had come tumbling
> clownishly after its dull day and, as he started through
> the dull square window of the schoolroom, he felt his
> belly crave for its food.

The repetition of "dull" and "dusk" throughout the opening
pages of the chapter suggests both habit and stasis, while the

meta-phorical language of dusk and dullness suggests just how plain and unappealing Stephen's lifestyle has become for him.

In a sense, this first paragraph represents Stephen's moral state at the start of this chapter. Chapter III is thematically concerned with Stephen's moral and religious state, which undergoes a major transformation over the course of the five days covered by the chapter. As the chapter opens, he is in class daydreaming about dinner:

> He hoped there would be stew for dinner, turnips and carrots and bruised potatoes and fat mutton pieces to be ladled out in thick peppered flourfattened sauce. Stuff it into you, his belly counselled him.

His intellect, or spirit, is subsumed in favor of his bodily appetites, a clear echo of the lustful nature of his sin. That this sin has become dull and unappealing in itself is suggested by the quality of food Stephen expects: bruised, fat, thick, and flourfattened. He does not indicate that there is something about the food itself which appeals to him. Rather, its chief quality that is that it will satisfy a bodily need, evidenced by the crudity of the phrase, "stuff it into you." Stephen is now motivated by the physical and worldly—his "belly" is personified as an entity separate from and dominant over his mind. His lust for food is clearly associated with his sexual lust, as his mind seems to progress naturally from thinking about dinner to thinking about wandering the brothel district. Both cravings are equally devoid of feeling.

As the novel's central chapter, Chapter III is the most temporally and thematically focused and concentrated. Whereas the other chapters in the novel cover anywhere from a few months to a few years in Stephen's life, Chapter III intensely focuses on five crucial days. Even within these five days, the narrative excludes everything except what specifically concerns Stephen's spiritual and religious status. We have the impression that this retreat consists only of Stephen hearing sermons, then cowering in his room, and eventually walking across town for confession. While he surely did many other things during these days, this narrator is interested only in presenting the details essential to the development of Stephen's soul. Therefore, the focus of the narrative in this chapter is intensely concentrated.

John Blades describes it as a "chapter of excesses." Father Arnall's sermons are excessive in their scope, and in their morbid and explicit attention to detail. The narrative is excessive in its unrelenting and comprehensive presentation of these sermons. It shifts from direct quotation of the priest to the style of paraphrase that seems to present Stephen's reactions to the sermon at the same time, but our overall impression of this section of the chapter is like sitting through these entire sermons. There is very little narrative presence interrupting the relentless flow of the priest's words. Stephen's response is also somewhat excessive, feeling that "every word was for him," and fearing an immediate death at the hand of God on his way back to his room.

One important change in Stephen's character in this chapter is in his attitude toward his peers. What we recognize in Chapter Two as a pose of detachment has now become a more explicit "contempt" for his peers. He perceives their acts of piety and religious devotion as hypocritical, easy and shallow, and feels no shame about his "double life" around them. The pose of exile and detachment here takes on a distinctly sinful quality—pride. This is an extreme manifestation of his feelings of uniqueness and exile in Chapter Two, and one which suggests the sinful state of his soul. The restlessness and impatience with the world of his family and his classmates, and the pervasive hope that some great calling awaits him, has now become a "cold lucid indifference" toward his own soul, and toward the extent to which he continues to live in sin.

While Stephen tries to convince himself that he is indifferent to his sin, and feels no regret or discomfort with "the falsehood of his position" as prefect of the sodality of the Blessed Virgin Mary, it is clear that he has been not able to escape the influence of the Catholic church. First of all, his sinful lifestyle does to constitute a rejection of or loss of belief in God:

> What did it avail to pray when he knew that his soul
> lusted after its own destruction? A certain pride, a
> certain awe, withheld him from offering to God even

one prayer at night though he knew it was in God's power to take away his life while he slept and hurl his soul hellward ere he could beg for mercy.

Stephen seems to fashion himself here after Milton's Satan; we can sense a romantic pleasure in his defiance of God's power. For Stephen never expresses disbelief of or lack of faith in God, and he is still intimately familiar with the tenents of the Catholic faith (evidenced by his role as resident expert in his class on obscure questions about the catechism). Stephen seems to take both pride and morbid and masochistic pleasure in his deep theological knowledge:

It was strange too that he found an arid pleasure in following up to the end of rigid lines of the doctrines of the church and penetrating into obscure silences only to hear and feel the more deeply his own condemnation.

His interest in the details of Catholic doctrine has a certain detached quality—as if religion were a series of puzzling intellectual questions and obscure knowledge. At the same time, however, Stephen seems to find a certain thrill in applying the consequences of these doctrines to his own sinful life. He is deeply aware of the "letter of the law," but this awareness never translates into a reaction to the "spirit of the law" until after the retreat. His interest in theological questions bears a very limited connection to his daily life. Up to this point, Stephen's relationship to the church is both an idle intellectual game, and a useful romantic trope for his imaginative construction of his own life.

Though he manages to remain detached to this degree, he is never outside of the structures of the church. He always refers to his "sin" and to his "condemnation," terms that have no application outside of the framework of religious doctrine and belief. By identifying his behavior as a "sin," and by dwelling on it to this degree, we can see how much the language and beliefs of the Catholic church continue to have a hold on him. We can see, from the start of the chapter, just how ripe Stephen is to be swayed by the sermon.

The centerpiece of this chapter is the pair of sermons Father

Arnall gives concerning hell and damnation. He quite literally puts "the fear of God" into Stephen, who, at the end of the
chapter, repents, confesses, and begins a new life in the service
of God. The narrator, as a recognizable presence, all but drops
out of the picture in this section. Stephen speaks very little in
this chapter, but listens and reacts internally to the sermon. The
narrator is able to illustrate this by recreating Stephen's experience for the reader—we are made to listen to the sermon almost
word-for-word, which recreates Stephen's experience in the congregation, continuing to align us exclusively with his perspective.

   Although the narrative starts by quoting large portions of
the sermon, we soon are able to recognize many characteristics
of Father Arnall's language in the narrator's "own" narration,
paraphrasing to the extent that the narrator's voice sounds like
the priest's:

> At the last moment of consciousness the whole earthly
> life passed before the vision of the soul and, ere it had
> time to reflect, the body had died and the soul stood
> terrified before the judgement seat. God, who had long
> been merciful, would then be just....

Eventually, the narration starts to present the sermon
directly, but without quoting, and without the marks of paraphrase in its syntax. The two voices seem to have merged
completely:

> And this day will come, shall come, must come; the
> day of death and the day of judgment. It is appointed
> unto man to die and after death the judgment. Death is
> certain. The time and manner are uncertain...

The narrator no longer seems to be telling us what the priest
said, so much as saying it directly. Our close alignment with Stephen's perspective allows us to "experience" this sermon more or
less from his position as an audience member in the congregation.

   The priest's rhetoric becomes the "action" of this chapter.
Since Stephen is convinced that "every word was for him," when
we read the narrator's paraphrase of the sermon, we are able to
gauge Stephen's reaction at the same time. Father Arnall, who

presumably gives the sermon (since he is running the retreat), is named initially before being reduced to "the priest." He eventually recedes as a direct presence in the narrative altogether. His language becomes, then, much less personalized, underscoring just how much Stephen is tending to take this as God's direct word, and as an unadulterated voice of absolute authority.

Stephen's reaction to the sermon, then, represents a kind of regression. Throughout Chapter II, as we recognized, Stephen was becoming increasingly suspicious of authority figures. In the early section of Chapter III, as his classmates are encouraging him to stall the teacher with a series of obscure and difficult theological questions, we are reminded of his lack of deep regard for authority. However, throughout Chapter Three, he becomes less critical and more accepting of the authority of the clergy, represent-ed by Father Arnall at the retreat, and the old priest at the chapel to whom Stephen confesses. His relationship to religion here is more emotional and simplistic. He does not question the authorities on the finer points of Catholic doctrine, but fears and respects them, and takes their words and their power directly to heart.

This is one of several ways in which Stephen's repentance represents a return to innocence. The reappearance of Father Arnall in the novel, whom we last saw in Chapter I, at Clongowes, recalls us to the time when Stephen was younger:

> The figure of his old master, so strangely rearisen, brought back to Stephen's mind his life at Clongowes: the wide play-grounds, swarming with boys, the square ditch, the little cemetery off the main avenue of limes where he had dreamed of being buried, the firelight on the wall of the infirmary where he lay sick, the sorrowful face of Brother Michael. His soul, as these memories came back to him, became again a child's soul.

Whereas in Chapter II, Stephen was eager to distance himself from those days, when "the memory of his childhood [was] dim" and he could not "call forth...vivid moments" but "only names," seeing Father Arnall calls up vivid and detailed memories for Stephen. In a sense, these are "memories" for the reader, too, as they cause us to recall how Stephen was then. The very appearance of Father Arnall symbolizes how this retreat will be a return to a state of innocence for Stephen, who assumes a childlike openness as he listens to the sermon. The narrator's language at the end of the chapter, after Stephen has repented and confessed, recalls the more childlike rhythms of Chapter I:

> He had confessed and God had pardoned him. His soul was made fair and holy once more, holy and happy. It would be beautiful to die if God so willed. It was beautiful to live if God so willed, to live in grace a life of peace and virtue and forbearance with others.

The convention of the priest calling him "my child" takes on special significance, as Stephen's confession represents a revision to his more childlike submission to voices of authority.

If the effect of Stephen's repentance is a seeming return to a state of lost innocence, then the priest's sermon certainly contributes to this. Stephen's repentance and change of heart are motivated by fear more than anything else. The sermon focuses solely on the threat of the tortures of hell; the method is to intimidate the young boys into behaving according to the law of God. His reason for living a pious life never move beyond intimidation. He spends a large portion of his sermon describing hell's geographical and physical characteristics with quasi-scientific exactness, comparing hell's heat and fire to heat and fire on earth, trying to impress upon the boys in earthly terms the inconceivable and unearthly extremity and eternity of hell's torments. The priest never offers a positive reason to believe in and follow God, but rests his argument solely on the consequences of a sinful life.

His very poetic and imaginative reconstruction of hell appeals to Stephen's artistic sensibility rather than to his intellect. Stephen's remorse, then, is not moral or intellectual in character—it is motivated primarily by fear of hell, God's wrath, and eternal damnation. Like the omnipresent threat of pandying or flogging at Clongowes, hell functions as an intimidation tactic, divorced from any moral choice. In Chapter Three, Joyce seems to be making his most explicit critique of the Catholic church. Although the church functions throughout the novel as one of the primary fetters which Stephen Dedalus tries to free himself from, in this chapter its mechanisms are portrayed most explicitly as coercive, simplistic, and reductive.

Stephen's repentance and spiritual rebirth has an immediate effect on his attitude toward his peers. Walking home from confession, he is pleased "to live in grace a life of peace and virtue and forbearance with others." At communion the next day, he partakes humbly of the communal spirit of the ritual:

> The boys were all there, kneeling in their places. He
> knelt among them, happy and shy....
> He knelt before the altar with his classmates, holding
> the altar cloth with them over a living rail of hands.

Stephen seems to feel a connection with his peers for the first time in the novel. His alienation and insecurity, which he felt as a child, and his proud exile, which developed as an adolescent, all seem to be abandoned in favor of this feeling of brotherhood and connectedness.

Before his confession, however, Stephen's sense of detachment and singularity is still present. His reaction to the sermon is intensely personal—he interprets it as a personal message from God, and the narrator illustrates how Stephen's extreme reaction is unique among his classmates. After the first sermon, while Stephen is vividly imagining his own death and damnation, the other students' voices serve to undercut and deflate his personal drama:

> His flesh shrank together as it felt the approach of the
> ravenous tongues of flames, dried up as it felt about it
> the swirl of stifling air. He had died. Yes. He was judged.
> A wave of fire swept through his body: the first. Again a
> wave. His brain began to glow. Another. His brain was
> simmering and bubbling within the cracking tenement
> of the skull. Flames burst forth from his skull like a
> corolla, shrieking like voices:
>
> —Hell! Hell! Hell! Hell! Hell!
> Voices spoke near him:
> —On hell.

—I suppose he rubbed it into you well.
—You bet he did. He put us all into a blue funk.
—That's what you fellows want: and plenty of it to make
you work.

The sound, *like* voices, in Stephen's imagination is juxtaposed with the actual voices of Mr. Tate and Vincent Heron. The
colloquial chattiness of their reaction—"he rubbed it into you,"
"you bet he did"—presents a plainer reality next to Stephen's
imaginative life, suggesting that Stephen's egotism results in
an overreaction on his part. Mr. Tate jokingly reduces the voice
of God which has quaked Stephen's soul to a mere scare tactic
to keep the students working. The narrator presents Stephen's
experience of these things literally, physically, which furthers
this sense of two separate realities here. Stephen's skull is melting, flames are shooting from his head, while Mr. Tate and Heron
joke about the students being put into a "blue funk."
     We might sense a tone of elitism or superiority in Stephen's
reaction, if we keep in mind his attitude of contempt toward the
other students' shows of piety earlier. It is easy to see how his
reaction would seem, to him, as the "real" or "righteous" one,
while theirs is shallow and trivial. The same kind of operative
distinction between Stephen's imaginative reality and ordinary
life, which characterized Chapter II, is at work here. We can see,
in this scene, Stephen's poetic and dramatic imagination coloring
his experience as unique and incommunicable, participating in
and contributing to his feeling of alienation.
     His feelings of contempt and disdain for his peers might still
be somewhat active as he decides that he must confess his sins,
"but not there among his school companions." Ostensibly, his
motive here is "shame" and "abjection of spirit"—he feels he is
not worthy to confess in the college chapel among their "boyish hearts." Implicit in this humility, however, is the same kind
of feeling of exile, detachment, and superiority which motivated
his "contempt" for them earlier in the chapter. Stephen does not
feel that he is a part of this community. Before, he had seen their
"boyishness" as a limiting and infuriating immaturity. Now,
however, he sees it as an innocence which he has lost.

As he is wandering the streets looking for a chapel, he sees "frowsy girls" along the side of the road. His "humiliation" that their souls may be dearer to God than his has its root in an implicit feeling of superiority or egotism. The implication, we suppose, is that he feels his soul should be dearer to God. Stephen's confession and repentance is motivated, in part, by a desire to change all this—while waiting his turn in the chapel, he is inspired by thinking about Jesus, and his love for the "poor and simple people." Before confession, Stephen's motivation is expressed thus:

> He would be at one with others and with God. He would love his neighbor. He would love God Who had made and loved him. He would kneel and pray with others and be happy. God would look down on him and on them and would love them all.

This communally oriented spirit is uncharacteristic of the Stephen we know. He seeks to identify himself with the group, to have his individual identity—which until now has been most important to him—subsumed under a group identity, and under God.

This represents another important reversion of the tendencies we recognized in Chapter II. Stephen is trying to relinquish the role of exile he began to assume then. His confession and repentance is motivated by and seems to result in a feeling of brotherhood and communion with humanity. His religious rebirth "sets back the clock" in various ways. It represents a return to a state of innocence, reconciling his sins with God; it represents a new, less critical attitude toward authority, and a less hostile attitude toward his peers. Up to this point, Stephen's individual identity was most important, and he sought only to find some means of escape from ordinary Dublin life, but he now seems reconciled to his peers and to his environment. The image of Stephen wandering the dark streets to find a chapel near the end of Chapter III is a clear echo of the end of Chapter Two, when he wanders the streets looking for a woman. Do we understand this as a kind of revision of this earlier scene, an attempt at starting over, this time on the "right foot"? Or do we hear an ironic echo of the earlier Stephen even here, suggesting that perhaps his change of heart is neither permanent nor desirable? He seems to have changed profoundly as Chapter Three closes—he seems happy to be a part of a "living rail of hands," to have conformed to the authority of God and the church. However, we should be suspicious, by now, of this novel's climaxes, and wonder, as we begin Chapter Four, whether this transformation is really for the better.

Study Questions

1. What is Stephen's attitude toward his sinful lifestyle as Chapter Three opens?

2. What religious office does Stephen hold at Belvedere?

3. What is important about St. Francis Xavier, according to the rector?

4. What are the "four last things" the sermons will cover during the retreat?

5. What effect does seeing Father Arnall have upon Stephen?

6. Why does Stephen feel he cannot confess at the college chapel?

7. Describe Stephen's vision of hell.

8. What effect does seeing the "frowsy girls" on the side of the road have on Stephen?

9. How old is Stephen in Chapter Three?

10. What does the priest tell Stephen after confession?

Answers

1. Stephen claims to be indifferent; he does not feel shame or guilt around his classmates, and is too proud to pray to God and repent.

2. Stephen is prefect of the sodality of the Blessed Virgin Mary.

3. The rector tells the boys that St. Francis Xavier was one of the original Jesuits, one of the first followers of Ignatius.

He was known for converting people in the Indies, Africa, and Asia. According to the rector, he once converted 10,000 in one month.

4. The "four last things" are death, judgment, hell, and heaven. The topic of the sermons never reach heaven, as promised.

5. Seeing Father Arnall recalls Stephen to his Clongowes days, making his soul "become again a child's soul," symbolizing how this retreat signifies a return to innocence for him.

6. Stephen does not want to confess along with his classmates out of shame for the extent of his sins.

7. Stephen imagines hell as peopled with goat-like, half-human creatures who encircle him, mumbling incoherently. It is a land of dry thistle and weeds, solid excrement, and dim light.

8. When Stephen sees the poor girls, he is ashamed and humiliated at the thought that their souls are dearer to God than his.

9. Stephen tells the priest during confession that he is 16 years old.

10. The priest tells Stephen to resist the Devil's temptation, to repent, and to give up his life of sin. He tells Stephen to pray to the Virgin Mary when he is tempted.

Suggested Essay Topics

1. In many ways, Chapter III represents a reversal of some of the tendencies Stephen developed in Chapter II. Discuss the changes in his attitude toward authority figures, his peers, and his identity as an individual. In what ways does Stephen seem to have changed as the chapter closes?

2. Stephen interprets Father Arnall's sermons as a personal message, sensing that "every word" of it was intended "for him." Reread the sermons carefully. What can you identify about the language and rhetorical strategy of the sermons that would appeal so strongly to Stephen? Some

things to look for in the descriptions of hell might include: the descriptions of hell's torments, the language of exile used here; the poetic and metaphorical language; and the language of the senses and the body.

3. What is the effect of the narrator aligning us with Stephen Dedalus' perspective during the sermons? How does this color our perspective toward the sermons, which seem otherwise to be presented word-for-word? How would the chapter read differently if it were aligned with the perspective of Vincent Heron, for example? Does our awareness of Stephen's idiosyncratic character affect our understanding of the communion scene at the end?

SECTION FIVE

Chapter IV
(pages 105–124)

New Characters:

The Director: *at Belvedere College, asks Stephen to consider joining the priesthood*

Dan Crosby: *a tutor, who goes with Stephen's father to find out
about the university for Stephen*

Dwyer, Towser, Shuley, Ennis, Connolly: *acquaintances of Stephen's; he sees them swimming near the strand*

Summary

Stephen has now dedicated his life to the service of God—
each day is structured around prayer, ritual, and religious devotions. He attends mass each morning, and offers ejaculations
and prayers each day for the souls in purgatory. He sees his daily
life now in terms of eternity, and senses an immediate connection between his acts on earth and their repercussions in heaven.
Each of his three daily chaplets is dedicated to one of the "three
theological virtues," Father, Son and Holy Ghost; each day of the
week is devoted toward gaining one of the seven gifts of the Holy
Ghost, and toward driving out each of the seven deadly sins.

Stephen views every aspect of his life as a gift from God; the
world now exists for him "as a theorem of divine power and love
and universality." He tries to mortify and discipline each of his
senses. He keeps his eyes to the ground, doesn't try to avoid loud
or unpleasant noises, intentionally subjects himself to unpleasant smells, and is strict about his diet, making sure he does not

enjoy his food. He goes to great efforts to remain physically uncomfor-table, both while sleeping and awake.

He is discouraged that, despite his efforts, he continues to get angry or impatient with others for trivial reasons. However, he takes great pleasure in being able to avoid temptation, though he periodically doubts how completely he has changed his life. In confession, he sometimes has to repeat an earlier sin because he sins so infrequently now. Stephen is frustrated, because it seems that he will never be able to fully escape the sins which he had struggled to confess at the end of Chapter III.

In the next section, Stephen is speaking with the director of Belvedere College. He has been summoned to the director's office, and, while making friendly and respectful small-talk, Stephen wonders why he has really been sent there. They begin talking about the Dominican and Franciscan orders, and of their respective styles of dress.

Stephen begins to think about his experiences with the Jesuits at school. He continues to hold them in high regard, although they sometimes seem "a little childish" in their judgments.

The director soon comes to the point, however, asking if Stephen has ever felt a vocation to join the priesthood. Stephen starts to answer "yes," but remains silent. He tells the priest that he has "sometimes thought of it." The priest tells him that only one or two boys from the college will be the sort who will be called by God, and suggests that Stephen, with his intelligence, devotion, and leadership qualities, might be one. The priest begins to talk of the power and authority a priest has, which reminds Stephen of "his own proud musings" on the subject, when he had imagined himself as a priest. The idea seems to appeal to him—he is attracted to the secret knowledge and power the priesthood could give him.

The priest tells him that his mass the next morning will be specially dedicated so that God may reveal His will to Stephen. He cautions Stephen to be certain of his decision, because it is a final one, on which the salvation of his soul may depend.

As he leaves the director's office, Stephen and the director shake hands. Stephen notes the gravity of the expression on the priest's face. Walking home, he tries to imagine himself as a priest. Remembering the "troubling odour" of Clongowes, he begins to feel restless and confused. He begins to imagine how restless and unhappy he would be, and quickly decides that he could not become a priest, that "he would fall," and that "his destiny was to be elusive of social or religious orders."

Stephen arrives at home, where his brothers and sisters are having tea. He learns that his parents have gone to look at another home. The family is moving again, under pressure from the landlord. The children start to sing, and soon Stephen joins them. It pains him to hear the "overture of weariness" in their young voices, and he thinks sadly of the "weariness and pain" of all generations of children.

In the next section, Stephen is pacing anxiously as his father and Dan Crosby, his tutor, have gone to find out about the university for him. After an hour of waiting, he leaves for the Bull, a sandy island near the mouth of the Liffey.

While walking, he thinks of the university. He knows his mother is hostile to the idea, which Stephen takes as an indication of how their lives are drifting apart. He still feels that he has been born for some special purpose, and he senses that the university will lead to new adventures.

As he crosses the bridge on the way to the Bull, he passes a squad of Christian Brothers, walking two by two. He has a moment of shame or regret for refusing to join the priesthood, but reassures himself that their life is not for him.

He thinks of a phrase he has read, "A day of dappled sea-borne clouds," and marvels at how the words seem to capture the moment so perfectly. He muses about what it is that fascinates him about words.

Having crossed the bridge, he heads toward the sea. Looking at the clouds coming in from the sea, he thinks of Europe, where they have come from. His reverie is interrupted, however, by a group of his classmates who are bathing in the sea. They call to him, and he stops briefly to chat, impatient with their immaturity, and repulsed by their adolescent nakedness. They call his name in Latinate and Greek forms, "Stephenos Dedalos" and "Stephanoumenos," which makes him think of his name as a prophecy. He understands Daedalus, the mythical artificer, as a "symbol of the artist forging anew in his workshop out of the sluggish matter of the earth a new soaring impalpable imperishable being," and wonders if this is an indication of his calling in life. He feels excited, and knows he must dedicate his life and soul to art.

He walks away from the boys, heading down the strand, along the sea. He sees a girl alone, wading in the sea, with her skirts pinned up around her waist. She seems to him like a bird, and he takes her as a sign of his newly chosen destiny. Their eyes meet, but they do not speak. Stephen wanders off, delirious with excitement. He has lost track of time and, realizing it is late and he has wandered far out of his way, he runs back toward the land. He lays down before long, and sleeps. When he awakes, it is evening, and the new moon has risen.

Analysis

In this crucial, climactic chapter, Stephen's awareness of his artistic vision begins to crystallize. Over the course of the chapter, he frees himself from the "nets" of the church, and from his family, embracing the role of the exile figure more explicitly than before. As the chapter ends, Stephen is alone on the seashore, facing away from Ireland, toward Europe. He has literally left his father behind, who had gone to see about the university for him. And he has left the church behind, as he decides he cannot become a priest, and must instead discover his destiny on his own, apart from the trappings of religion, family, or nation. Just as, over the course of Chapter Three, Stephen had undergone an almost total religious transformation, over the course of this chapter his outlook changes greatly. There is a progression in Chapter IV from the rigid order of Stephen's religious devotion and the promise of an even more rigid order in the priesthood, to uncertainty and loss of faith, disorder and confusion, and back to a certainty in a different kind of calling, that of creative art.

Stephen's religious devotion, at the start of this chapter, has none of the passion of his conversion. Stephen's piety is rigidly structured, almost monkish—the narrator's language in this first section is prosaic, dry and businesslike, cataloging Stephen's tight and orderly schedule of religious devotion.

Again, we see how what had seemed a passionate and climactic epiphany—Stephen's repentance and religious awakening at the end of Chapter Three—seems to become, at the start of the next chapter, a dull and habitual routine.

Stephen's religious devotion has a particularly mathematical and economical character, which tends to undercut our sense of his seriousness. The weeks and even the days of his life are broken down into numbered segments. His prayers for the souls in purgatory are described as a kind of transaction with God; Stephen is anxious that he "could never know how much temporal punishment he had remitted by way of suffrage for the agonizing souls." He constantly frets that he has not been able to amass enough to make an appreciable difference. The economic metaphors are made more explicit further on, as Stephen imagines the immediate repercussions in heaven of his acts of devotion on earth:

> At times his sense of such immediate repercussion was so lively that he seemed to feel his soul in devotion pressing like fingers the keyboard of a great cash register and to see the amount of his purchase start forth immediately in heaven.

Though Stephen is certainly adamant in his dedication to the religious life, the narrator seems to be subtly parodying his piety in passages like this. When Stephen views his prayers in terms of "the amount of his purchase," imagining a "great cash register" in heaven, his religious dedication seems simplistic and reductive.

While on the one hand this portrayal of Stephen's faith seems rather ridiculous and simplistic, on the other hand, it represents a vividly imaginative kind of belief. In a manner which is typical of Stephen, his religious life colors his daily life in every aspect—he now understands his life in terms of eternity, and imagines heaven's response to his every action. His imagination is typically poetic and metaphorical in character. For example, when he recites the rosary prayers while walking down the street, he imagines the beads "transformed . . . into coronals of flowers of such vague unearthly texture that they seemed to him as hueless and odorless as they were nameless." His daily rituals, although certainly routine and habitualized to an extreme degree, represent for Stephen an active and vivid imaginative life.

Religion, for Stephen, serves to keep him detached from ordinary Dublin life—its effect on his imagination can be accurately compared to the effect of the *Count of Monte Cristo in* Chapter II. Although it is imaginative, however, his devotion becomes less and less passionate. He can comprehend minute theological details, but cannot conceive of the notion of God's eternal love:

> The imagery through which the nature and kinship of the Three Persons of the Trinity were darkly shadowed forth in the books of devotion which he read...were easier of acceptance by his mind by reason of their august incomprehensibility that was the simple fact that God had loved his soul from all eternity, for ages before he had been born into the world, for ages before the world itself had existed.

It is not just God's love which Stephen finds difficult to understand or to feel:

> He had heard the names of the passions of love and hate pronounced solemnly on the stage and in the pulpit, had found them set forth solemnly in books, and had wondered why his soul was unable to harbour them for any time or to force his lips to utter their names with conviction.

Books do not connect to life for Stephen, and his faith is more intellectual than emotional. Once the lust from which he suffered has been effectively banished, his mind is left "lucid and indifferent." The same kind of indifference that had characterized Stephen's spiritual life before his conversion is used to characterize him now—the narrator suggests that in some sense maybe Stephen's life has not charged as completely as it may seem.

He is still cut off from other people, for example. There is a detached, intellectual quality to his religious faith. He looks at the world as evidence of divine power, but in a way that does not necessarily reveal any appreciation or love for the beauty in the world:

> The world for all its solid substance and complexity no longer existed for his soul save as a theorem of divine power and love and universality.

Stephen is certainly "otherworldly" in his religious devotion. It is as if his life is only a brief preparation for eternity, part of some "divine purpose" that he "dared not question." It is difficult for him to "understand why it was in any way necessary that he should continue to live."

The absurdities of his efforts to mortify his senses illustrate how his religious faith is cutting him off from the world around him. This contrasts strongly with the extremely physical language which characterized Stephen at the start of Chapter III, and represents one way that he has changed in Chapter IV. One way he has not changed, however, is how detached he is from life around him. In Chapter III, it was as a result of this physicality, and the nature of his sin, that he felt no sense of community with those around him. In this chapter, after the communion scene with Stephen kneeling among his classmates, we might assume that he is now on some common ground with them, and is a part of their community. Instead, however, he finds that "To merge his life in the common tide of other lives was harder for him than any fasting or prayer." Despite his efforts, he is still isolated from his peers. Religion for Stephen is an intensely private, almost solipsistic experience, and becomes only one more way that he feels alienated from those around him.

In some ways, we might suspect that Stephen's religious transformation is incomplete. But his dedication is so extreme that when the director of Belvedere asks him if he has considered joining the priesthood, we may very well assume that he will accept the offer. His devotion is already very priestlike in its rigid self-discipline, and in its effect of keeping him cut off from the flow of ordinary life. He indeed seems, as the priest suggests, an ideal candidate.

At the same time, however, many aspects of the language used to describe this scene prefigure Stephen's rejection of the offer, and ultimately of the church and religious life altogether. The priest himself is described in the language of death and stagnation:

> The priest's face was in total shadow but the waning daylight from behind him touched the deeply grooved temples and the curves of the skull.

His face, which we would associate with a living individual, is not visible in the dim light. Only his skull, which we associate with anonymity and death, can be perceived. His voice is described more than once as "grave and cordial," and the double meaning of "grave" resonates strongly. The hour of dusk suggests a fading and waning life.

When they begin talking about the styles of dress of different orders of the priesthood, and how they are often impractical and ridiculous, the extent to which a priest must remain detached from normal life is emphasized. This, of course, should appeal to Stephen, as he has seen himself as detached from normal life for some time now. But the wandering of Stephen's mind as the priest is slowly leading up to his point suggests that perhaps he is not ready for this kind of commitment:

> The names of articles of dress worn by women or of certain soft and delicate stuffs used in their making brought always to his mind a delicate and sinful perfume....It had shocked him too when he had felt for the first time beneath his tremulous fingers the brittle texture of a woman's stocking....

It is not an encouraging sign that Stephen is thinking, with no sign of guilt or regret, of his experiences with the prostitutes while the priest is building up toward asking him to consider joining the priesthood.

Stephen's attitude toward the priest is similarly suggestive of his eventual refusal. He is respectful, but also somewhat impatient and indulgent as he waits for the priest to stop beating around the bush. This reflects his overall attitude toward the Jesuits these days. He is respectful of the order, and all they have done for him, but he is also subtly dissatisfied with them.

He thinks fondly and without resentment of the way they ran the schools he has attended—he has even forgiven the pandying incident from Chapter One. However, he associates the Jesuits with a younger phase of his life, and it does not seem that he will continue among them:

> Lately some of their judgments had sounded a little childish in his ears and had made him feel a regret and pity as though he were slowly passing out of an accustomed world and were hearing its language for the last time.

He remembers an incident where a priest was condemning Victor Hugo for turning against the church, which incites an "unresting doubt" in Stephen's mind. He associates Jesuit authority with his childhood, and it is apparent that he has matured since then, and is beginning to feel superior to them in some ways.

Despite these numerous suggestions to the contrary, the idea of the priesthood does appeal to Stephen initially. He has indeed thought of it before this, and the priest speaks directly to the aspects of the priesthood that appeal most to Stephen: the privilege, power, and prestige of the office. His initial response is positive:

> A flame began to flutter again on Stephen's cheek as he heard in this proud address an echo of his own proud musings. How often he had seen himself as a priest wielding calmly and humbly the awful power of which angels and saints stood in reverence! His soul loved to muse in secret on this desire. He had seen himself, a young and silent mannered priest, entering a confession swiftly, incensing, genuflecting, accomplishing the vague acts of the priesthood which pleased him by reason of their semblance of reality and of their distance from it.

Both the priest's description and Stephen's response recall one of his earlier vices: pride. The appeal of the priesthood for Stephen involves power, secrecy, and access to privileged knowledge. He pictures himself a priest, in a highly dramatic and literary fashion. It represents for him a "secret desire," a fantasy. There is an unhealthy degree of sexual voyeurism and self-satisfied pride in his hope to "know the sins, the sinful longings and sinful thoughts and sinful acts, of others, hearing them murmured into his ears in the confessional under the shame of a darkened chapel by the lips of women and girls."

Stephen imagines taking pleasure in hearing other people's sins, and in the pride he would feel at being above and beyond such a sinful existence: "no touch of sin would linger upon the hands with which he would elevate and break the host." It is almost as if the priesthood would afford an opportunity to vent the desires he apparently is not free from, but in a "safe," sinless environment.

His reasons for being attracted to the priesthood are all self-indulgent and proud. He has no thoughts of helping others, of the benefits of his works on the world around him. The priest's description of the power and privilege, and Stephen's fantasies, all glorify the priesthood for the wrong reasons. This suggests again that Stephen is perhaps not as changed as it would seem.

Stephen's picture of a priestly life is one of isolation, which is consistent with the role of exile which has appealed to him in different forms throughout the novel. As he comes out of the director's office, this isolation from his peers is emphasized:

> Towards Findlater's church a quartet of young men were striding along with linked arms, swaying their heads and stepping to the agile melody of their leader's concertina.

Stephen stands apart, alone; we could never picture him strolling across campus in this manner. The students' "linked arms" recall the "living rail of hands" of which Stephen is a part in the communion scene at the end of Chapter III. His aspiration to become a part of his community has been abandoned, and indeed his imaginative visualization of himself as a priest emphasizes his singularity and detachment.

In fact, it is the thought of the community of the priesthood which changes his mind. He realizes that life as a priest would cost him the individuality he has cultivated for so long:

> The chill and order of the life repelled him. He saw himself rising in the cold of the morning and filing down with the others to early mass and trying vainly to struggle with his prayers against the fainting sickness of his stomach. He saw himself sitting at dinner with the community of a college. What, then, had become of that deeprooted shyness of his which had made him loth to eat or drink under a strange roof? What had come of the pride of his spirit which had always made him conceive of himself as a being apart in every order?

Again, he imagines himself, pictures himself a priest, but this time in a more negative light. The idea of being part of a community of priests, one among many, does not appeal to Stephen's sense of pride or individuality. He remembers that his sense of a special purpose for his life had always been rooted in the keen sense that he is special, that he is unlike other people, a "being apart in every order":

> He would never swing the thurible before the tabernacle as a priest. His destiny was to be elusive of social or religious orders. . . . He was destined to learn his own wisdom apart from others or to learn the wisdom of others himself wandering among the snares of the world.

The commitment involved in joining the community of the priesthood threatens to stifle Stephen's individual ego. When he rejects the priesthood, he affirms the "snares of the world," and accepts the idea that to fulfill his destiny, he may have to sin in the eyes of the church:

> The snares of the world were its ways of sin. He would fall. He had not yet fallen but he would fall silently, in an instant. Not to fall was too hard, too hard. . . .

Stephen accepts the idea that to sin is human, and that the rigid constraints of his religious faith will continue to threaten his freedom to develop.

As he returns, the disorder of the Dedalus household symbolically contrasts with the "order" of the priesthood. While earlier in the novel, the declining status of the family's wealth had
caused Stephen despair and shame, he now embraces it. This
represents his new perspective on his life: Stephen affirms disorder, fluidity and change over the rigidity and commitment of
the priesthood. As he joins his younger brothers and sisters in
song—probably the most notable example of familial love in the
novel—he seems to feel more at home with them than he would
ever feel in the company of priests. As this section ends, Stephen
is thinking of the privileges he has had, which his younger sib-
lings will not have. "All that had been denied them had been
freely given to him, the eldest: but the quiet glow of evening
showed him in their faces no sign of rancour." In a rare selfless
moment, Stephen seems to appreciate the opportunities he had
despite his family's decline.

In the final section of the chapter, we have what is considered by most readers to be the major climax of the novel. Stephen
has gone off alone, along the seashore. Seeing a girl bathing
alone, he has an intense vision of his life as an artist. However,
the narrative leaves open the possibility that this climax may
be somewhat ironic, and that Stephen might be under a delusion. After all, Chapter Three had ended with a spiritualclimax
of comparable energy—by now we are perhaps more suspicious.

Stephen's artistic awakening is spawned initially by a poetic
phrase, "A day of dappled seaborne clouds," which came to mind
as he walked alone. Stephen has been fascinated by language
since he was a young boy, only here his enthusiasm is given a
more complete expression, and more directly affects his conception of his life. He turns this phrase over and over in his mind,
fascinated by the sound and rhythm of the words themselves.

His reverie is interrupted, however, as he comes across a
group of his classmates bathing. Once again, Stephen's imaginative "voices," in this case the European voices "from beyond
the world" of Dublin, are interrupted by literal, earthbound
voices, those of the boys calling his name. This is similar to the
moment when, in his religious trance, Stephen heard the voices
of hell and the narrator juxtaposed those against the voices of

Mr. Tate and Vincent Heron speaking in ordinary, casual voices. Here, the narrator creates a stark contrast between the world of Stephen's imagination and the reality that surrounds him. He is repulsed by the sight and sound of these boys, and sets himself apart from them:

> He stood still in deference to their calls and parried their banter with easy words. How characterless they looked: Shuley without his deep unbuttoned collar, Ennis without his scarlet belt with the snaky clasp, and Connolly with out his Norfolk coat with the flapless sidepockets! It was a pain to see them and a swordlike pain to see the signs of adolescence that made repellent their pitiable nakedness....But he, apart from them and in silence, remembered in what dread he stood of the mystery of his own body.

There is an interesting combination of identification and distance in this passage. Stephen is still clearly trying to separate himself from the other boys his age—he stands apart, silent, and only engages with them in a superficial and detached manner. He is pained by what he has in common with them, but in this pain he recognizes a kind of common bond with his peers, a limit to his pose of detachment. The narrator shows us both how distinct Stephen is from others his age, while at the same time suggesting that his dreams and fantasies are primarily imaginative. He is perhaps not as different from other boys as he thinks.

When Stephen sees the girl bathing in the sea, he interprets every aspect of their wordless encounter in symbolic terms—she seems to him like a bird, representing Ireland, sexuality, femininity and creation all at once. The image of a bird suggests Stephen's new desire for flight from Ireland, to be free of the "nets" of religion, nation, and family. He interprets this encounter as an otherworldly visitation, a profound spiritual experience that validates and christens his new conception of himself as an artist.

When he encounters the girl, we already know that Stephen is especially ripe to interpret things symbolically. This new capacity is one manifestation of his artistic and poetic awakening, and stems directly from his meditation on language and its mysterious appeal. When the boys interrupt his thoughts about language and poetry, they call his name in pseudo-Greek and Latinate constructions. Stephen then recognizes an aspect of his name that he had not considered before—he thinks of the mythological figure of Daedalus, the great artificer, and Icarus his son, who escaped from Crete using wings which Daedalus created out of feathers and beeswax. He takes this as a kind of "prophecy," a sign that the role of creator is the special purpose he has sensed since childhood. The figure of Daedalus also suggests the escape Stephen imagines his art will be able to provide—an escape both from dull, ordinary life, and from Dublin and Ireland:

> Now, at the name of the fabulous artificer, he seemed to hear the noise of dim waves and to see a winged form flying above the waves and slowly climbing the air. What did it mean? Was it a quaint device opening a page of some medieval book of prophecies and symbols, a hawklike man flying sunward above the sea, a prophecy of the end he had been born to serve and had been following through the mists of childhood and boyhood, a symbol of the artist forging anew in his workshop out of the sluggish matter of the earth a new soaring impalpable imperishable being?

The reference to a "hawklike man flying sunward" suggests Icarus rather than Daedalus, who disregarded his father's advice and flew too close to the sun, fatally melting his wings. This suggests the amount of risk involved in Stephen's imaginative bid for freedom, and how the pride that has been his vice in the past might ultimately lead to his destruction.

Thinking about his name and the vision it inspires, Stephen immediately asks himself, "what did it mean?" He now assumes that things around him can have symbolic import, and so when he encounters the girl in the water, his immediate perception reveals a complex process of interpretation:

> A girl stood before him in midstream, alone and still, gazing out to sea. She seemed like one whom magic had changed into the likeness of a strange and beautiful

seabird. Her long slender bare legs were delicate as a
crane's and pure save where an emerald trail of seaweed
had fashioned itself as a sign upon the flesh.

This scene, like any in the novel, is mediated by Stephen's
consciousness. We observe him interpreting her as a symbol,
rather than reading her as one ourselves. Stephen is transform-
ing everything about her as he perceives it, and we are always
aware that this is only a representation of how she "seemed" to
him. And his interpretive process is complex and multi-leveled:
she is as a seabird, and both the sea and the potential for flight
suggest Stephen's turn of attention away from Ireland and
toward Europe. The "emerald" trail of seaweed clearly suggests
Ireland (the "emerald isle), and he interprets this immediately
and without hesitation "as a sign."

This scene is richly suggestive in its symbolism in its own
right, and can indeed inform and influence our interpretation of
the novel and Stephen's artistic awakening. This double-leveled
structure, by which we are experiencing the symbol at a remove,
seeing him make a symbol out of her, allows us a distinct distance
from the scene. We might feel that this is not "really" a symbol at
all, but merely an example of the narrator showing us the temper of Stephen's mind at the time, which causes him to see his
life in a symbolic light. We might feel that the narrator is creating another "false climax," as he has in every chapter so far, and
that Stephen is really deluded in his enthusiasm and certainty.
By now we are certainly suspicious of Stephen's revelations; we
might not be as sure as Stephen that his name is a "prophecy."

The narrative artfully leaves all its options alive. The tone
of these closing pages is genuinely triumphant, and these symbols, which Stephen recognizes, are indeed richly suggestive
and multivalent in their own right, and really do offer some useful interpretive perspectives on the meaning of the novel as a
whole. At the same time, the pace of this narrative has fostered
in us a suspicious and subtly ironic attitude toward Stephen.
We are not easily convinced, by this point in the novel, that Stephen's epiphanies are genuine. Our experience of this profound
moment of significance in Stephen's life remains contingent on

the developments of the next chapter. Either Stephen has had a spiritual awakening and will dedicate his life to artistic creation, and will continue to distance himself from his religion and nation in an effort to serve this end, or, like his religious awaking, this will prove to be another instructive delusion.

Study Questions

1. Describe Stephen's daily life at the start of Chapter IV.

2. Why does Stephen have trouble mortifying his sense of smell?

3. What is Stephen's opinion of the Jesuits now?

4. How does Stephen reply when the director of Belvedere asks him if he feels he may have a vocation for the priesthood?

5. What appeals to Stephen about the priesthood?

6. What repels Stephen about the priesthood?

7. Why aren't Stephen's parents at home when he gets in?

8. What phrase comes to Stephen's mind as he crosses the bridge to the Bull?

9. What symbolic import does Stephen recognize in his name?

10. How does Stephen interpret his encounter with the bathing girl along the strand?

Answers

1. Stephen's day is structured around religious devotions—he attends morning Mass each day, carries his rosary in his pocket, and prays systematically throughout the day. He says three chaplets a day for the three theological virtues, while dedicating each day toward gaining one of the seven gifts of the Holy Ghost, and toward driving out each of the seven deadly sins.

2. Stephen has trouble mortifying his sense of smell because he finds that he has little natural repugnance to odor, and

it is difficult for him to find a smell unpleasant enough to disturb him. He ultimately finds that the smell of "long-standing urine" does the trick.

3. Stephen still respects the Jesuits, and is grateful for all they have done for him, but he admits that their judgments and opinions now seem "a little childish" to him. It is clear that Stephen feels that he is outgrowing a phase of his life that the Jesuits represent.

4. Stephen replies that he has "sometimes thought of it," but he remains noncommittal.

5. Stephen is attracted to the power, privilege, and secret knowledge that the priesthood would offer. He is eager to learn the theological secrets, and to hear people's secret confessions.

6. Stephen realizes that to become a priest would be to sacrifice an important degree of his individuality. The idea of being an anonymous member of a community of priests ultimately causes Stephen to reject the director's offer.

7. His younger sister tells him that they have gone to look at another house. Apparently, the family will have to move again, under pressure from the landlord.

8. Stephen thinks of the phrase "A day of dappled seaborne clouds," and is fascinated by the way it seems to capture the moment perfectly. Stephen is fascinated by the sound and rhythm of the words as much as their sense.

9. Stephen reads his name, Dedalus, as a "prophecy." Daedalus was the mythical artificer who escaped from Crete with his son Icarus, using wings built from wax and feathers. Stephen sees Daedalus as a symbol of both art and flight.

10. Stephen interprets her as a symbol, an affirmative sign of his new understanding of his destiny as an artist. She seems to him like a seabird, who represents art, sexuality, femininity, and Ireland.

CH. IV

262 *A Portrait of the Artist as a Young Man*

Suggested Essay Topics

1. Consider the narrator's description of Stephen's daily religious devotions. What does the language used suggest about the nature of Stephen's piety? Does it foreshadow in any way his ultimate rejection of religious life?

2. Compare Stephen's artistic awakening in Chapter IV to his religious awakening in Chapter III. How are they similar in their effects on Stephen's life, and in the language in which they are presented? In what ways are they different? What do these similarities and differences suggest about the larger themes of the novel?

3. At the end of Chapter IV, Stephen begins to read his name symbolically, as a "prophecy." Then, as he sees the girl bathing on the strand, he interprets this, too, as a "sign." Reread these scenes carefully. What do the symbolic meanings suggested here tell us about the novel as a whole? How do they add to our understanding of Stephen's character?

SECTION SIX

Chapter V
(pages 125–185)

New Characters:

Temple: *a gypsy socialist student, he is the instigator of the debate*

Lynch: *student at the university, to whom Stephen sounds off about his theory of aesthetics*

Donovan: *student whom Stephen dislikes; Stephen and Lynch see him on their walk*

Father Moran: *priest with whom Stephen thinks Emma flirts*

Dixon: *medical student at the library with Cranly*

The Captain: *a dwarfish old man, whom Stephen sees at the library*

O'Keefe: *student who riles Temple outside the l-library*

Goggins: *stout student outside the library*

Glynn: *young man at the library*

Summary

At the start of the final chapter, Stephen is sitting at breakfast in his parents' house. Pawn tickets for clothing are on the table next to him, indicating that the family had to sell more possessions. He asks his mother how fast the clock is, and she tells him he had better hurry. His sisters are asked to clear a spot for Stephen to wash at the sink, and his mother scrubs his neck and ears for him, remarking how dirty he is. His father shouts down to ask if Stephen has left yet, and his sister answers "yes." Stephen makes a sarcastic remark and leaves out the back.

As he is walking, he hears a mad nun yelling in the mad-house, "Jesus! O Jesus! Jesus!," which disturbs and angers Stephen. He is trying to forget about the "voices" of his parents, and religion. Walking alone, he thinks of plays and poems, and the aesthetic theories of Aristotle and Aquinas. He passes a clock that tells him it is eleven o'clock. He tries to remember the day of the week, thinks of the lectures he is scheduled to attend, and realizes that he is late for English. He thinks of that class, and begins to think about his close friend, Cranly. He composes nonsense verse idly in his head, and thinks of the etymology of the word "ivory." He thinks of his Latin studies and Roman history. He sees Trinity, which depresses him, and he looks at the statue of Thomas Moore, the national poet of Ireland. He thinks with affection of his friend Davin, the peasant student, and of Davin's nationalistic sympathies for Ireland. Stephen remembers a story Davin told him once, about encounter-ing a woman alone at night while he was walking on the road, and being invited to her house to spend the night.

His reverie is interrupted by a flower seller, whom Stephen tells he has no money. He walks on and, when he arrives, he realizes it is too late for his French class, too. He goes in early to physics, instead. The physics hall is empty, except for the Dean of Studies, who is lighting a fire. The dean tells Stephen to pay attention, and learn the art of firestarting, one of the "useful arts." Stephen watches silently. They begin comparing different conceptions of art and beauty. Stephen quotes Aquinas, and defines beauty as "that which, when seen, pleases us." The priest asks Stephen when he plans to write his aesthetic theory, and Stephen humbly says he hopes to work up some ideas from Aristotle and Aquinas. Stephen begins to feel uncomfortable around the dean, and perceives the dean's partial attention to what he is saying. They begin to casually debate the usage of the world "funnel," which Stephen does not recognize because in Ireland it is called a "tundish." The priest is English, and Stephen thinks his interest in the new word is feigned. Stephen tries to return to his original subject, and thinks with some distress that the language they are speaking is the dean's national language, not his. Stephen becomes disheartened with their conversation, and the class begins to fill with students. The priest gives Stephen some conventional advice, and hurries away. Stephen stands at a distance and watches him greet the students.

When the professor comes in, the students respond with "Kentish fire"—a stomping of the feet which could represent either applause or impatience. The professor calls roll, and Stephen's friend Cranly is not in class. A student named Moynihan sarcastically suggests that Cranly is at Leopardstown, a horse racing track. Stephen borrows a piece of notepaper from Moynihan, and idly begins to take notes. Moynihan whispers a ribald joke about "ellipsoidal balls," which causes Stephen to imagine the faculty of the university playing and laughing like animals. A northern Irish student, MacAlister, asks a question, and Stephen thinks about how much he hates this student.

After class, as the students file into the hall, they encounter a student named MacCann who is gathering signatures for a political petition. Cranly, who is waiting outside for Stephen, says, in Latin, that he has signed the petition "for universal peace," in support of Czar Nicholas II. He asks if Stephen is in a bad mood, and Stephen answers, "no." When Moynihan walks by, makes a sarcastic comment about MacCann, and then proceeds to sign the petition, Cranly expresses his disgust. MacCann then sees and greets Stephen, gently teasing him for being late. Students begin to gather, anticipating a "war of wits." MacCann asks Stephen to sign, and a "gipsy student" named Temple begins to talk about socialism and universal brotherhood. Stephen finally responds that he is not interested, and MacCann insults him by calling him a "minor poet." Stephen tells then "keep your icon," referring to the picture of the Czar, and begins to walk away with Temple following him. Cranly leads Temple and Stephen away.

As they talk, it is clear that Temple is annoying Cranly, who attacks him periodically, and pleads with Stephen to ignore Temple. They stop with Davin to watch handball, and Cranly becomes increasingly impatient with Temple. Though Temple appears undaunted by Cranly's insults, he soon leaves. Stephen and Cranly then see their friend Lynch, and Cranly and Lynch begin to wrestle. Stephen asks Davin if he has signed the petition, and Davin nods yes. When Stephen says he hasn't signed,

Davin calls him a "born sneerer." When Davin asks why he does not study Irish, Stephen implies that it is because Emma flirts with the teacher of the Irish course. They begin to discuss Stephen's attitude toward Irish nationalism and culture. Stephen claims to want to "fly by" the "nets" of nationality, language, and religion.

Davin walks off to join Cranly and the handball players, and Stephen and Lynch walk away. They share a cigarette, and Stephen begins to explain his aesthetic theory to Lynch, who pretends to resist, claiming to be hung-over. Stephen defines "pity" and "terror" as they relate to tragedy, defining the "dramatic" and "esthetic" emotions as "static," or arrested, "raised above desire and loathing." Stephen feels that art should not excite "kinetic emotions" like desire, but should serve a more "detached" function, calling forth an "ideal pity" or "ideal desire."

Lynch continues to listen to Stephen, although reluctantly, claiming that he doesn't care about it. Stephen continues to define beauty, using Aquinas' definition, as he did while speaking to the dean earlier. He then discusses the relation between beauty and truth, according to Plato and Aristotle. His discourse is interrupted first by a drag full of iron, then by another student, Donovan, who tells them about exam results, and the field club. As he leaves, Stephen continues to detail his concept of universal beauty, and its relation to perception, and artistic structure, with Lynch now egging him on. Stephen is concerned with what he calls the three basic forms of art: lyrical, epical and dramatic, and the inter-relationship between them. Stephen's picture of artistic creation is of the artist as a kind of God, indifferent to his creation, "paring his fingernails."

As it starts to rain, they head to the library. Lynch tells Stephen that his "beloved" (presumably Emma) is there. He stands with the group silently, glancing at her from time to time. She ignores him, and soon leaves with her friends. Stephen is first bitter and resentful, but then wonders if he has judged her harshly.

As the next section begins, Stephen is waking up at dawn. He feels a seemingly divine inspiration, and begins almost spontaneously to compose lines of verse in his head. Fearing he may lose his inspiration, he gropes around and finds a pencil and cigarette pack, and writes down the first two stanzas of a villanelle. It is clear that he is thinking of Emma as he writes, and he begins to imagine himself singing songs to her. He recalls a brief exchange with her at a dance, and imagines himself as a heretical monk. He thinks of her flirting with a priest, and tells himself that he scorns her, though he admits that this is also a "form of homage."

Having composed an entire villanelle, Stephen recalls writing a poem for her ten years before (in Chapter II), after they rode the last tram home together. He imagines sending her the poem, and thinks of her family reading and mocking it over breakfast. He then corrects himself, and says that she is "innocent," though still a "temptress." The section ends with Stephen's villanelle:

> Are you not weary of ardent ways,
> Lure of the fallen seraphim?
> Tell no more of enchanted days.
>
> Your eyes have set man's heart ablaze
> And you have had your will of him.
> Are you not weary of ardent ways?
>
> Above the flame the smoke of praise
> Goes up from ocean rim to rim.
> Tell no more of enchanted days.
>
> Our broken cries and mournful lays
> Rise in one eucharistic hymn.
> Are you not weary of ardent ways?
>
> While sacrificing hands upraise
> The chalice flowing to the brim,
> Tell no more of enchanted days.
>
> And still you hold our longing gaze
> With languorous look and lavish limb!
> Are you not weary of ardent ways?
> Tell no more of enchanted days.

In the next section, Stephen is standing on the library steps, watching birds in the sky. He is thinking about his mother, and his plans to leave the country. He thinks of a line from Yeats' play *The Countess Cathleen*, and delights in the pleasurable sound of the words. He thinks with disgust of the opening night of the national theater, where the Dublin audience booed Yeats' play.

Stephen goes inside and meets his friend Cranly, who is talking with a medical student named Dixon. A priest has gone to complain about their chatter, so they decide to leave. They encounter an old man they call "the captain," who is known for his fondness for reading Sir Walter Scott. They encounter a group of students, with Temple at the center. They are joking around, for the most part, teasing Temple. Temple tries to engage Stephen into the discussion, asking if he believes in the law of heredity, while Cranly expresses his disgust. Temple says that he admits that he is a "ballocks," but that Cranly is too, and won't admit it. Emma walks past them, and greets Cranly casually. Stephen thinks of his friend Cranly, and wanders about, on the outskirts of the group thinking to himself. His reverie is interrupted as he picks a louse off his collar—his thoughts then revert to his despair about his impoverished state.

Stephen walks back to the group just as a student named Glynn has come out. They engage in further discussion, this time around the biblical phrase "suffer little children to come unto me." Temple tries to engage the group in a theological debate, but they disregard him. He pursues this, until Cranly chases him away. Stephen tells Cranly he wants to speak with him, and they walk away together.

Cranly stops to say some parting words to the other students, and Stephen goes on ahead to wait. While waiting, he looks in the window of a hotel drawing room and thinks angrily of the "patricians" of Ireland. Stephen wonders how, with his art, he could "hit their conscience" or "cast his shadow over the imaginations of their daughters."

He is soon joined by Cranly, and as they walk off arm in arm Cranly makes an angry remark about Temple. Stephen tells Cranly that he had an "unpleasant quarrel" with his mother over religion earlier that night. Mrs. Dedalus wants Stephen to observe his Easter duty, but he refuses to. Cranly calls Stephen an "excitable man" and warns him to "go easy." Cranly ask Stephen if he believes in the Eucharist, and Stephen answers that he neither believes nor disbelieves, and does not wish to overcome his doubts. Cranly remarks that Stephen's mind is "supersaturated" with the religion he professes to disbelieve.

When Cranly asks if Stephen was "happier" when he believed, Stephen responds by saying that he was "someone else" then. Cranly asks Stephen if he loves his mother, and Stephen says he does not understand the question. He says that he tried to love God, but is not sure if he succeeded. Cranly asks if Stephen's mother has had a "happy life," and Stephen responds, "how do I know?" Cranly asks about the Dedalus family's economic history, and learns that they were once much wealthier than now. Cranly then supposes that Mrs. Dedalus has suffered much, and encourages Stephen to try to "save her from suffering more." Cranly says that a mother's love is the one sure thing in this world, and tells Stephen that this is more important than this "ideas and ambitions."

Stephen counters by naming prominent intellectuals who placed their "ideas" before their mother's love, and Cranly calls them all pigs. Stephen suggests that Jesus too treated his mother with "scant attention in public," and Cranly replies that perhaps Jesus was "not who he pretended to be," and that he was "a conscious hypocrite." When Cranly asks if it shocked Stephen to hear him say this, Stephen admits that it did. Cranly asks him why a blasphemy would shock someone who professed not to believe, and Stephen replies that he is "not at all sure" that the Catholic religion is false. Stephen admits that part of the reason he will not take communion is because he fears that God might be real. Stephen then checks himself, saying that it is not the power of the Roman Catholic version of God that he fears, but the danger to his soul of committing false homage. When Cranly asks if he will now become a Protestant, Stephen replies dryly that he has not lost his self-respect.

They pass a servant singing in a kitchen as she sharpens knives, and they stop to listen. As they move on, Cranly asks Stephen if he considers the song she sang, "Rosie O' Grady," to be "poetry," and Stephen replies that he would have to see Rosie before he could say. He then announces his plans to go away from Ireland. Cranly suggests that the church is not driving Stephen away, and that if he leaves he leaves of his own accord. He questions Stephen on some moral issues, and Stephen responds by saying that he will not serve any church or country, but will seek the freedom to express himself apart from these bonds. He says that he is not afraid to live alone, or to have made a "great," eternal "mistake." The section ends as Cranly asks Stephen how he could live with no friends at all. Stephen suspects that Cranly is thinking of himself, but when he asks Cranly does not answer.

The novel ends with excerpts from Stephen's journal, beginning with an entry for the night following his conversation with Cranly. He writes about following women with Lynch, discussing religion with his mother (who claims he has a "queer mind" and that he reads too much), arguing about heresy with other students, and wondering what Emma is doing and thinking. He writes of his plans to leave, and he writes about a final encounter with Emma when he told her he was leaving. They shook hands, and Stephen concludes that it was "friendly." He tells himself, however, that he is over his obsession. The journal ends as Stephen is about to depart—as he vows "to encounter for the millionth time the reality of experience and to forge in the smithy of [his] soul the uncreated conscience of [his] race."

Analysis

If the novel had ended with Chapter IV, it would have been an unambiguous climax, an affirmation of Stephen's artistic vision. Such an ending would, however, have left many important questions unanswered. How would Stephen reconcile his new vision for his life with the reality of his surroundings? After all, we might say, deciding to become an artist does not make you an artist. By including Chapter V, Joyce makes Stephen's vision more realistic. By showing the day-to-day reality the artist will still have to face, we are given a sense of how Stephen's newly understood role will play out in his life—we can see how he attempts to live up to his new ideal. Though the tone of this chapter is harder to gauge perhaps than the ending of Chapter IV—there are many instances where we suspect that Stephen is being treated somewhat ironically by the narrator—Chapter V represents the culmination of the main themes of the novel. In this chapter we read about Stephen's developing aesthetic or artistic theory, we see the first example of his own artistic composition, and we hear of his preparation to leave Ireland for Europe.

In Chapter V, Stephen fully articulates and defends his conception of what it takes to be an artist, and we see him progress further toward assuming and embracing the role of solitary exile which we have seen him tending toward all along. Though this chapter consists of a good deal of dialogue—Stephen speaks with others more than in any other chapter of the novel—these conversations serve to gradually set him further and further apart from his surroundings. In them, Stephen articulates his need to be alone, free of the "nets" of family, religion, and nation. As the chapter, and the novel, ends, we have Stephen's voice all alone, addressing himself in the form of a journal, unmediated by any narrative presence. Over the course of this chapter Stephen moves closer to the solitude he deems necessary for artistic creation.

As with other chapters previously, the opening pages of Chapter V serve as an abrupt anticlimax after the triumphant and inspired tone in which Chapter IV ended. We have already recognized that of all the potential climaxes of the novel, Stephen's artistic awakening in Chapter IV seems least prone to the narrator's irony. In Joyce's novel, the ideal of a "climax" is not the same as in more conventional fiction, where the climax is defined by the progression and culmination of a plot. In *A Portrait of the Artist as a Young Man,* all the significant "action" is internal, and therefore the climax of the novel will be in the form of a significant moment for the protagonist—a moment of "epiphany." The moment where Stephen decides he must reject his country and his religion in the name of art, when he begins to perceive his life in symbolic terms and therefore to "understand" the significance of his name, is clearly a pivotal and climactic moment in the novel—one on which our ultimate understanding of Stephen's character rests. However, this tone of triumph is sobered dramatically as Chapter Five begins.

The language with which the narrator describes Stephen at breakfast is dismal and depersonalized:

> He drained his third cup of watery tea to the dregs and set to chewing the crusts of fried bread that were scattered near him, staring into the dark pool of the jar. The yellow dripping had been scooped out like a boghole....

The way his eating is described makes it seem mechanical and numb—he "drains" the cup of tea, and "sets to chewing" the crusts of bread. The sense of images in this opening paragraph are all rather unpleasant—the "dark pool," "yellow drippings," and "boghole" are all distinctly unappetizing. We are reminded that the family is in dire economic shape by the pawning tickets on the table—Mr. Dedalus has made some of them out under false names, presumably out of shame. These first pages represent a marked drop in intensity from the previous chapter.

There is some suggestion in these opening pages that Stephen has perhaps not grown past the trappings of his surroundings at all, and that indeed he has regressed. In the first paragraph, we are told that the contents of the jar remind him of "the dark turfcoloured water of the bath in Clongowes, and we recall Stephen's younger days in the first chapter. By pulling our attention backwards in this way, after the forward-looking ending of the previous chapter, the narrator reminds us of Stephen's past, and how illusory some other "awakenings" have proven. This is further emphasized as Stephen's mother must remind him of the time, chastise him for being late for class, and even wash his face and neck for him.

His lackadaisical attitude toward his classes might seem at odds with the "new adventures" the university represented to him in the previous chapter. While Stephen's idleness and casualness at the start of the chapter might on the one hand seem like laziness or lack of energy, it also suggests a kind of patience, an attitude of inner peace and calm in the midst of his chaotic surroundings. For it is apparent that the *effects* of the previous chapter's climax are still active in Stephen's mind. There is a distinct sense, which Stephen shares, that his surroundings are holding him back, and this is the reason for the anticlimax in this chapter. It is not the case, as before, that we feel that Stephen is somehow deluded. When we saw how his religious fervor deteriorated into a dry and lifeless routine, our sense was that Stephen did not recognize this, and that the narrator was, through his choice of language, showing us that Stephen was deluded. The difference in Chapter Five is that Stephen understands that his surroundings are profoundly at odds with his conception of himself as an artist. The major substance of this chapter consists of Stephen attempting to change the squalid circumstances of his life by leaving. His daily existence then becomes a kind of challenge to his will, a test of his convictions.

That the ideals of his artistic awakening are still fully present in Stephen's mind is made clear as he leaves his house. He hears a mad nun wailing in an insane asylum, and his reaction symbolically leaves religion and family behind:

> —Jesus! O Jesus! Jesus!
> He shook the sound out of his ears by an angry toss
> of his head and hurried on, stumbling though the
> mouldering offal, his heart already bitten by an
> ache of loathing and bitterness. His father's whistle,
> his mother's mutterings, the screech of an unseen
> maniac were to him now so many voices offending and
> threatening to humble the pride of his youth. He drove
> their echoes even out of his heart with an execration. . . .

He can now reduce the effects of the "voices" of family and church to simple personal threats—threats to his freedom, which he attempts to shake away with an "angry toss of the head." This chapter represents Stephen's articulation and defense of his motives and methods for seeking to distance himself from all such obligations. The calmness and quite priestlike seriousness with which he conducts himself around his friends should not be understood as a lazy kind of idleness, but rather as an attitude of patience in preparation for his life's calling. Stephen attempts to assume such a detached and disengaged posture because this is how he conceives of the proper attitude of artists in relation to their surroundings.

Stephen's artistic conversion, as he understands it, means

that he must try and set himself apart form national, political, religious, and familial concerns. We have such a clear understanding of Stephen's conviction on this point because a large portion of this chapter consists of Stephen engaged in a series of significant conversations in which he defines and defends his understanding of art and its purpose, his attitude toward his country and toward political concerns, and his attitude toward his family and religion. Whereas he had been a silent observer for the greater part of the novel up to this point, now Stephen is portrayed as a relentless talker, sounding off about his developing theory of aesthetics to anyone who will listen. Four such significant conversations are the structuring principle of this chapter. We understand crucial aspects of Stephen's point of view, as well as some serious objections to it, through the conversations he has with the dean of studies, Davin, Lynch, and, most importantly, Cranly.

Stephen's conversation with the dean of studies reveals a marked change in his attitude toward authority figures once again. Priests have occupied a role of religious and practical authority for Stephen throughout the novel, though, as we observed in the last chapter, his attitude toward them had been changing of late. The subtle dissatisfaction he had felt with the Jesuits in general is now manifest in an almost condescending attitude toward the dean, who is for Stephen supposed to be a figure of academic as well as religious authority. As the dean promises to teach Stephen the art of lighting a fire, Stephen reflects to himself that the dean seems fawning and servile:

> Kneeling thus on the flagstone to kindle the fire and busied with the disposition of the wisps of paper and candelbutts he seemed more than ever a humble server making ready the place of sacrifice in an empty temple, a levite of the Lord....His very body had waxed old in lowly service of the Lord...and yet had remained ungraced by aught of saintly or of prelatic beauty.

Stephen now sees no value in such servitude—indeed, the theme of this chapter for him is an attempt to separate himself from all sorts of service to others. His disdain for the priest's air of servitude recalls his reaction to the "droll statue" of the national poet of Ireland on his way to class, in which he detects "sloth of the body and of the soul," and a "servile head...humbly conscious of its indignity." Stephen is now eager both to judge, and to set himself apart from, figures of authority both in the artistic and religious realms.

Stephen's attitude toward the dean during their brief discussion is one of polite impatience, almost condescension. While he sets the dean up in his mind as an example of all that is wrong with the priesthood, there is much about this man's manner in particular which irritates Stephen. When the dean invites him to learn one of the "useful" arts, this sets up Stephen's discourse about aesthetics perfectly, since his conception, as we will see, is that "usefulness" is not one of the proper purposes for art. The priest asks Stephen how he would define the "beautiful," and Stephen quotes Aquinas—"beauty is that which, when seen, pleases us." The dean encourages Stephen to pursue these questions, and to write something on them, but his responses to Stephen indicate that he is not especially interested. He is noncommittal and unconvincing in his remarks. When the dean says, "Quite so, you have certainly hit the nail on the head," or, "I see. I quite see your point," we are not at all convinced that he either understands or is interested. We can perhaps read his words of encouragement more as a somewhat perfunctory exercise of his duties as dean of the university. Stephen seems to perceive this, and eventually loses interest in the conversation. The dean does not function for Stephen here as an intellectual peer to engage and interact with in a discussion of ideas. Rather, Stephen takes this opportunity to speak about himself and his interests (an opportunity, as we will see, that he rarely passes up), and we can tell by his private responses to the dean that he is never seriously considering the dean's remarks, but rather using him as an example of the priesthood in general.

Part of Stephen's feeling of distance from the dean seems to come from the fact that the dean is English. When the dean uses the word "funnel," Stephen says that he has not heard this word before. Stephen calls this a "tundish," a word the priest claims not to have heard before. The priest concludes that "tundish" must be the Irish word for the English "funnel," and he offers a halfhearted interest in the question, claiming, "That is a most interesting word. I must look that word up. Upon my word I must." This marks a turning point in Stephen's attitude toward the priest, as he becomes less patient, and effectively stops the conversation. This apparently is a nationalistic issue for Stephen, as he reflects to himself:

> —The language in which we are speaking is his before it is mine. How different are the words *home, Christ, ale, master,* on his lips and on mine! I cannot speak or write these words without unrest of spirit. His language, so familiar and so foreign, will always be for me an acquired speech. I have not made or accepted its words. My voice holds them at bay. My soul frets in the shadow of his language.

Stephen seems to be voicing his anxiety over the fact that the Irish people, as a whole, no longer speak the Irish language. The priest then would be a representative of the conquering country, England.

These quasi-nationalistic sentiments certainly seem uncharacteristic of Stephen. English, we might say, has not seemed "uncomfortable" for him before—it was the English language in fact which he found so beautiful and rhythmic at the end of Chapter Four. Rather than take this passage at face value, as representative of Stephen's true feelings toward the language question, it is more likely that he is finding reasons to dislike the priest. The funnel/ tundish debate seems to bring the issue of nationality to the foreground, but Stephen had been getting impatient with the priest's noncommittal politeness before this. The issue stays on his mind, however, as we learn in his journal that he has looked up "tundish," and found it to be an English word after all. Stephen's resentment toward the priest as it is expressed in the journal seems more personally than nationally motivated: "Damn the dean of studies and his funnel! What did he come here for to teach us his own language or to learn it from us? Damn him one way or the other."

On the same day as this conflict with the dean, we see Stephen discussing this very question with his friend Davin. Davin comes from the country, in the west of Ireland, and represents Irish nationalism in the novel—he seeks both political and cultural independence for Ireland, and believes that it is people's foremost responsibility to serve their country. In the brief conversation between Stephen and Davin, we get a clear and useful exposition of Stephen's point of view on these issues, which is consistent with his intention to remain detached from all external responsibilities.

Stephen calls Davin a "tame little goose" for signing the petition, thus equating his nationalistic ideals with subservience. Stephen is especially prone to recognize and condemn subservience lately, as he implies that Davin's enthusiasm for Irish independence is on the same scale as the bowing and fawning servitude he saw in the dean. Davin, on the other hand, criticizes Stephen as a "sneerer," indicating his dissatisfaction with Stephen's pose of detachment. A "sneerer" would not consider the issues at stake carefully, but would criticize from a safe distance. In Davin's view, to be Irish is not merely hereditary or racial—it necessarily involves a responsibility to the cause of the Irish people, and a love for the Irish culture and language. He asks Stephen, "Are you Irish at all?" When Stephen offers to show him his family tree to prove it, Davin's response is, "Then be one of us." To *be* Irish means to demonstrate your affiliation through your actions. When he asks Stephen why he dropped out of a class on Irish language and culture, Stephen indicates that "one reason" is because Emma was flirting with the priest who teaches the class. His other remarks indicate, however, that his objections run much deeper—Stephen is not very interested in Irish culture, and especially Irish nationalism. Stephen expresses his view of the situation in the following exchange:

—This race and this country and this life produced me, he said. I shall express myself as I am.
—Try to be one of us, repeated Davin. In your heart you are an Irishman but your pride is too powerful.
—My ancestors threw off their language and took another, Stephen said. They allowed a handful of foreigners to subject them. Do you fancy I am going to pay in my life and person debts they made? What for?

Stephen perceives the Irish as "subjects" to another power—a situation that he cannot abide. He feels that his ancestors made the mistake, and that it should not be for him, as an individual, to pay for it. Stephen accepts the political (and therefore linguistic) circumstances of his birth and, far from feeling any responsibility on this count, seeks rather to escape the constraints these circumstances impose upon the individual:

> When the soul of a man is born in this country there are nets flung at it to hold it back from flight. You talk to me of nationality, language, religion. I shall try to fly by those nets.

We can read Davin's response to this proclamation—"Too deep for me, Stevie"—in at least two ways: either as a "serious" expression of bafflement (which would fit into Stephen's sentimental picture of him as a simple peasant), or as a critique of Stephen's extreme pose of detachment. Perhaps Davin is saying that to be "deep," in this case, is not necessarily good, if it causes one to avoid all immediate responsibilities.

Whereas Davin challenges Stephen, and provides a serious foil to his point of view, Stephen apparently finds a much more receptive audience in Lynch, whom he speaks with extensively just after his conversation with Davin. Though Lynch seems to be a more receptive audience, he is actually only a more appealing version of the dean. He playfully resists Stephen's "lecture," claiming that he has a hangover, and never seems particularly interested in the question of aesthetic value which Stephen is so fascinated by. His sarcastic commentary is his version of the dean's polite pretensions of being interested. There is the sense that no one will argue extensively with Stephen on these points because aesthetic questions are not as important to anyone else as to him.

Stephen's conversation with Lynch is more like a lecture, or a monologue, than a dialogue in earnest. Stephen is espousing his aesthetic theory, while Lynch serves as the opportunity for Stephen to talk. His contributions to the conversation are in the form of crude jokes, mock protestations, and halfhearted objections. Their long conversations, while they walk through

Dublin on the way to the library, represents Stephen's intellectual development up to this point—he gives a detailed exposition of his aesthetic theory, which is impressive in its scope and sophistication.

Stephen is seeking both to define beauty and the concept of the beautiful, and to define the proper place of the artist in relation to his or her creation. Stephen bases his definition of beauty mostly on the work of Aristotle and Aquinas. He describes it as a "static" emotion—the beautiful does not evoke the "kinetic" emotions of desire or loathing, but exists outside of this realm in a state of purity. Stephen's view emphasizes the structure, wholeness, and harmony of a piece of art, and asserts that we can in fact define the "necessary qualities of beauty" despite the fact that different people in different cultures perceive and appreciate different qualities as beautiful:

> Though the same object may not seem beautiful to all people, all people who admire a beautiful object find in it certain relations which satisfy and coincide with the stages them-selves of all esthetic apprehension.

Stephen identifies three essential forms of art: the lyrical, epical, and dramatic. Stephen values the dramatic most highly, in which the author is most removed from the work of art, when the "personality of the artist...finally refines itself out of existence." Stephen's ideal image of the artist is:

> Like the God of the creation, [who] remains within or behind or beyond or above his handiwork, invisible, refined out of existence, indifferent, paring his fingernails.

This passage is often cited as Joyce's own credo of artistic creation, although, paradoxically, this would be used to warn us against identifying Joyce with his fictional self, Stephen Dedalus, too completely. Here we see how Stephen can justify his rejection of national and political concerns in favor of his pose of detach-ment. In his conception, the duty of the artist is first to the unity and beauty of the work of art itself—the less the personality (and therefore the political or religious agenda) of the artist comes into play, the better.

The seriousness with which Stephen's sophisticated system of aesthetics is presented to undercut significantly, however, by Lynch's persistently crude and sarcastic humor, and his only partial engagement with Stephen's monologue. Stephen seems to like Lynch, however, perhaps because he will not challenge Stephen's assertions the way Davin or Cranly will. As soon as their conversa-tion begins, Stephen recognizes with pleasure evidence of Lynch's "culture":

—Damn your yellow insolence, answered Lynch.
This second proof of Lynch's culture made Stephen
smile again.
—It was a great day for European culture, he said, when
you made up your mind to swear in yellow.

Apparently Lynch is more cultured than Davin, which encourages Stephen that he will be a better (less hostile) audience, although Stephen's evidence for considering him cultured amounts to nothing more than the fact that he curses in a literary way.

Earlier, Stephen had been offended by the sound of Cranly's accent, associating it with all that is ugly and unpleasant about Dublin:

Cranly's speech, unlike that of Davin, had neither rare
phrases of Elizabethan English nor quaintly turned
versions of Irish idioms. Its drawl was an echo of the
quays of Dublin given back by a bleak decaying seaport,
its energy an echo of the sacred eloquence of Dublin
given back flatly by a Wicklow pulpit.

Surely Davin's speech, though "quaint," is not "cultured," and neither is Cranly's. However, from what we can tell, Lynch's "culture" amounts to a habitual repetition of stock literary phrases, in order to curse. Lynch's appeal is as artificial as Cranly's offense. In neither case is Stephen interested in the substance of the person, but in how good they sound. After Stephen remarks about how fond he is of Lynch "cursing in yellow," almost every remark out of Lynch's mouth involves some variation on "yellow." Stephen exercises a certain amount of control over Lynch, and seems to have his respect. But the overall sense is that this is still something of a joke to Lynch; he still seems like little more than Stephen's "yes man." When Stephen finishes a long tirade, and Lynch does not reply right away, he imagines "that his words had called up around them a thought enchanted silence." The narrator is clear to phrase this as Stephen's perception of the scene; we may suspect, instead, that Lynch merely has not been paying attention.

In his conversation with Cranly, which marks the end of the narrative proper, Stephen finds a much more challenging audience. There is the distinct sense that Stephen values Cranly as a friend whose opinion is important. In their dialogue, there is none of the condescension which characterized Stephen's attitude toward Davin, Lynch, and even the dean of studies. Cranly is not afraid to be directly critical of Stephen's ideas and actions, and he raises significant and considerable objections to Stephen's plan to forsake his country and family in favor of art. Stephen recognizes a certain connection between the two of them early in their conversation:

> Their minds, lately estranged, seemed suddenly to have been drawn closer together, one to the other.

Cranly is perhaps the first person in the novel who Stephen seems to engage with on equal terms—earlier in the novel he had been intimidated by his peers and authority figures, and later in the novel he generally feels superior to both his peers and authority figures.

Cranly raises humanistic objections to Stephen's plan, trying to show him how his rejection of church and family will cut him off from those close to him. For Cranly, it is not a matter of rejecting "religion" or "family" or "nation" in the abstract—he reminds Stephen of the real people who will be hurt by his actions. Cranly tries to turn Stephen's attention away from the abstract principle (which Stephen expresses by quoting Lucifer, "I will not serve") and toward a more practical and human level. Stephen does not view his quarrel with his mother in terms of *her* feelings—from his point of view, she is asking him to observe a false homage, a move which his integrity of soul cannot abide.

Cranly urges him to consider how much she has suffered in her life, and how Stephen, by compromising and observing his Easter duty, can reduce her suffering a little. When Cranly asks him, however, if he loves his mother, Stephen claims not to understand the question. Just as Stephen tried and failed to love God, he has not been able to feel any meaningful connection with any people in his life, family or otherwise. His one-sided obsession with Emma can hardly be called "love," and his relationship with his family is, by now, as distant and detached as can be. When Cranly asks Stephen if his mother has had "a happy life," Stephen responds honestly "How do I know?" It is clear that her feelings do not come into play in his decision not to observe Easter—it is a personal matter, that has to do in his mind with his rejection of the Catholic church. Cranly's sentimental language of human compassion provides a stark contrast to Stephen's self-centered ethic of isolation and individualism:

> —Whatever else is unsure in this stinking dunghill of a world a mother's love is not. Your mother brings you into the world, carries your first in her body. What do we know about what she feels? But whatever she feels, it, at least, must be real. It must be. What are our ideas and ambitions? Play. Ideas! Why, that bloody bleating goat Temple has ideas. MacCann has ideas too. Every Jackass going the roads thinks he has ideas.

Cranly tries to appeal to Stephen's (or the reader's) sentimentality. He attempts to deflate Stephen's emphasis on the unassailable virtue of an individual pursuing his destiny outside of all society by claiming that this is not so unique, that everyone thinks his or her ideas are most important. Stephen, however, appears unaffected, and quickly moves the discussion away from himself and to the subject of other famous intellectuals in history who have offended their mothers. Cranly, however, offers a perceptive critique of Stephen's assumed pose of detachment, one which many readers will take to heart.

Cranly also challenges Stephen on the more abstract, theological and philosophical bases for his rejection of Catholicism. When Stephen assumes his pose of detachment, relishing the role of religious rebel by saying he "neither believe(s) nor disbelieve(s)," and "do(es) not want to overcome" his doubts, Cranly points out that Stephen's mind is "supersaturated" with the tenents of Catholicism. Stephen cannot set himself fully outside the structure of the church, because his pose of detachment is compromised by his long history in the church. His disbelief then is necessarily rebellious, and not disinterested and detached, since he very recently did believe. While Stephen claims that he "was someone else then," there are many indications that he is perhaps not so changed from the days when he was a believer. His conception of himself and his "mission" as an artist uses the language of the priesthood. He admits that his intellectual interests make his mind a "cloister," and cut him off from the outside world just as much as the priesthood would have.

The hold the Catholic church still has upon his mind, despite his rejection of its tenets, is made clear as Stephen admits that he is not "sure" that the religion is "false," and this is part of the reason he refuses to take communion falsely. Stephen admits that he still has a certain fear of blasphemy, although he quickly checks himself and says, "I fear more than that the chemical action which would be set up in my soul by a false homage to a symbol behind which are massed twenty centuries of authority and veneration," asserting his devotion to a personal ethic which would be morally superior to the church.

Stephen's "supersaturation" with Catholicism, despite his apparent rejection of it, is demonstrated by his reaction to Cranly's blasphemy. When Cranly suggests that Jesus was "a conscious hypocrite," and "not what he pretended to be," Stephen admits that he was "somewhat" shocked to hear Cranly say this. When Cranly asks if this is why he will not take communion, because he feels and fears that God might indeed be real, Stephen admits that this is true. It seems that Cranly is really affecting Stephen here. He seems to puncture Stephen's pose of indifference and nonchalant rebellion, showing that Stephen is still profoundly affected by the religion he claims to reject. However, Stephen's tone is difficult to gauge here. He quickly checks himself, claiming "I fear many things: dogs, horses, firearms,

the sea, thunderstorms, machinery, the country road at night."
He tries to lump his lingering fear of God in with other "irratio-
nal" fears.

When Stephen announces his plans to leave Ireland, Cranly
is quick to point out that the church is not driving Stephen away,
but that he is leaving of his own accord. When Stephen says that
he "has to" go, Cranly replies, "You need not look upon yourself
as driven away if you do not wish to go or as a heretic or an outlaw." Cranly is saying that Stephen is assuming this role of exile
himself, that he seems to *want* to be a heretic or outlaw. This, as
we know, is largely true. Stephen's conception of the artist is that
he must live free of all familial, patriotic and religious obligations, and he now sees Europe as the place where this is possible.
Near the end of their conversation, Stephen repeats his credo
again:

> I will not serve that in which I no longer believe whether
> it call itself my home, my fatherland or my church: and
> I will try to express myself in some mode of life or art
> as freely as I can and as wholly as I can, using for my
> defense the only arms I allow myself to use—silence,
> exile, and cunning.

Stephen's emphasis is all on himself—he detaches himself from any obligation by dismissing his family, religion, and
country as something which might "call itself" home, fatherland, or church. Stephen sees himself not necessarily as "driven
away," although it is clearly necessary, for him to fulfill his vision
of art, to remove himself from the circumstance, the "nets," of
his birth. Cranly has pointed out, throughout their discussion,
the ways this is selfish and insensitive. When he suggests that
Stephen, by doing so, will alienate himself from others perma-
nently, that he will "have not even one friend," Stephen appears
unaffected. As we know, he has been alone his whole life.

Although Cranly seems to raise some serious objections,
and Stephen seems to respect his point of view profoundly,
we can see from his first journal entry that he has not taken
Cranly's remarks to heart. Stephen's account of the situation is
superficial:

> Long talk with Cranly on the subject of my revolt. He
> had his grand manner on. I supple and suave. Attacked
> me on the score of love for one's mother.

Stephen describes it as if they both had been play-acting, rather than talking about issues of real consequence in both of their lives. He is more interested in Cranly's "grand manner," and proud of his own appearance of being "supple and sauve," than any of the issues their discussion raised. Cranly's passionate appeal in favor of Mrs. Dedalus' suffering, and her love for her son, is reduced to a depersonalized move in a formal debate: "attacked me on the score of love for one's mother." Stephen shows no evidence that this conversation, which voices many reasonable and serious objec-tions to Stephen's plan of "revolt," has had any affect on him whatsoever. It is as if his mind has been made up throughout the chapter, and it shows no tendency to change now.

Stephen in his journals appears superficial and affected. He is not afraid to be alone, and has by now embraced the role of exile fully. His brief and unemotional account of his conversation with Cranly shows how his perception is limited, and we may indeed wonder what kind of artist he will be if he has no conception of human affection or connection. His act of creation, the centerpiece of Chapter Five, bears this out. He wakes up, and almost spontaneously composes a villanelle. We have already seen him in the role of art critic, or aesthetic theorist. This is the first evidence of Stephen as artist in the novel.

Stephen's artistic inspiration is presented in religious or spiritual terms—his mind is portrayed as "pregnancy" with inspiration that came from a mysterious, divine source:

> In the virgin womb of the imagination the word was
> made flesh. Gabriel the seraph had come to the virgin's
> chamber.

He imagines himself like the Virgin Mary, and while he continues to compose the poem in his head he imagines "smoke, incense ascending from the altar of the world." As Cranly will suggest, Stephen's mind is indeed still "supersaturated" with religion, and this language suggests that in some ways his new life may not be so radically transformed from his former life. He imagines himself "a priest of eternal imagination, transmuting the daily bread of experience into the radiant body of everlasting life"—his act of creation seems to give him the same kind of power he dreamed he would have as a priest.

The "subject" of his poem is presumably Emma, although the way he imagines her while he is composing suggests how much their "relationship" exists only in his mind. As with the poem he composed for her ten years earlier, the villanelle is highly abstract, and seems to be "about" or "for" her in only the most indirect way. In some ways, his composition is quite impressive. Stephen shows a definite sensitivity to the sounds of the words, and a villanelle is a rigid and strict form—using only two rhymes, repeating the lines in a regular pattern for five three-line stanzas and a quatrain. The villanelle requires discipline, skill, and control, and gains its effects more from the formal interplay of sound and repetition than it does from emotion or passion. Therefore, Stephen's first poem is abstract, symbolic, and clearly removed from anything in his immediate life. Just as his first attempt, ten years earlier, had failed by being too far removed from the situation which had inspired it, this poem, too, is emotionally flat and detached from life. Stephen, it appears, has little conception of human love or emotion, and his art serves the purpose of removing him from daily life into the realm of fantasy and escape, sound without sense. While his poem is a somewhat impressive technical and formal achievement, we may wonder if Stephen's rigid code of individualism will cause him to suffer as an artist.

In the journal entries at the end of the novel, we have Stephen's voice directly, without the potentially ironic narrator. Over the course of the chapter we have seen him gradually become more and more alone, and this is emphasized by the univocal final pages, where Stephen is essentially "talking to himself." His tone is somewhat dramatic, and it is clear that the defense mechanisms and affectations we recognized in his interactions with his peers tend to carry over into the journals, too. However, there is a definite eagerness in the passages where he anticipates his flight to Europe. At the end of the novel, we see the young man, whom we have followed since early childhood, now an "artist," eager to leave his dreary homeland behind in favor of life, art and experience:

> *26 April:* Mother is putting my new secondhand clothes in order. She prays now, she says, that I may learn in my own life and away from home and friends what the heart is and what it feels. Amen. So be it. Welcome, O life! I go to encounter for the millionth time the reality of experience and to forge in the smithy of my soul the uncreated conscience of my race.
> *27 April:* Old father, old artificer, stand me now and ever in good stead.

The novel in Stephen's voice, seems to end on an optimistic and forward-looking note. Most of the novel has been about rejection—Stephen has had to reject the "nets" which Dublin and Catholicism have laid upon him at birth. But his attitude now is of expectation and anticipation. Our sense is that "experience" and "life" lies elsewhere, in Europe, and that his art will feed on these. Although the narrator has been puncturing his "epiphanies" throughout, here we just have Stephen's voice in what seems to be an unambiguous affirmation. But the narration's ironies, and in particular Cranly's objections, have not been forgotten by this point, giving us a complicated and multifaceted picture of the artist. We can see many of Stephen's shortcomings, but we can also recognize in him a definite skill and ambition. We may feel, as the novel ends, that he will go off and succeed in Europe, experiencing life and creating life. Or, we may feel that this is the common delusion of youth, that, as Cranly puts it, "everyone has ideas," and we have no reason to believe that Stephen Dedalus is special. If we are willing to look outside of the text, we will see that in Joyce's next novel, *Ulysses,* Stephen Dedalus is back in Dublin—he has returned for his mother's funeral and ended up staying in town for months. In light of this later novel, the ending of *A Portrait of the Artist as a Young Man* will perhaps seem to be "punctured" much as the climaxes of the individual chapters were. The symbolism he recognizes in his name suggests both the need for flight or escape, as well as the potential hazards—Icarus, Daedalus' son, flew too high and his wings were melted by the sun. The ending of the novel is suggestively ambiguous—we may see Stephen in either, or indeed both, of these ways.

Study Questions

1. Describe Stephen's attitude toward school at the start of Chapter V.

2. What does Davin call Stephen?

3. What is the "useful art" the dean of studies promises to teach Stephen?

4. What are the two primary influences on Stephen's artistic theory?

5. What is Davin's objection to Stephen's "revolt" against religion, family, and nation?

6. What characteristic of Lynch's speech does Stephen identify with "culture"?

7. What, according to Stephen, are the three basic forms of art?

8. What kind of poem does Stephen compose in the middle of Chapter V?

9. Describe the attitude which the other students take toward Temple.

10. When Lynch asks Stephen if he loves his mother, what does Stephen say?

Answers

1. Stephen has a casual, even lackadaisical attitude toward his schoolwork at the start of Chapter V. He is late for lecture, and has to borrow a scrap of notepaper from Moynihan.

2. Davin calls Stephen "Stevie."

3. The dean of studies promises to teach Stephen the "useful art" of starting a fire in a fireplace.

4. Stephen's artistic theory is based heavily on the work of Aristotle and Aquinas.

5. Davin feels that an individual's primary responsibility is to his or her country, and feels that Stephen is betraying Ireland in favor of abstract, selfish aims—a view with which Stephen does not disagree.

6. Stephen recognizes Lynch's use of "yellow" as an expletive to be an example of his "culture."

7. Stephen recognizes the three basic forms of art as the lyrical, the epical, and the tragic. The tragic is the most important, since it is when the artist is able to remove himself or herself from the creation as completely as possible.

8. Stephen composes a villanelle, a strict form which consists of only two rhymes ("ways" and "rim"), five three-line stanzas, a final quatrain, and a pattern of repetition.

9. The other students tease Temple constantly, and don't take his ideas seriously.

10. Stephen replies that he does not understand the question.

Suggested Essay Topics

1. In Chapter V, we are given a detailed exposition of Stephen's theory of aesthetics, as well as the text of his first poem since his artistic transformation. Discuss the villanelle, using the terms of Stephen's theory as he describes it to Lynch. What can this theory tell us about the poem? How does this relate to the thematic issues in this chapter?

2. Cranly suggests that, despite his claims of rejecting the Catholic church and its faith, Stephen's mind continues to be "supersaturated" with Catholicism. Discuss how this view might be used to illuminate his character in this chapter. Aspects you may want to examine include: how the narrator describes Stephen, how he describes himself, how his inspiration and act of artistic creation is described.

3. After the entire novel has been narrated through Stephen's consciousness by a third-person narrator, the

novel ends with some excerpts from Stephen's journal, as he makes final preparations to leave for Europe. How does the recession of the narrative presence affect our understanding of the ending of the novel? What are some of the effects of Joyce ending the novel this way?

Bibliography

Blades, John. *A Portrait of the Artist as a Young Man.* Penguin Critical Studies. London: Penguin Books, 1991.

Ellmann, Richard. *James Joyce.* Second Ed. New York: Oxford U.P., 1982.

Joyce, James. *A Portrait of the Artist as a Young Man: Text, Criticism, and Notes.* Ed. Chester G. Anderson. Viking Critical Library. New York: Penguin Books, 1968.

Schutte, William M. ed. *Twentieth Century Interpretations of A Portrait of the Artist as a Young Man.* Englewood Cliffs, NJ: Prentice-Hall, 1968.

Seed, David. *James Joyce's A Portrait of the Artist as a Young Man.* New York: St. Martin's Press, 1992.

DOVER·THRIFT·EDITIONS

FICTION

ADVENTURES OF HUCKLEBERRY FINN, Mark Twain. (0-486-28061-6)

THE ADVENTURES OF TOM SAWYER, Mark Twain. (0-486-40077-8)

ALICE'S ADVENTURES IN WONDERLAND, Lewis Carroll. (0-486-27543-4)

THE AWAKENING, Kate Chopin. (0-486-27786-0)

THE CALL OF THE WILD, Jack London. (0-486-26472-6)

CANDIDE, Voltaire. Edited by Francois-Marie Arouet. (0-486-26689-3)

A CHRISTMAS CAROL, Charles Dickens. (0-486-26865-9)

CRIME AND PUNISHMENT, Fyodor Dostoyevsky. Translated by Constance Garnett. (0-486-41587-2)

DRACULA, Bram Stoker. (0-486-41109-5)

ETHAN FROME, Edith Wharton. (0-486-26690-7)

FLATLAND, Edwin A. Abbott. (0-486-27263-X)

FRANKENSTEIN, Mary Shelley. (0-486-28211-2)

THE GIFT OF THE MAGI AND OTHER SHORT STORIES, O. Henry. (0-486-27061-0)

GREAT AMERICAN SHORT STORIES, Edited by Paul Negri. (0-486-42119-8)

GREAT EXPECTATIONS, Charles Dickens. (0-486-41586-4)

GULLIVER'S TRAVELS, Jonathan Swift. (0-486-29273-8)

HEART OF DARKNESS, Joseph Conrad. (0-486-26464-5)

JANE EYRE, Charlotte Brontë. (0-486-42449-9)

THE JUNGLE, Upton Sinclair. (0-486-41923-1)

THE METAMORPHOSIS AND OTHER STORIES, Franz Kafka. (0-486-29030-1)

MOBY-DICK, Herman Melville. (0-486-43215-7)

THE ODYSSEY, Homer. (0-486-40654-7)

THE PICTURE OF DORIAN GRAY, Oscar Wilde. (0-486-27807-7)

A PORTRAIT OF THE ARTIST AS A YOUNG MAN, James Joyce. (0-486-28050-0)

PRIDE AND PREJUDICE, Jane Austen. (0-486-28473-5)

PUDD'NHEAD WILSON, Mark Twain. (0-486-40885-X)

THE SCARLET LETTER, Nathaniel Hawthorne. (0-486-28048-9)

THE SCARLET PIMPERNEL, Baroness Orczy. (0-486-42122-8)

SIDDHARTHA, Hermann Hesse. (0-486-40653-9)

THE STRANGE CASE OF DR. JEKYLL AND MR. HYDE, Robert Louis Stevenson. (0-486-26688-5)

DOVER · THRIFT · EDITIONS

FICTION

A TALE OF TWO CITIES, Charles Dickens. (0-486-40651-2)

TREASURE ISLAND, Robert Louis Stevenson. (0-486-27559-0)

THE TURN OF THE SCREW, Henry James. (0-486-26684-2)

UNCLE TOM'S CABIN, Harriet Beecher Stowe. (0-486-44028-1)

WUTHERING HEIGHTS, Emily Brontë. (0-486-29256-8)

NONFICTION

THE IMITATION OF CHRIST, Thomas à Kempis. Translated by Aloysius Croft and Harold Bolton. (0-486-43185-1)

NARRATIVE OF SOJOURNER TRUTH, Sojourner Truth. (0-486-29899-X)

WIT AND WISDOM OF THE AMERICAN PRESIDENTS, Edited by Joslyn Pine. (0-486-41427-2)

CIVIL DISOBEDIENCE AND OTHER ESSAYS, Henry David Thoreau. (0-486-27563-9)

UTOPIA, Sir Thomas More. (0-486-29583-4)

WALDEN; OR, LIFE IN THE WOODS, Henry David Thoreau. (0-486-28495-6)

UP FROM SLAVERY, Booker T. Washington. (0-486-28738-6)

ON THE ORIGIN OF SPECIES, Charles Darwin. (0-486-45006-6)

THE DECLARATION OF INDEPENDENCE AND OTHER GREAT DOCUMENTS OF AMERICAN HISTORY, Edited by John Grafton. (0-486-41124-9)

GREAT SPEECHES, Abraham Lincoln. (0-486-26872-1)

GREAT SPEECHES BY AMERICAN WOMEN, Edited by James Daley. (0-486-46141-6)

INCIDENTS IN THE LIFE OF A SLAVE GIRL, Harriet Jacobs. (0-486-41931-2)

THE SOULS OF BLACK FOLK, W.E.B. DuBois. (0-486-28041-1)

THE AUTOBIOGRAPHY OF BENJAMIN FRANKLIN, Benjamin Franklin. (0-486-29073-5)

COMMON SENSE, Thomas Paine. (0-486-29602-4)

NARRATIVE OF THE LIFE OF FREDERICK DOUGLASS, Frederick Douglass. (0-486-28499-9)

THE WIT AND WISDOM OF ABRAHAM LINCOLN, Abraham Lincoln. Edited by Bob Blaisdell. (0-486-44097-4)

GREAT SPEECHES BY AFRICAN AMERICANS, Edited by James Daley. (0-486-44761-8)

THE CONFESSIONS OF ST. AUGUSTINE, St. Augustine. (0-486-42466-9)

THE PRINCE, Niccolò Machiavelli. (0-486-27274-5)

REA's Test Preps

The Best in Test Preparation

- REA "Test Preps" are **far more** comprehensive than any other test preparation series
- Each book contains full-length practice tests based on the most recent exams
- **Every** type of question likely to be given on the exams is included
- Answers are accompanied by **full** and **detailed** explanations

REA publishes hundreds of test prep books. Some of our titles include:

Advanced Placement Exams (APs)
Art History
Biology
Calculus AB & BC
Chemistry
Economics
English Language &
    Composition
English Literature &
    Composition
European History
French Language
Government & Politics
Latin
Physics B & C
Psychology
Spanish Language
Statistics
United States History
World History

**College-Level Examination
    Program (CLEP)**
Analyzing and Interpreting
    Literature
College Algebra
Freshman College Composition
General Examinations
History of the United States I
History of the United States II
Introduction to Educational
    Psychology
Human Growth and Development
Introductory Psychology
Introductory Sociology
Principles of Management
Principles of Marketing
Spanish
Western Civilization I
Western Civilization II

SAT Subject Tests
Biology E/M
Chemistry
French
German
Literature
Mathematics Level 1, 2
Physics
Spanish
United States History

Graduate Record Exams (GREs)
Biology
Chemistry
Computer Science
General
Literature in English
Mathematics
Physics
Psychology

ACT - ACT Assessment

ASVAB - Armed Services
    Vocational Aptitude Battery

CBEST - California Basic Educa-
    tional Skills Test

CDL - Commercial Driver License
    Exam

CLAST - College Level Academic
    Skills Test

COOP, HSPT & TACHS - Catholic High
    School Admission Tests

FE (EIT) - Fundamentals of
    Engineering Exams

FTCE - Florida Teacher Certification
    Examinations

GED

GMAT - Graduate Management
    Admission Test

LSAT - Law School Admission Test

MAT - Miller Analogies Test

MCAT - Medical College Admission
    Test

MTEL - Massachusetts Tests for
    Educator Licensure

NJ HSPA - New Jersey High School
    Proficiency Assessment

NYSTCE - New York State Teacher
    Certification Examinations

PRAXIS PLT - Principles of
    Learning & Teaching Tests

PRAXIS PPST - Pre-Professional
    Skills Tests

PSAT/NMSQT

SAT

TExES - Texas Examinations of
    Educator Standards

THEA - Texas Higher Education
    Assessment

TOEFL - Test of English as a
    Foreign Language

USMLE Steps 1,2,3 - U.S. Medical
    Licensing Exams

*For information about any of REA's
    books, visit www.rea.com*

Research & Education Association
61 Ethel Road W., Piscataway, NJ 08854
Phone: (732) 819-8880